"Harper creates a fascinating world of devices, conspiracies, and personalities. . . . Alice and Gavin fight to survive and to find love in this steampunk coming-of-age story. Harper's world building is well developed and offers an interesting combination of science and steam."

—SFRevu

"You'll have great fun exploring the Third Ward, and the author created such a rich and lavish world for his characters. . . . Twists and turns abound, and the author managed to lob some shockers at me that I'll admit I didn't see coming. . . . If you love your Victorian adventures filled with zombies, amazing automatons, steampunk flair, and an impeccable eye for detail, you'll love the fascinating (and fantastical) *Doomsday Vault*."

—My Bookish Ways

"*The Doomsday Vault* is a good way to start off a new series in a highly specialized genre. Its combination of science and fantasy and good versus evil works well . . . a clever and worthwhile take on the steampunk universe."

—That's What I'm Talking About

"A fun and thrilling fast-paced adventure full of engaging characters and plenty of surprises. . . . I particularly enjoye...   twists that kept p...   e story figured ou...   —SFF Chat

...ntinued . . .

Books by Steven Harper

THE CLOCKWORK EMPIRE

THE
DRAGON
MEN

A NOVEL OF THE
CLOCKWORK EMPIRE

STEVEN HARPER

A ROC BOOK

ROC
Published by New American Library, a division of
Penguin Group (USA) Inc., 375 Hudson Street,
New York, New York 10014, USA

Penguin Group (Canada), 90 Eglinton Avenue East, Suite 700, Toronto,
Ontario M4P 2Y3, Canada (a division of Pearson Penguin Canada Inc.)
Penguin Books Ltd., 80 Strand, London WC2R 0RL, England
Penguin Ireland, 25 St. Stephen's Green, Dublin 2,
Ireland (a division of Penguin Books Ltd.)
Penguin Group (Australia), 250 Camberwell Road, Camberwell, Victoria 3124,
Australia (a division of Pearson Australia Group Pty. Ltd.)
Penguin Books India Pvt. Ltd., 11 Community Centre, Panchsheel Park,
New Delhi - 110 017, India
Penguin Group (NZ), 67 Apollo Drive, Rosedale, Auckland 0632,
New Zealand (a division of Pearson New Zealand Ltd.)
Penguin Books (South Africa) (Pty.) Ltd., 24 Sturdee Avenue,
Rosebank, Johannesburg 2196, South Africa

Penguin Books Ltd., Registered Offices:
80 Strand, London WC2R 0RL, England

First published by Roc, an imprint of New American Library,
a division of Penguin Group (USA) Inc.

First Printing, November 2012
10 9 8 7 6 5 4 3 2 1

 REGISTERED TRADEMARK — MARCA REGISTRADA

Printed in the United States of America

ALWAYS LEARNING   **PEARSON**

*To my son, Maksim, who sees adversity
and keeps on going.
You're the bravest little boy I know.*

ACKNOWLEDGMENTS

Thanks must go to my long-suffering editor, Anne Sowards, and my hardworking agent, Lucienne Diver.

THE STORY SO FAR

Once again, we feel it necessary to pause our thrilling narrative to catch our readers up. Friends familiar with events in *The Doomsday Vault* and *The Impossible Cube* should immediately flip to chapter one and begin there. Those who have not read those most excellent and fascinating volumes are discreetly encouraged to find and peruse them forthwith.

However, should those books (enthralling though they are) be unavailable, or should the gentle reader simply need a reminder about the various events leading up to the ones in this volume, the following information may prove useful.

In 1750, a new plague entered the world. Most who caught it died of fever and respiratory distress. Those few who survived this stage were often left crippled or scarred. A great number experienced dementia, loss of muscle tone, photosensitivity, and thinning of the skin, which led to open sores and necrotic tissue. These unfortunates were inevitably dubbed *plague zombies*, and they lurched through towns and cities, spreading the disease even further.

However, for perhaps one plague victim in a hundred thousand, the disease made the brain come together instead of fly apart. For these rare people, fields of study such as physics, mathematics, biology, and even art became simplicity itself. They created wonderful and terrifying inventions with the power to touch tiny microbes or rend the world in two. These men and women became known as *clockwork geniuses* or *clockworkers*. Unfortunately, their grip on reality inevitably slipped, and they thought nothing of destroying human life, or even the entire world, in the pursuit of their own experiments. Within three years of contracting the plague—often sooner—each one went utterly mad and died, allowing others to rise.

Most countries feared plague zombies and clockworkers, but China and the British Empire cheerfully set about harvesting the latter, using their inventions to divide the world between the empires. The delicate balance of power was maintained by England's captive clockworkers and China's hidden force of Dragon Men, which is the name by which clockworkers were known in Asia.

As a precautionary measure, the British Crown created the Third Ward, an underground police force dedicated to hunting down clockworkers anywhere in the world and bringing them back to London, where they were sequestered in hidden laboratories and encouraged to create their fantastic inventions for the benefit of the Empire. One of the more notorious examples was a German clockworker named Dr. Clef, who created a device known as the Impossible Cube, with which he could manipulate time itself.

The Third Ward worked hard and in secret to maintain the balance of power between the two world empires. After all, with balance comes peace. However, recent events have threatened this balance.

In 1842, England managed to gain a distinct advantage through a conflict that eventually became known as the First Opium War. In the aftermath of this conflict, England forced China into a number of trade concessions that severely damaged China's economy. Most notably, British merchants were now allowed to sell their (much cheaper) goods to Chinese buyers. The conflict also demonstrated to China that when it came to war, the British clockworkers had gained a definite edge over the Dragon Men. By 1857, China's economy had only recently begun to recover.

It was then that Gavin Ennock and Alice, Lady Michaels, accidentally destroyed the British Empire.

Perhaps *accidentally* is too strong a word. The destruction was actually more of a side effect. The reader must understand that, for reasons detailed in that most compelling of books, *The Doomsday Vault*, Gavin became infected with the clockwork plague, and Alice learned that the Third Ward, fearing an upset in the balance of world power, had locked the cure away in that eponymous repository. The only way to save Gavin's life was to steal the cure from the Doomsday Vault.

This Alice and Gavin did quite handily. In the process, Gavin destroyed Dr. Clef's Impossible Cube (much to that clockworker's chagrin), and Alice found herself in possession of an iron gauntlet that used her own blood to cure plague victims. Recipients would also spread the cure each time they coughed or sneezed, allowing the cure to diffuse more quickly.

Unfortunately, this meant the end of British clockworkers and the end of new clockworker inventions. In the four or five years it would take for the cure to spread to Asia, China would gain an insurmountable advantage over Britain and forever rule the world.

With no more clockworkers to hunt or guard, it was also the end of the Third Ward.

All this meant very little to Alice Michaels and Gavin Ennock, for the cure had one catch—it didn't help clockworkers. And Gavin turned out to be one of the few.

While the clockwork plague elevated Gavin's intelligence and eroded his sanity, Alice determined that if the Third Ward held a secret cure for plague zombies, China's Dragon Men might have one for clockworkers. Alice and Gavin fled across Europe toward China in the *Lady of Liberty*, Gavin's own airship. Joining them were Dr. Clef and a clockwork cat named Click. Pursuing them with the intent of bringing them to justice was Lieutenant Susan Phipps, at one time the head of the Third Ward and more recently out of a job.

During an eventful stop in Luxembourg for events chronicled in a delightful book titled *The Impossible Cube*, Gavin heard an astonishing rumor that his father, thought long dead, might still be alive, and Alice heard a dreadful prediction that if she didn't let Gavin go, the world would perish in flood and plague.

When the group arrived in Kiev mere steps ahead of Lieutenant Phipps, Dr. Clef managed to open a portal through time and reach backward through the timestream to snatch his Impossible Cube at the moment it was destroyed. A related outcome would also have destroyed the entire universe, a possibility which caused everyone concerned a certain amount of alarm. Alice and Gavin did manage to stop him, but only at great personal cost.

Unfortunately, the time portal, which proved deadly to all who touched it, remained open and was drawing Alice and Gavin in. They were rescued at the last moment by Lieutenant Phipps, who had come to realize saving millions of actual lives from the clockwork plague took precedence over her perceived duty to the British Empire. Once the consternation of the near destruction of the universe faded, Phipps insisted on accompanying Gavin and Alice to China and on helping them spread the cure along the way.

The clockwork plague continues its terrible march through Gavin's mind, and time is running short. Dr. Clef once estimated Gavin had at most three or four months to live, and their journey to China would take a minimum of ninety days. Gavin might, of course, go mad and die much sooner.

Meanwhile, the Impossible Cube sits in a cupboard aboard the *Lady of Liberty* while Gavin pilots the ship to China and Alice prays they make it in time.

We also wish to let the reader know that when transliterating Chinese into English, it is customary in some circles (including this one) to render the *sh* sound with a *q* or an *x*. Therefore *Qing* is pronounced *shing* and *Qilin* is pronounced *sheelin*, while *Xianfeng* is *sheeanfeng* and *Cixi* is *keeshee*. Why transliterators use a *q* or *x* instead of the more straightforward *sh*, we cannot hazard a guess, beyond the possibility that both letters simply look smashing.

Chapter One

"I still think this is a terrible idea," said Alice.

Gavin spread his mechanical wings, furled them, and spread them again. He shrugged at Alice's words and shot a glance across the deck at Susan Phipps, who set her jaw and tightened her grip on the helm. Her brass hand, the one with six fingers, gleamed in the afternoon sun, and a stray flicker of light caught Gavin in the face. The world slowed, shaving time into transparent slices, and for one of them he felt trillions of photons ricochet off his skin and carom away in rainbow directions. His mind automatically tried to calculate trajectory for them, and the numbers spun in an enticing whirlpool. He bit his lip and forced himself out of it. There were more important—more *exciting*—issues at hand.

"I completely agree," Phipps said. A brass-rimmed monocle with a red lens ringed her eye. "But he's the captain of the ship, and he can do as he likes, even if it's idiotic."

"Captains are supposed to listen to common sense," Alice replied in tart British tones. "Especially when the common sense comes from someone with a decent amount of intelligence."

At that Gavin had to smile. A soft breeze spun itself across the Caspian Sea, winding across the deck of the *Lady of Liberty* to stir his pale blond hair. He started to count the strands that flicked across his field of vision, noted the way each one was lifted by the teamwork of gas particles, then bit his lip again. Damn it, he was becoming more and more distractible by minutiae. More and more individual details of the world around him beckoned—the drag of the harness on his back, the creak of the airship's wooden deck, the borders of the shadow cast by her bulbous silk envelope high overhead, the sharp smell of the exhaust exuded from the generator that puffed and purred on the decking, the gentle thrumming of the propellered nacelles that pushed the *Lady* smoothly ahead, the shifting frequency of the blue light reflected by the Caspian Sea gliding past only a few yards beneath the *Lady*'s hull. Sometimes the world seemed a jigsaw puzzle of exquisite jewels, and he needed to examine each piece in exacting detail.

"Gavin?" Alice's worried voice came to him from far away, and it yanked him back to the ship. "Are you there?"

Damn it. He forced the grin back to full power. "Yeah. Sure. Look, I'll be fine. Everything'll work. I've been over the machinery a thousand times, and I've made no mistakes."

"Of course not." Alice's expression was tight. "Clockworkers never make mistakes with their inventions."

Gavin's grin faltered again, and he shifted within the harness. She was worried about *him*, and that both thrilled and shamed him. It was difficult to stand next to her and not touch her, even to brush against her. Just looking at her made him want to sweep her into his arms, something she allowed him to do only sporadically.

"Alice, will you marry me?" he blurted out.

She blinked at him. "What?"

"Will you marry me?" Words poured out of him. "I started to ask you back in Kiev, but we got interrupted, and what with one thing and another, I never got the chance to ask again, and now there's a small chance I'll be dead, or at least seriously wounded, in the next ten minutes, so I want to know: Will you marry me?"

"Oh good Lord," Phipps muttered from the helm.

"I—I . . . Oh, Gavin, this isn't the time," Alice stammered.

He took both her hands in his. Adrenaline thrummed his nerves as if they were cello strings. Alice's left hand was covered by an iron spider that wrapped around her forearm, hand, and fingers to create a strange metal gauntlet, and the spider's eyes glowed red at his touch. Gavin had his own machinery to contend with—the pair of metal wings harnessed to his back. They flared again when he shifted his weight.

"The universe will never give us the right time."

Gavin's voice was low and light. "We have to make our own."

"Dr. Clef tried to make time," Alice said, "and look where it got him."

"He wanted to keep it for himself." Gavin looked into Alice's eyes. They were brown as good clean earth, and just as deep. "We'll share it with the world. I can't offer you more than the open sky and every tune my fiddle will play, but will you marry me?"

"There's no minister. Not even a priest!"

"So you're saying you don't want to."

She flushed. "Oh, Gavin. I do, yes, I do. But—"

"No!" He held up a hand. "No *yes, but.* Just *yes.* And only if you mean it."

"Ah. Very well." Alice, Lady Michaels, took a deep breath. Her dress, a piece of sky pinned by the breeze, swirled about her. "Yes, Gavin. I will marry you."

With a shout of glee, Gavin leaped over the edge.

Air tore past his ears, and his stomach dropped. The *Lady's* hull blurred past him, and only two dozen yards below, the calm Caspian Sea shimmered hard and sharp and a little angry. Gavin spread his arms, moved his shoulders, and the wires attached to his body harness drew on tiny pulleys. The wings snapped open. The battery pack between his shoulder blades pulsed power, and blue light coruscated across the wings with a soft chime like that of a wet finger sliding over a crystal goblet. A matching blue light current glowed through a lacy endoskeleton underneath the *Lady's* envelope above, giving her a delicate, elegant air. The endoskeleton and the wings were fashioned from the same alloy, though the wings consisted of tiny interwoven links of metal, much like chain mail. And when electricity pulsed through the alloy—

Gavin dove toward the water a moment longer, until the glow and the chime reached the very tips of his wings. In that moment, the alloy pushed against gravity itself, and abruptly he was swooping back up, up, and up, and by God he was rising, climbing, ascending, *flying*, and the wind pushed him higher with an invisible hand, and the deck with Alice and Phipps upon it flashed by so fast, Gavin barely had time to register their surprised expressions, and then the *Lady*'s curli-blue envelope plunged toward him like a whale falling onto a minnow, and the wind tore his surprised yell away as a sacrifice, giving him just enough time to twist his body and turn the unfamiliar flapping wings—God, yes, they were *wings*—so that he skimmed up the side of the envelope so close, his belly brushed the cloth, and with dizzying speed he was above the ship, looking down at her sleek envelope and her little rudder at the back and the fine net of ropes that cradled the ship like soft fingers, and his body stretched in all directions with nothing below or above him. Every bit of his spirit rushed with exhilaration, flooded with absolute freedom. His legs in white leather and his feet in white boots hung beneath him, deliciously useless. His muscles moved, and the wings, made of azure light, flapped in response, lifting him into the cool, damp air, with bright brother sun calling to him, lifting body and soul. A rainbow of power gushed through him, and he was part of the heavens themselves, a whole note streaking through infinity, cleansed by wind and mist and shedding worries like grace notes. Gavin yelled and whooped, and his voice thundered across distant clouds as if it might split them in two. *This* was what he'd been born for. This was home.

He hung in the blue nothing for a tiny moment. His wings glowed and sang softly behind him. The clouds spread a cottony pasture far away, and he could almost—almost—see gods and angels striding across them. A calm stole over him. It didn't matter how many trillions of particles held him aloft or how gravity failed to function. It didn't matter that a disease was coursing through his body and killing him bit by bit. Here was blessed nothing. His mind slowed and joined the stillness. The wind sighed, and Gavin hummed a soft note in response as the breeze curled about his white-clad body. Harmony. Peace. How perfect it was here.

A shadow below caught his eye. The *Lady* was still hovering just above the surface of the calm Caspian Sea. This was at Phipps's insistence—if Gavin's wings had failed, he wouldn't have fallen far, and the ocean would have provided a more pleasant landing than hard ground. Perhaps five miles ahead of the ship lay a sliver of an island, and just beyond that, a rocky coast. The shadow was moving beneath the water, growing larger and larger beneath the *Lady* as whatever cast it moved up from the bottom of the sea. The thing was nothing natural. Unease bloomed quickly into concern and fear. Gavin tucked and dove, his wings pulled in tightly. He didn't dare dive too quickly—he didn't know how much the harness could take, even though his mind was automatically calculating foot pounds and stress levels. He shouted a warning to Alice and Phipps and felt the vibration of his vocal cords, sensed the compression of air, knew the sound would scatter helplessly long before it reached Alice's eardrums, and still he shouted.

Half a mile below him, a pair of enormous black tentacles rose up from the shadow and broke the surface of the water. At seven or eight feet thick, they easily looped themselves up and around the *Lady* with incredible speed, even though she was the size of a decent cottage. Fear chased Gavin's heart out of his rib cage as he dove closer. He could hear Alice shrieking and Phipps yelling in thin, tinny voices that were ballooning into full volume. Air burned his cheeks as he dove past the envelope, now wrapped in suckered black flesh, and he caught the rank smell of ocean depths and old fish.

Instinct rushed him ahead. He had to reach Alice. He had no other thought but to reach her, get her to safety. Even the *Lady*'s distress didn't matter.

Below and just behind the ship, a black island rose from the waves. Eight other tentacles trailed in oily shadows beneath the ship, and a wicked horned beak large enough to crack an oak tree snapped open and shut. A single eye the size of a stagecoach stared up at Gavin, and he caught his own reflection in the dark iris. Inside Gavin, a monster equal to the one below him roared its anger. For a mad moment, he wondered if he could dive into the eye, punch both fists straight through the cornea into vitreous goo, and force the creature away. Grimly, he ended that line of thought as foolish. Instead, he made himself fling his wings open and end the dive with a sharp jerk that sent a red web of pain down his back and into his groin, where the flight harness was strapped to his lower body. He skimmed through a gap in the tentacles and the rope web that supported the *Lady*'s hull, twisting his body in ways that were already becoming reflexive, until he could drop to the deck. His wings folded back into a metallic cloak that dragged at his back and shoulders once the blue glow faded and the chime stopped.

Susan Phipps had drawn a cutlass of tempered glass— only fools used sparking metal on an airship—and was hacking at one of the loops of tentacle that encircled the ship in a rubbery tunnel. Her mouth was set in a hard line, and her graying black hair was coming loose from under her hat and spilling over her blue lieutenant's uniform. The blade gleamed liquid in the sun and it distorted the black tentacle as Phipps slashed again and again, but the edge made only shallow cuts in the rubbery surface, and if the creature noticed, it gave no indication.

Alice, meanwhile, kicked open a hatchway on deck, and a finger of relief threaded through Gavin's anger when he saw she wasn't injured.

"Are you all right?" he demanded.

"I'm fine," she barked, then shouted into the hatchway, "Out! Out, out, out!"

From belowdecks burst a cloud of little brass automatons. Some skittered on spider legs; others flew on whirl-igig propellers. They sported arms and legs and other limbs of varying sizes and shapes, but most had points, and a little pride fluttered in Gavin's chest at the way they obeyed Alice. She pointed at the tentacle above Phipps's head with her gauntleted hand. "Attack!"

The little automatons rushed at the tentacle. Their blades and pincers slashed and poked. The cuts oozed bluish ichor but otherwise seemed to have no impact. Wood creaked in protest beneath the smelly tentacles, and Gavin felt the *Lady*'s distress as his own. His stomach tightened. Water sloshed below, and a breeze stirred.

"We *told* you we knew something like this would happen, Ennock!" Phipps shouted. She was still slashing at her tentacle with the help of the little automatons. "We *told* you dropping this close to the water in unknown territory was foolish."

"Does that matter now?" Alice yelled back. She cast about the deck, looking for something to do, then flung her arms around Gavin's neck. "I'm so glad you're all right. I was terrified the entire time you were up there."

Suddenly the squid didn't matter. He held her even as wood and rope creaked all about them and seawater dripped from loops of black tentacle; his wings, no longer glowing and heavy now that he had landed, cupped protectively around them both. For a tiny moment, he let himself feel as if he had created a safe island for them both, and Alice was warm against him. It seemed they never really had moments to themselves, when they could enjoy just being together. Their time together burned away like a dying candle, and Gavin hated it. He just wanted to spend time alone with Alice, love her, raise children with her, but one crisis after another stormed over them. For one moment, at least, he held her, and she let him.

"Oi! Lovebirds!" Phipps called over her metallic shoulder. The red lens of her monocle was hard as a ruby. "We need to figure out how to handle this before it drags us under!"

"The creature isn't dragging us down." Gavin released Alice. "It's towing us."

Phipps stopped hacking, and even the little automatons above her paused for a moment. "What?"

Alice ran to the gunwale and peered over. The ship shuddered and creaked, moving forward instead of down. The creature's tentacles were towing the *Lady* the way a child carried a balloon on a string. "Good heavens—he's right. How did you know, darling?"

"I felt the breeze. Besides, this thing could crush the *Lady* in seconds," Gavin said. "It hasn't, which means it doesn't want to, or someone is stopping it from doing so. I don't think this creature is natural. Someone made it. Someone's *controlling* it. Someone who wants to capture us, not kill us."

"That makes me feel so much better," Phipps snapped. "Instead of being crushed or drowned, we're being kidnapped by someone who breeds giant squid for private amusement."

Jaw set hard, Alice swatted controls on a deck panel, sending the nacelles into full reverse. The engines whined and protested. The *Lady* bucked and shuddered, fighting the creature's grip, but the towing barely slowed. Alice was growing desperate. Gavin knew she hated and feared being unable to control her world, and her fear made him angry at whoever—whatever—was causing it.

"We need more weapons," she said, still pounding at the controls. "What do we have?"

Gavin shook his head. The *Lady* used to have a number of weapons, but they'd all been destroyed or rendered useless during recent events in France and Ukraine, and Gavin hadn't had time to make any more. In fact, the only real weapon they had was—

His blue eyes met Alice's brown ones, a meeting of sky and earth. In that instant, the same thought went through both their heads; Gavin could see it.

"No," Alice said. Her eyes showed the whites.

"We don't have anything else," Gavin countered.

"No."

The *Lady* picked up speed. Ahead of them lay the island, thin as a knife, and it was growing larger.

"No what?" Phipps demanded. Then she got it. "Oh. Oh God. No, Gavin. We can't. Can we?"

"Do we have a choice?"

The *Lady* bucked again as Alice revved the nacelles with her spider-gauntleted hand, but it didn't slow one iota. Gavin glanced at the island and ran automatic calculations. Ten minutes, nine seconds at their current rate of speed, assuming the island was their destination.

"Go," Phipps ordered. "Get the Cube."

Wings clutched tightly to his sides, Gavin ran to the main hatch Alice had kicked open and dropped into the dark hold. Halfway down, his plague-enhanced reflexes let him snag a ladder rung that broke his fall and allowed him to sidestep the next hatchway that would have dropped him farther belowdecks. He ran down the narrow passageway past facing doors to the end. With every hurried step, the *Lady* moaned in the creature's grip.

The door at the end of the corridor opened into Gavin's laboratory, a small but efficient space with two little worktables, floor-to-ceiling shelves and cupboards, and several racks of scientific equipment. He yanked open one of the cupboards. Inside sat the dented brass head of a mechanical man with flat, motionless features, lightbulbs for eyes, and a speaker grill where his mouth should have been. The lightbulbs were dark, and one was shattered.

"'Scuse me, Kemp," Gavin muttered, and reached for the shelf above. It held a cube-shaped object of struts and mesh made from the same blue metal as his wings. The cube was the size of a hatbox and felt light and springy in Gavin's hand. It also twisted the eye and made it go strange places. One of the rear struts seemed to fold over the front of the cube, or perhaps it was that one of the front struts was slipping behind the rear. At the same time, the top overlapped the bottom, which similarly overlapped the top. The Impossible Cube. Dr. Clef, Gavin's friend and mentor, himself a clockworker, had nearly destroyed the universe with it, and Gavin had nearly killed himself last month using it to save the citizens of Kiev from a devastating flood. He hadn't touched it since then out of fear and respect. Gavin hesitated for a fraction of a second, then fled the lab with it, along with a small box of tools.

Topside, the *Lady* was now skimming along just above the flat waters at greater speed than before. Below, the creature knifed through the water, pulling the ship with thoughtless power. Its stagecoach eye stared up, flat and expressionless. The island was less than half a mile ahead of them, and they would reach the shore in less than five minutes.

"What are you going to do with the Cube?" Alice asked tightly.

"I have to charge it. No one's touched it since Kiev." Gavin knelt next to the small generator that puffed and purred on the deck, exuding steam and the smell of paraffin oil exhaust. Needles on readout dials flicked back and forth, indicating strength of current and health of machinery. A set of heavy-duty cables snaked from one side, across the deck, up the rigging, and into the center of the envelope. Trying not to think about the monster grasping his ship, Gavin set the Impossible Cube on the deck, pulled on a pair of rubber gloves, and snatched tools from the box. A moment's work with a wrench loosened one of the cables from the generator.

"Whatever you're going to do, hurry up!" Phipps called. "We're nearly at the shore!"

His fingers protected by rubber, Gavin jerked the cable free of the generator. Instantly, a large section of the envelope's endoskeleton went dark, and the *Lady*, unable to retain proper buoyancy, dropped straight down. Gavin's stomach lurched, his feet left the deck for a moment, and his wings automatically snapped open to slow his fall. Alice yelped. Gavin reached for her, though he was too far away to do anything. But four of the whirligig automatons caught at her arms and shoulders, the propellers spinning madly to keep her aloft. Phipps gave a shriek such as Gavin had never heard from her and dropped with the ship.

"Phipps!" Gavin shouted, but the lieutenant was already in action. A wire whipped out of her brass palm and wrapped around one of the tentacles still encircling the ship. The *Lady* hit the water with a spectacular *boom*. Water exploded in all directions. Phipps flicked the wire around her wrist, bent at the waist, and swung in a graceful arc to land beside Alice and Gavin, who had come down on the deck as well. With a jerk, Phipps released the wire from the tentacle, and it sucked itself back into her palm. Then she smacked Gavin on the back of the head. He grunted.

"Idiot," she said.

"Sorry."

The two women exchanged a glance they thought Gavin didn't see. The glances said *clockwork plague* in silent, pointed words. The plague killed most of its victims. It usually crippled survivors, though in most cases it ate the flesh from their bones and chewed through their brains, leaving behind demented, oozing zombies that shambled through shadows, spreading the disease even further. But in the brains of a tiny minority, the plague burned like a star and illuminated the dark corners of the universe, revealing impossible secrets and allowing the victim to create inventions both terrifying and benign. But such stars consumed themselves quickly, and Gavin's time was growing short. He was already finding the tiny details of what was before him more and more intriguing, and he tended to forget the bigger picture, such as the fact that diverting power to the Impossible Cube would drop the *Lady of Liberty* several feet into the Caspian Sea. Gavin's mentor, Dr. Clef, had felt sorry for Gavin and Alice and had tried, quite literally, to give them more time together, but he hadn't considered that by doing so he would destroy the universe. Gavin hadn't traveled quite that far down the clockwork road, but he could feel his grip slipping, and he hated that Alice and Phipps had noticed. It also scared the hell out of him.

The *Lady* was now floating on the water. Her partially charged envelope continued to hover above her, though it couldn't lift the hull any longer, and the creature still held the ship firmly in its grip. Wood groaned, and the rubbery stench of the sea creature stung Gavin's nose. Beneath his boots, the deck moved sickeningly up and down in a completely unnatural motion for an airship. The shore was now perhaps a hundred yards away. An enormous cave gaped like an open mouth, and the ship was moving inexorably toward it, skimming over the waves.

Alice looked over the gunwale again, her automatons following like a flock of nervous birds. "I don't think we've harmed the creature by landing on it. More's the pity," she said with forced calm. "How did a clockworker create something so large? That's biology, not physics."

Phipps growled, "Strange questions coming from a woman whose aunt could cure clockwork zombies. You've *seen* what they can do with biology."

"Not on this scale." She grimaced. "Or tentacle."

"Can you see any damage to the *Lady*?" Gavin called. Now that Alice had come up unharmed, his concerns had shifted.

"No, though I'm no expert." The breeze from the monster's towing had pulled Alice's long, honey brown hair out of its twist and it blew in soft waves around her face. She was so beautiful, even when she was disheveled and nervous. He wanted to scoop her off the deck and fly her to a secluded hilltop where she would be safe, but he hadn't tried carrying another person yet and didn't know if the wings could take it.

Alice added, "Now that you nearly killed us, darling, perhaps you could get that Cube charged? If that's what you insist on doing."

Her tone was artificially light, and it didn't take clockwork genius to read the grim undertone. Gavin jammed the business end of the live wire against the Impossible Cube. Electricity cracked and fizzled, and the Cube glowed a faint blue that grew brighter as the object powered up. While it did so, it grew lighter and lighter until it was floating within Gavin's hands, for it was forged of the same alloy as Gavin's wings and the *Lady*'s endoskeleton. The Cube was a truly singular object. Dr. Clef, its inventor, had claimed it had no parallel object in any other universe; it twisted gravity and energy and even time itself in ways Gavin was only beginning to understand. As a side effect, the Cube converted sound waves into other forms of energy, making it a potent weapon for anyone with a good set of tuning forks—or perfect pitch.

The Cube continued to drain the generator. Ahead of them loomed the dark cave, and the *Lady* seemed to groan in fear. Gavin thought about telling the women to swim for it while he stayed behind to defend the ship, but one glance at Alice's heavy gauntlet and Phipps's equally heavy brass arm reminded him that neither of them was effective in the water.

"Hurry up." Phipps's jaw was tense. "That cave won't be a holiday resort."

Gavin gritted his own teeth. "I can't make the power flow faster, Lieutenant."

The black tentacles continued to hold the *Lady* in bands of iron. Alice hovered anxiously over Gavin, and her automatons hovered over her.

"What are you going to do with it once it's charged?" she asked.

"Something horrible," he said shortly. The initial shock of fear had worn off, and he was getting angry again. This monster had taken *his* ship and threatened *his* fiancée. It was *his* duty to fend off the beast and set things right. Waves spumed and broke on rocks as the *Lady* reached the mouth of the cave and slid inside. The light faded. Beneath the surface, the dark creature squirted along under the ship, hauling her forward by orders understood only to itself. The Impossible Cube glowed a full sapphire blue that indicated it had reached a full charge just as the *Lady* glided into the cave entrance. Gavin disconnected it from the wire and held it aloft in triumph at the exact moment the squid men attacked.

Chapter Two

Alice, Lady Michaels, jumped away from the gunwale as the first squid man shot from the ocean in a fountain of water and landed on the deck with a rubbery *thwap* that echoed through the huge cave. The creature had a man's body, though its skin was covered in greenish blue slime, and its head was that of a squid. Tentacles formed a horrid squirming bush around its neck, and enormous dark eyes too round and large to be human glistened in the half-light of the cave. Its fingers and toes were webbed, and they dripped more slime. Although it was naked and had a male build, it showed no male accoutrement. With a frightened squawk, Alice stepped back and bumped into Gavin as another squid man vaulted onto the deck, and another and another and another. In seconds, the deck was teeming with more than two dozen of them.

The sight of those doll-like eyes, the smell of the oozing slime, and the sound of the writhing tentacles crawled over Alice's skin like cold worms. The creatures spoke no words and closed in around the trio with outreaching arms and faint squishing sounds. A fear she didn't know she possessed poured ice water down Alice's back and froze her voice. She had faced down zombies, gargoyles, and a mechanical war machine several stories tall, but these creatures touched something primordial. She wanted to leap behind Gavin and Phipps, or even hide in a closet.

"Good Lord," Phipps breathed. She had her cutlass out, but it seemed small and senseless compared to the crowd facing them. Gavin didn't react. He simply stared at the squid men, either fascinated or mesmerized, Alice couldn't tell which. Thanks to the clockwork plague, Gavin fell into these fugues more and more often, and it wasn't just when they came across something as strange as a school of squid men. A simple leaf or air current could capture his fancy with equal ease. This unnerved Alice even more than his recent dive over the side of the ship. Right now, the clockwork fugue was proving dangerous—Gavin had lost track of himself while he held their only weapon.

Alice tried to speak, but no words came out. She coughed and tried again. "Gavin! The Cube!"

Gavin came to himself with a snap. The eye-twisting Impossible Cube glowed in his grip, and he held it out in front of him. Metal wings formed a chain mail cloak that rippled down his back, and the blue light of the Cube lit his white-blond hair with an unearthly glow. The squid men oozed closer in eerie silence, and Alice's breath came in fearful gasps. She couldn't stand such horrible creatures, and she felt foolish and helpless hiding behind Gavin, who was four years younger than she. Still, she had rescued him from danger more times than she could count, so what was the harm in letting him and his powerful weapon take the forefront?

The squid men reached for Gavin with their dripping arms. He opened his mouth and sang a single, clear note. Alice had no idea which—Gavin had perfect pitch, not she—but the impact was electric. The Impossible Cube flickered in Gavin's strong hands, and his voice . . . changed. It roared from his throat with the sound of a thousand tigers. A cone of sound thundered across the deck and flung squid men aside like toys, clearing a corridor all the way to the gunwale. The sound continued to boom from Gavin's throat, and pride fluttered in Alice's chest. He looked handsome and powerful and, God, he was so young, but Alice loved him with every particle in her body. The squid men crashed into one another and tumbled across the wood without uttering a sound.

Phipps was also busy. She slashed one creature with her cutlass, slicing off its arm at the elbow. Blue blood gushed over the deck and her victim staggered back, but Phipps was still in motion. She gave another squid man a side kick to the midriff. It fell back into the attacker behind it while Phipps back-punched another squid man in the face with her metal hand. Her knuckles sank into the flesh between its eyes, then pulled free with a sucking sound. Undaunted, the squid man grabbed her wrist. Like a cat, she twisted round and bent her attacker's arm, sending the creature to the deck with its neck tentacles writhing in what Alice assumed was pain.

Meanwhile, the squid men Gavin had scattered began to recover. Their movements changed from slow and shambling to quick and nimble. The ones that had fallen rolled to their feet, and the rest surged forward. Strangely, they seemed to be ignoring Gavin and reaching for Alice.

"What the hell is going on?" Phipps panted. She took a punch to the jaw, staggered, righted herself, and kept on fighting. Her monocle gleamed an angry red, helping her aim.

"Shout at them again!" Alice cried. "Shout at—"

One of the squid men grabbed her from behind with cold hands. Alice screamed as nightmares she didn't remember having smeared her mind with slippery darkness. She struggled and kicked, and another grabbed her as well. Gavin turned, the Impossible Cube still glowing in his hands. Phipps was raising her cutlass against another group of squid men.

And then Alice noticed the spider on her arm.

Last spring, the iron spider had wrapped itself around her hand and forearm at the behest of her aunt Edwina, a world-class clockworker. Soft, flexible tubules had burrowed into her flesh and gorged themselves on her blood, which now bubbled and flowed up and down the spider's body and legs. The spider's head and five of its legs clutched the back of her hand and each of her fingers, creating a strange gauntlet. Alice had tried to get it off, but it refused to budge, and it had quickly become so much a part of her that she was now afraid to try more drastic methods such as cutting it away. These days, she didn't entirely want to. What currently caught her attention were the spider's eyes. They glowed red. Her fear vanished despite the rubbery arms that held her.

"Wait!" she cried. "These . . . people have the clockwork plague!"

Before Gavin could respond to this news, Alice swiped at the arm that held her with the claws that tipped her left hand. The hollow claws sprayed her own blood over the wounds she created, mixing scarlet and azure. The squid man released her and reeled away. Two more stepped up to grab at her, but Alice swiped both of them with quick, darting motions. More blood mixed in the scratches, and they staggered away, too. The first squid man was now writhing on the deck. Soft clicking sounds emerged from either its neck or chest; Alice couldn't tell which. The other two soon joined it. Their skin tone was changing, shifting from dark blue to a mottled pink.

All this happened in just a few seconds. Phipps had dispatched or driven back half a dozen squid men of her own. Her cutlass and metal arm dripped with blue blood, and she had lost her hat. A wild look had come over her eyes as more squid men crowded toward her. Gavin opened his mouth to roar again.

"That's enough!"

The new voice echoed through the cave. The squid men all froze, except for those writhing and clicking on the deck because Alice had scratched them or Phipps had lopped pieces off. Alice turned. What *now*?

Skimming across the channel that cut through the cave floor came a man. He was barefoot and wore a black bathing costume with short sleeves and leggings. Around his waist he had an elaborate, heavy-looking belt with a number of clunky pieces of machinery attached to it. Over everything, rather strangely, he wore a long gray cloak. He was standing sideways and seemed to be riding a low wave until he came closer and Alice realized he was standing on the back of another creature. How he kept his balance she couldn't imagine until it came to her that, like Gavin, he was a clockworker and had the requisite enhanced reflexes that he would enjoy until plague burned out his brain. No doubt this was the man who had created both the giant squid and the squid men. Alice pursed her lips.

Gavin traded a look with Phipps while the scratched and wounded squid men squirmed on the deck. The ones Alice had slashed continued their metamorphosis, with their skin growing paler and their neck tentacles going still. Alice wanted to examine them, see if they were in pain, but she didn't have the chance. The clockworker skimmed closer to the ship, and in moments he vaulted from his creature's back and scrambled onto the deck, his gray cloak fluttering behind him. He had a Persian's dark hair and complexion, and the wrinkles around his eyes and mouth put him somewhere in his forties, or perhaps near fifty.

"That's enough," he repeated in accented English. "Leave my poor men alone!"

Phipps, Gavin, and Alice stared. The crowd of squid men remained motionless. Alice recovered herself first.

"And you are?" she asked.

"You may call me Prince Mehrad al-Noor," he said. "I already know who you are—or one of you, at any rate."

"And that would be?" Phipps said.

"Alice, Lady Michaels, late of London," al-Noor said. "You are the one with the cure to the clockwork plague, and you have demonstrated it on my poor men."

"What are you talking about?" Alice said, still trying to get a full grip on herself. "Why did you bring us here? I assume that this creature"—she gestured at one of the tentacles still encircling the ship—"attacked us at your behest."

"Yes, yes." Al-Noor waved his hands in a series of complicated gestures, and several of the squid men dragged the ones Alice had scratched and those Phipps had wounded to the side and leaped overboard with them. Splashes followed. They left trails of blue blood on the deck. "Why else would a giant squid attack a passing airship?"

"How do you know the name Lady Michaels?" Gavin demanded.

"Everyone knows this name," al-Noor replied with a white grin. "She is the angel with a sharp metal hand who spreads the cure to the clockwork plague. She coasts through the heavens in a glowing blue airship piloted by her lover, dropping to Earth to bestow her blessings wherever people are good and kind and deserving of her notice."

Alice felt her face turn hot. "Gavin's not—"

Phipps trod on her foot, cutting her off. "So you've heard of me," she interrupted, holding up her metal arm. "I'm flattered. That doesn't explain why you intercepted us and tried to destroy my ship."

For a split second, Alice found herself wanting to correct Phipps. Then she shut herself up. Any advantage they could take, including a case of mistaken identity, could work in their favor.

"I apologize if I gave you that impression, Lady Michaels. I got wind that the very famous angel of mercy was coasting over my ocean, and I merely wanted to invite you for a visit. Unfortunately, giant squids are not good at subtlety. We will, of course, repair any damage to your fine ship."

"And your . . . men?" Gavin gestured at the crowded deck. The Impossible Cube glowed close to his chest.

"They guard the mouth of the cave and became too enthusiastic when your ship appeared. Again, I do apologize." Al-Noor gave a little bow. "You will come with me, have a wonderful meal, spend the night in comfortable rooms, and in the morning, you will go on your way."

"Oh?" Phipps said. "Well, if you—"

"Liar," said Alice.

Al-Noor looked taken aback. "I do not understand. You refuse my hospitality?"

"Was I unclear?" Alice snapped. "Let me be blunt, then. You did not invite us here. You captured us, and now you're acting polite to put us off our guard. Once we've eaten at your table, the laudanum you put into our food will send us to sleep, allowing you to do whatever you wish. So let's skip over the bad food and the drugs and go straight to what you wish. What might that be, Mr. al-Noor?"

For a moment, al-Noor looked hurt and astonished, and Alice thought she had made a terrible mistake. Then a cool, calculating look slid over the man's face. "You are a clever woman, Miss . . . ?"

"Susan Phipps," said Alice. "At your service."

"Miss Phipps," al-Noor said. "Yes, very clever indeed."

Phipps wiped her cutlass clean on a handkerchief. "Flattery from a liar doesn't sit well, al-Noor. What do you want, then? Do tell, before my friend here blasts you into your component bits."

At this, Gavin waved the Impossible Cube. It hummed softly and left a blue trail hanging in the air. His face was set hard. The squid men stood motionless on the deck, though their dark eyes seemed to be following the Cube.

"I think he will not." Al-Noor pressed a switch on his belt, and a tremor went through the black tentacles wrapped round the *Lady*. Wood groaned and cracked.

Gavin cried out and lowered the Cube. "Wait!"

"Yes," said al-Noor. "A flick of my finger, and electric impulses will force the squid to crush this ship to flinders. That famous metal arm of yours, Lady Michaels, will drag you to the bottom, and you will drown."

Alice shot Gavin a hard look. He seemed upset, but was it over the idea that she was in danger or that the sea monster might destroy his ship? He was a clockworker and could get strange ideas about what was important.

Her glance flicked about the deck, looking for solutions. Her gaze inevitably came back to the Impossible Cube resting in Gavin's hands. It was the most powerful weapon on Earth, but the moment Gavin tried to use it, al-Noor would try to kill all three of them, and chances were better than even that he would succeed at least once. The Cube was useless in these circumstances.

There was one alternative. An obvious one, really. Alice could see that Gavin knew what it was, but he was hesitating to take it, waiting for her to give the word. One word. Alice started to speak, but her throat closed around the word, trapping it like hope at the bottom of a box. Gavin looked at her, his soul in pale blue eyes. Alice clamped her lips shut, and her chin trembled with the force of holding it in.

Phipps did it for her. "Fly," she hissed.

Gavin gave her a sharp look.

"Fly," Phipps hissed again.

He gave Alice a wild look, then ran for the gunwale through the gap in the crowd of squid men the Impossible Cube had created. Before the squid men could react, he hurled himself over the side. Alice held back a cry but still reached for him. She felt that her heart might spring out of her chest and follow after.

"Gavin!" Phipps cried, making a halfhearted leap after him that effectively covered Alice's own movement. "Oh, what will I ever do?"

It would have been funny under other circumstances. Gavin's wings snapped open. Still clutching the Impossible Cube to his chest, he caught the air with the grace of someone who had been flying all his life and glided away, trailing blue light behind him.

"You leave him alone, you awful, awful man," Phipps simpered at al-Noor. Her monocle made the gesture even more ridiculous. "You have me. He can't hurt you."

"Indeed so, Lady." Al-Noor looked after Gavin's retreating form. He had already reached the mouth of the cave and vanished into bright light. "But you will pardon me for docking this ship and taking you somewhere more secure."

"So, what is it you want from—from Lady Michaels?" Alice demanded.

"Exactly what is your position here, Miss Phipps?" al-Noor replied.

"I never go anywhere without her," Phipps put in quickly. "She's my maid."

"Maid?" The word popped out before Alice could stop it.

"Well, you're not a valet, *Susan*," Phipps said pointedly. "And someone has to polish all this brass. You *have* to be my maid."

Alice gritted her teeth. "Yes, mum," she said between them.

"But regardless of her station, sir," Phipps continued, "the question still stands. What exactly do you want?"

Al-Noor was still looking after the fading light trail left by Gavin's wings. He thought a moment, then shrugged and turned back to the two women.

"I want all the tea in China," he said. "Or perhaps its weight in silver."

Phipps crossed her arms, flesh over metal. "No clock-worker riddles. Be specific."

"I noted your trajectory before I sent my pet to fetch you," al-Noor said. "Based on that and on the rumors I have managed to intercept about you, I have decided you are trying to reach China. Is that correct?"

Alice kept her face expressionless, taking her cue from Phipps, though her insides were tight. Al-Noor had the right of it—they were indeed headed for China. A number of events allowed her and Gavin to hope that China could cure clockworkers. Weeks ago, Alice had discovered that over the years, a number of British clockworkers had found different cures for the clock-work plague—Alice wore the handiwork of one of them around her arm—but the Crown had suppressed them so the plague would continue to produce clockworkers, who would, in turn, produce useful inventions for the Crown. Never mind that the disease also slaughtered millions, including most of Alice's family. What mattered to the Crown was that China was doing the same thing so its Dragon Men could produce similar inventions, maintaining a careful balance between the two empires.

Although the remedy Alice herself was spreading could heal the plague in zombies and in people who had recently fallen ill, no one in England had managed to cure a clockworker. That meant Gavin was doomed.

With Gavin's help, Alice had ended the clockwork plague in England and was spreading the cure across Europe, though her ultimate goal was still China. Britain had never managed to cure a clockworker, but China . . .

the Oriental Empire was known for its introspection, do-ing research about research. If anyone had a clockwork cure, it was the Dragon Men.

"We are traveling to China, yes," Phipps said cau-tiously. "What does it matter to you?"

"I am doing you a favor. China has recently closed its borders. No one gets in these days. Or out."

A pang jolted Alice's stomach. "What? They can't do that!"

"Hm," al-Noor said. "This is not the place to discuss such things. Come and eat, and I promise—no drugs."

A few moments later, the *Lady* had been dragged to a little stone quay and a contingent of squid men with clammy hands was escorting Phipps and Alice—without her little mechanicals—down a cavern tunnel and into a chilly, high-ceilinged cavern the size of a formal dining room. Stalactites dripped water from the ceiling, and the sandy floor felt gritty under Alice's feet. The squid men shut and barred a thick door at the entrance to the cav-ern and brought the two women to a low table surrounded by pillows. Foods Alice couldn't begin to identify heaped the dishes and filled the air with strange, spicy smells that turned Alice's stomach. Electric lights clung to the walls to cast a hard, unmoving light over everything. The whole place looked like a dining room designed by, well, a madman. Alice stood unhappily next to the table with Phipps while al-Noor, still in his damp swimsuit and belt, seated himself on a plump pillow. A squid man took his gray cloak, and Alice belatedly realized it was made of sharkskin.

"Please, sit, eat," he said as one of the squid men piled food on his plate.

Alice remained standing. Sitting cross-legged on the floor would put her at a further disadvantage, and she was too tense to sit in any case. Her muscles felt stiff as whalebone, and sweat trickled down her back despite the chill of the cave. She forced herself to relax—or try to. Gavin would come for them. He had the Impossible Cube, the most powerful weapon in the world.

A weapon they only barely understood. A weapon that had nearly destroyed the entire universe by stopping time. It hadn't even been two weeks since she and Gavin had faced down plump, merry Dr. Clef at the bottom of the dam in Kiev, not fourteen days since she had watched in horror as he charged up the Impossible Cube with half the power of a city and reached for a switch that would freeze everything forever between two ticks of the universe's clock. He had been her friend, a kind, slightly eccentric old man with strange theories that bent her mind and made her see the world on different terms. And she had taken a hand in his death. Feng Lung, another dear friend, had died as well, messily and horribly. She often saw the image of their mingled blood hanging in the air before she fell asleep in her bunk at night.

"Get to it, al-Noor," Phipps snapped, also refusing to sit. "What do you want?"

"You are not in a position to shout." Al-Noor stuffed a wad of flat bread into his mouth. "With a word, my men could kill you. Or perhaps they will pull your brass arm off so I can study it. Have some coconut milk."

"My name is Lady Michaels, a peer of the British Empire. You will use that title when you address me."

Alice wished Phipps wouldn't antagonize the man. Although al-Noor clearly wanted them alive, he *was* a clockworker, and who knew what he might decide to do. The overpowering presence of more than a dozen squid men in the room made her continually nervous, and she found herself fingering her spider gauntlet like a security blanket.

Stop it, she told herself. *You're better than this.* But the slimy squid men and the dank cave continued to press in all around her.

"Even a lady must eat." Al-Noor waved away Phipps's comment with a forkful of noodles. "But it is your prerogative to go hungry if you wish. A pity, when so many others in the world are starving."

"What do you want with us, Mr. al-Noor?" Alice asked carefully. "You said something about China's borders."

"I did, I did." Al-Noor sipped noisily from a porcelain cup, which was instantly refilled by one of the squid men. A bit of slime from its neck tentacles dripped into the cup. Al-Noor drank again, and Alice's gorge rose. Phipps looked a bit green. "The borders are closed."

"They can't do that," Alice said again. "The Treaty of Nanking opened free trade between China and England after that fight over opium—what?—nine years ago? Ten?"

"Nine, yes." Al-Noor toyed with an oily bit of fish. "But the treaty was not about free trade. It was about letting

British merchants ram Indian opium down Chinese throats. And the Chinese finally had enough. Fellow named Prince Cheng teamed up with a Manchu warlord named Su Shun, and they closed the borders, treaty or no."

"There'll be a fight," Phipps predicted. "A big one."

"Yes. I think Cheng and Su Shun are counting on that. You British took Peking by sheer luck. Everyone knows that if General Zexu Lin's war machines hadn't broken down at Canton and let the English forces through, the Chinese would have thrown the British out quite handily. And even so, the British took huge losses at Peking before the emperor surrendered. If General Lin had not backed down, the British might have still failed."

"Ancient history," Phipps said. "The Chinese lost. They signed the treaty."

"And now they have decided to fight again." Al-Noor popped something blue and rubbery into his mouth. "Perhaps they have heard that the British are losing their clockworkers and they have decided to flex their muscles. It will be interesting to see how the British fare now that no new clockworker has been spotted in Europe for nearly two months and the ones they already have are dying out. Who will create and repair their engines of war?"

"So they've closed the borders to keep the cure out." Alice sank to a pillow despite herself.

"It is what I would do were I ruling China."

"But it doesn't explain why you captured us," Phipps pointed out.

"Ah, but it does. In a way." Al-Noor checked the contents of a serving bowl, discovered it was empty, and made a face. A squid man snatched it up and hurried away with it. "I myself know quite a lot about the clock-work plague. I suffer from it."

"Do you?" Phipps said without a trace of sarcasm.

"It was why my countrymen sent me here. This island is a men's leper colony, you know. Up top, that is. They also send people who suffer from the clockwork plague here, but we, poor souls, are lepers among lepers and are forced to scuttle about down here. After nearly a year of hard work, I discovered how to alter the plague a bit, combine it with proteins from sea animals."

"Squid," Alice whispered in horror.

Al-Noor nodded with enthusiasm. "My process changes them. It slows the plague considerably but does not halt it. The two you cured, Lady Michaels"—he gestured at Phipps, and Alice remembered she had scratched the squid men before al-Noor boarded—"have died. Only my altered plague was keeping them alive, and you took that away from them."

Guilt engulfed Alice, and she folded her arms across her stomach. The iron spider made a cold, dreadful weight.

"I still don't understand why you captured me," Phipps growled. "And I'm growing impatient."

"My research is expensive," al-Noor replied simply. "Do you have any idea how much I pay in bribes just to get a ship's captain to land here, let alone bring me what I need? It is ungodly. Fortunately for me, a source of revenue skimmed across my little sea directly at me."

"We don't have much money," Alice said, not quite lying. "We can pay a little—"

"Not you," al-Noor interrupted. "The Chinese."

That stopped Alice. "The Chinese?" she repeated.

"The emperor, to be specific. His Imperial Majesty Xianfeng is offering four hundred pounds of silver for the capture of Alice, Lady Michaels. Alive." His eyes glittered. "I can breed a lot of squid with that much money."

"Four hundred pounds of silver," Phipps breathed.

"Good heavens," Alice whispered.

"Wait—he wants me alive?" Phipps said. "So when you were threatening to drown me aboard our ship—"

"An excellent bluff," al-Noor agreed. "I'm very good at them."

Phipps closed her uncovered eye for a moment. "Why does the emperor want us? Me?"

"Rumor has it Xianfeng fears the clockwork plague. Perhaps he wants to ensure he avoids it forever. He's also known for keeping pretty concubines, especially unusual ones. You can keep him occupied in any number of ways, I am sure."

A chill slid over Alice, and her fingers automatically went to her spider gauntlet. Phipps caught her eye and gave a tiny shake of her head, which stiffened Alice's spine.

"In any case," al-Noor finished, "once I turn you in, I will have enough silver to buy everything I need for the next stage of my research."

"And what is that?" Alice couldn't help asking.

"A female squid."

"Oh good Lord," Phipps muttered. "Look, al-Noor, my maid is worthless to you. There's no need to hold her hostage. Let her go as a sign of good faith, and I'll do whatever you like."

"No." Al-Noor slurped more tea and held out his cup for a refill, which one of the squid men instantly gave. "I already regret letting that stunning young man go. This maid of yours will guarantee your good behavior. If you try anything strange, she will suffer for it."

"I give you my word as a . . . as a lady that I won't—"

Al-Noor cut her off with a sharp gesture. "Your pardon if I do not accept your word. I will alert the Chinese border authorities by wireless transmission in a moment, but first I want a demonstration of this cure."

A sour worm crawled through Alice's stomach. Phipps glanced at her again, then said, "I don't understand."

"I want to see this cure at work. You used it on two of my squid men before I arrived on the airship, and I had no chance to study the reaction before the two of them died. I wish to see it now."

Alice's earlier guilt returned in a black cloud. Who had those squid men been? Did they have families? Children? Had they understood what was happening to them? It had been an accident—she'd had no intention of killing them, or even hurting them. But she had done it nonetheless, and they were dead because of her.

Phipps crossed her arms. She was still standing. "What do you mean by *see it*?"

"Cure one of my squid men. Now."

Uh-oh. Alice licked dry lips. The masquerade was going sour. She cast about for something to say, something to do.

"I feel I should ask," she said, trying to stall, "exactly why you sent that enormous creature out to capture us. My . . . employer, Lady Michaels, is well-known for curing people with the plague. If you had sent her a message to say you had an entire island of plague victims who needed help, Lady Michaels would have sailed into this cave of her own accord and you could have betrayed her at your leisure, no squid necessary."

"Oh," said al-Noor. A long moment of silence followed. Then he added, "But that would have been dull."

"Indeed," Phipps said.

"In any case," al-Noor continued, "I must insist that you show me the cure, Lady Michaels."

"I am not a circus act, Mr. al-Noor." Phipps's posture stiffened. "And in any case, the cure kills your men. I won't be responsible for more deaths."

"They are all dying anyway," al-Noor replied reasonably. "Fortunately, the mainland sends me a fresh supply of plague victims every few months. They do not even know what becomes of them—nor do they care."

"And you don't, either?" Alice burst out.

"As we already observed, they are dying anyway. Please, Lady Michaels."

"No," Phipps said.

Al-Noor snapped his fingers twice, and one of the squid men whipped the cover off a serving platter. On the platter lay an ugly brass pistol with a glass barrel. Almost languidly, al-Noor plucked the pistol from the table and aimed it at Phipps. A thin whine shrilled through the cavern, and the glass snapped with yellow sparks as the weapon powered up. "Cure one of my men or I will shoot."

"No, you won't," Phipps sniffed. "The reward is to capture me alive. If I'm dead, you get nothing. And if you shoot my maid, I'll be too upset to cure anyone, so don't bother threatening her."

"Oh, I will shoot you, all right," al-Noor said. "And you, Lady Michaels," he added to Alice, "will watch her die. Slowly."

This caught Alice completely off guard. She sprang to her feet, not sure if she was more angry or afraid. *"What?"*

"I deduced it some time ago. This woman—is her name actually Susan, perhaps?—speaks and carries herself like a military officer and, oh yes, she wears a uniform. Lady Michaels serving in the military? I hardly think so. And you, madam, do not walk or talk like a maid. So, Lady Michaels, demonstrate the cure on one of these men here, or I will shoot your friend. I have the feeling you will prove rather more compliant."

"If you shoot her," Alice said, trying to imitate Phipps's bravado and not quite succeeding, "I won't help you."

Al-Noor fired. A red energy beam slashed through the air and struck one of the squid men in the chest. It fell to the floor with a terrible squeal amid sizzling skin. The smell of cooked fish filled the air. The squid man twisted and screamed in agony, even though it had no mouth, and Alice watched in horror as its chest melted into a blue mass that bubbled like a witch's cauldron. The squid man screamed and screamed. Alice clapped her hands over her ears in horror. The spider claws cruelly raked her skin, but she left them there through a century of seconds, until the squid man died. The other squid men remained motionless and impassive, their dark eyes reflecting the mess on the floor.

"That is setting one." Al-Noor cranked a dial on the stock of the pistol and aimed at Phipps, who blanched despite herself. "This is setting seven."

"Wait!" Alice cried.

"Yes, Lady?"

Alice looked down at the table and unhappily ran her hands around the rim of the empty plate before her. The spider's claws scraped over china. Two awful choices, and no one to hide behind, no one to turn to. Just herself. Just as it always was. A wave of homesickness swept over her, and more than anything in that moment she yearned to be back in London, in the little house she had rented, with Gavin sitting across the kitchen table from her while they shared a meal and talked about nothing in particular. No clockworkers, no squid men, no iron spiders. Just she and Gavin, with his kind voice and blue eyes and that way he had of looking at her that made her feel like the only woman in the entire world. Her fingers continued their crawl around the plate.

"Very well, Mr. al-Noor," she said. "I will 'cure' one of your squid men. Just don't—"

She flung the plate at al-Noor. It glanced off his pistol and shattered. He yelped. The pistol fired, but the beam went wide. Phipps leaped across the table at him, brass arm outstretched. Dishes scattered and broke as she grabbed his fleshy wrist with her metal fingers. Except with the clockwork plague came enhanced reflexes, and al-Noor was quick to recover. He went down beneath Phipps but managed to keep his weapon hand free. The pair rolled across the stone floor as al-Noor brought the pistol around to press against Phipps's temple. Phipps knocked it aside. Alice threw another plate at him and missed. It crashed next to his ear, and he ignored it. She dashed around the table, cursing her bulky skirts and looking for an opening.

"Take them, you fools!" al-Noor barked. "Hit this stupid woman!"

The squid men in the room moved. Two grabbed Alice from behind, and their cold hands chilled her skin through her dress. Another pair hoisted Phipps straight off al-Noor while a third cracked her over the ear with a hard fist. Phipps staggered, stunned but still conscious.

Al-Noor hauled himself to his feet. Blood from a split lip spattered his ridiculous swim costume, and Alice loathed him with a black hatred. She struggled within the grip of the squid men, but they held her like iron.

"That was a mistake." He spat blood and raised the pistol. "The reward for your dead body is lower, but still sufficient."

Alice forced herself to remain calm, though fear and adrenaline zipped through every artery and vein. *Think, girl,* she told herself. Al-Noor was a clockworker. Clockworkers were geniuses, but their thinking was far from perfect. *Remember what happens to Gavin.*

"I like what you've done with those droplets of blood," she said with quiet desperation. "They're so round, so smooth, so clear. There must be millions, billions, trillions of cells in each drop, spinning, whirling, swirling through liquid. How beautiful, how lovely, how perfect."

Al-Noor looked down. Scarlet drops fell from his lip, just as Alice described, glistening in the air before they landed on the broken table, and the sight seemed to grab his attention. A drop fell, and his eyes followed it until it hit the wood with a tiny *tip* noise. Another followed. A third landed in his cup, spreading like a tiny fractal flower, and his attention remained rooted. He had the same expression on his face Gavin did when he became fascinated by something, and the similarity unnerved Alice. She ground her teeth. Gavin had nothing in common with this man, and he never would.

"The blood disperses through the water, expanding, flowing, moving. The blood is beautiful, the blood is entrancing," she forced herself to chant.

Nothing in common? Truly? An icy finger of doubt slid around her thoughts. Gavin was a clockworker, and clockworkers always went mad. Always. Al-Noor was just further along than Gavin. How would she react if—when—Gavin decided her life was worth less than some new bit of technology?

Her voice faltered. "The blood is . . . is . . . ," she said, trailing off, tried again, and failed to come up with a single thing to say. All she could see was Gavin's face superimposed over al-Noor's. The squid men, bereft of further orders, remained in place, holding the stunned Phipps upright and keeping Alice in their cold grip. She considered scratching the one on her left with her spider, but that would mean the poor creature's death, and she couldn't bring herself to do it, even to free herself.

Al-Noor looked up. His attention had only been barely diverted, and when Alice stopped chanting, he lost interest in the blood.

"Very good, Lady," he said. "You have shown yourself more dangerous than I knew. You will die now."

He aimed the pistol at Alice. The last thing Alice heard was the pistol's high-pitched whine.

Chapter Three

Peking was burning. The flames lit the night sky with phoenix wings, and smells of smoke and gunpowder stung Cixi's nose, even here at the Mountain Palace for Avoiding Heat, far from the Forbidden City in Peking. Behind her in the spidery palanquin, her maids hid their painted faces in their sleeves and wept. Cixi, the Lady Yehenara, kept a carefully mild expression, as if she were out enjoying an evening ride, though inside she was weeping just like the maids. For a second time the British barbarians had invaded Peking, and now they were do-ing what they did best—destroy. Automatically she reached down to her lap to stroke one of her dogs for comfort, forgetting that her lap was empty. During the hasty evacuation of the Forbidden City, the eunuchs had thrown all her dear little lion-faced dogs down the well so the barbarians wouldn't be able to touch them. She wondered if any of them were still alive, struggling to stay afloat in the cold water and begging for someone to take them out.

The spider palanquin came to a halt. Its legs lowered it to the ground, stirring the silk curtains that preserved the privacy of the riders. Li Liyang, her chief eunuch, personally helped her out and guided her toward the steps of the Pavilion of a Thousand Silver Stars, her own residence within the palace. The palace wasn't a single building but was actually a compound that took up most of the little town of Chengde. Dozens of pavilions and temples and bridges and palaces lay scattered artfully about the lush lawns and gardens of perfumed flowers chosen for their complementary scents. Cixi, who pronounced her imperial name *kee-shee* in the Manchu fashion, paused at the top of the steps to look at the too-bright sky again. The city was dying as slowly and steadily as her dogs.

"My lady, we should not remain outdoors," said Liyang in his high-pitched lilt. "It is too upsetting for a delicate constitution."

"Where is my son?" she asked as she mounted the steps.

"He is safe," Liyang replied. His head was shaved, and he wore a conical hat of gold silk that matched the elaborate geometric designs on his gold robe. Like most eunuchs, he smelled vaguely of urine—the knife that stripped away a boy's three preciouses took with it the ability to control the bladder, a problem that remained through adulthood and led to the saying "smelly as a eunuch." At his belt, Liyang carried a pouch with a small jar in it. The jar held his preciouses preserved in oil, and when he died, they would be buried with him so he could join the ancestors as a full man. Cixi thought of her dogs again and wondered how long it would be before such a thing happened to Liyang.

"*Safe* does not tell me where he is, Liyang," she said. "Bring him to me immediately."

"My lady—"

"You have disobeyed me, Liyang. Fortunately, you are my favorite eunuch, and these are trying times. Therefore I will not have you beaten for disobedience—*if* my son Zaichun is at my side by the time I reach the front door."

Liyang scurried away. To be nice to him, Cixi took her time with the steps, pausing to allow her maids to smooth the wrinkles from her silken split-front robe and straighten the wide trousers beneath. Cixi was beautiful and knew it, but in the Imperial Court, beauty was common and cheap. Cixi's lustrous hair, fine features, and smooth skin had gotten her chosen as a concubine of the fifth rank when she was sixteen, but poise, wit, and her skill in the bedroom had caught the emperor's fancy, and by age twenty-two, Cixi had spun that fancy into a pregnancy and finally her current rank as Imperial Concubine. Beauty had its uses, and it had to be maintained, but it was nothing without a mind behind it.

Liyang was lucky that beauty requirements for Manchu women such as Cixi did not extend to binding their feet as some of the concubines did. Otherwise someone would have carried her up the steps in an instant and she would have been forced to have Liyang beaten with bamboo rods regardless of how she felt about him. She supposed she could order it done with the thicker ones that broke bones and left bruises instead of the thinner ones that split skin and laid flesh open. But that might show too much favoritism, even for Liyang, and when things were chaotic, people craved order. It wouldn't do to go back on the rules for any reason. No, if Liyang didn't produce her son within the allotted time, she would have to have the Imperial Master of a Hundred Cries mete out a severe beating with no intervention from Cixi. It would make everyone feel better.

She reached the top of the steps. The Pavilion of a Thousand Silver Stars was three stories tall, bright and airy even in the night. Lacquered pillars held up the portico, which looked out over the serene waters of a lotus pond. She had ordered the pavilion painted a soft pink, the exact shade of an orchid, because her girlhood name had been Little Orchid. Cixi was the name given her on the day she had been chosen as an Imperial Concubine. A year after the birth of her son—so far the emperor's only son—Cixi had been promoted to the position of Noble Consort, which put her second only to the empress. This meant she had the emperor's ear and could do things such as build pink pavilions in the Mountain Palace for Avoiding Heat.

Cixi glanced at the fiery sky again. Last year, just before the signing of the awful Treaty of Tientsin—the treaty that granted the British power to travel within China and sell their filthy opium—a fleet of British ships carrying diplomats, envoys, and thousands of soldiers sailed up the Peiho River near the fortress at Taku. The emperor and his generals didn't want an armed force coming so close to Taku, and so the emperor sent a message asking them to anchor at a harbor farther north. Although the request was perfectly reasonable and not even inconvenient, the English envoy Wright Frederick—or Frederick Wright, as Cixi supposed the barbarians put the name—ordered the fleet to attack Taku to teach the Chinese a lesson. No doubt to the great surprise of the English, the fortress at Taku had turned out to be more heavily fortified than expected. The automatons and soldiers at Taku had turned back the English forces with little effort. The easy victory emboldened the emperor to declare the entire Treaty of Tientsin in abeyance and the borders closed.

Now, a year later, the English responded in force. They fought their way up the river all the way to Peking, despite the best efforts of the emperor's generals. Emperor Xianfeng had been forced to flee to the Mountain Palace for his own safety. A difficult thing it had been, too, with hundreds of soldiers, slaves, and eunuchs, and an equal number of mechanical carts filled with their minimal possessions and treasures, preceded by fifty spiders to sweep the road ahead of the emperor's palanquin and strew the stones with rose petals.

Cixi reached the pavilion doors, gridded with flawless glass, and her maids hurried to slide them open. She glanced about. No sign of Liyang or Zaichun. Ah well.

Cixi raised her foot, clad in a bejeweled slipper, to step over the threshold.

"Honored mother!" Her son Zaichun dashed up the steps, his dark eyes sparkling beneath his round cap. He was not quite six, and to him this was a grand adventure that kept him up well past his normal bedtime. Behind him came an entourage of eunuchs and his wet nurse, all of them carrying any toys, foodstuffs, and articles of clothing the boy might need. The servants looked frazzled, and their clothes were in disarray. Cixi made a mental note to have a sharp word with Liyang about that. Servants in the presence of the emperor's son and the Imperial Concubine had no place to appear less than respectable. Disarray led to fear, fear led to panic, and right now, no one could afford to panic.

"You wished to see me, Mother?" Zaichun continued.

"I did, Little Cricket." She touched his hair, careful not to the let the long jade coverings on her nails jab his face. "I wanted to see for myself that you were safe."

"I am. I spoke with Father, too. He even let me ride behind his palanquin so I could watch for invaders!"

"That was kind of him. I hope you remembered to give him your thanks."

"Of course, Mother. I heard him talking to General Su Shun about how well-mannered I was when we entered the palace."

"That is good to hear, my son, and I am glad to see that you are safe, but perhaps you should sleep in my pavilion tonight."

"I can sleep in my own pavilion," he said sulkily, betraying his earlier good manners. "It's bigger. And I'm not sleepy."

"Mother has had a trying day. She hopes her son won't make things more difficult."

"I don't like pink. It's for girls."

"Your words are very interesting." Cixi's tone remained mild, but her hand dropped to his shoulder, and the points of her nail covers dug into his flesh. He gasped. "But I'm sure you would rather spend the night here, where it's safer. Is that not true?" She tightened her grasp.

"Yes, Mother." He was struggling not to show the pain, and she was proud that he didn't do so, though she didn't loosen her grip.

"It would be good if the eunuchs knew."

He cleared his throat. "I believe I will spend the night in my honored mother's pavilion. See to it."

The eunuchs bowed and swarmed into the pavilion through a series of side entrances—no one but Cixi and her guests used the main door.

"You are a well-mannered boy. Perhaps you would like to run along now." She released him, and he fled into the pavilion.

She held out her hand and said, "Tea." A porcelain cup was placed in it, and she let the warm drink wash the road dust from her throat as she strolled across the threshold. Inside the pavilion, a maid carrying a heavy feather bed froze as she realized whose presence she was in. She tried to bow and keep the precious feather bed from touching the floor all at once, though she didn't dare flee without permission. Cixi dropped the cup—a spider caught it before it hit the ground—and was about to enter the pavilion fully when she changed her mind and paused in the doorway again. The bowing maid holding the heavy feather bed bit her lip, and sweat was making her makeup run. A bit of down worked its way out of the feather bed and, caught on a draft, drifted out the open door and away to the east, toward the place known as the Cool Hall on the Misty Lake, the emperor's residence. Cixi watched it go. The fear she had been keeping firmly at bay gave way to a new nervousness she couldn't name. The feather vanished into the darkness.

"Liyang!" she said.

Liyang came to her side. "My lady?"

"What is the latest news of Peking?"

"The Army of a Thousand Tigers continues to fight the English north of Peking, my lady, while Su Shun and the Dragon Men use the Machines of Wind and Thunder in the south."

"But who is winning?"

Liyang hesitated. "The Tiger Army is . . . rather . . . it is encountering quite a challenge, one worthy of its fighting prowess. The Machines of Wind and Thunder fight bravely under Prince Kung and will do so until nothing is left but a pile of melted brass."

"I see." They were losing, but Liyang couldn't say such a dreadful thing to the Imperial Consort. She kept her face calm with effort. "How is the emperor?"

The arms of the bowed maid were now trembling with

the effort of holding up the bulky feather bed. Letting the silk cover touch the floor would mean her death. Liyang shot her a glance and said quickly, "I am told he is resting very comfortably."

Resting comfortably was Liyang's way of saying Xianfeng had taken a great deal of rice wine. *Very comfortably* meant he had used his opium pipe as well. Cixi knew she shouldn't be surprised. The man had turned thirty only last month, and already he had smoked more opium and drunk more wine than any four emperors before him. Small wonder he had produced only one child, and how lucky for Cixi it had been her son. The maid was panting now, and one corner of the bed drooped toward the floor. Another feather floated away to the east, drawing Cixi's eye with it. The nervousness wouldn't leave her alone. Two feathers in a row. A sign?

"I heard him talking to General Su Shun about how well-mannered I was when we entered the palace."

Two drifting feathers. Rice wine and opium. Strange. If Xianfeng had been drinking and smoking long enough to be "resting very comfortably," how could he have been coherent enough to comment on his son's manners?

"I believe I will call on the emperor," Cixi said, then remembered herself and coughed to cover her lapse. "Rather, please let the emperor know the Imperial Concubine would be pleased and honored to find herself summoned to his heavenly presence."

"But the emperor is resting— Yes, my lady," Liyang said. He snapped his fingers, and one of his apprentices, a eunuch of perhaps six or seven, rushed up, clutching at the jar at his own belt. "Run to the Cool Hall on the Misty Lake and deliver the lady's message."

The boy dashed away. Cixi turned to follow more sedately, and her maids slid the doors shut on the relieved face of the maid with the feather bed.

The palanquin delivered Cixi, her maids, and her eunuchs to the Cool Hall on the Misty Lake, the emperor's residence at the palace. The palanquin skittered faster than the little apprentice eunuch could run, and he would actually not have been able to deliver the message yet, something Cixi was counting on. Cixi swept toward the main doors of the Hall, and the startled eunuchs on duty hurried to slide it open. Again, she halted in the doorway. Why was she here, ahead of the messenger she herself had sent? Foolishness. This was a strange day, and she was on a strange errand. But her instincts told her to continue, and she had learned to trust her instincts.

"The back of the mind is wiser than the front," her mother liked to say.

"I wish to proceed completely alone," she announced, and continued inside.

For the Imperial Concubine, *completely alone* meant her, four maids (one for each sacred direction), Liyang, his three assistants, and a spider to run ahead with a lantern. At one time, the Hall had been fitted for electric lights, with each lightbulb personally designed and blown by one of the Dragon Men at great effort and expense. The lights were an artistic triumph, each one a delicate work of art that captured the sun itself. But the moment Xianfeng entered his new apartments, he fell victim to a headache that lasted three days. The chief eunuch declared electricity was the cause, and he ordered all the wiring pulled out and every bulb smashed. The Dragon Man had drowned himself in a fishpond, and no electric light had been allowed in the Hall since.

Cixi strode through the dark corridors, following the spider. She could tell the place was bustling with activity as frightened servants rushed about, finding places to store the clothing and treasures brought out of the Forbidden City, but this was merely a sense she had, a change in the night and feeling of tensions. She actually saw nothing—everyone cleared the way for Cixi, and she walked through empty hallways, alone but for her spider, maids, and eunuchs, and eventually she came to Xianfeng's chambers. Outside the sliding door stood twelve muscled guards with swords, armor, and pistols. All of them sported metal limbs or partially armored skin, as was proper for a soldier and taboo for nobility.

Cixi hesitated. Something was wrong here. The soldiers' builds weren't soft and flabby like those of eunuchs. Only a few highly trusted male advisers were allowed to enter the Forbidden City back in Peking, and not one of them was allowed to remain inside after nightfall, not even in the most dire emergencies, because the integrity of the emperor's wife and concubines had to be protected. Even one man left on the grounds overnight meant the origin of any baby born to a wife or concubine later might not be the emperor's. Yet here stood a dozen powerful, virile men. True, some rules were bent at the Mountain Palace, but never this one. Cixi's own integrity could be called into question by just standing in their presence. Why would—

Then Cixi noticed the corner of a bandage sticking out from the waist joint of the armor of one of the guards, and she understood with great relief. These men had only recently been castrated, probably in the last day or two, when it became clear the emperor would have to evacuate the Forbidden City and would need strong guards. She wondered where their jars were.

"I wish for the emperor to know I am here," she said to one of the guards. "You know who I am?"

"Yes, great lady." The guards bowed and looked at one another uncertainly. It occurred to Cixi that these guards were unschooled in proper etiquette. A flabby eunuch would have politely enquired about her business, or more likely have long been aware she was coming and admitted her immediately or turned her aside in such a way as to make it seem that leaving were her idea.

"You are honorable men who are guarding the emperor's heavenly presence during these trying times," she said. "I am sure he appreciates your service." And boldly she stepped forward to reach for the door. Horrified, two of her maids leaped forward to whip it open, their fear of the guards overcome by the idea that the Imperial Concubine might touch a door for herself. Cixi sailed through as if she had done nothing at all unusual, and before the guards could decide what to do, her maids and eunuchs also boiled through and the doors snapped shut. The chaos of the evacuation worked in her favor.

Moments later, she was entering Xianfeng's bedchamber, with its wide, curtained bed, treasure boxes, windup machines, and red wall hangings drilled with spy holes. Eight perfumed lanterns threw down a glow that held back the darkness. A silver nightingale trilled soothing music from a bejeweled cage, and a small crowd of eunuchs knelt around the bed, awaiting the emperor's slightest desire. Above the bed hung a painting of a seated man dressed in black. His bare head was shaved, and his piercing eyes stared through the viewer. He held a human hand made of brass and jade and a box of blackest ebony inlaid with gold dragons. The man was Lung Fei, China's first Dragon Man, and his image was prominent everywhere in every imperial palace.

Against one wall, another man dressed all in black occupied a black pillow. A brass salamander curled around his ear with its tail inserted into his ear canal. The man was sitting down in the presence of the emperor, a capital offense for most people, but the disease known as the blessing of dragons made Dragon Men forget many social protocols, and if they were punished or executed every time they forgot one, soon there would be no Dragon Men left, and China needed Dragon Men. They wore unadorned black silk to show they had no time to worry about clothing and to quickly identify their position even to the uneducated.

This Dragon Man held a board and paper in his lap, and he was scribbling madly. "Cixi," he said without looking up or stopping. "A paper cut. One bleeds without knowing."

Cixi ignored this nonsense, knelt, and tapped her forehead on the floor at the bedchamber's threshold, as did her maids and eunuchs. Then she waited, facedown.

"The Son of Heaven won't give his permission to rise, great lady," said a voice from a corner. "He is resting very comfortably, and it is a surprise that you were allowed to enter."

Since the owner of the voice clearly wasn't on the floor, Cixi remained in her daring mood and took it as a sign that she could rise anyway. She did so, though her entourage remained on the floor.

The speaker, a tall, muscled man in his midforties, moved into the lantern light. He had the swarthy complexion that bespoke hours spent outdoors, and his hair was streaked with gray under his high red cap. His straight nose and long jaw gave him a regal air, and he wore pieces of red-lacquered armor over his Manchu robe and trousers. The armor pieces were purely decorative, indicating his rank. Half the man's face was covered in intricately etched brass, and riveted brass ringed his neck. The man's name was Su Shun. Cixi narrowed her eyes. Last she had heard, he was commanding troops in the city.

"One has to wonder," she said, "what the emperor's most trusted general is doing in Jehol when he is likely needed in Peking."

"I like the ducks on the canal," said the Dragon Man. "They don't wind down."

Su Shun ran a finger down the side of his metallic face, almost as if he were scratching. Members of the nobility did not modify themselves with metal—such modifications were reserved for the lower classes. Su Shun was an exception. The blessing of dragons had ruined his face, forcing him to have the disease's damage repaired by a Dragon Man. Cixi knew Su Shun felt a deep disdain for anyone who had not served in the military, including the emperor. That he looked down on mere women was a given.

"The emperor needs an experienced general to coordinate military movements at his side," Su Shun replied. "I am, of course, here at his request. Prince Cheng is easily able to command Peking."

"I believe Prince Kung runs Peking."

"Prince Kung was not available, and I was forced to turn command of the troops over to Cheng. I am confident he will do a good job."

"Cheng does admirable work," Cixi said smoothly. "A hard worker who never speaks for himself. Somehow, his superiors always take credit for what goes right, and Cheng takes the blame for what goes wrong." She paused. "Who is Cheng's superior in this conflict, Su Shun? Would he be in this room?"

"The emperor," Su Shun replied, equally smoothly, "is everyone's superior."

"Hm." Cixi sniffed. The oily perfume of the lanterns was the only scent on the air. On the bed lay Xianfeng, hidden beneath a pile of embroidered scarlet coverlets. "I am happy to see that you are here to comfort the emperor in his hour of need, Su Shun, but perhaps the Son of Heaven will require comfort from his Imperial Concubine as well as his general."

Su Shun stepped forward, between Cixi and Xian-feng's bed. His partially brass face distorted his expression, giving him a half-dead look. "As the lady can see, he has already been well comforted."

At that, Cixi noticed for the first time a young woman kneeling among the eunuchs. Her robes indicated her position as a concubine of the fifth rank, the lowest rank. "Who is that?" Cixi demanded, and the girl flinched, though she didn't rise from the floor or even look up.

"A new nothing," Su Shun said dismissively. "The emperor wanted company, and I brought her here myself."

"Into his bedchamber?" Cixi's voice had nearly become a squawk. The emperor saw only select concubines in his own bedchamber. Lesser concubines he visited in their rooms. A sound came from one of the eunuchs, and Cixi regained control of herself. "That is surprising, Su Shun."

"Unusual circumstances, one supposes," he said, his tone still mild. "The journey was difficult, and he wanted comfort."

"Comfort from an untutored girl rather than his Imperial Concubine or a concubine of the second rank?" Her voice shook at the outrage, though she didn't know whom she was outraged at. The emperor could do as he wished, of course, and it wasn't her place to be angry, or even to be mildly unhappy.

"It would seem so."

Cixi was steadily losing ground. The more she lost her temper, the more she looked the fool, and the more face she lost. She had to get control of herself and of the situation. But the awful evacuation and the death of her dogs and the long journey were taking their toll, and the words snarled free before she could stop them. "Get out, you piece of pig filth," she snapped at the girl. "And do not return."

The concubine scurried backward to the door, hurriedly knocked her head on the floor the prescribed number of times, and fled. Cixi hoped she would have a bruise in the morning.

"You'll disturb the emperor's rest, Lady Yehenara." Su Shun was suppressing a smile, or as much of one as his brass cheek allowed.

Cixi closed her eyes and forced her anger back like a dragon forcing a tiger into a cage. "An Imperial Concubine is better able to ensure the emperor has a proper rest, General."

"This is not true," Su Shun said mildly. "Her proper position is to disturb him in his bed as often as possible. Nothing more."

"An Imperial Concubine's proper place is indeed in the emperor's bedchamber." Cixi felt more in control now that the girl had gone. "On the other hand, some may wonder why a general is spending so much time there."

The left side of Su Shun's face flushed. The eunuchs and maids, still on the floor, were watching from the corners of their eyes and listening hard, even as they pretended they weren't there. Within moments, this conversation would be repeated all over the Mountain Palace. Everything was. Su Shun drew himself up.

"Now that the other concubine has left, you may approach the emperor if you wish," he said, taking the upper hand by giving permission, even though he had no right to grant it. His magnanimity, false or not, pushed Cixi down another level. She cast about, but she was still tired, and she couldn't find a counter response.

"Very well," was all she could think to say.

"And if the great lady does not mind," he continued, oozing politeness, "I have other duties to attend to. If she will allow me to withdraw?"

Cixi ground her teeth, feeling the secret eyes of the eunuchs and slaves and the spies through their spy holes on her. Su Shun had scored yet more points with too-precise manners. If she dismissed him, she was giving in to his sarcasm. If she refused, she would look peevish, and she wouldn't have the chance to approach Xianfeng.

"Very well," she murmured.

"What was that?" he said. "If the lady could speak more clearly?"

He was truly in his element now. Cixi's face flamed. He had embarrassed her, here in the imperial bedchamber, a place where she was supposed to have the most power, and he was flaunting the fact that he knew it. Before sunrise, the whole Mountain Palace would know Su Shun had bested Cixi in the imperial chambers. Cixi wanted to crawl under the bedcovers and hide from all the eyes in the room, those she could see and especially those she couldn't. But she kept her back straight and her head high. *"Face what you cannot avoid"* was another piece of advice from her mother, and it had never failed her.

"Very well," she repeated, briskly this time. "Thank you, Su Shun. Your service in the imperial bedchamber is appreciated."

But Su Shun was already leaving with his own eunuchs, and her final remark was delivered to his back.

"Paper cuts," said the Dragon Man.

Refusing to feel defeat, Cixi approached the bed. The eunuchs shuffled out of the way, and she ignored them. The nightingale in the corner stopped singing, and Xianfeng stirred. He had remained asleep during an argument between his general and his Imperial Concubine, but this woke him up. The coverlets fell away from his right hand, which wasn't flesh and blood, but jade inlaid with wires of gold and brass. The wires were twisted into impossible shapes, and the hand seemed to quiver with quiet power, even when the owner was partially asleep.

"I want a different song for my bird, Lung Chao," Emperor Xianfeng murmured. "Make it sing a different song."

The complicated wiring on the Jade Hand glowed faintly at his words, and the salamander in the Dragon Man's ear made an answering glow. The Dragon Man twitched once, then set his drawings down and scuttled over to the nightingale. He plucked it from its cage, flipped it open, and did something to the insides that

Cixi didn't see. The emperor, meanwhile, drifted back to sleep, the Jade Hand lying still on his chest.

Cixi looked down at Xianfeng's sleeping form. His cheeks were hollow, his skin sallow, his build thin and only filled out by the voluminous silks that enshrouded him. He looked like a man of fifty, not a man who had just celebrated his thirtieth birthday. Cixi's eyes, however, were mostly drawn to the Celestial Scepter, the Jade Hand. The top of the hand pierced Xianfeng's flesh and connected with the tissue inside, allowing the hand limited motion. The Scepter was the creation of Lung Fei and had become the symbol of office for every emperor since Lung Fei's time more than a hundred years ago. It would fall off when the emperor died, and it would graft itself onto the stump of the new emperor. Lung Fei had written that willingness to give up a hand for the empire indicated proper character for a ruler and set him apart from lesser nobility, but the thought that she would eventually watch her own son's hand be chopped off turned Cixi's stomach, no matter how much he—and she—stood to gain by the gesture.

The Dragon Man rewound the nightingale and replaced it in the cage. It started to sing a different song, just as the emperor had ordered. More of Lung Fei's work. He had written that Dragon Men were too dangerous to be allowed free rein, and the Celestial Scepter, paired with the salamanders, allowed the emperor to keep them under control.

Cixi leaned over Xianfeng but didn't touch him—she

had no desire to. She didn't love him, or even like him very much. It was a concubine's job to be beautiful and entertaining and give advice when asked, and she did this job spectacularly well. It was not a concubine's job to fall in love. She did feel a certain fondness for Xianfeng, and a definite sense of possessiveness. He was her emperor. *Hers.* Thanks to him, she had risen from a childhood of poverty and become the second-most-powerful woman in China, just behind the empress herself. In some ways, Cixi was even more powerful than the empress because Cixi had borne the emperor a son, and it didn't look as if he would have any others. Usually emperors had too many sons, but Xianfeng had spent his youth in brothels and opium dens, and she could see close up the impact such activities had on a man and his fertility. It was possible he had a few dozen bastard children out there, sons of prostitutes, but they were of no consequence. Only a son born of the empress or an Imperial Concubine could inherit the Celestial Throne.

Greatly daring, Cixi put out a hand and touched the lapel of his pajamas. The trouble was, Xianfeng wasn't ruling China in any real sense. The eunuchs and generals handled everything while Xianfeng sucked his opium pipe and drained his wine cup and spent himself uselessly on concubines and prostitutes. It was no wonder the English had managed to invade China and force opium down Chinese windpipes, not when the emperor himself partook of the stuff at every opportunity. Meanwhile, the generals wanted only to fight, and the eunuchs wanted only to line their pockets with silver. No one truly wanted to lead China.

Thoughts of Xianfeng's death made Cixi's eyes go to the corner of the bedchamber. An ebony box carved and inlaid with golden imperial dragons and sealed with a latch shaped like a phoenix perched on a jade table. The flickering lantern light made it appear as if the sinuous dragons were chasing one another around the box, either in play or battle. The box was another invention of Lung Fei, and inside, Cixi knew, lay a piece of paper, and on the paper was written the name of the man—or boy—the emperor had designated as his heir. The box would be opened at the moment of the emperor's death. The heir was supposed to be Zaichun, but Cixi had never seen the paper, and given Xianfeng's state of mind, nothing was certain.

Cixi leaned over Xianfeng and sniffed again. A soft scent of rose petals floated over the bedcovers to mingle with the perfume from the lanterns. She set her face. There was no hint of rice wine or opium about him; there hadn't been since she walked into the room. Her suspicions must be correct—he hadn't taken any opium at all. Yet he had somehow remained asleep throughout Cixi's argument with Su Shun, and he didn't stir now. A tray of jade dishes sat on a small table next to his bed. Bits of food were left on them, and the tiny serving spider lay motionless and unwound nearby. Things were truly out of order if dirty dishes were left in the emperor's presence. She straightened and passed by the tray. As she did, she slipped the little spider into her sleeve. No doubt *someone* had noticed, but it didn't matter quite yet.

Cixi lingered a while longer in the imperial bedchamber, establishing and reinforcing her right to be there, and then finally left, backing away from the bed and knocking her forehead on the floor as she did so. Liyang, the eunuchs, and her maids followed.

"Liyang," she murmured as they strolled slowly through the corridors.

"My lady?"

"In the morning, everyone will be discussing that conversation, and the emperor will certainly hear of it. One wonders if I will come across as . . . less than I am."

"I will personally see to it that some of the correct eunuchs are on hand when the emperor wakes in the morning," Liyang said instantly. "They will feed the emperor a flattering version of the story along with his breakfast."

"Thank you, Liyang. You are most skilled."

"My lady. Will there be anything else?"

With that, she knew he had seen her take the spider. "Tell Lung Fan I wish to see him tonight."

"Yes, my lady."

Fingering the cup in her sleeve, Cixi passed by the imperial dining hall, with its low tables, sumptuous pillows, and careful wall hangings. One of the sliding doors, covered in frosted glass, was partly open, and Cixi saw light and a hint of movement inside. Curious as to who could have business in the dining hall at this time of night, on *this* night in particular, she stopped and motioned for Liyang to remain silent, knowing the others would follow suit. She leaned forward to peer through the crack. What she saw made her knees go weak, and she stifled a gasp of horror.

Su Shun was sitting at the head of the table. A small banquet was spread out before him, sweetmeats and delicacies on jade plates and bowls rimmed with gold. As Cixi watched, a spider ran down his arm to the table, speared a dumpling from a bowl, and ran back up Su Shun's arm to drop the morsel into his open mouth. Cixi staggered, and one of her maids hurried to help her upright. Horrifying. Unthinkable! Su Shun was sitting in the emperor's place at the emperor's table eating from the emperor's dishes. Anyone who dared such a thing would be instantly put to death.

Anyone but the emperor.

Su Shun's intent couldn't be more clear. He saw himself in the emperor's place and was indulging himself in a bit of predictive fantasy. The eunuchs who were with him wouldn't say a word, since they were in a position to be chief eunuchs once Su Shun took the throne.

Su Shun ate another dumpling. Cixi hung in the hallway, wracked with indecision. Should she burst into the dining hall and confront him? That would be satisfying and even fun, and the little girl in her longed to see the look on his brassy face when she did so. But the Imperial Concubine in her paused. Su Shun was a highly trusted general. He had just had an argument with Cixi in the emperor's chambers, an argument that Cixi had clearly lost, and Cixi had definitely not been summoned to the imperial bedchambers while Su Shun just as definitely had been. All of this meant that if Su Shun claimed Cixi—and her servants—were lying out of spite, and if Su Shun's eunuchs backed him up, the emperor would have no choice but to believe Su Shun, and Cixi would lose considerable status. The emperor might refuse to see her entirely, putting her position in court into great jeopardy. Although her son was the emperor's only male offspring, the emperor needed only Zaichun. Cixi had finished her part in this and could still be dismissed at any time.

Therefore it was time to go. Cixi and her servants fled as silently as they could in their silken slippers down the corridors to the main doors, where her spider palanquin awaited her. No one would have known of this if Cixi hadn't come to the Hall at this late hour, or if that door hadn't been left open. Or if that maid hadn't walked by with that feather bed, or if that errant feather hadn't drawn Cixi's attention to the Cool Hall on the Misty Lake. She shook her head. It was impossible to track down the first event that led to anything. One might as well argue that all this was coming about because Cixi herself had been born, though that had happened only because her father had met her mother and they had copulated at a particular time in a particular place. How differently history might go if one tiny event changed along the way.

Back at the Pavilion of a Thousand Silver Stars, Cixi entered her own chambers, her mind churning. Soft rugs hushed her footsteps, and the spy holes on the walls were well crafted, barely noticeable between the wall hangings. Since this was not the emperor's residence, electric lights were allowed, and the maids set about flipping switches on intricate jade lamps. Cixi sighed as shadows fled the room and the place brightened. She felt more at ease in the light. The water clock on the wall told her dawn was only three hours away, and now that she was slowing down, exhaustion settled over her. Had it only been this afternoon that her eunuchs had thrown her dogs down the well? They were no doubt dead now. She hoped their little corpses rotted quickly and that a barbarian might sicken and die from tainted water so her dear pets' deaths wouldn't be completely in vain.

A woman was waiting for her, another Dragon Man dressed all in black with her hair worn in a man's long queue. They were all called Dragon Men and referred to using *he* and *him* in conversation whether they were male or female to ensure that everyone treated even the women with deference, allowing them to build the all-important inventions and weapons that kept the empire on an even footing with the West. Her face was plain, her cheekbones broad and flat, but her eyes burned with intelligence. This Dragon Man was Lung Fan, and she— he—was personally assigned to Cixi just as Lung Chao was assigned to the emperor.

"My lady wished to see me?" said Lung Fan without bowing.

"I did." Cixi handed her the spider. "I want you to test this."

Lung Fan turned it over, examining it with long fingers. "An eating spider? What for?"

"For—"

"No, wait." Lung Fan sniffed the spider's legs and the little chopsticks it used to hold morsels of food. Then she took a metal instrument from her pocket. It was shaped like a serpent, a very wise creature. By law, all automatons and machines in China were shaped like animals or mythical creatures. Man-shaped automatons were strictly forbidden, lest the automatons begin to think themselves human beings. Lights along the serpent's body flickered in strange patterns, and it hissed in short bursts.

"There is good news," Lung Fan said.

Cixi furrowed her brow, puzzled. "Good news? But I haven't told you what I was looking—"

"The battle in Peking has taken a turn for the better. Based on what I have learned from the eunuchs, the concentration of paraffin in the atmosphere, and the contents of a coded message the emperor has not yet read, our troops stand slightly more than a ninety percent chance of winning."

Cixi realized her mouth was hanging open, a most unbecoming gesture. She shut it. "You are sure?"

Lung Fan sniffed the air again. "No. It's ninety-two percent."

A soft ripple went through the eunuchs and maids, though none spoke. A great deal of tension evaporated. Cixi herself felt a little giddy. "So all we need do is wait for a while, and we can go home."

"Duck tongues," said Lung Fan. "Bear paws, beef marrow."

"I—what?"

Lung Fan held up the little automaton. "Those are the foods that were most recently eaten with this spider. I can do a much longer examination and tell you more, if you like."

"Is that all?" Cixi asked, disappointed. "Because I was wondering—"

"Yes, they were all drugged," Lung Fan added as an afterthought. "A powerful sedative also designed to stop a cough. I believe there is also willow bark distillate, which will reduce a fever."

"Drugged." Cixi didn't know whether to be relieved or alarmed that her theory had been correct. It was so much news so fast, she was having a hard time taking it all in. Perhaps this was the reason Dragon Men went insane.

"With medicine," Lung Fan said.

"Is the emperor ill?" Liyang asked doubtfully. "I heard nothing of it."

"The sedative would make him sleepy and would explain why he was resting very comfortably, even without his opium," Cixi said. "But why something for fever and cough when he had problems with neither?"

"Perhaps the sedative was all Su Shun wanted," Liyang hazarded, "and the other effects are coincidental."

"You believe Su Shun was behind it?"

"I have no proof, of course," Liyang said. "But he was there, and he brought in the concubine, and I assume she served the food to the emperor, perhaps even tasted it herself beforehand to show it was not poisoned. And it was not. Quite." Liyang paused thoughtfully. "Perhaps Su Shun knows the emperor is ill and is trying to hide it?"

"The food served by this spider was definitely not poisoned," Lung Fan said. She dropped into a lotus position on the floor and fiddled with the spider. One of the maids made a disgusted noise, but Dragon Men were allowed to sit in the presence of the Imperial Court.

"The food was not poisoned," Cixi repeated slowly. And then a dreadful thought stole over her, a terrible, world-wrecking thought. She also sank to the floor, and a maid pushed a padded stool under her. One of the seams burst as Cixi sat on it, and little feathers puffed out. The maid rushed about, gathering them up. "The *food* was not poisoned. Liyang, go now and find that concubine. Bring her to me immediately. If you cannot find her, find out everything you can about her. This is urgent. See to it yourself."

"My lady." Liyang bowed and vanished out the door with his apprentices and assistants.

"So, what are you thinking, concubine woman?" Lung Fan asked. "You look as if you swallowed a frog."

"I do not wish to say."

Lung Fan grinned, and the expression looked ghoulish in the bright lights. "I actually know what you're thinking. And I think you're right. Can I be reassigned to someone else?"

Cixi didn't answer. For a long time, she waited in tense silence. The only sound was the dripping of the water clock and the clicking of the spider against the serpent in Lung Fan's lap and the footsteps of the maids who were gathering feathers. Eventually, Liyang rushed back into the room with his apprentices panting behind him.

"Where is the girl?" Cixi asked without waiting for formalities.

"She is dead, my lady. Drowned in a lotus pool. Already the story is going about that she killed herself because she displeased you, or that you yourself are directly responsible."

Cixi waved this aside. One fewer low-ranking concubine was of no importance. "And where did she come from?"

"That is the startling thing, my lady. No one seems to know. All the records are in disarray, thanks to the evacuation, of course, but no one I talked to seems to remember her, or when she joined the Imperial Court."

"I thought as much," Cixi muttered. "Su Shun arranged for her to slip into the evacuation caravan. Where is the body?"

"I anticipated your wishes, my lady, and my assistants are bringing her here. She is on the back lawn."

A feather drifted across Cixi's nose as she rose to her feet. "Come, Lung Fan. Bring your device."

The dead girl was still soaked through. Her hair had come undone and lay tangled about her neck and shoulders. She huddled on her side in her ruined green robe on the grass. Cixi guessed she was no more than sixteen, the same age Cixi had been when she became a concubine. Lung Fan squatted next to her and punctured her skin with the serpent's teeth. The lights along the serpent's back glittered, then settled into a steady scarlet glow.

"Well?" Cixi asked. "Was I thinking right?"

"Were *we* thinking right?" Lung Fan corrected. "And yes. The girl was in the early stages of the blessing of dragons."

Cixi stepped back, as did all the maids and eunuchs. The girl carried the blessing of dragons, and Su Shun had arranged for the girl to share Xianfeng's bed. Thanks to Su Shun, the emperor now had the plague.

Chapter Four

Gavin slipped down the dark tunnel, the Impossible Cube clutched tight to his chest. The sandy floor ground unpleasantly beneath his boots, and he was uncomfortably aware that he stood out like a torch with his white leathers and blue wings. Fortunately, he hadn't met any squid men. For once the clockwork plague worked in his favor—clockworkers sometimes became so engrossed in something fascinating that they forgot mundane duties, such as posting guards.

Back in the main cavern behind him, the *Lady* was moored at a small stone quay, her half-lit envelope glimmering like a tethered star. The giant squid that had towed her there was nowhere to be seen. Gavin had slipped aboard and quietly reconnected the generator so her envelope would lift her again, but he didn't power the machine up fully to avoid calling attention to the situation. Now he just had to rescue his reason to escape.

Doors faced the tunnel, all of them heavy, all of them shut. He tried one and found it unlocked. On the other side was a laboratory—sharp glassware, smoking burners, gooey things in jars, a rubbery segment of tentacle on a dissecting table. An operating table with blue bloodstains hunkered in the corner amid a nauseating smell of sulfur. The sight oozed over Gavin's skin and made him shiver. Thank God Alice and Phipps weren't here. He slipped back into the tunnel.

The Cube shifted in Gavin's hands, almost as if it resisted being moved. Dr. Clef had once said the Cube always stayed in a fixed point in space and time, that it never actually went anywhere and instead forced the universe to move around itself, like a rock in a river. It rather felt to Gavin that if he lost control of the Cube, it might go spinning away from him, punching holes in space-time like a hot needle, and the possibility unnerved him.

His fingers tightened around the Cube's springy surface as he slipped down the long cave, trying to listen, but the heavy doors trapped sound and light. The only noise was the soft clink of metal wings on his back and his heart pounding in his ears while he searched. He was always looking for something. It had started when pirates attacked the *Juniper*, the airship on which he had spent most of his childhood. That attack had stranded him in London, forcing him to search for a way home. Then he had met Alice, and he had found himself constantly searching for a way to have her in his life. Then he had been infected with the clockwork plague, and he searched for a cure. And just lately, he had learned from a woman who could see the future that his father, the man who had abandoned him, was still alive and his destiny was somehow "entwined" with Gavin's. The thought both thrilled Gavin and angered him beyond measure. He wanted to find his father and grab him in a big bear hug even as he wanted to punch him in the gut.

To his horror, he realized he was singing under his breath:

I picked a rose, the rose picked me,
Underneath the branches of the forest tree.
The moon picked you from all the rest
For I loved you best.

He stopped himself. Gavin used to think his grandfather had taught him that song, but lately he'd begun to wonder if it had come from his father instead, if his father hadn't sung it to his mother when they were young and in love. If so, it was more than a little unsettling that Gavin had gotten Alice to fall in love with him by singing it to her. Or maybe that was just fitting. He would have to ask his father. If he could find him.

Tension tightened every muscle and joint, and anger burned in his belly. Alice. Al-Noor would pay for touching Alice. The thought of the man laying a hand on her unleashed a red, snarling fury and made his fists clench until they ached. He wanted to storm through the caves, brandishing the Impossible Cube like Zeus with a bucketful of thunderbolts. The Cube bit into his fingers.

Calm, he told himself. *Calm.* He had a right to be angry about al-Noor taking Alice, but actual murder . . . That still lay beyond him. Not even the plague could make him into a murderer. Not yet. Though it was true that he could use the Cube to bring down the entire cave and peel the flesh from al-Noor's bones with—

Gavin ground his teeth, and a bead of sweat ran down the side of his head. Damn it, he had to get control of himself. He didn't *really* want to kill al-Noor, and the squid men were his innocent pawns. At least now al-Noor wasn't in a position to destroy the *Lady* and drown Alice, which freed Gavin to effect a rescue. If he could just find her.

He was putting out his hand to try another door when he heard the crash of breaking crockery. Gavin turned, trying to orient on the sound. A moment later, he heard the scream. An icy spear drove through his heart. Alice! He tried to find the source of the sound, but the tunnel echoed and he couldn't pinpoint it. Frantic, he ran up and down the stony path. Alice was hurt. Alice was dying. He had all this power, and he couldn't help her. More than a dozen doors faced him, and he had no clue which was the right one. It was like one of those dreams in which he had something to do but couldn't do it, no matter how hard he tried.

Another crash brought his head around. This time he was able to get a better sense of the noise—it seemed to come from one of the first doors, some thirty yards behind him, but he still couldn't tell exactly which one. Gavin didn't even think. He opened his mouth and *sang*.

A hard, crystalline note streamed from his throat. The Impossible Cube drank the note in, twisted it, changed it into something alien. Power poured out of the Cube in all directions, and the wings on his back quivered with sympathetic vibrations as every door smashed into splinters. Chunks of wood pelted the air. From one of the newly open doorways, light streamed. Gavin cut the note short and dashed into the stony room while bits of sawdust bounced off his face like warm snowflakes.

Al-Noor was aiming a large pistol at Alice across the ruins of a dinner table while two of a group of squid men held a struggling Phipps. The dead squid man on the floor barely registered. A red haze descended over Gavin. The man had threatened Alice. With a snarl, Gavin launched himself at al-Noor. Al-Noor saw him coming. He flicked the pistol around to orient on Gavin and pulled the trigger. Alice screamed. The universe slowed down. Air became fluid as water. His body floated in it. He calculated how fast he was moving, the arc of his travel. He was aware of the temperature heating the barrel of the pistol and how brass and glass expanded with tiny crackling noises. He saw where the pistol barrel was pointed and in a fraction of a second assessed the eventual path of the emerging energy. In midair, his plague-enhanced reflexes lined up the Impossible Cube to match it. A yellow lightning bolt cracked from the pistol, crawled slowly through the air, and struck the Impossible Cube. The Cube sucked the bolt down, and the energy vanished.

The universe snapped back to normal speed. Gavin slammed into al-Noor. Both pistol and Cube went flying.

The glass parts of the pistol shattered, but the Cube bounced, unharmed. Both clockworkers rolled across the floor, trading and blocking blows so fast, their hands blurred. Gavin was younger and stronger, but he was hampered by his wings, and al-Noor had the advantage of height and a longer reach. Any thought of plan or strategy fled Gavin's mind. He didn't feel any of the hits that landed. Nothing but the animal fury burned in him. Al-Noor's face was twisted in an equally horrible rictus of rage.

"Sing, damn it!"

"Sing what?"

"Any note! Just sing!"

Gavin remained only vaguely aware of the two female voices speaking somewhere behind him. Al-Noor flicked a fist through Gavin's defenses and caught Gavin on the chin hard enough to make him see stars. Gavin kneed al-Noor in the belly. Fetid air rushed out of him. Al-Noor straightened his right hand, and a needle sprang from his index fingernail. A clear liquid glistened at the pointed tip. He tried to stab Gavin's face, but Gavin caught his wrist. The older man forced his hand inward, pressing his weight into Gavin, shoving the needle closer to Gavin's eye. Gavin gritted his teeth and fought back, but al-Noor had the advantage now. The needle crept toward Gavin's eye, and the light glittered hard and sharp off the tip. It brushed his eyelashes.

A terrible sound smashed through Gavin's head. The needle jerked back. Al-Noor and Gavin both screamed and clapped their hands over their ears. The sound tore through Gavin's mind. It was worse than countless claws screeching across a blackboard the size of a galaxy, and he felt as if his nerves were sizzling in acid. A part of him recognized the horrible noise as a tritone—two notes separated by three full steps. The two notes that made up the tone vibrated against each other at a ratio of one to the square root of two, an irrational, impossible number that couldn't exist. Like all clockworkers, Gavin had perfect pitch, and the tritone, the *idea* of the tritone, spun him around, threatened to swallow him in the same way that infinite swallowed a whole number. He screamed and tried to shut the sound out, but his hands couldn't quite mask it. Al-Noor writhed on the floor beside him, and Gavin was dimly aware that all the squid men had fallen to the floor as well.

And then the sound stopped. The pain ended, but the disorientation continued. Hands hauled him to his feet.

"How did you do that?" he gasped.

"I may not have perfect pitch," Phipps said in his ear, "but after twenty-five years in the Third Ward, I can make a tritone with any note you—or Alice—can sing. Now, let's get out of here before al-Noor and his squid men recover."

"I'm so sorry we had to do that," Alice said in his other ear as they stumbled toward the doorway. "Are you all right?"

"I—I think so." Gavin shook off the disorientation and regained enough presence of mind to snatch up the Impossible Cube. It glowed pure azure, and it squirmed in his hands. The lattices twisted in ways he had never seen before, moving over and behind themselves, and his own hands seemed both close and far away at the same time. When he moved forward with Alice and Phipps, he could feel it tugging in his grip like a dog that wanted off its leash.

"The Cube," he said. "It took in a lot of strange energy. I don't know what that means."

Phipps glanced back at the room. The squid men, who were plague zombies in their own way and who were also flattened by tritones, were stirring. Al-Noor was sitting up, his heavy belt askew and his black bathing costume torn. "Unless we want to kill them," Phipps said, "we need to run now and worry about the Cube later."

They ran. Phipps, whose monocle let her see best in the dim light, led the way. Alice noted the shattered doors they passed. "Good heavens, darling. Did you—?"

"Yeah." The rage rose at the memory, and he forced it back down. "I'd do it again. Did he hurt you?"

"No, though he planned to. Your timing was perfect."

The tunnel opened up into the enormous cavern. Most of the floor was taken up with the ocean, with a rim that ran around the edge. The *Lady* was moored to the quay, her envelope glowing softly, and he heaved a sigh of relief that she was still there. Bright sunlight outdoors made the mouth of the cave painful to look at.

They hurried aboard the *Lady*. When they reached the helm, the Impossible Cube twisted almost painfully in Gavin's hands and began to pulse in colors: red, orange, yellow.

"What is it doing?" Alice asked, unmooring the lines.

Her little automatons streamed out of a hatchway to flitter and skitter in a brass cloud around her.

"No idea." Gavin held up the Cube. The lattices slid and twisted around so fast, he couldn't watch them. It was like looking at the sun. "It feels like it's going to go off or something, but I don't know what to do about it."

"Are we cast off?" Phipps threw switches on the generator, and it rumbled to full power. Electricity scrambled up the wires to feed the endoskeleton, which came to blue life. Gavin set the Cube down and took the helm. The *Lady* shuddered once and rose gracefully toward the cavern ceiling, streaming water from her lower hull. The nacelles were unaffected by their seawater bath, and Gavin spun the helm, pointing her toward the mouth of the cave and freedom. The Cube pulsed green.

"No!" Al-Noor was standing on the quay, alone. His cloak was missing, his hair rumpled, his silly swimsuit still torn. His belt was crooked. "Return at once! I will have the reward! I will!"

The rage threatened again, but Gavin still kept it under control. Al-Noor had no weapons in his hands and was no threat. The plague would kill him in a few months. No point in risking Alice's life over further retaliation. Gavin spun the dial that cranked up the power to the nacelles and felt the *Lady* thrum forward. She skimmed toward the cave opening. Gavin felt himself relax a little. Alice was unhurt, and soon they'd be in open air again, on their way toward China. The Cube pulsed blue, then indigo.

"What's the bloody Cube *doing*?" Phipps called.

With the sound of a hundred waves rushing the shore, the giant squid rose from the water in front of the ship. Alice screamed. Phipps yelled. The squid reached for the *Lady* with its dripping tentacles. Gavin snatched up the Impossible Cube and held it out before him. It pulsed violet. His wings snapped open, quivering and ringing out a clear blue tone.

"Gavin!" Alice cried. "What are you—?"

Gavin sang one note, the first note that came to mind. It was the note Alice had sung back in al-Noor's lair, a D-flat. Only later would he remember that he had also used a D-flat as the base for the paradox generator, which Dr. Clef had stolen and hooked to the Impossible Cube as part of his scheme to halt time. The Cube absorbed the clear tone and *TWISTED.*

Blackness engulfed Gavin, and for a horrible moment he was falling through ice water. Then the world exploded in a billion colors that pulled him downward into a pattern that became more complicated as he dropped toward it, the tiny particles themselves made of tiny particles made of tiny particles made of tiny particles. He shouted as he fell, not knowing if he would ever stop. He had no wings, no clothing, no body. He was nothing but a voice tumbling endlessly through chaotic patterns. The colors swarmed and drew together into a single pinpoint of light that exploded in all directions, and Gavin tried to hold his breath, but he could no longer breathe or move. Intense heat and brilliance flashed around him—

And then he was lying facedown on the hard deck of the *Lady.* Wood mashed against his cheek. He lay there a moment, unwilling to move. His sleeve blocked his view. A blob of grease marred the white leather. The generator puffed and rumbled nearby, and the soft vibration of the nacelles purred through him. Ropes creaked. His wings and the power pack pressed down on his back. He became aware that he was breathing, pulling air steadily into his lungs and pushing it back out again. His heart beat in his chest. He blinked, then cautiously moved his arms, bracing himself for pain. He got none. Well, that was a relief. After this kind of thing, Gavin had come to expect blinding, tearing pain, and then he wondered when he had become the kind of man who regularly participated in events that caused blinding, tearing pain.

He pushed himself upright and immediately looked around for Alice. She lay curled on her side in a puddle of blue skirts with her mechanicals scattered around her. Phipps was on her hands and knees nearby, shaking her head. Gavin was about to run over to see to them when he remembered the squid. He tensed and glanced at the bow of the ship. Empty cavern, empty air. The squid was gone. Puzzled and relieved, he ran to the gunwale to make sure. The water beneath the ship lapped calmly at the stones. There was no sign of the giant squid, or even any indication that such a monster had ever existed. Behind the ship, the little quay was also empty. Al-Noor had disappeared as well.

Reassured but mystified, he hurried over to Alice and Phipps. Alice was already stirring, and he helped both women to their feet. The mechanicals came to life as well. The whirligigs started their propellers in short spurts and hovered uncertainly in the air while the spiders staggered about the deck like sailors on three-day leave.

"What in God's name was that?" Phipps's hair had come down completely, and she was trying to wind it back into a knot, but her hands, both metal and flesh, were shaking, and she wasn't having much success.

Alice leaned on Gavin for a moment, and he could smell her hair. He allowed himself a moment to hold her, glad she was safe. Then she broke away from him and, as he had, ran to the gunwale to look around. Her mechanicals followed.

"They're gone," she said. "The squid, al-Noor—gone. I don't see any squid men, either. What happened?"

The Impossible Cube was laying on the deck. Gavin picked it up. It felt heavier than usual. The glow had gone out, and the lattices, while still confusing, didn't twist the eye nearly as much. It appeared to be nothing but an odd piece of machinery.

"Did the Cube destroy them?" Phipps conjectured.

"I've never seen it do anything like that," Gavin replied, "though I don't know half of what it can do. I can't think of how it could destroy just al-Noor and his squid and leave us and the ship unharmed. And what were those lights about?"

"This isn't the best place to have this discussion," Alice said briskly. "Let's leave, please."

Phipps and Gavin agreed this would be a good idea. Under Gavin's hand, the *Lady* glided out of the cavern into the sunlight. The fresh, salty air cleared his head, and he pushed the generator into adding more power to the *Lady*'s envelope, increasing their altitude until they were safely out of tentacle range. Below, waves broke against the long blade of the rocky island. Gavin checked the compass, reoriented east, and set the *Lady* skimming away in that direction. The Impossible Cube sat near his foot like a cat in a coma.

"Are we away?" Phipps asked. "Are we safe?"

Alice stared over the gunwale. "I don't think al-Noor or his weapons could reach us at this distance. So I would give a qualified *yes*, myself."

Phipps crossed the deck in three steps. In a quick motion, her brass hand caught Gavin by the throat and lifted him above the deck. Her harsh grip cut off both air and circulation so fast, even his clockworker reflexes were dulled.

"What the *hell* did you do with that Cube, you fool?" she snarled.

Gavin grabbed her wrist with both his hands, but her brass arm was impervious to anything he could do. He tried to kick, but spots swam before his eyes, and he couldn't move.

"You detonated the world's most powerful weapon at our bloody feet!" Phipps's face was a rictus of fear and fury. "After everything we went through in Kiev, and you *still* used it!"

The only sound Gavin could make was a faint gurgle. The spots spread and grew blacker.

More gleaming brass whirled into view. Alice was there, surrounded by a dozen angry-looking whirligigs and spiders, and they were all staring at Susan Phipps. Sunshine gleamed off blades and spikes.

"Put. Him. Down." Alice's voice was perfectly steady. "Now."

Phipps glared at Alice for a long moment. Then she released Gavin. He dropped to his knees, sucking in lungfuls of air. Phipps stalked away and dropped into a deck chair. The whirligigs stayed in place but oriented on her. Alice helped Gavin to his feet, and he braced himself on the helm.

"Are you all right, darling?"

"I'll be fine," he gasped.

"That went beyond the pale, Lieutenant," Alice snapped. "He rescued us."

"By detonating that . . . *thing*," she shot back.

"Which you yourself told him to fetch, as I recall."

"And which you yourself had doubts about."

"That's no reason to lay hands on him like a common thug! We'd be dead if not for him."

Phipps folded her arms. "We still don't know what it did, either."

"Just *shut* it, Phipps."

"Or what? Your spiders will tickle me to death? Your whirligigs will—oh, never mind." She rested her forehead in one hand. "It's been a bloody difficult day. I'm sorry, Ennock. I shouldn't have done that."

The abrupt apology caught Gavin off guard. "Uh . . . sure. It's all right."

Alice didn't look nearly as forgiving, but the whirligigs and spiders dispersed to different areas of the deck.

A moment of awkward silence followed as Gavin took up the helm again.

"Are those wings getting heavy, Gavin?" Alice ventured at last. "I can help you out of them while you fly the ship."

Gavin had completely forgotten he was wearing them. Now that Alice mentioned it, they were starting to drag, and the harness was chafing. At his grateful nod, Alice gestured, and her little mechanicals zipped about Gavin's body, unbuckling straps and untying knots while Phipps stared into space from her deck chair. One of the whirligigs slowed, and its movements became listless. Alice plucked the whirligig out of the air, extracted a key on a long silver chain from her bodice, and wound the whirligig with it. The other automatons continued their work as Gavin piloted.

"Exactly what did happen with the Cube?" Alice said.

"I have no idea," Gavin replied. He shrugged out of the last part of the harness and helped the automatons set the wings on the deck. "And I don't have any means to find out, unless we want to go back and look for clues in al-Noor's cave."

"No, thank you," Alice said with an exaggerated shudder. "Once was quite enough."

"I'm also still trying to wrap my head around the fact that you're my fiancée now."

"Oh! I'd almost forgotten it myself. The attack quite drove it from my mind." Alice turned pink, then gave a little laugh. "Where shall we publish the banns?"

"Not many newspapers hereabout read English."

Phipps had conjured up a bottle of sherry from somewhere and was pouring herself a glass. "Though I suppose that means you could say anything you like and no one would know."

"'Mr. Gavin Ennock, not of any nearby parish, thoroughly disreputable street musician and airman,'" Gavin said, "'intends to marry the talented and beautiful Alice, Lady Michaels—'"

"'Impoverished and social outcast baroness who rescued a handsome man with a golden voice from a tall tower,'" Alice put in, moving closer to him. "'And quickly, please, because she desperately wishes to take this wildly handsome musician to her—'" She suddenly remembered that they weren't alone and stopped.

Phipps raised her glass at them. "Don't stop on my account."

They were saved from further discussion when from the open hatchway clambered a tomcat made of brass. His green eyes glowed phosphor, and his segmented tail twitched high in the air as he picked his way across the deck, his claws making little sounds on the wood.

"Click!" Alice scurried over to pick the cat up. "I should have looked for you. Are you all right?"

Click remained aloof for a moment, annoyed that he had been ignored during what had clearly been a dreadful afternoon, but finally allowed Alice to rub his head.

"Don't be upset," she crooned, still stroking him. "We all had a difficult time of it."

"You don't pet *my* ears like that," Gavin breezed.

"Fiancé or not," Alice sniffed with mock sternness,

"one does not address a lady in such a manner, Mr. Ennock."

Gavin bowed over the helm. "My deepest apologies, Lady Michaels. My heart rends in twain."

"Do you even know what *twain* means?"

"I think he's a travel writer who wrote a story about a frog."

Phipps spoke up from her chair. "Pleasant as it is to eavesdrop on a lovers' spat, we do need to determine where we're going." Then she quickly added, "Other than China. Because China has become somewhat problematic."

Gavin rounded on her, startled. "What? Why?"

"Oh dear." Alice continued to stroke Click, who made a purring noise like an engine that couldn't quite get started. "We didn't have time to explain what al-Noor told us."

"Is this about the reward?" Gavin's stomach was tense again. "I heard al-Noor shouting about one."

"It is." Alice explained, and every word dragged Gavin's spirit lower. With China's borders closed and an incredible reward for Alice's capture offered, they had no chance of finding out if the Dragon Men could cure a clockworker, and without the cure, he would go mad and die before winter. The fury and fugue he had experienced in al-Noor's lair was just the beginning. He could almost feel the plague burning inside him, consuming brain and body and leaving behind nothing but empty ashes.

Gavin clutched the helm with white fingers and tried

to think, but his normally busy mind only ran in little circles. "What are we going to do?" he asked at last.

"I'll tell you what we're *not* going to do." Phipps was consulting a large map she had unrolled across her lap. "We're *not* going to panic. Got that? For one thing, al-Noor could have his facts wrong, or he could have been lying, or he could have been saying whatever came into his head. He's a clockworker, after all. We need to find out more before we proceed, and the best place to start is going to be here." She pointed to the map, though Gavin couldn't read it from his vantage point. "Tehran. It's south, so you'll have to change course, Gavin, but it shouldn't take more than two or three hours to get there."

"Why Tehran?" Alice asked.

"It's the nearest city of any size," Phipps replied. "And Tehran has large petroleum reserves. China and the Empire have been quietly fighting over control of this region for several years now because of them. At the Third Ward, we called it the Great Game. Russia used to be a player in it, but once Catherine lost control of Ukraine, she didn't have the resources to keep playing. At any rate, the petroleum reserves mean we can top off the paraffin oil kegs as well as pick up other supplies. Tehran also used to be a stop on the Silk Road back in the caravan days, so there's likely information to be had about China. It may be al-Noor's source of news, but we'll see."

"And if al-Noor was right?" Gavin said, hands still tight on the wheel. The *Lady* creaked as if in protest, and he forced himself to loosen his grip.

"No use inviting trouble." Alice's tone was light, but Gavin could read the tension in her voice. She put Click down, and he trotted to the gunwale where he reared up and put his paws on the edge so he could look over the side, as was his habit. "We'll deal with that if it comes up."

"I still want to know what happened to al-Noor and that squid." Phipps rolled up the map and picked up her sherry glass. "My father liked to say that a loose end cracks like a whip."

Gavin said nothing but adjusted the *Lady*'s course at Phipps's direction, then glanced at the Impossible Cube, still lying dark and quiet on the deck as the ship turned south.

Chapter Five

A flock of airships hovered over Tehran, hungry as crows for the paraffin oil that poured from the city's distilleries. The sharp smell of petroleum stung the air, even as high as the *Lady* was. High towers with golden minarets poked up like gold-tipped fingers all around the city, and the white stone buildings reflected harsh desert sunlight back into Alice's eyes. The place looked strange. Foreign. When they arrived, she wouldn't know the language or the customs or any of the rules. That made her anxious and set her on edge.

Knowing the rules made life possible for Alice. When you knew the rules, you knew what you were about, what to do, what to say. Everything was regular and straightforward as a clockwork automaton. True, not all situations were *likeable*. Regular wasn't the same as pleasant. Regular trains got their passengers to their destinations on time, but they didn't care if they ran over a cat on the tracks. Still, you knew the train was coming and had time to get yourself out of the way.

And then a year ago Gavin had blasted into Alice's life, like a fox into a covey of quail. He broke every rule Alice knew. At the time, Gavin owned a bare eighteen years to Alice's stately twenty-two. He was a fallen airman turned ragged street musician to her titled ladyship. He declared his love for her when she was already engaged to someone else. He should have disgusted her, horrified her, sent her fleeing to the safety of her then-fiancé's arms. Instead, she found Gavin excited her, exhilarated her.

Freed her.

Her wretched, treacherous heart hadn't cared one bit who he was or where he had come from. Her heart didn't mind being turned into an outlaw and flung from pillar to post. In fact, and rather surprisingly, she liked it. Good heavens, she *loved* it. Without him, she would this moment be living in London with a dreary, lifeless husband in a dreary, lifeless mansion, enduring a dreary, lifeless marriage. Instead, she was gadding about the world in an airship with a collection of mechanicals and a disreputable former lieutenant, wanted by both the British and Chinese empires. Chaos personified! She wouldn't change a single, glorious thing.

Except . . .

One glance at Gavin, stalwart at the helm, told her that the glory was a sham. On the surface, with the wind teasing his white-blond hair and his keen blue eyes scanning the horizon for obstacles and airships, he looked every inch the capable airship captain. But underneath, the red worm that was clockwork plague ate steadily away at him. She saw it nearly every day now, and so did Phipps. The wings he had built in his spare time in Germany and Ukraine were a symptom. He was brilliant, perhaps more brilliant than Dr. Clef, but he was steadily losing touch with reality.

With her.

She had to admit to a certain amount of fear. Clockworkers always turned into lunatics who lashed out at the people around them. Always. She had already encountered him once during a fugue, and he hadn't even recognized her; he had snarled at her and nearly struck her. The plague made him strong and fast. Would he eventually . . . ?

No. He wouldn't. Quite impossible. He loved her deeply, just as she loved him. They had fought long and hard to be together. Not even the plague could destroy something so fundamental.

She shook her head. The conflicts were always there — law against chaos, love against fear. She didn't know how to resolve them. Instead, she kept moving forward. It was a lesson she had learned from Gavin: If you kept moving, you didn't have to stop and think about why you were moving.

Alice put a hand on Click's metal head at the gunwale, wanting to feel the familiar pattern of rivets on his skin, as the *Lady* glided closer to the group of airships hanging over the city of Tehran. The place looked nothing like London, and as she had done in so many other places before it, she would have to find a way to work around her ignorance of the local rules. So far she had learned to live with the nervousness created by that particular problem. A larger issue loomed. Tehran was supposed to be the first step on the road to China.

That road was now closed.

The *Lady* reached the edge of the city and slid over the top of the ancient walls, gentle as a cloud. Several of her whirligig automatons dashed into the open air as if scouting ahead, then zipped back to the safety of the deck while her spiders clung to the netting and watched with glittering eyes. They were perhaps half a mile from the ground, and a steady updraft from the heated earth tried to push the ship higher. Gavin was compensating by edging the power levels down and making the *Lady* heavier. The deck rocked, but Alice had long ago earned her air legs and she scarcely noticed. So much was happening so fast, she barely had time to consider any of it.

Al-Noor had claimed China had closed its borders to all foreign traffic, presumably to keep the cure out. Alice flexed her ironclad hand. The spider's eyes glowed green, indicating no one with the plague was within close range, though her blood continued to burble through the tubes running up and down the spider's legs. The cure created by her blood could spread from person to person like a cold or influenza, leaping from one body to the next with every cough or sneeze. If no one went in or out of China, her cure couldn't get anywhere. Still, China couldn't keep the cure out forever, could it? China did have a reputation for keeping strict order. On the other hand, its border was long, and it took only one person to penetrate the embargo and spread the cure. On yet another hand, that probably didn't matter. China needed only to delay the cure's arrival, the longer the better. Every day that China kept the clockwork plague meant one more day that another Dragon Man might arise from the pool of victims and invent fantastic devices for the Chinese Empire. England, meanwhile, had lost the plague—and her clockworkers—entirely. China had the upper hand, and China didn't much care for England.

All this meant that the three of them weren't in a position to travel to Peking and beg, borrow, or steal the Chinese clockwork cure, if one even existed. And that meant Gavin would soon—

Unbidden, an image slid into Alice's mind: the *Lady* gliding through the sky with an empty space at the helm. Gavin's mechanical wings lying in a wiry pile on the deck, their owner long since vanished. Alice swallowed the lump that came to her throat and tried to dash at sudden tears with her hand, but the cold spider bumped her face, which only made things worse. She turned her back on Gavin and fumbled for a handkerchief with her good hand, only to discover she had none. With a small choking sound, she leaned over the gunwale as if she were looking at the buildings below and let the tears drop into the city. Click pressed his cool nose against her side.

After a full half minute, she forced herself upright. *That's enough now,* she thought. *Whimpering like a helpless maiden never gets anything done. Perhaps you can't get into China, and perhaps the Chinese Empire has put*

*a price on your head. If that's true, your choices are either
to alter your goal or find a new way to attain your current
one. Get the information you need and make a plan.
Meanwhile, straighten up, girl!*

This was supposed to be a happy day, a thrilling day.
Gavin had, at long last and after many delays, asked for
her hand in marriage. And he had built a successful pair
of wings, for heaven's sake! At the end of such a day, they
should be drinking champagne while he slid a ring onto
her finger, and then there should be music and dancing,
or at least a good meal.

Gavin was still guiding the ship across the city while
Phipps watched from her deck chair. The majority of the
ships were clumped on the southern side of Tehran,
which presumably meant there was a mooring yard over
there. Alice could also make out large, round buildings
that her experience in Kiev told her were petroleum distilleries. It made sense—dirigibles were a major market
for paraffin oil, and there was no sense in paying to haul
the stuff any farther than necessary. The ship dipped
lower, and the smell of petroleum grew stronger. It was
hardly the romantic place she had imagined spending
the first night of her engagement.

Well, really! she told herself. *Have you learned nothing in the last few weeks? If no one gives you what you
want, you must take it.*

With that, she strode across the deck, trailing little automatons and snatched the sherry bottle from Phipps's
brass hand with her ironclad one.

"Oi!" Phipps protested. "That's mine!"

"What the heck?" Gavin said.

"Go away," Alice snapped at Phipps. "Belowdecks."

Phipps rose slowly to her feet and stared at Alice for a long moment, the red lens of her monocle glistening bloodred in the late light. Then she nodded once and picked up the dark Impossible Cube from the deck. "I think I'll stash this and perhaps take a nap. Wake me when we've moored." With that, she went below.

"All of you, too," Alice said to the automatons, who were chasing one another about the deck. "Now!"

Startled, the flock of automatons froze for a moment, then skittered into an open hatchway. The only one left up top was Click, who pointedly continued staring over the side as if Alice hadn't spoken.

"Bloody cat," Alice muttered.

"What was that all about?" Gavin enquired. "We're almost to the mooring field, you know."

In answer, Alice grabbed the front of his jacket with her free hand and pulled him in for a long kiss. He smelled of mist and leather, and he tasted of salt. Gavin stiffened, startled. Then his hands left the helm, and his arms went strong around her. She pressed against him, feeling both safe and hungry. Her hand ran through his hair, silky as feathers, and his callused palm caressed her face and neck, then stole over her breast. Her breath quickened, and a warmth spread through her. Then she pulled back.

"Wow," he said. "What was that for?"

"I call for a toast, Mr. Ennock"—she raised the sherry bottle—"to celebrate our engagement and those brilliant, beautiful wings you invented. If I can't have you for long, I intend to enjoy your company for every moment we have left." Her voice quavered for a moment, and she covered by taking a pull directly from the bottle. The sherry, too sweet and too warm, burned all the way down. "To the best damned clockworker in the whole damned world!"

"Why, Lady Michaels," Gavin laughed, taking the bottle from her, "you foul-mouthed hussy! I never thought I'd see the day!"

"You've seen nothing, Mr. Ennock," she replied, and kissed him again. This time her hands wandered greedily over his chest and back, wanting to touch him, drink him in as she had the sherry. She moved her body against his and felt him harden, which caused her own deep self to pulse.

When they separated, he took a swig from the bottle. "To the best and most talented woman in the god-damned universe!"

"And don't you forget it, sir," Alice said. She slid her hands around his strong, solid body again, not wanting to let go for a moment. Never, ever letting go. "I have many talents, some of which I haven't yet developed."

He buried his face in her hair. "I look forward to charting unexplored territory."

They stayed like that for several moments while air and sky played over them. Then Alice reluctantly stepped away. What she intended to say next was difficult, but it needed to be discussed. The words stuck in her throat at first, but she decided she wasn't having any of that nonsense anymore, and she would speak. The words came in a rush.

"So, what are we going to do about getting you into China, darling? I refuse to let something as petty as an empire stand in the way of finding your cure."

She gave a short, sharp sigh. A burden she hadn't realized she was carrying lifted and floated away. What a strange thing—once the words were said aloud, they lost their power.

"I've actually been thinking about that," Gavin replied.

"Have you?" she said with a smile.

"It's an occupational hazard with clockworkers. We never stop."

"Truly? This strikes me as more of a social problem," Alice said. "And with the sole exception of my aunt Edwina, I've yet to meet a clockworker who excelled in the social arena."

"I'm also an airman," Gavin pointed out, "and you might remember how the *Juniper* did her share of . . . untaxed shipping."

"Smuggling," said the newly forthright Alice.

"If you like," Gavin sniffed. "Anyway, you can't possibly make a border that big airtight, and I happen to know that for the right price, an untaxed shipper—"

"Smuggler."

"Smuggler will move anything you like. That includes people. We just need to find such a person."

"Iffy," Alice mused. "We'd be putting our trust in a criminal."

"Not all smugglers are bad people," Gavin said in a pained voice. "Some of them are just trying to avoid stupidly high tariffs."

Alice narrowed her eyes. "You're smuggling right now, aren't you? What have you hidden on this ship?"

"Well, technically . . ."

"Gavin! What are you—?"

They were interrupted by a mechanical yowl. Click was arching his back on the gunwale at a looming airship ten times the size of the *Lady*. Gavin had taken his hands off the helm during the . . . discussion with Alice, and neither of them had noticed the ship veering into danger. Gavin spun the helm with a yelp and Alice slapped switches on the generator. The *Lady*'s glow dimmed, and the little ship swooped starboard even as it dropped, missing the other ship by a mere few yards. Alice's stomach lurched, and she caught faint shouts of outrage from the deck of the other ship. The *Lady* sped away like a minnow fleeing a whale. Gavin caught Alice's eye. And they both started to laugh. Click pulled his claws out of the decking and turned his back on them in disgust.

"Well, Mr. Ennock," Alice said, "we seem to have a knack for attracting and averting disaster together."

"True, Lady Michaels. It's the second talent that gives me hope."

Later, they were mooring the ship at the edge of the dusty landing field just outside the walls of Tehran. Hot sunlight mixed with the unpleasant smells from the distilleries, which also clanked and grumbled like metal jungle animals. There were only a few of the enormous, rounded hangars available, and Gavin said the rent for them was atrocious, so they powered down the *Lady*'s envelope and together staked her to the ground outside among other airships, and even for this there was a fee that set Gavin to grumbling. Puffs of dust rose up like tiny djinn every time Alice took a step.

"You'd better hide in the hold while I pay," Gavin said. "Al-Noor might have been lying or mad or both, but if there really is a price on your head, we don't want the controller to be the person who recognizes you. Stay down there until I have the chance to run into town and find something appropriate for you to wear."

Alice looked down at her modest blue dress. "Appropriate?"

"For a Turkmen woman," Gavin clarified. "We're in Persia, you know. You need some native clothing so you can blend in. Don't let anyone aboard while I'm gone."

"What are you smuggling, Gavin?" she asked. "Technically?"

"Technically? My wings. The Impossible Cube. And probably you," he said lightly, and kissed her cheek before sliding down a rope to the ground below.

Alice dutifully climbed up to hide in the hold with Gavin's new wings at her feet and her automatons perched on her shoulders. She peeped out a porthole while Gavin talked to a swarthy man in red blousy trousers and a tall, furry hat. A considerable amount of money exchanged hands. Alice held her breath, but the man strutted away without demanding to inspect the cargo hold. Gavin followed a moment later, heading toward the city walls and leaving a trail in the dust. She waited for a considerable time in the afternoon heat, but after a short while her eyes started to droop, and she found she couldn't stay awake. The day's excitement and the sherry were having an effect. Perhaps she could creep off to her stateroom bunk as Phipps had done. But no—simpler just to curl up on this pile of sacking near the bulkhead. The automatons would wake her if a stranger—

The next thing she knew, Gavin was shaking her awake. Outside the sun had dropped, and it was nearly dark. Phipps was with him, her hair restored to its usual neat twist and her lieutenant's hat firmly in place above her monocle. She was holding the Impossible Cube, and her expression was grim. Alice's sleepy languor jerked away, replaced by dread.

"What's wrong?" she said, instantly alert. The automatons clustered about her with little peeping sounds.

Gavin set a bundle of cloth on the wood next to her little nest and handed Alice a newspaper. "After I bought clothes, I found this. Take a look."

The curly Persian letters meant nothing to Alice, and for a moment she realized that this was how it felt to be illiterate. It was an odd sensation, being unable even to sound out individual letters. She started to ask why Gavin would give her a paper she couldn't read. Then her eye lighted at the top-right corner. A string of numbers, the same in English and in this language, tugged at her attention. Her stomach went cold.

"1681," she said aloud. "That—that can't be the year, can it?"

"Persian reads right to left." Her voice was tight, as if she were trying not to fly apart. "Today is August 20, 1861. About three years after we met al-Noor."

A small sound escaped Alice's throat. The cargo hold spun, and she put out a hand to steady herself, glad she was still sitting down. Her breath came in short gasps. Automatically, her gaze went to the Cube in Phipps's hands. It sat there, innocent as a baby. Alice couldn't wrap her mind round the idea. It was like trying to spin a rope from sand; the harder she tried, the more it fell apart.

"Three *years*?" she cried. "Holy Mother of God! That thing moved us three *years*? Why? How?"

"I don't know." Gavin knelt next to her and took her hand. His fingers were cold. "Al-Noor's pistol fed it a lot of strange energy, and I sang one of the notes from my paradox generator. Don't forget that Dr. Clef used the generator and the Cube to stop time—or he tried to."

Alice felt the wooden deck pressing against the backs of her legs. She saw her little automatons and heard their little whirs and peeps. Gavin's white-blond hair fell soft over his forehead, and Phipps stood straight as a yard-stick next to him. It all looked perfectly normal, perfectly sane. Yet every scrap, every particle was three years wrong.

Alice's mind was racing now. She remembered the strange lights and the falling sensation when Gavin had sung into the Cube back in al-Noor's cave. "Perhaps we didn't move through time. If a series of notes was instru-mental in stopping time everywhere, perhaps one note in the series *stopped* time. Just for us. Or something."

"Or something," Gavin agreed. "God, Alice, I'm sorry. I didn't realize—"

"Sorry? You're *sorry*?" Her words were rising toward hysteria, and she bit them back. Get a grip, woman! Would a tantrum change anything or make the situation better? She forced out a breath and wrenched her thoughts into something resembling rationality. How much did it truly matter?

Alice straightened, and her air of ladyship returned. The more she thought about it, the more she realized this could work to their advantage.

"Well. Yes," she said. "There's nothing to be sorry about, darling. Now that I think of it, this is the best of all possible worlds. It explains why al-Noor was gone—he and his squid men couldn't have survived three years with clockwork plague. They're long dead, poor souls. We escaped them completely unharmed. Additionally, I've managed to elude capture by the Chinese government for three years, so perhaps the reward has expired. At minimum, the furor would have died down."

Her right hand hurt. A glance downward told her she was unconsciously gripping Gavin's hand so tightly, her knuckles were white, and Gavin had set his jaw to avoid crying out. She forced herself to let go.

"Well," she said again. "Yes. Best of all possible worlds."

"Can we use the Cube to go back?" Phipps asked. "Just a thought."

Gavin shook his head. "I wouldn't even know how to begin. Besides, you saw what happened when I tried to charge it again just now."

"You tried what?" Alice asked, bewildered. "When? What happened?"

"I connected the Cube to the generator while you were sleeping, but it won't accept a charge," Gavin explained. "No matter what I do, it stays dark."

"Can you repair it?"

Gavin shrugged. "I don't know. Maybe. If I study it long enough."

"Just because something can be done," Phipps said, her voice still tight, "doesn't mean it *should* be done. I tried to put this . . . thing into the Doomsday Vault, you may remember. I'd be for dropping it into the ocean if I weren't afraid it would wash up on shore one day."

"Hm," was all Gavin said.

"What's next, then?" Alice asked briskly. "Is it too much to hope that China has reopened the border?"

"It is." Gavin sighed. "That's one of the reasons this place is so busy. It's one of the last stopping points for Western merchants."

"And for smugglers?" Alice asked with a smile.

But Gavin shook his head. "No. No smugglers. The Chinese have invented automatons to patrol their borders. They don't eat or sleep or rest. You can't bribe them or distract them, and when they notice anyone crossing the border—in or out—they run him down with intent to kill. Smugglers from both sides are too frightened to try anything."

"Good heavens," Alice breathed.

"The border can't be completely closed," Phipps said.

"What about ambassadors and delegations? And trade? China can't get along without *some* outside trading."

"I don't know," Gavin admitted. "The people I spoke to had limited English, and my Persian is nonexistent. Besides, I couldn't appear *too* interested, you know?"

Alice leafed idly through the newspaper in her lap while they talked, more for something to take her mind off the sudden bad news than anything else, since the writing still made no sense to her. Partway through, she stopped and stared down at the page. There was a head-and-torso drawing of a young woman in a high-necked dress and her hair pulled up in a French twist. She was holding up her left hand, which was encased in an ugly metal gauntlet tipped with razor-sharp knife blades. The woman looked cruel and evil, but she was obviously meant to be Alice.

"What on earth?" she said, turning the page so Gavin and Phipps could see it. "Is that a notice about me?"

Phipps looked it over. "My Persian is poor," she said, "but yes. Here it gives your name and a description, and it names the reward—four hundred pounds of silver, alive only."

"Four hundred pounds?" Alice said, affronted despite herself. "Is that all?"

"Not pounds, the unit of currency. Pounds, the measure of weight. You could bribe the pope and a pair of kings with that much silver. It appears the emperor is still eager to acquire a concubine who can cure the plague."

"It's nice to be wanted," Alice said tartly. "Though I doubt this is what my father had in mind for me."

"It does mean," Gavin put in, "that there's *some* contact between East and West. Without it, how would the reward notice get into the newspaper and how would anyone collect on it?"

"Good point," Phipps said.

"Er, just out of intellectual curiosity," Alice asked carefully, "how *does* one collect this reward?"

"It says here to contact a man named Bu Yeh at the Red Moon Hotel."

"Hm," Alice said.

"I still think this a terrible idea," Gavin hissed.

"Do you?" Alice said. "I seem to remember hearing those very words directed at someone else recently, someone who ignored them just as I'm about to do."

Gavin straightened the glass cutlass at his belt. "Lieutenant, how about some support?"

"Far be it from me to get in *her* way," Phipps said, holding up a metal hand. "According to the great lady here, my sole job is to watch for—"

"Plague zombie!" Gavin interrupted.

Alice halted. They were threading their way through the dim, dusty streets of Tehran. A scattering of torches and lamps in odd windows lit the way. Unfamiliar food and spice smells swirled around them, along with the people clad in loose-fitting desert clothes—men in trousers tucked into high boots and long tunics split for riding; women in loose dresses with round, elaborately embroidered caps covering their hair. Alice and Phipps wore similar outfits to blend in better. The undergarments that came with the dresses were shockingly lightweight and brief, and Alice felt half naked even though her outer garments covered more of her than her previous dress had done. It was a strange feeling, and a little daring. And exciting. She and Phipps had both wrapped scarves loosely around their metal limbs to keep them from view, and Phipps had adjusted her cap to hide her monocle. No one paid the slightest attention to them.

Countless narrow alleys led off the streets, twisting away into noisome darkness. Within one of these stirred the plague zombie. It was—had been—a man, though how old he was, Alice couldn't guess. His hair had come out in clumps, and open sores leaked pus. His skin had thinned and split, revealing pink and gray muscle. He was gaunt from malnutrition, and his mouth hung open as the plague ate its way through his brain. His clothing hung in filthy rags. Alice would have once recoiled from such a creature, both from the disease and the dreadful sight. Now, however, she saw a person, a patient who had lost everything. She stripped the cloth from her metal-clad hand. The spider's eyes glowed red to indicate the presence of plague as she reached for the unfortunate man and swiped her clawed fingertips across his chest. Automatically, the tubules that ran up and down the spider's legs sprayed a fine mist of Alice's blood across the scratches. The cure, what Aunt Edwina had called a *virion*, attacked the bacterium that caused the plague and, additionally, turned the patient into a host that would spread the cure with every cough and sneeze, inoculating others he encountered. The virion also worked fairly quickly. When Alice scratched the zombie, he staggered backward. In a few moments, his eyes cleared. He looked at Alice, then held up his pus-speckled hands and stared at them as if seeing them for the first time in years. He made a small sound in the back of his throat. Then he turned and shuffled away, still staring down at his hands.

"What do you think will happen to him?" Phipps asked quietly.

"I've no idea." Alice sighed. "I can only cure them. I can't give them their old lives back. At least now he has a chance to live. The worst are the children."

Gavin put an arm around her. "I was hoping that after three years, your cure would have wiped out the plague entirely."

"Clearly not." Suddenly she was very tired—tired of travel, tired of strange places, tired of pitiable plague victims and a world that shunned them or used them. It didn't feel as if she were having any impact whatsoever, and therefore why bother? It all seemed very sad.

"Are you all right?" Gavin asked solicitously.

"I will be," she said, straightening. She was an English lady. Did the Queen whine to herself? What nonsense! Soldier ahead, girl. Always ahead. "Take me to that hotel now."

The Red Moon Hotel sat at one corner of a five-way intersection. A pair of towers topped by little minarets flanked the square white building, and strange music mingled with strong tobacco smoke in a courtyard behind it. The place had been fitted with electric lights, and all three stories cast stiff beams of illumination in all directions. The lobby struck Alice as distinctly threadbare, even a little shabby. Before she could lose her nerve, she strode to the battered front desk, where a man in a turban was holding forth.

"Do you speak English?" she asked.

"Yes, little," he said.

She put a coin on the desk. "I am looking for a man named Yeh."

"Eat. There." The coin vanished, and the man pointed to a doorway that seemed to lead into a restaurant. "Wears green."

Alice swept away with Gavin and Phipps in tow, her regal bearing hiding a pounding heart and a stomach tied in knots. This had the potential to explode in her face, and the closer she came to Bu Yeh, the more she wondered at her chances of success.

You are a baroness, blast it. Act like one.

The restaurant was crowded with customers sitting on cushions at low tables. They ate and drank and pulled fragrant smoke from enormous bulbous water pipes that Alice had never seen outside a storybook illustration. Loud conversation swirled around the room and bounced off the walls. The crowd was largely swarthy Easterners with a sprinkling of white Westerners, and they all gesticulated wildly when they spoke. Alice and Phipps were the only women present. Waiters rushed about with trays of food and silver coffee services. At a corner table by himself sat an enormously fat Chinese man wearing a green embroidered tunic that tied shut over his left shoulder. A large, puffy green hat covered his head, and a black braid ran down his back. His face was clean-shaven but for a sparse mustache and a pointed bit of beard in the center of his chin. On his shoulder sat a brass spider. The man stared about the room with a look of contempt on his round face. Every so often, the spider skittered down his shoulder, hooked a bit of food from one of the plates on the table, and skittered back up the man's shoulder to pop it into his open mouth. Alice remembered the meal she and Gavin had shared with the Chinese ambassador back in London—had it only been a few months ago?—and the way spiders had fed every morsel to her instead of allowing her to touch anything with fork or fingers.

Before she could lose her nerve, Alice strode across the restaurant and plumped herself down across from him at his table with Gavin and Phipps standing guard on either side of her. Startled, the man reared back, and two large Persian men appeared from the shadows to flank him. One had a pistol, the other a sword. Gavin put a hand on the glass cutlass at his belt.

"No need," Alice said in a calm voice completely at odds with her churning insides. "Mr. Yeh, I presume?"

"Mr. Yeh does not speak to filthy Westerners," one of the guards said. His accent was faint.

"He will speak with me." Alice took out the newspaper page with the dreadful drawing on it and laid it on the table, then unwrapped her spidery hand and laid that on the table as well. "Do you recognize this?"

Yeh's eyes widened. His mouth fell open. For a moment, no one around the table moved. Then the spider on his shoulder scampered down to the table and flipped a chickpea into Yeh's mouth. Yeh sputtered and coughed and slurped down some tea.

"You Alice Michaels lady," he said, recovering. "Angel of death."

"I wouldn't put it that way, but yes."

Yeh's eyes glittered. "Why come here? Why see me?"

"Isn't it obvious, Mr. Yeh? I wish to claim the reward."

Chapter Six

The emperor was dying. Everyone knew it, but no one would say it. Everyone also knew Su Shun had arranged for the emperor to sleep with a false concubine who carried the blessing of dragons. No one would say that, either. Su Shun was powerful, and there was no real proof. The official prognosis was smallpox, and the imperial physicians could only ensure that Xianfeng rested very comfortably until the end came. The only people allowed to see the emperor were eunuchs who had survived the blessing and were therefore unable to transmit it. They, and Su Shun.

"It's a disaster," Liyang said, wringing his soft hands. "A disaster! Cheng defeated the British in Peking, but Su Shun has already taken credit for it, just as you predicted, and now Su Shun intends to use this bit of popularity as an excuse to take the Celestial Throne."

Cixi tried not to grimace. "We are definitely in trouble. Su Shun is indeed popular at the moment, and the emperor has not publicly declared Zaichun as his heir. So unless Xianfeng put Zaichun's name in that box, my son's claim on the throne will be tenuous at best. At least Xianfeng has not publicly declared Su Shun his heir, either. That's something, at least."

"It pains me to say it, my lady," Liyang said, "but the emperor isn't . . . he hasn't been at his strongest. . . ."

"I know. No need." Cixi sipped from her teacup. It was now a month after the evacuation to the palace at Jehol. Life was comfortable in the Pavilion of a Thousand Silver Stars, and no one would have known that just to the south, sections of Peking lay in shambles and thousands were dead. The British were slaughtered or had fled, and Su Shun, speaking for the emperor, had ordered all borders sealed again. Still, people were working hard in Peking, and, in a few months, life would be normal once more. The streets would be clean, the buildings rebuilt, the parks green and quiet. Except that the emperor was dying. Except that Su Shun intended to steal the throne the moment he was dead. Except that Su Shun intended to go to war as soon as he had the throne.

"The only thing that keeps Su Shun from attacking England right now," Cixi mused, "is this cure I've heard about. What is that woman's name?"

"Alice, Lady Michaels," Liyang supplied. He fingered the jar at his belt. "Minor nobility in England, and of no consequence. That is, until she and her courtier, Ennock Gavin, began spreading this cure. Then she became consequential indeed. The irony is, Xianfeng worried that the blessing of dragons might fall on him one day, and he ordered Su Shun to put out a reward for her capture so he—the emperor—could bring her here for himself."

"I hadn't heard," Cixi lied, not wanting to give away the fact that her own spies kept her better informed than Liyang did.

"Oh yes. He offered four hundred pounds of silver. That should have flushed anyone into the open. Michaels and Ennock were spotted three years ago in a leper colony near Tehran, but no one's heard from them since. Su Shun has left the reward in place, but with one small change."

This *was* news to Cixi. "And what is that?"

"He wants Lady Michaels brought to him alive so he can kill her himself."

"Ah." Cixi thought about that. "He wants personally to see her dead. Su Shun does not trust someone else for something this important."

"But why? This I do not understand."

"He needs to stop her from spreading the cure. The only reason Su Shun hasn't started a march across Mongolia to Europe in the emperor's name is that he is worried our troops will be infected with that filthy cure and bring it home. He wants to make absolutely sure this Alice woman is dead before he invades."

Liyang bowed. "My lady is brilliant. Of course she is correct. Unfortunately for Su Shun, even four hundred pounds of silver have not brought her to him. She is most likely dead. Still, Su Shun isn't sure, because he has not begun the invasion."

A fly buzzed about the room, and one of the maids chased it away with her fan. Cixi said only, "Hm."

"All reports say the cure stalled in Europe," Liyang said. "It has not touched India or the United States of America. We are not sure about Africa."

"We certainly don't need it in China," Cixi said firmly. "No more Dragon Men? The empire would collapse."

"Collapse," said Liyang. "Yes."

Cixi gazed out a latticed window at a tranquil pool covered with white lotus flowers. Neither of them was talking about the other problem, the main problem, the problem that once Su Shun took the throne, he would ensure no one who could challenge his rule would be left alive. The death of Zaichun, her little boy, was inevitable. Su Shun would trump up charges of treason and have the boy's mouth and nose stopped up with wet silk. Cixi would be forced to watch while he struggled and kicked and slowly suffocated.

A golden fish leaped out of the lotus pool and vanished with a tiny splash, no doubt fleeing a predator. Once Zaichun was dead, Su Shun would almost certainly order Cixi's execution as well, followed by the deaths of Liyang and all the eunuchs who served under him, including his boy apprentices. No one with strong allegiances to the rightful emperor could be allowed to live. Cixi had tried to see the emperor on several occasions despite the order that only immune eunuchs were allowed in, but the soldiers on duty outside Xianfeng's chambers now knew not to let her in, and her polite and kind requests were always met with equally polite and kind refusals. Cixi had tried every trick she knew, and none of them worked. Time was working against them.

"There is one way to save China and the Celestial Throne," Cixi said quietly.

"My lady?" said Liyang.

"Everyone knows Su Shun's rule would destroy China," she said, vocalizing thoughts that had been going through her head for a long time. "Everyone also knows my—the emperor's—son is the proper heir."

"My Lord Zaichun is a bright and intelligent boy," said Liyang with proper deference. "The most intelligent boy the world has ever seen. But even the most intelligent boy cannot truly rule an empire."

"No. Someone would have to be regent. Make decisions in his name. Someone who knows the empire. Someone who knows what is best for China. Someone who can make good decisions. Someone who isn't hot-blooded like so many men."

"Not I, my lady," said Liyang quickly.

"No. You are a eunuch, but you still think like a man. Your advice would, of course, be instrumental in all decisions, Liyang." Cixi smoothed the front of her silk tunic and its elaborate embroidery. "No, the time for men to rule China has come to an end, I think."

"Ah," said Liyang. "I see, my lady. Yes. I agree. But how will this happen?"

Lung Fang, seated in her corner, ran a finger over the salamander in her ear. "I have calculated that the emperor has twelve minutes left to live."

"What?" Cixi sprang to her feet. Her kneeling maids scrambled to follow suit.

"Eleven minutes and fifty-five seconds, actually," said Lung Fang.

Time had run out. Cixi stood for a moment, thinking furiously. Years of training in court etiquette warred with looming necessity. In the end, necessity won. She rushed out of her chambers, out of the Stars Pavilion, and down the front stairs. Zaichun was playing with a set of small mechanical animals on the front lawn under the watchful eye of a dozen eunuchs and his wet nurse. Without pausing, she snatched him up, eliciting gasps from her maids and eunuchs.

"My lady, I'll carry him!"

"My lady, it is not seemly—"

"My lady, do you want your palanquin?"

She ignored them all and all but ran across the lawns toward the Cool Hall on the Misty Lake. By the time the palanquins was summoned and readied, everything would be over. Zaichun clung to her, wide-eyed and without speaking. He was heavy, but she didn't set him down. She was panting and her arms were aching to fall off by the time she reached the Hall, but she kept going, trailing a line of frantic maids and eunuchs. She stormed up the step and through the front doors. Servants and courtiers leaped to get out of her way as she stormed down hallways and across courtyards, ignoring the pleas of her servants, knowing if she slowed for even a moment, she would lose her nerve.

She was turning a corner to come down the final corridor to the emperor's chamber when she slipped. Her feet came out from under her, and she landed hard on the polished floor. Zaichun landed on her, knocking the breath from her lungs. A squawk went up from the flock of maids and eunuchs, who quickly took the crying boy away and helped her to her feet. Thanks to her voluminous clothing, it took considerable time to get to her feet. As she rose, she saw a white feather detach itself from her slipper and float away. She must have slipped on it.

But no time to consider further. She snatched the bawling prince away from the maid and ran down the hallway, every muscle in her body aching now. "Enough, child," she murmured into his ear. "We are going to see your father, and you do not want him to see you weeping as he departs this world."

Zaichun got himself under control as Cixi reached the muscled eunuchs at the door. They tensed, having been through Cixi's attempts at entry before, but before they could speak, Cixi held Zaichun out before her.

"Make way for Prince Aisin-Gioro Zaichun, the Celestial Gift of China!" she boomed. "Make way for the emperor's son!"

As they had the first time Cixi had come through, the guards looked uncertain and puzzled. Cixi had been forbidden to enter the imperial bedchamber, but the prince and presumptive heir outranked everyone except the emperor himself. The guards were unwilling to lay a hand on him—or on the woman carrying him.

Cixi didn't hesitate. Holding the boy before her like a living battering ram, she bullied past the waffling guards and kicked the doors open. The eunuchs gathered around Xianfeng's bed jumped in bewilderment at Cixi's unannounced entrance. She didn't bow, she didn't kneel, she didn't kowtow. Forgetting these things meant her death, but she was dead anyway and had nothing to lose.

Su Shun stood beside the emperor's scarlet bed, his brass half face gleaming in the sunlight filtered through the frosted glass of the doors. He was bending over Xianfeng's wasted form. The blessing of dragons turned a tiny number of people into Dragon Men, it turned a certain number of people into shambling zombies, but most people it simply killed. And emperor or not, Xianfeng turned out to be no better than a commoner in this case. Xianfeng's breathing came in short gasps as the blessing progressively paralyzed his muscles and fever ravaged his body.

"Father!" Zaichun cried from Cixi's arms. He squirmed away from her and ran to Xianfeng's bed. The eunuchs boiled out of the way, and Cixi followed in the path he cleared. "Father!"

"What are you doing here?" Su Shun snapped. "Guards!"

Xianfeng turned fever-bright eyes on Zaichun. "My . . . son!"

The guards from outside rushed into the room, swords and pistols drawn. But Xianfeng raised the Jade Hand. "No . . . back . . ."

The guards obediently backed away. Su Shun looked

outraged, but he could say nothing. Cixi gave him a grim smile.

"What of your succession to the throne?" Cixi said urgently. "My lord, who shall rule after you die?"

Xianfeng dropped his hand. The light was fading from his eyes. The water clock in the corner ticked away the time. Thirty seconds left, according to what Lung Fan had said. The room was dead silent. Everyone—guards, eunuchs, Su Shun—was listening with every fiber of his being. Cixi held her breath.

"My . . . throne . . . ," Xianfeng whispered.

"Your son is here!" Cixi said. Even now she couldn't bring herself to order the emperor to choose Zaichun, but she slid the boy closer to the emperor's side. Zaichun looked confused and unhappy, and he reached for his father's Jade Hand. Everyone held his breath. The water clock dripped away the seconds.

"My . . . throne," said Xianfeng. "Eighteen. Eight . . . teen."

He exhaled once more, then went still.

Several things happened all at once. The Celestial Scepter dropped off Xianfeng's forearm and fell toward the floor. The water clock chimed. A fast-thinking eunuch dove sideways and caught the Jade Hand before it could touch the ground. Cixi's maids and the other eunuchs set up a screaming wail and tore at their clothes. Su Shun's eyes met Cixi's, and she knew they both had the same thought. The emperor had not declared Zaichun his heir. He had declared no one his heir. And Su Shun was the most powerful man in the room.

Both Cixi and Su Shun moved at the same time. The eunuch was cradling the precious Jade Hand against his chest. Su Shun snatched a pistol from one of the guards and shot the eunuch in the head. The pistol boomed against Cixi's very bones. She caught up the shocked Zaichun and ran for the door. For a fraction of a second, Su Shun started to aim his pistol at Cixi, then changed his mind and grabbed the Jade Hand from the dead eunuch instead. The pause gave Cixi extra time, and when she passed one of the tables, something made her snatch up the Ebony Chamber, with its gold dragons and phoenix latch. She ran for freedom, clutching the box and towing Zaichun with her. As she left, she had just enough time to see Su Shun raise a guard's sword high and hear the meaty *thunk* as Su Shun chopped off his own hand.

"What now, my lady?" Liyang panted. "Oh, what now?"

They were in Cixi's dressing room at the Pavilion of a Thousand Silver Stars. Terrified maids were rushing about the room, looking busy while accomplishing nothing. Zaichun sat on the floor beside her, trying to be a man and not cry. Cixi idly stroked his hair. She herself felt a strange, icy calm, as if she had gone through terror and come out the other side. She had faced down the emperor and lost, but she was still alive. Once Su Shun recovered from attaching the Heavenly Scepter, he would doubtless come after her, but she should have a few minutes, and she meant to make them count. At the moment, she was examining the Ebony Chamber. The inlaid dragons seemed to move in impossible patterns, and when she looked at them, she realized the dragons were actually created of a design of smaller dragons, and those smaller dragons were made of yet smaller dragons. It hurt her eyes. The phoenix latch had three numbers on it, all on little wheels that could be spun to create numbers between zero and 999. She thought a moment. Xianfeng's official lucky number was seven, but that was too obvious. This was the eleventh year of Xianfeng's reign. But no, that would mean resetting the Chamber every year. Wait—when Xianfeng died, he had said *eighteen*. Cixi also knew that Xianfeng's official lucky number was seven, but when the emperor was young, a fortune-teller had once said his lucky number was eighteen, and that he secretly preferred that one. Cixi set the latch to 018.

The lock popped open. Heart beating fast, Cixi opened the box. A single piece of paper with her son's name and the emperor's seal on it would change everything. She looked inside.

The Chamber was empty.

Despair washed over her. It didn't seem to matter what she did or how hard she tried. The universe was conspiring against her with tiny events. The emperor had failed to sign a small slip of paper. That feather she had slipped on had delayed her a few crucial seconds. Now the empire had chaos instead of a tidy succession. She and Zaichun were as good as dead.

But, no. Sometimes the universe could not be allowed to win. Sometimes one had to strike back at the universe. Resolve filled Cixi. There was no time to stop, no time to give in. The Chamber was still open. Cixi swept the contents of one of her jewelry cases into it, sending jade and gold and silver tumbling inside. Two pieces—a jade leaf and a gold hairpin—fell to the floor, and these she kept separate. Then she scrambled out of her elaborate concubine's clothes with the help of her startled maids and, in her underthings, grabbed the arm of a passing chambermaid, the lowest ranking girl in the room.

"Give me your clothes," she said. The girl stared, open-mouthed, until Cixi slapped her across the face. "Now, girl!"

The move galvanized the girl into action. She stripped and handed her much plainer clothes over to Cixi, who got into them. "Liyang, have your apprentice trade clothes with Zaichun. Quickly!"

"What will you do, my lady?" Liyang asked while this was being accomplished.

"I will not say," Cixi said, then turned to address the entire room. Everyone froze and fell silent. "Listen to me, all of you. The Celestial Throne has been taken by a usurper, one who has good reason to fear the true emperor and his supporters. If you feel your lives are in danger, take the remaining gold in my storehouse and the jewelry in my cases and flee. Do it now! Su Shun is not a patient man."

Silence for a moment, and then chaos as several maids and eunuchs bolted for the storerooms and strongboxes. So much for loyalty. Cixi, in her plain clothing, was at the door with the Ebony Chamber in a sack when Liyang stopped her.

"You can't go alone, my lady," he said. "Who will sweep the road before you? Who will steer the palanquin? Who will—?"

She touched his arm to silence him. "Su Shun will be looking for a concubine traveling with her servants. It will simply not occur to him to look for a maid in plain clothes traveling on foot with a servant boy. You have been a good servant and a good friend. You should run as well. Alone."

Liyang pursed his lips and nodded.

The salamander in Lung Fan's ear glowed softly. She twitched once, then rose. "I must go. I must go now. Yes, now. Right now." Cixi's stomach went cold as the Dragon Man walked out the door without a backward glance. Outside, she joined other Dragon Men who streamed from halls, palaces, and pavilions in an eerie stream of black silk, all marching toward the Cool Hall on the Misty Lake. Cixi's mouth was dry. Were they marching in from Peking as well?

"Mother?" Zaichun asked. "Are we truly leaving?"

"We must, Little Cricket. We will play a game as we go. Pretend you are a servant boy and keep your eyes down."

"What do I win?"

"Your life." She handed him the sack containing the Ebony Chamber. "Quickly, now."

Keeping her own head down, Cixi ran with Zaichun through the pavilion and out a servant's door. With the palace in disarray and without their usual clothing, no one recognized them, or even looked at them closely. The jade leaf fell into the hands of the bribe-hungry eunuch who guarded one of the gates, and then they were on the streets of Jehol.

Cixi looked around. Word of the emperor's death hadn't leaked out yet, and people passed by on the street outside the palace walls as if nothing abnormal were happening. She felt naked without her layers of clothing and her maids and her eunuchs. Still, that was an acquired sense. Her father had been a low-ranking army officer, quite poor, and she had chopped vegetables and scrubbed floors and sewn seams like any other girl for the first sixteen years of her life. It was time to become that girl again, at least for a while.

"Did I play the game well, Mother?" Zaichun asked.

"You did, Little Cricket. But we must play a little longer. From now on my name is . . . Orchid, and yours—"

"I want to be Cricket!"

"As you like."

"Where are we going?"

She thought again. A little voice told her she had enough money in the form of her jewelry to go anywhere in China. There were a number of nice small cities to the south, where she could live a quiet existence as a moderately wealthy widow.

But that would leave China in the hands of a usurper warlord, a foolish man who intended to wreck the world. Her back straightened. No. Just as she had told Liyang, it was time for man's rule in China to end. And although she herself could not ascend the throne—women were not allowed to rule—she held in her hands the means to govern China properly.

"We're going to Peking," she said to Zaichun. "I have friends there who will hide us." *And there I will make this cricket into a dragon,* she added to herself. *A dragon with an orchid in its ear.*

Chapter Seven

Yeh laughed and laughed. His jowls jiggled, and he slapped the table, nearly upsetting his teacup. For his part, Gavin nearly whipped his sword from his belt to chop the man's hand off for such effrontery. His fingers itched to dig into the fat man's neck and snap his vertebrae one by one. The bastard was—

He ground his teeth and pushed the thoughts back. Not now. Perhaps it was the plague running away with his emotions, or perhaps it was his own reaction to a man mocking his Alice. In any case, he was in control here. He shot a glance at Phipps, who looked perfectly calm, and at the guards, who also remained perfectly calm.

No, wait—that wasn't true. Gavin studied them sidelong. The one with the pistol ... his left leg was jumping up and down just a little, and tiny movements in his face said he was chewing on the inside of his mouth. He was nervous, very nervous, and trying to hide it. The older man, the one with the sword, was calmer, but he was as coiled as a clockwork spring. They weren't as in control as they thought.

"You want to claim reward for you," Yeh snickered. "Funny."

"The notice does not say anything about who may or may not claim the reward," Alice replied. "It only offers one such. Are you a man of honor or not?"

Yeh blinked at this. "Why I give you reward? Why I not knock you on head, take you back to Peking?"

Gavin locked eyes with the younger guard, who stared back. Phipps folded her arms and looked at the ceiling, seeming to ignore her own opposite number, but Gavin knew she was keeping an eye on the room. Men continued to eat and laugh and smoke with no indication they understood the world-class drama playing out in the corner nearby. Gavin wondered how many of them would die if—when—a fight broke out.

Alice gave Yeh a little smile and reached delicately across to the table to take his plump hand in both of hers. As if soothing a child, she stroked the back of his hand with her spidery fingertips.

"Mr. Yeh," she said, "you're an expatriate, am I right? You are not allowed to cross the border back into your dear homeland, and you are forced to live among us Western barbarians. You find this horrible, I can see."

"Yes," Yeh spat, though he didn't move his hand away.

"Now why is it you have been banished, hm? Is it because you and a few others like you haven't tracked me down yet? Because someone has to stay outside the borders to coordinate the search for me?"

"It is so." Yeh leaned forward, his hand still in Alice's. "We are sacrifices for empire. But now that I find you, I go home. Emperor will use you as he likes."

"Now, now." Quick as a flash, Alice jabbed an iron finger into the flesh of Yeh's hand without quite breaking the skin. He inhaled sharply at the unexpected pain, a sensation he was unaccustomed to. "Do you know what this spider does?"

Yeh trembled, and his eyes rolled until the whites showed. A trickle of sweat ran down the side of his head. The guards tensed, and this time Gavin half drew his cutlass.

"Don't," Gavin said, knowing that at least one of the guards spoke English.

"I see you do know, Mr. Yeh," Alice said. "I also see you've worked out what will happen if I break the skin on your hand with this claw. How likely is it the emperor will ever let you reenter your homeland if you carry the cure for the clockwork plague?"

Yeh remained silent, his gaze rooted on Alice's finger.

"Let me tell you what will happen now, Mr. Yeh," Alice continued. She sounded like a woman entertaining in her drawing room over tea, and admiration for her swelled in Gavin's chest. "You will give us that delightfully enormous reward, and we will put it aboard our airship. Then you yourself will board, and we will all fly to China. You will authorize us to cross the border—I assume you can do that—and once we arrive in Peking, you will be hailed as a hero for single-handedly delivering the notorious Alice, Lady Michaels, to the emperor. You will be able to go home, and we will be in Peking for reasons of our own. This offer is nonnegotiable and expires in one minute. If you refuse, we will walk out that door and vanish forever. An airship covers a lot of ground, Mr. Yeh, and you will never have this chance again. The time begins now."

Phipps pulled out a pocket watch and flipped it open with her metal hand.

"You dictate nothing," Yeh said. "Filthy white woman."

"You are quite correct, Mr. Yeh," Alice said with a nod. "I dictate nothing. I am merely giving you the conditions under which I will surrender myself to you, making it easy for you to return to China a hero. Whether you accept these conditions or not is purely your choice."

"Forty seconds," said Phipps.

"Women set no conditions," Yeh said. "They obey them."

"As you like, Mr. Yeh. But please note whose claw is digging into your hand."

"Thirty seconds," said Phipps.

"How I know you no try to kill me and run with reward?"

"Because I need you, Mr. Yeh. We can't get to Peking without you."

"Why you go to Peking?"

"That will have to remain a mystery."

"I say we leave," Gavin put in. "This mongrel has no

idea what honor is. His country means nothing to him. He *wants* to live in exile. I think he enjoys living among foreigners, eating our food, and enjoying our women."

Yeh's jowls quivered. "You pay for that, boy."

"I hope so," Alice said. "In silver, if you please."

"Ten seconds," said Phipps.

Alice shifted on her pillow. "Well, it was nice meeting you, Mr. Yeh. A pity we couldn't come to—"

"Wait," Yeh said.

"Three seconds."

"Yes?"

Yeh ground his teeth. "I accept."

"You are a wise man," Alice said, and Gavin held back a smile.

The arrangements went quickly and smoothly, mostly because Alice refused to leave Yeh's side. "One strange move, Mr. Yeh," she said, "and I'll poke you in a tender place." In his rooms at the hotel, he dismissed his guards, packed a trunk, and produced a number of bearer bonds printed in several languages, including Persian, Chinese, and English. Together, they granted the bearer the right to four hundred pounds of silver. With the new telegraph system that allowed bankers and merchants to talk to each other over long distances, that meant the silver could be withdrawn from any participating bank in the world, with appropriate notice.

Gavin read through the bonds with Phipps peering over his shoulder. Each was printed on smooth, creamy paper, and the stack of them felt weighty and important.

They represented more wealth than he had ever dreamed existed. Odd. This pile of paper could support his entire neighborhood back in Boston for a hundred years. He thought of his grandfather and his mother and his siblings. Gavin's father had disappeared when Gavin was young, leaving his family to fend for themselves in a two-room flat that didn't even have running water. Most of Gavin's childhood memories involved cold, hungr-filled winters.

When he had shown an ability to coax tunes from his grandfather's battered fiddle at age nine, Gavin took to playing street corners, trying to scratch up a few coins to help out. At first he'd come home every day with sore fingers and little money. Then Patrick, a year his junior, told Gavin to wear the best shirt he could find, and to wash his hands and face at the corner pump, and to smile at every person who passed his corner. *"People only give money to the ones who don't seem to need it,"* he said. *"Look like a beggar, and they'll hate you. Look like a musician, and they'll pay you."*

He was right. When Gavin washed up and smiled, his take for the day tripled. Patrick was so smart, and it broke Ma's heart that there was no way to send him to school. Gavin missed him terribly. And he missed Jenny, who got a job as a hotel maid and fell in with a window washer who made less money than she did but treated her nicely. And Harry, who tried to be dad and big brother and breadwinner to everyone, but who drank his drover's paycheck away and stayed too late at dice games. And Violet, who just wanted to help and was frustrated because she was the littlest.

When Gavin was twelve, Gramps had taken him down to the shipyards where sailors moored the floating mountains that were their airships and introduced him to Captain Felix Naismith. As a newly minted cabin boy, Gavin hadn't earned much, but he was able to send some money home. Later, when pirates had stranded him in London, he had joined the underground police force known as the Third Ward, at a much better salary. That money had allowed his family to install a better stove and buy better food, at least. With a pang, he realized that thanks to the Impossible Cube, they hadn't heard from him in three years. He had effectively vanished and left them in the lurch, just as his father had. They all probably thought he was dead. Now he was sitting atop a pile of treasure with no way to send any of it to them. Although the silver itself could be transferred from bank to bank with relative ease, the bonds that indicated the silver's ownership were tied to the physical piece of paper. And thanks to the interference of the Chinese Empire, there was no American embassy in Tehran, no good post office, no trustworthy way to deliver even one of the bonds to his family in Boston. Suddenly the thick paper seemed flat and worthless.

Back at the airfield, Phipps ordered paraffin oil from the nearby petroleum yards, which operated twenty-four hours a day, while Gavin stowed Yeh's trunk in the *Lady*'s hold. The bonds he put into a secret compartment in his own cabin. As an afterthought, he put the Impossible Cube in with them. Whether the Cube was working or not, he didn't want it falling into Chinese hands. As Phipps had already pointed out, he didn't dare drop it into the sea or bury it somewhere—it would inevitably come to light—and he had no idea how to destroy it safely. He grimaced. It was like traveling with a bomb strapped to the hull.

Yeh puffed up the ladder with Alice boarding behind him. Gavin decided the man must be desperate indeed to return home, since he had only Alice's word that she wanted to go to China and that the three of them wouldn't kill him and make off with an empire's ransom in Chinese silver. Even now, Gavin wondered if that wouldn't be wiser.

Alice whistled to her automatons, and they scampered over to her. "Guard this man at all times," she said. "Don't hurt him, but don't let him touch anything, either."

Moments later, the *Lady* was flying again with Gavin at her helm. Clockworkers slept very little, so it wouldn't be a problem for him to stay up all night, or even for the next several nights. The moon scattered silver across papery forest leaves, and the cold air smelled spicy. Yeh estimated it would take them two days to pass through Bactria, then another day or two over Samarkand to reach the Chinese border just west of the city of Kashgar, assuming everything went well. After pointing out the route on Gavin's charts, he waddled below to the cabin Phipps had assigned him, accompanied by his new brass entourage. Phipps went below as well.

"I hope you know what you're doing," Gavin said uneasily as the *Lady* glided through the night.

"For the most part I'm confident," Alice said. "The emperor is offering an enormous amount of money for me, and he wants me alive. That means it's safe to hand myself over to him. For now. It's the only way into Peking with the border sealed."

"Have you seen the hole in this? The emperor wants you because he wants to ensure you don't spread the clockwork plague. That means the Chinese don't have a cure themselves. If they can't cure the clockwork plague among regular people, how can they cure a clockworker?"

"We've been over this before, darling. The British Empire had a cure, but they tried to suppress it for the same reason China is. I think the Chinese have a cure of their own."

"But if they want to suppress the cure, you're just handing it to them. I have the feeling the emperor just wants to see you dead personally. That's why he's bringing you in alive."

"That possibility did cross my mind, and I've accounted for that." Alice held out her spidery hand. "I can cure ordinary clockwork plague, but I can't cure clockworkers. I think the Chinese can do the reverse. It would be yet another reason they want this cure so badly. A total monopoly over the clockwork cure would grant them a great deal of power on the world level. Imagine if a great leader took ill with the plague, and only China could cure it. But I am thinking we can arrange a trade. If they will administer their cure to you, I will give them this one. I am sure their Dragon Men can find a way to take the gauntlet off without injuring me."

He worked his jaw back and forth. Everything Alice had just said he had pretty much worked out for himself. But there was one question that bothered him quite a lot, and it was difficult to ask aloud. It was like holding a box that contained a paper with the date of his death written on it. In many ways it was better just to leave the box shut and walk away, but in the end, he knew he would have to open it to learn the truth.

"You're willing to hand your cure over to the Chinese if they can cure me," Gavin said slowly. "But if you stop scratching people, thousands—maybe millions—of other people would die. Should we be trading their lives for mine?"

Alice didn't move. Gavin held his breath. The box was open, and the paper lay folded at the bottom. Gavin didn't want to die, and he definitely didn't want to go frothing mad, but the thought that he might live only at the expense of all those other lives brought a leaden lump of guilt to his stomach. Did Alice feel the same way? If she did, how could they go through with this? And if she didn't feel the same way . . .

If she didn't, that would be a cold thing indeed. Could he continue to love someone so cold? And how long before her love for him turned into something icy and dead?

A long silence hung dark between them. Finally Alice said in a low voice, "I don't have it all worked out. Perhaps I can persuade them to give you their cure in exchange for all this silver. Or perhaps I can prevail upon their sense of . . . fairness. I severely weakened the British Empire, which let China come into greater power, so perhaps the emperor will feel an obligation and grant my request to cure a single clockworker. Or perhaps I will simply scratch a few dozen people on my way to the emperor's palace and spread the cure no matter what."

"That's a lot of *ifs*, Alice."

"That's true." Her face grew serious. "The problem is, we're facing a definite *when*. By that I mean *when* the clockwork plague gets worse. That is worth facing any number of *ifs*." She paused. "I don't want more innocent people to die when I can save them. But I can't let you die, either, darling. I'm torn between a lion and a tiger, and I don't know entirely what to do."

Gavin put his arm around her shoulders. Strangely, the revelation that she was anything but certain made him feel better. She wasn't quite willing to trade millions of lives for his, but she *was* willing to fight for him. The box was open, and he didn't feel the need to read the date on the paper. The leaden lump evaporated. "Maybe I could cure myself."

She looked at him. "Could you? Honestly?"

"Probably not." He sighed. "I've thought about it, but I don't know much about biology. The plague tells me about energy, and sound, and physics, and the mechanics of flight. Sometimes I think it's all related somehow, at the base level, but not in any way that would help me."

They stood in melancholy silence for a long moment. Then Alice said, "Do you know what I miss? I miss Kemp."

"Kemp?"

"Right about now, when I'm feeling unhappy—when *we're* feeling unhappy—he would bustle in with a tea tray and demand that we have something to eat or that I put on a pair of slippers. And the way he found a way through the Gonta house in Kiev—masterful! We wouldn't have gotten this far without him."

"He was good, wasn't he?"

"I know he was only an automaton, but . . ."

"Yeah. I know."

Gavin peered forward into the darkness, though the only light was the soft blue glow of the *Lady*'s envelope. The only way to navigate was by star and compass, and peering ahead was his way of not looking at Alice. His thoughts drifted away from Kemp and back to China again. He was frightened for Alice, and his fear for her chewed at his bones. Gavin had never visited China and knew little about the place, but he did know people, and anyone who offered such a large reward for someone usually had something fairly unfriendly in mind for him—her. He was afraid that if he looked at Alice, he would turn the ship around and fly west toward safety, hang the reward, and hang Yeh. Maybe that would be the best idea anyway.

Alice's arm slid around his waist. She was still wearing the voluminous Turkmen dress, and the cloth whispered against his white leathers. "I know what you're thinking," she said quietly. "And we're doing the right thing."

"How do you know?" A lump formed in Gavin's throat, and the words came out sounding harsher than he intended.

"Because I can't imagine a world without you in it," she said. "Because I don't want to live in such a world, and because I'm quite comfortable risking my life to extend yours."

"What if we get to China and they kill you?" His arm was still around her shoulders, and he pulled her closer while he stared fiercely ahead. "I can't live knowing I caused your death. I can't let anything happen to you."

"It's my decision, darling." Alice leaned into him, and he held tightly to her. The eyes on her spider gauntlet glowed red between them. The clockwork plague was always there.

After a moment, she said, "Play for me?"

Gavin couldn't have refused her request any more than rain could refuse to fall. Alice took the helm while he retrieved his fiddle from his cabin and tuned it.

"Something quick," she said. "If you play something slow, I'll melt. I just know it."

With a small smile, Gavin took out his fiddle, tuned up, and played the first song that came to mind. His voice rang off the ropes and bounced off the envelope:

Still I sing bonny boys, bonny mad boys
Bedlam boys are bonny
For they all go bare and they live by the air
And they want no drink nor money.

"Tom o' Bedlam" was the unofficial anthem of all airmen. The endless verses and a tune made for pounding out on a wooden deck teamed with the idea that airmen were handsome, a little bit crazy, and never wanted for drink or money. It created immense appeal, so much so that the ritual for a cabin boy becoming a true airman at age eighteen involved his climbing in his underwear from the lowest deck below to the highest point of the envelope above—going bare and living by the air. Pirates had attacked Gavin's ship the *Juniper* and beaten Gavin when he was only a few weeks shy of his eighteenth birthday, and he had missed this ritual. Instead of airman's wings, he got nightmares and an inability to awaken in the morning without a jolt of fear.

He shook his head and kept singing, the fiddle his accompaniment.

The moon's my constant mistress,
And the lonely owl my marrow;
The flaming drake and the night crow make
Me music to my sorrow.
And still I sing bonny boys...

Alice was tapping her hands on the helm to the song, and even though Gavin had played the song a thousand times, he became nervous about making a mistake. He always felt this way when he played for an audience, no matter how sympathetic. It always seemed as if the listeners were waiting for him to make an error, ready to laugh or pounce.

"This is an A, this is an E. Go back and forth between the two. No! Hold the bow right. You can do this."

For a flicker of a moment Gavin was in a different place. A tall, tall man was standing over him, a man with pale hair and broad shoulders and strong hands. Gavin's fingers felt tiny on the strings; the bow grew larger. *"Keep trying. One day, you'll play better than your old man, but only if you do better."*

> *By a knight of ghosts and shadows*
> *I am summoned to a tourney*
> *Ten leagues beyond the wide world's end—*
> *Methinks it is no journey.*
> *And still I sing bonny boys . . .*

The memories were little more than shades, but he could almost touch them. For years Gavin had thought he had no memories of his father, but after he had been infected with the clockwork plague, some of them had come back. His father had left long ago, leaving a hole in Gavin's life. He wanted to know what his father was like, who he had been.

Why he had left.

A deep ache made his ribs hurt. He knew he must have done something terrible to drive his father away. Ma never spoke of him. Gavin didn't even know his name. It was ridiculous to miss someone he had never really known, and yet he did. The music was a gift left behind by a faceless angel, a man dead and gone.

> *I now repent that ever*
> *Poor Tom was so disdainéd*
> *My wits are lost since him I crossed*
> *Which makes me thus go chainéd*
> *And still I sing bonny boys . . .*

But a circus fortune-teller named Madam Fabry had told Gavin with absolute certainty that not only was his father still alive, but that their paths would cross soon. He still remembered every detail of the card she had shown him, the fair-haired king holding a cup while water flowed all around him. Gavin didn't much believe fortune-tellers, but everything else Madam Fabry had predicted had come true. He found he was hoping and dreading at the same time—hoping because he wanted to talk to his father before the plague took him, yet dreading because he knew that finding out the truth about his father's leaving would hurt in some way.

The song ended. He lowered the bow.

"Thank you, darling," Alice said. "You saw your father, didn't you?"

"How do you always know?" he asked, half in complaint.

"I remember what Madam Fabry said, too," she said, ignoring the question. "If you believe in that nonsense. Which I don't."

"Linda's usually right," Gavin reminded her. "And

Monsignor Adames said flood and plague will destroy us if I don't cure the world, and he said you have to let me go or the world will die."

"Now, you see?" Alice sighed. "This is exactly what I mean. I'm the one carrying the cure, not you, and it's not as if you're my prisoner to release. Prophecies and fortunes work only in storybooks."

"God, I hope so. The thought that you and I could be responsible for saving—or destroying—the world—"

"Again," Alice put in.

"Again," Gavin agreed with a laugh, but it sounded forced. Suddenly his boots felt heavy, and the ship felt small and confining. He looked at the open sky beyond the ship. "Listen, Alice . . ."

"Go," she said. "I don't mind."

"You don't?"

"I can't sleep anyway, and you know they work, so there's no danger." She corrected their course. "Now what was that about my having to let go?"

Gavin ran down to the hold. Moments later, he reappeared on deck with his new wings strapped on and ready to go. The power dial said the battery was half full, plenty of charge left. Already he felt lighter, freer. He activated the power, and the wings glowed blue with the soft chime that was already becoming familiar. Alice blew him a kiss. He stepped up to the gunwale, wings spread, then from his pocket pulled a small bird. It was a clockwork nightingale made of silver, encrusted with gems. It had been a present from Feng Lung, whose life Gavin had saved last year. It recorded the last thing it heard and returned to the last person who had touched it. Originally the nightingale had been created as a way for lovers to communicate, and Feng had laughed at the confused look on Gavin's face when Gavin learned of this.

Gavin pressed one of the nightingale's gleaming eyes and whispered, "I love you always," to it, then flung the bird into the air. It fluttered fluid wings and zipped across the deck to alight on Alice's shoulder. Gavin had time to hear it repeat in his own faint voice, "I love you always," and see Alice's soft smile before he leaped over the edge.

The trip to Kashgar actually took a week. Not long after they passed out of the forests and into the deserts around Samarkand, a sandstorm swept in, forcing the *Lady* to climb high above it. Unable to see any landmarks on the ground during the day, Gavin lost his bearings and drifted off course, losing most of a day. They lost another day outrunning another airship that Yeh vociferously said was a notorious pirate vessel. It was Gavin's first brush with pirates since the loss of the *Juniper*. During the chase, he found himself sweating with terror, and in that moment, he knew that if the Impossible Cube had still been working, he would have used it, regardless of the consequences.

But in the end, the smaller, lighter *Lady* escaped, and Alice, who understood what Gavin had been going through, knew better than to say anything, but merely stood next to him at the helm to let him know she was there, and for that he was grateful.

Yeh spent most of the time in his cabin with Alice's

tireless automatons standing guard outside. Click often joined them, crouching near the door as if waiting for a mechanical mouse to emerge from a hole. Phipps spelled Gavin at the wheel. Alice busied herself spotting and making small repairs to the ship. None of them spoke of what was coming, though Gavin's nerves grew with every passing mile. He didn't even fly anymore.

Just after dawn, when they were passing over yet more hot desert, a brass nightingale, similar to the one Gavin had given Alice but plainer, fluttered out of the bright sky and landed on the helm in front of Gavin. Startled, he looked at it. The bird cocked its head, staring back. Its eyes were flat and black, but its movements were very lifelike, except for the tiny winding key sticking out of its back. The bird opened its beak and a tinny voice spoke what Gavin assumed was Chinese.

"Alice!" he called. "Go get Yeh!"

A second nightingale landed beside the first one. It spoke the same message. Then the first one repeated the words, and the second one said it again, a second behind, creating a strange echo. Another nightingale landed, and another and another. Gavin stepped back from the helm with a gasp. More and more nightingales arrived, landing on the guylines and gunwale and the envelope and the generator. The sky was agleam with tiny brass bodies and madly fluttering wings, their metallic voices echoing and chattering. The *Lady* groaned and lost altitude, tipping under the uneven new weight. Gavin frantically maneuvered to keep her upright.

Yeh appeared at Gavin's elbow with Alice's flock of

brass mechanicals in tow and with Alice and Phipps pale behind him. One of the whirligigs dive-bombed a nightingale, which dodged away and returned with three friends. The whirligig squeaked and fled back to Alice's shoulder.

Yeh, meanwhile, yelled over the noise. "When they come?"

"Just now!" Gavin yelled back. "Do something!"

Yeh shouted something in Chinese. To his surprise, Gavin understood a few words: *bring, lady, border, fly.*

When Yeh finished, the birds stopped their chatter, and abrupt silence rushed in to fill the space. Then, as one, they gripped wood and rope in their claws and flew. Wind whistled through thousands of tiny wings all working in concert. The *Lady* shuddered and seemed to pull back for a moment; then she smoothed out and glided forward. The birds moved in liquid synchronicity, as if guided by a single mind, gently hauling the ship. Gavin's mouth fell open. He had never seen anything like it, and he longed to pull the birds apart, examine their tiny gears and switches, understand them.

"I know what you're thinking again," Alice said beside him, "because I'm thinking it, too."

"Just one," Gavin said. He was breathing hard, and copper tanged his mouth. "Just one little bird. No one'll notice."

Gavin's hands were still on the helm. Just to see what would happen, he tried turning it. The *Lady* shuddered, and the nightingales all shrieked as one. It made a sound like a drill going through glass. The terrible noise ripped through Gavin's head. He let go the helm and clapped his hands over his ears. The ship smoothed out, and the shrieking stopped.

"What was that for?" Phipps gasped.

"Bad to fight with ship," said Yeh. "Don't repeat."

"Thanks for the warning."

One of the birds circled Gavin three times, then settled on his shoulder and pecked his neck once, hard enough to draw blood. Gavin yelped and slapped at the little machine. The bird shot away, blood on its beak. It vanished into the sky.

"What did I do to him?" he asked aloud of no one in particular. No one answered.

Phipps shaded her eyes with one hand. "I assume the birds are taking us to Kashgar."

"No. To border guard. I tell them we have Lady Michaels. He check for truth, kill us if we lie."

"But we aren't lying," Alice said.

"Hope border guard believes you."

Chapter Eight

The trip to Peking was difficult and stressful. They were forced to walk most of the way or beg for rides on the back of farm carts because Cixi didn't want to call attention to herself by hiring a carriage or a palanquin, and Su Shun would watch the trains. They also had little money. Cixi risked selling the hairpin in Jehol but got only a fraction of its worth because a woman in maid's clothing selling a noblewoman's pin must have stolen it, and she could only approach a stingy black market buyer. Cixi didn't dare sell any more jewelry for fear the jeweler, already nervous, would call a guard. As a further disguise, Cixi traded the maid's clothing and Zaichun's eunuch's clothing in favor of simple peasant garb.

Peking was more than a hundred miles from Jehol, and the journey would take at least two weeks on foot, but there was nothing for it. To stretch out their meager supply of cash, they slept on the ground and begged food from other travelers. It had also been years since she had been required to perform even simple tasks like urinating without at least three maids in attendance, let alone walk so many miles without aid. The hunger and the dust and the unrelenting heat sent Cixi straight back to her youth. What made things worse was the constant fear that a troop of soldiers would descend on them and haul them back to Jehol for a long, painful death.

Zaichun, for his part, became surly as he became hungry and tired, and when at one point he started to complain — and no doubt say something that would have revealed their identity to the farmer on whose cart they were riding — Cixi slapped him hard, as any peasant mother would.

"Shut your foul mouth," she snapped. "Do not complain when this honored farmer has given us a free ride."

Zaichun stared at her. No one in his life had ever given him a direct order. To him, it was more shocking than the slap, as she intended. It sharply brought his attention back to their position.

"Yes, Mother," he said, both sullen and meek, and neither of them spoke of it again.

They finally arrived in Peking through the peasant's gate, the ill-kept one that was open for only a few hours a day and for which there was no charge, but which carried with it a long wait on the hot, dusty road. Cixi carried the sack now, unwilling to let it out of her sight. It would require money to take back the throne, lots and lots of money, and she would need every tael.

They walked down the streets of Peking, among the market stalls and braying donkeys and oozing sewage and press of people. News of the emperor's death two weeks ago had reached the city, and everywhere Cixi looked, people who could afford it wore white. A constant parade of mourners made a wailing train of ghosts through the city and would continue for a full hundred days after Xianfeng's death. No musicians performed in the streets, no acrobats or tumblers, no singers or dancers. Theaters bore padlocks. All the men looked strange—their heads and faces were covered with untidy fuzz because for one hundred days they were not allowed to shave as proper men did. The emperor died; performers and barbers starved.

A number of buildings lay in ruins from the war, though as Cixi had predicted, people were already rebuilding, and the city echoed with the sounds of hammering and sawing and the thud of stones being set. A nobleman on a horse trotted down one byway, causing everyone to dive out of his way. The horse kicked up manure that spattered Cixi's cheek. She wiped it away with her dusty sleeve and pulled Zaichun along. He followed like a wax doll, dull with fear and hunger. She felt the same but didn't dare give in to it.

After what felt like hours of walking, Cixi and Zaichun finally arrived at a luxurious mansion compound with red peaked roofs and gutters surrounded by a high wall. The front gate was actually a section of wall that had been pulled back to create entrances to the left and right—demons and evil spirits traveled in straight lines, so gates into houses forced a turn to deflect them. A pair of brass lions stood guard.

"The emperor is dead. There is no work," said one of them said in a rumbling voice. "The emperor is dead. There is no work."

"I have a delivery," said Cixi, holding up the sack. "It is for Prince Kung."

"Deliveries are at the back gate," said the lion. "There is no work."

Peasants did not enter at the front gate. She had forgotten. Cixi took Zaichun's hand. The mansion grounds were enormous, and it took a long time to walk around to the back. The sun was setting, and the alley was already growing dark. Here there were no lions, but bars forbade entry through the gate into the courtyard beyond. Cixi pulled a cord and heard a bell ring inside. Moments later, a plump woman rushed to the bars. She wore a white tunic that made her look like a snowball.

"The emperor is dead. There is no work," she said.

"I have a delivery for Prince Kung." Cixi held up the sack again.

"Of course you do," the woman said. "Everyone has a delivery for Prince Kung."

Cixi set her mouth. This woman had no way of knowing who Cixi was and was only doing as she was instructed. Still, Cixi wanted to order the cow beaten. "Nevertheless, it is true. I must present this to him personally."

The woman eyed Cixi's filthy clothes and Zaichun's filthy face. "Hm."

"Tell him," Cixi said through clenched teeth, "the Little Orchid is waiting to see Devil Number Six and that she has a gift from the Jade Hand for him." Here she glanced left and right to ensure the alley was empty and opened the sack so the woman could see the Ebony Chamber. The woman would never have seen the object in her life, but she would recognize the richness and beauty of the box and would know that such a thing must be highly important. She wavered a moment, then produced a key and unlocked the gate.

"Wait here," she said when they were in the stone courtyard. "Do not move from this spot."

She bustled away.

"I remember Prince Kung," said Zaichun. "He is my uncle. I rode his horses."

Cixi clutched the bag to her chest, darting uneasy looks in every direction. Prince Kung was Xianfeng's half brother, though Cixi knew they weren't close, and his home occupied the largest and most luxurious compound within Peking. The compound covered hundreds of acres that included ponds, bridges, trees, gardens, and elaborate fountains that gave the illusion of country life in the middle of the world's most magnificent city. The luxury was lost on Cixi. Now that they weren't moving, she felt exposed and vulnerable, like a piece of meat on a butcher's chopping block.

The snowball woman returned. "The prince will see you, Orchid. Though first," she continued with a small sniff, "you will have to be prepared."

Cixi was never so glad for a bath and fresh clothes in

her life. There was even a maid to help her, though throughout the process she never took her eyes from the grubby sack and the treasure within. Zaichun was bathed in another room, and although she was sure he would be safe, she insisted the doors between their chambers be left open so she could hear everything. They were even brought small plates of food, which Cixi forced herself to eat with proper decorum and manners. Zaichun gobbled his down. Their borrowed clothes were simple and white, the color of mourning.

At last they were ushered in to see Prince Kung. He was sitting at an elaborate writing desk, murmuring to a spider, which painted his words on rice paper with blurry speed. He wore a white robe he seemed to have thrown on quickly. To Cixi's surprise, there were no soldiers or other servants in the room. The servant who showed Cixi and Zaichun in bowed and withdrew. Prince Kung touched the spider. It shut down, and Kung turned to face them. Cixi bowed, still clutching the sack with the Ebony Chamber in it. Zaichun did not bow—he had forgotten himself already. Cixi kicked his leg. He started, then bowed as well.

Kung was a worried-looking man who was not yet thirty. The pouches under his eyes and his slender build made him look older than he was, and his unshaven head beneath his round cap gave him a disheveled look. Cixi, newly bathed and dressed, felt better-dressed than he, though her clothes barely amounted to more than a white sheet. Kung's tired eyes widened when he recognized Cixi and Zaichun.

"What—?" he began, so startled he didn't even touch formalities.

"Who is listening?" Cixi interrupted, necessity also forcing rudeness.

Kung shut his mouth and pursed his lips. Then he reached under his desk and pulled a hidden lever. There was a cranking, grinding noise, followed by a series of small thumps. When they ended, Kung said, "The spy holes have been stopped up. We can talk freely."

"Not even the emperor has such power," Cixi said, impressed.

"I am not the emperor. Nor do I wish to be." He gestured at a laden table. "Please, sit. There is food. You will have to feed yourself, I'm afraid. Even food spiders may carry messages. And you are safe here, Orchid."

Cixi almost wept with relief at those words. She and Zaichun gratefully sank to the pillows and took up chopsticks. It felt so fine to be clean and sitting down, with food on a table and fresh clothes on her back. In that moment, if Kung had requested it, she would have offered herself to him as a concubine in his household.

"Please tell me what really happened at the Cool Hall in Jehol," Kung said as they ate. He clearly wasn't hungry, but he nibbled a cake and sipped tea to be polite. "I only hear official stories, and my spies are giving me conflicting information."

Cixi obeyed, omitting no details. To her surprise, she found herself choking a little as she described the death of the emperor. She hadn't realized she felt enough attachment to him to grieve. Zaichun stared fixedly into his lap, and a tear dropped onto his knee. Cixi ignored this breach, trying to keep herself under control. But as she told the story, her sorrow dissolved into an anger that hissed like a serpent, and then roared like a dragon. At one point, there was an odd snap, and she realized she had broken an ivory chopstick in two. Embarrassed, she set it aside and stopped eating.

"You acted with admirable forethought," Kung said when she finished. "I can think of no concubine who would do what you have done."

"Thank you," she said, surprised at the praise.

"You may know that I have long felt that the empire's policy of antagonism and isolationism toward the West has been a bad idea."

"One has heard," she murmured. Kung's ideas about peaceful contact and exchange of ideas with the West were actually considered scandalous by Xianfeng's advisers, and they had convinced Xianfeng to push his half brother to the margins, leave him with a largely administrative post in Peking, and all but banish him from the Forbidden City. However, over the years, he had cleverly consolidated his position into one of great power. The emperor ignored Peking itself in favor of the Forbidden City, which meant every time he left for Jehol or the Summer Palace, Peking was basically left in the charge of Prince Kung. He'd had little power within the Imperial Court, but outside it, he was arguably the most powerful man in China. He also did not get along with Su Shun, which was why Cixi had come to him in the first place.

"The continual conflict we have with Britain drains treasure and people on both sides," Kung said. "Imagine what we could accomplish if we worked together! The British are making extraordinary leaps forward in the fields of medicine and public education, for example, but their people starve in the streets because British farmers are ignorant of agricultural secrets we have hoarded for centuries. Yet we fight and keep our people apart because we look different and act differently. Foolishness!"

"I met a few bar—Westerners when I was younger," Cixi said. "They don't have proper manners, you know. It makes it very difficult to talk to them."

"They say the exact same thing about us," Kung replied. "Do you think we Chinese are so stupid that we can build a wall halfway around the world but we cannot learn to talk to Englishmen? Or that the English are so stupid that they can build ships to fly through the air but cannot learn proper etiquette? No, both sides are narrow-minded, and it costs us dearly."

"I do not disagree," Cixi put in. "I lived on the streets of Peking as a child, and I have lived in the Imperial Court. From these vantage points I have seen how . . . insulated our society has become. The emperor is— was—a symptom of that. We seal ourselves off as we sealed off the emperor, and the only thing that gets in is sickness."

"Exactly! When the emperor is sealed off, he stagnates like bad water in a pond. You yourself saw the proof. We need someone to sit on the throne who is willing to listen to new ideas."

"But not you," Cixi said.

"By the heavens, no." Kung drank tea in obvious distress. "I have more than enough difficulty with Peking, let alone an entire empire."

"You would make a wonderful adviser to an emperor," Cixi said. She hesitated a moment. Bluntness was never a part of politics. No one at the Court was ever able to speak in private, and everyone's words were quickly spread by spies and servants throughout the Forbidden City, which meant all comments had to have multiple meanings—one for the spies and one for the actual recipient. It made for twisted, difficult negotiations that lasted days or weeks. But here there were no listeners, and the longer they delayed, the longer Su Shun had to consolidate his hold on the throne. She decided to plunge ahead. "You could also be an adviser to a regent. Even if that regent were, say, a mere woman."

Kung looked at her for a long time. Cixi looked back. "Yes," he said at last. "That's true. I think that would be a fine idea. A woman who ruled from behind a silk curtain, as the saying goes."

"But not alone," Cixi added quickly. "As I said, this woman would need advisers, generals, trustworthy eyes and ears. No one can run an empire alone."

"And this woman would want peace with the West, not war as Su Shun does."

"I imagine she would." Cixi found she couldn't quite bring herself to be completely blunt after all. "Especially if working for peace meant she enjoyed the support of important people."

"It would." Kung drummed his fingers on the table-top. "If we want to put the proper heir on the throne, we need proof that Xianfeng intended this heir to sit there."

"Unfortunately," Cixi said, "he made no such declaration. Many, many witnesses know this. And the Ebony Chamber"—she gestured at the sack on the floor beside her—"was empty."

"Hm. And I am even farther from the throne than we knew. Did you know I was in charge of the army that defended Peking from the British?"

"I thought it was Prince Cheng."

"It was. Su Shun wrested that honor away from me and gave it to that toad Cheng—"

"In order to take credit for it because Cheng always does as he is told and never speaks for himself," Cixi finished for him. "Yes. I wondered at that."

"For once Cheng will be rewarded." Kung sighed. "Su Shun intends to give my position as governor of Peking over to Cheng. He is handing out many civil positions to military friends of his without regard to their skill at administration. I have been deliberately excluded. My influence at this new Imperial Court is nonexistent."

"If we have no heir and no paper, we will need the Jade Hand," Cixi mused. "Though acquiring the hand will be much the same thing as assassinating Su Shun."

Kung nodded. "There is another factor. You know of the cure for the blessing of dragons."

"The one carried by that Western woman, Lady Michaels. Yes. She is the main reason Su Shun has continued to seal the borders—he does not want the cure to enter and wreck the Dragon Men. She is the most dangerous person in the world right now after Su Shun himself. Su Shun has put out an enormous reward for her capture so he can personally ascertain her identity and see to her death."

Kung toyed with his teacup. "It may interest you to know that Alice, Lady Michaels, was captured not long ago in Tehran. In a fascinating turn of events, she turned herself in and claimed the reward for herself."

"What?"

"My sources are impeccable. Imperial troops are escorting her to Peking even now."

Cixi realized her thumb was in her mouth and she was gnawing on the nail, a habit her mother had long ago broken in her. She put her hand down. "I think," she said slowly, "that if Su Shun wants her so badly, we cannot afford to let him have her. I also think that whoever controls Michaels Alice controls the empire."

"Oh?"

"Think of it. Releasing her cure would abruptly put our empire on equal footing with the West. It would destroy Su Shun's chances of going to war. The cure destroyed the British Empire's ability to fight us, after all. Since he is using this war on the West as a distraction from his weak hold on the throne, no war would mean we would have a better chance to unseat him."

"I concur. And, my lady, I must say I like the way your mind runs. You think on a grand scale, and that is what we need for an empire."

"Thank you, my prince."

Zaichun, who hadn't spoken a word, had finished stuffing himself and was now drooping over his plate. Cixi laid him down on the pillow as she had done many times before with the emperor. He sighed and fell more deeply asleep. Cixi drank more tea.

"So," she concluded, "we need to divert Lady Michaels and bring her here. Can this be arranged?"

"I will see what I can do," said Prince Kung.

Chapter Nine

The border guard was a serpentine mechanical dragon, long and segmented and at least a hundred yards in length. Smoky steam puffed from its nostrils, and a metal beard dripped from its chin. Its jaws could easily bite a man in half. Gavin couldn't see any human controlling it, though he supposed one might be inside. Like the nightingales, it skimmed with lithe grace when it moved. The birds pulled the *Lady* down to the sands, and the dragon raised its huge head to peer onto the deck. Steam puffed across the ship like a locomotive's. The whirligigs and spiders made yipping noises and scampered belowdecks. Gavin automatically backed up a step and put his hand on his cutlass, though the glass blade had as much a chance of harming the beast as did a pin of harming a turtle.

Yeh stepped fearlessly up to the dragon, bowed, and spoke to it while the birds huddled in the rigging and on the deck. Once again, Gavin caught words, the same ones as before, and this time *emperor*, *permission*, and *cross*.

"I think I'm learning Chinese," he murmured to Alice. "Can the plague do that?"

"Shush," she said.

Alice had to present herself to the dragon, which huffed warm steam over her and blew her skirts about. Gavin held his breath and kept his hand on his useless cutlass, but the dragon seemed satisfied. The dragon spoke to Yeh in a thunderous voice.

"The guardian birds will take you to Kashgar," it said, and Gavin gasped. The dragon spoke Chinese, but Gavin understood it perfectly well. Definitely a function of the clockwork plague. Yet it hadn't done this for him in France or Germany or Ukraine. Was it a sign of the disease's acceleration? If he was learning languages in moments, how much time did he have left?

"Do not leave the ship," the dragon continued. *"Soldiers who are immune to the blessing of dragons will board in Kashgar and accompany you to Peking. If you leave the ship, you will die. Do you understand?"*

Yeh bowed again. *"Yes, my lord."*

The dragon turned toward Gavin and whuffed out more warm, damp steam. It said in English, "You are . . . special."

Surprised, Gavin said, "Am I?"

"Indeed," the dragon growled, then dipped its head. "I will alert the proper people."

"I don't understand," Gavin said.

But the dragon merely dropped out of sight. The brass

birds sprang back to life and hauled the *Lady* back into the air while Yeh turned to the three Westerners to translate the dragon's instructions about not leaving the ship. Gavin thought about doing it himself, then decided to keep to himself the fact that he knew Chinese. Who knew what might be said in front of him if the speakers didn't know he understood?

Hours later, the city of Kashgar hove into view. Gavin's nerves hummed with tension. He tried to tell himself that the Chinese wanted Alice alive, that if they wanted her dead, the dragon would have destroyed her in a moment. It didn't help. Alice appeared cool and unflappable, but he noticed a tightness around her mouth and in her neck.

Just outside high brown city walls, the birds halted the ship and flew away in a chattering metal cloud. The ship lurched under the abrupt change, and Gavin steadied the helm just in time. A cloud of dust emerged from one of the city gates and grew closer. It was caused by a contingent of soldiers—twenty-four of them, at Gavin's count— on horseback galloping toward the *Lady*. They wore scarlet coats and carried curved swords. All of them sported metal: a brass hand with blades for fingers, iron claws, a fitted monocle like Phipps's, a pistol mounted on a forearm. At Yeh's word, Gavin dropped a ladder, and the men swarmed up it while below a groom strung the horses together. The *Lady* settled lower under the weight again. Alice moved closer to Gavin, and Phipps tensed. One man whose coat was of a different cut came forward. He glanced at Alice, who glanced coolly back.

Then he and Yeh bowed to each other, and they spoke at length. Gavin's understanding grew with every word, like a wireless radio that tuned out more and more static until the signal became clear. It was a strange sensation, and oddly exhilarating.

"This Lieutenant Hing Li," Yeh translated when they finished. "He and his men stay on ship until we arrive in Peking. No one leaves ship. You try, you killed. You fly ship in direction Lieutenant Li say. You change course, you die. We stop for supplies when he say, and soldiers bring them. You no leave ship. All soldiers have survived blessing of dragons—you say clockwork plague—so cure from Lady Michaels not affect them."

"They're survivors," Gavin said. "That's why all the metal, isn't it? The plague crippled them."

"You Westerners call it a plague," Yeh spat. "Treat it like a curse instead of honorable blessing. In China, those who survive blessing of dragons bring great honor to families, and as a reward for strength, are allowed to join army or work for empire. Those who become Dragon Men are exalted."

"So why doesn't everyone try to contract the plague?" Alice asked.

"Not everyone strong enough to face it," Yeh replied. "Not everyone strong enough to face death."

Next, Lieutenant Li handed Yeh a handful of bottle corks, and Yeh turned back to Alice. "You wear these on claws so you not spread cure. You take them off—"

"I die, yes, yes." Alice accepted the corks and pushed them onto her clawed fingertips with little squeaking sounds. "Is that the only consequence you hand out in China?"

"Only one people listen to."

The soldiers, meanwhile, spread out all over the ship, over the deck and down below, swarming into every space, every nook, every cranny, calling to one another in coarse Chinese. Gavin could almost feel their greasy fingers running over the *Lady*'s wood, hear them scraping her decks with their gritty boots, sense their prying eyes. He thought about the reward bonds and the Impossible Cube hidden in their secret compartment and resisted the impulse to check on it. That would only draw attention to the place. His glance met Phipps's, and he knew she was thinking the same thing.

One of the men came up from below holding Click. The cat hissed and tried to swipe at the man's arm, but his claws only raked brass. The soldier held Click up by the neck, laughing. Outrage swept over Gavin. Before he could respond, Alice stepped forward and snatched Click from the surprised man's grasp.

"Don't touch him!" she snapped. "Who do you think you are?"

There was a whisper of sound as every soldier on deck drew a weapon. All were pointed at Alice. Tension hummed in the air. Gavin's gaze flicked around the deck, and his mind ran a hundred calculations, none of them successful. He jumped in front of Alice, and a soldier grabbed his arm.

Gavin rounded on him in a fury. "One of us is going to remove that hand."

"Your father was a turtle," the man snarled, and his sword—metal, not glass—moved toward Gavin's throat.

"Gavin!" Alice cried.

Then Susan Phipps stepped forward.

"That's quite enough," she said, and repeated it in accented but perfectly serviceable Chinese. Gavin blinked at her. "Everyone calm down. You are all honorable men, and your duty is to keep Lady Michaels from harm. If you fail, the emperor will be displeased. If you complete your task, you will be rewarded. In the meantime, we ask you to leave us and our possessions alone. In return, we will not try to escape. Agreed?"

Lieutenant Li came up on deck in time to hear her speech. He cocked his head. *"Where did you learn our language?"* he said. *"It falls strangely from a Western tongue."*

"I served in the East for several years," Phipps replied with a bow. *"But my skills are poor."*

"Not so poor," Li said. *"In any case, it shall be as you say. Soldiers!"*

The soldier holding Gavin's arm let go. Gavin straightened his jacket as the men put their weapons away. The tension left the air, and Gavin relaxed. A little. Alice stroked Click, who was muttering to himself.

"Is it going to be like this all the way to China?" she asked.

"It had better not be," Gavin muttered back.

"Oh?"

"At least one of us will be dead if it is," he growled. "And it won't be me."

*   *   *

But to Gavin's surprise, the next several days went smoothly. Phipps and Li, both military, seemed to have forged a wary respect. Alice stayed close to Gavin, and Click stayed close to Alice. The only other incident was when a soldier discovered Alice's spiders and whirligigs, still hiding in the hold from their encounter with the brass dragon. A great commotion came from one of the hatchways, and the soldier bolted across the deck with several little mechanicals in hot pursuit. He yelped, *"Turtle turtle turtle turtle turtle!"* as he ran, something Gavin had only recently come to understand was a swear word or insult in Chinese. It was only with great effort that Gavin kept his face neutral. Alice's skin went pink.

"Tell me," Phipps said to Li at one point, *"why did the emperor close the borders?"*

"You do not know?" Li replied.

They were standing near the main hatchway, not far from the helm where Gavin was piloting, and Gavin was easily able to overhear them. By now, he had listened to hundreds of conversations among the soldiers and gotten some translations from Phipps, and his mind made leaps and connections, untangling syntax and extrapolating vocabulary. He wondered if this was how Dr. Clef, a native German, had learned English.

"I would like to hear the Chinese perspective," Phipps replied smoothly. *"I am sure it differs from the English one."*

"To be sure," Li said dryly. *"I assume you know of the first battle over opium."*

The soldier dove back below, and there was another crash. A moment later, Click emerged with the soldier's hat in his mouth. He dropped it on the deck and strolled innocently away. The other soldiers laughed, and for that Gavin was grateful. It would have been all too easy for the mood to run the other way. The *Lady* had passed the desert some days ago and was now gliding over lush green farms and pine forests blanketed in drowsy mist. The air was cool and damp, a refreshing change from hot, arid winds. They had stopped twice for supplies, and both times the local farmers in their peaked straw hats had given the soldiers everything they demanded with a fawning deference that clearly masked an underlying fear.

"I know the Opium War well," Phipps said. *"We English were flooding China with cheap opium from India—"*

"Creating addicts everywhere and taking silver out of China," Li interrupted. *"It was a terrible problem. You Westerners have no idea what your greed for silver was doing to us."*

"Of course I know. Just as I know what your greed for petroleum has done to the Middle East and what your greed for metal has done to the United States." Phipps stroked her monocle with a brass fingertip. *"Perhaps, for the sake of this conversation, we could acknowledge that both empires have done good and evil."*

Li gave a nod. *"Perhaps. In any case, all that opium created an entire class of addiction in China, and it meant tael after tael of silver left our country. England also had the right to sell factory-made products in China, and they were cheaper than those we make in small shops or at home, which meant our people bought them and pushed Chinese workers out of their jobs. The last straw came at Taku."*

"What happened at Taku?"

"A fleet of British ships carrying soldiers and diplomats sailed up the Peiho River toward Taku. It's an important fortress, and the emperor was afraid—"

"You mean his generals were afraid," Phipps interrupted.

Li waved a hand. *"It is the same thing. The emperor was afraid that so many armed soldiers in the same area might lead to fighting, so he asked the fleet to anchor farther north. It was a reasonable request. Unfortunately, your envoy deliberately took it as an insult and decided to attack Taku. It sparked a war, one that we initially won. We threw the British out of China, and the emperor closed the borders."*

"Interesting." Phipps scratched her nose. *"But that's—"*

"It's not the entire story, if I may," Li said. *"A year later, the British invaded in force. They fought all the way to Peking. There was a sort of desperation to the attack, actually."*

"The cure was pushing them," Phipps said.

Li nodded. *"The British knew they had only limited time with . . . what is your word?"*

"Clockworkers," Phipps said.

"A pejorative in your language."

Phipps glanced at Gavin, who kept his face neutral, as if he had no idea what they were talking about. *"Depending on how it's used."*

"The English Dragon . . . clockworkers were dying out, and soon our Dragon Men would have the upper hand worldwide. If the English were going to invade, it had to be right then. But in the end, the British lost at Peking. General Su Shun—or rather, Emperor Xianfeng—ordered the execution of everyone who had any contact with British soldiers to ensure the destruction of the cure within China, and then he sealed the borders again. Our Dragon Men are safe."

"And so is your ability to invade the rest of the world once British and European builders of clocks have died," Phipps added with a bitter note. Gavin uneasily concurred. It was the only conclusion.

Li shrugged. *"I do as the emperor commands."*

At that moment, a single nightingale flittered across the deck. It was carrying something in its claws. The little metal bird dropped the small object in Lieutenant Li's hand, then perched on his shoulder. Gavin heard a faint voice, though he didn't catch the words. He glanced at Alice's pocket, where his silver nightingale currently resided. Li's face went pale at the nightingale's recorded message. The military demeanor left him. Slowly, with deference and fear in every movement, he sidled across the deck toward Gavin, the object clutched to his chest and the nightingale on his shoulder. Gavin exchanged puzzled looks with Alice. What now?

"Do you need something, Lieutenant?" Gavin asked.

With a lightning movement that caught even Gavin's clockworker reflexes off guard, Li clapped his hand to Gavin's left ear. A hot needle pierced his eardrum with white pain. Gavin howled. He snapped out a hand and stiff-armed Li so hard, the man flew backward across the deck. Gavin dropped to his knees, still screaming, his hand on his ear. The hot pain was excruciating. It went on and on. He was vaguely aware that Alice was kneeling next to him with her arm around his shoulder and that most of the soldiers on deck were standing around him with their swords and pistols out. The pain drilled a molten hole through his skull, leaving a trail of coals behind it.

And then it stopped. The pain vanished as if it had never been. The change was so abrupt, he became light-headed.

"Gavin!" Alice was saying. "Darling, what's wrong? What did he do to you?"

He got to his feet. The hand at his ear was a little warm and sticky, and he felt bumpy metal beneath his fingers. The soldiers kept their weapons at the ready. Outside their circle, Li had already risen. He looked unhappy. Phipps looked furious.

"How dare you attack him!" she said in Chinese. *"You bring shame to your—"*

Gavin brought his hand down, revealing his ear. There was a group gasp. A tinkle and clank of dropped weapons indicated numb fingers all round. Every soldier, including Li, dropped to his knees and knocked his forehead on the decking.

"What the hell?" Gavin looked at the soldiers, then at the little smear of blood on his palm.

"Oh!" Phipps wove her way among the kneeling soldiers, who kept their facedown position, and put out a finger to touch Gavin's ear. "I didn't even consider. Oh, damn it. I'm sorry, Ennock. I should have thought—"

"What's going *on*?" Alice demanded.

"Li put a salamander in Gavin's ear," Phipps said. "That messenger bird brought it. I'm guessing it also told him Gavin is a clockworker—a Dragon Man."

"So?" The salamander lay curled around the outside of Gavin's ear. He followed its contours with his finger. The tail seemed to be lodged in his aural canal. He tugged at it, and a blinding pain came over him again. He staggered and let go. The pain stopped.

"Don't touch it," Alice cautioned. "Let me have a look."

"You can't take it out," Phipps said. "Not without killing him."

"What?" Gavin almost tugged at it again, then thought better of it. "What do you mean? What's it for? What's it doing?"

"Dragon Men are revered in China." Phipps gestured at the kowtowing soldiers. "But they're also feared, and with good reason. Clockworkers—Dragon Men—always put rulers in a tough spot. They have great power, but they're deadly lunatic. The British Empire coped by creating the Third Ward and building the Doomsday Vault. China has a different solution."

"A salamander?" Alice was examining the object as best she could. Gavin remained still, though he felt sick.

It seemed as if he could feel the thing's tail worming into his skull.

"All Dragon Men in China have to wear one," Phipps said. "It's the law. Rogue Dragon Men are executed."

"But what does it do?" Gavin demanded.

"Hold still, darling."

Phipps hesitated. "It ties each Dragon Man to the emperor. I've never seen it in action myself, but I'm told no Dragon Man can disobey a direct order from the emperor, and it's the salamander that forces obedience."

Gavin was almost panting. He felt panicky, hemmed in. The idea that some despot could give him an order and he'd have to jump at it like a puppet horrified him deeply. He supposed it wouldn't bother the Chinese or even the British, people who were used to kings and emperors, but Americans didn't have kings, and he had only recently found his freedom in the air. Now a fiery salamander was going to drag him back down?

He suddenly remembered Feng Lung again. The Gonta family had captured Feng in Ukraine and experimented on him; into his head they had drilled an enormous spider that forced Feng to obey any orders given to him. He couldn't even sit down unless someone told him to. In the end, he had let himself die, partly to save Gavin and Alice's lives, but also to end his own pain. Was this how he had felt? Nausea oozed around Gavin's stomach, and he took several deep breaths to keep from throwing up.

"Lieutenant Li was put in a terrible spot," Phipps continued. "The nightingale brought him the salamander and the news that you were a Dragon Man. No doubt this is what the border guard meant when it said you were special. It must have alerted the authorities, who sent the bird and the salamander."

Gavin remembered. Alice's hand was gentle but insistent on his ear. She could use only one hand because the other had corks on the fingertips. He braced himself for more pain, though it didn't come. The soldiers didn't move.

"It's illegal for someone of his rank to lay hands on a Dragon Man." Phipps crossed her arms. "It's also illegal for a Dragon Man to run about within Chinese borders without a salamander. Clearly, the emperor wants Alice in his hands immediately, so they didn't want to delay the ship at the border until someone of the correct rank could arrive with a salamander. Someone would have to put this salamander on you now, and that fell to Li."

"Good for him," Gavin growled. "I hope he gets a raise."

"You don't understand, Ennock," Phipps said. "You're flying with dead men."

Alice dropped her hand, and both she and Gavin looked at Phipps. The soldiers still hadn't moved. The *Lady*'s engines purred along, and more farmland coasted beneath them, the fresh green fields below at odds with the conflict in the clouds above.

"Go on," Alice said tiredly. "Tell us the rest."

"Li laid hands on a Dragon Man," Phipps said. "It's a form of treason, really. And when a commanding officer commits treason, he and his men are put to death. All these men will be executed the moment we reach Peking."

"But that's terrible!" Alice protested. "Li only did as he was ordered, and these men did nothing."

"In China," Phipps said, "the emperor's merest word is more important than a thousand human lives, and every command must be obeyed, even if it means death. They see it as an honor to sacrifice themselves to the emperor, and they'll be buried with great ceremony."

Gavin belatedly realized no one was guiding the ship. He set the *Lady* to hover and walked over to Li. It felt odd to stand over a kneeling man. "Is this true?" he asked.

Li said something, but his face was still facing the deck and Gavin couldn't hear.

"Get up and talk to me," Gavin said, not sure whether to be uncomfortable or outraged. The salamander made an unfamiliar weight on his ear.

Li came reluctantly to his feet and bowed deeply. The treacherous nightingale was still on his shoulder. *"My deepest apologies, my lord. You will, of course, want to strike off my head immediately."*

Phipps translated, and Gavin let her.

"I will, of course, want to do no such thing," he said. "What were you thinking?"

Li looked stricken. *"If I am not properly executed, my lord, my family will live in shame for generations."*

Gavin thought of his friend Feng and his complicated views on what was just and honorable, and how those views had ultimately cost him his life. He understood, though he didn't sympathize. He fingered the salamander in his ear. Part of him was furious and wanted to wield the executioner's sword himself. But how many of these men had wives? Children? How many little ones would cry because Daddy's head had been cut off? His own father had disappeared, dead or as good as such. Could he take the responsibility for putting all those other children through the same thing?

No. The person responsible for the salamander was not on board this ship, and it wasn't right for Gavin to take his anger out on any of them. He thought a long moment with the ship hovering high over foreign farmland. Despite his decision, it was hard to make the words come—the anger was still there.

"Thank you, Lieutenant," he said at last, with Phipps translating. The words were clipped and forced.

"Thank you?" said Li.

"For delivering the salamander. To me." The men. The innocent families. He had to think of the families. Abruptly, and to Li's surprise, Gavin switched to Chinese.

"I am glad you were able to properly give me my salamander. As I requested. Because I know you would never touch a Dragon Man without his express request. And I clearly requested it." Gavin ground his teeth. *"Because, as we all saw, I wanted the salamander, and I needed your expertise for its insertion. I . . . thank you, Lieutenant."*

Li dropped to the deck and kowtowed again. *"My gratitude, great lord."*

Gavin couldn't bring himself to respond. Instead, he

strode to the gunwale and stared at nothing for a long time. Eventually, Li and the soldiers rose and silently stole away, as if they were afraid Gavin was a bomb that might go off at any second.

Alice slipped up beside him without speaking for some time. Then she said, "That was a good thing you did. Phipps tells me that as long as you keep the salamander in, the men's lives may be spared."

"May be?"

"Nothing's certain. Phipps says this is a strange area for Chinese law. But you've helped, and I know it hurt you a lot." She stroked his arm. "You're the bravest man I know, Gavin Ennock."

"There's other difficult news, I think," he said to change the subject, and he repeated the conversation between Li and Phipps to her, the one about the emperor's planned invasion of Europe to take place once he was sure the clockworkers were gone and Alice's cure was neutralized.

"You're right," she said. "That is bad news. The question is, how do we stop it?"

"I don't know." He glanced at the spider on her arm. "You can start the cure spreading through China, if you get the chance."

Alice's face was tight. "If they don't kill me."

"You only have to scratch one person to spread it."

"It's not that simple, and you know it. Any number of factors could slow or even halt the cure entirely. The person I give it to might die or stay home or simply not transmit it to anyone who can carry it. A mountain range can block its passage for years, as could a desert. Or it could simply fade away like some illnesses do. That's what seems to have happened in Europe, anyway. No one truly understands how diseases spread, and my cure spreads like a disease. I need to 'infect' as many people as possible, and even then, there's no guarantee it'll reach the entire world." She sighed sadly. "Sometimes I think the plague will be with us forever."

He didn't know what to say just then, so he kept silent, though he tightened his grip on her hand. Phipps had taken the helm and was piloting.

"And now it occurs to me to ask," she continued, "how you learned Chinese so quickly."

"The plague is accelerating. A bad sign."

"But you haven't had a fugue in days, darling," she said. "That must be a good sign. I think it's those clock-worker fugues that are bad for you. They burn out your mind faster, like a candle or even a firework. The more you give in to the plague, the more it takes from you. Perhaps," she continued hopefully, "you're going into re-mission or even getting better."

"Don't do that." Gavin rapped the wooden helm with his knuckles, then stamped his foot and whistled two notes. "It's bad luck on an airship to say what you think will happen. It means the opposite will come true."

"Is that what that little dance was about?"

He looked sheepish. "You have to distract the sprites so they don't remember what you just said."

"It certainly distracted me. I thought it was boyishly handsome."

Without thinking, he said, "Am I that?"

She blinked. "Are you what?"

"A boy. To you?" He hadn't realized the idea had been bothering him until he said it aloud. Now he held his breath, feeling tense again. Of course she would say he wasn't. Of course he would pretend to accept what she said at face value. But no matter what she might say, he wasn't the traditional sort of man, and even though she had left England behind, Alice had brought a great deal of its traditional mind-set with her. She still refused to do more than kiss him until they were married, even though his body ached for her, and he knew she wanted him. Just standing next to her aroused desire in him, even with the soldiers looking on. They hadn't begun a physical relationship largely because Alice didn't want to risk getting pregnant, not when Gavin was living under a death sentence. Gavin himself didn't want to create a child who would grow up without a father as he had done. But he also suspected that Alice was holding back a little. The acceptance of his marriage proposal on the Caspian Sea had been tentative, hesitant. Was her love the same way?

"Listen to me, Gavin Ennock." Alice placed her hand atop his on the rail. "When I look at you, I don't see an airman. I don't see a fiddler or a singer. I don't see a nineteen-year-old. The one thing I see is the man I love."

Gavin stared ahead into empty sky, not convinced.

"And not only that, darling." Alice leaned closer to his ear. "I destroyed one empire for you, and now I'm going to destroy another. How can you doubt anything after you hear that?"

Something broke inside, and he had to laugh. "All right," he snorted. "You win."

"That's not a joke, darling." Her eyes were smoke. "When your strong arm pushed me behind you, I never wanted you more."

Desire for her made his skin hot, and he lowered his voice. "Really?"

"Oh yes."

"Now I really wish those soldiers weren't aboard."

She sighed. "As do I, darling. As do I."

Lieutenant Li, who was at the front of the ship standing lookout, shouted, *"Peking!"* just as the explosion knocked Gavin to the deck.

Chapter Ten

A hatchet was splitting Alice's head in two. A dull hatchet. With chips in the blade. She groaned and tried to open her eyes, but they were gummy and stuck shut. Her mouth tasted like dry paper.

A gentle grip closed her hand around a cup and pushed it toward her mouth. Alice resisted at first, but her body was tired and heavy and great clods of pain kept thudding about her skull, and she finally drank. The warm liquid was overly sweet and tasted of licorice. Absinthe. Alice grimaced, but after a few swallows, her headache receded and the heaviness left her. The gentle hands helped her sit up, and a damp cloth washed her eyes open. Alice blinked uncertainly. She was sitting on a bed in a smallish room crammed with furniture, most of it red, all of it Chinese. What looked like plain white sheets had been hung over other wall hangings for reasons she couldn't fathom. A small barred window let in a bit of breeze. The person helping her up was a maid in Chinese dress, though her clothes were white. Her upper lip had been split all the way up to her nose, giving her something of a canine appearance.

In another bed sat Susan Phipps, her uniform rumpled, her hair down and tangled in her monocle. Alice automatically put her hand up to her own head and found herself in a similar state. The corks on her fingertips caught in her hair. She cast about, befuddled. The last thing she remembered was talking to Gavin aboard the *Lady*.

"Are you all right?" Phipps asked.

"What happened?" Alice said, pulling her hand free. "Where are we?" To the maid, she said, "Who are you?"

A gleam caught her eye. Click was curled up on the bed. Alice felt a little better at seeing him, though she was still confused. Automatically she picked him up and checked his windup mechanism. He was running down. She took the key from around her neck, inserted it, and started winding. He slitted his eyes in contentment.

"How did we get here?" Alice asked Phipps. "Why won't this woman speak to us?"

"I don't know. We—"

The door opened, and in came another woman, also dressed in a white Chinese outfit—wide trousers beneath a full-length tunic split in the front and held together with a silver clasp. Her hair was elaborately twisted around her head, and her every movement was graceful as a measure of music. She was Alice's age and very beautiful. Alice glanced down at her wrinkled, travel-stained clothes and forced herself to sit erect like the baroness she was.

The woman said something in Chinese, and it annoyed Alice now. The lack of understanding made her feel like a lost child.

"She says there's no point in asking the maid questions," Phipps said from her own bed. "Her tongue has been torn out."

"That's terrible!"

"She's a former opium addict who probably lied to obtain money for the drug," Phipps said. "The punishment for opium addiction is to split the upper lip so as to prevent the ... patient from sucking smoke from a pipe, and the punishment for lying is to cut the tongue out. She was fortunate to be hired here. No doubt she was chosen to wait on us because she can't tell anyone we're here."

Alice shuddered but set that aside as something she could do nothing about for the moment. "Where are we? Is Gavin all right?"

At this, the beautiful woman, who had been waiting with hands clasped, spoke at some length. Phipps translated.

"My name is Lady Orchid," she said. *"Please accept my apologies for the way in which you were treated. We had no time to explain. You are in the palace compound of Prince Kung, half brother to Emperor Xianfeng, who died recently. When the prince and I heard you were on your way to Peking, we knew we had to intercept you. Prince Kung sent a number of men with a device that re-*

leases a special type of tree pollen that, when breathed, sends one into a deep sleep. Absinthe is the antidote."

"Why, we have the same thing in England," Alice said, then shot Phipps a guilty look. The lieutenant had been on the receiving end of the stuff during Alice and Gavin's raid on the Doomsday Vault last spring. Phipps crossed her arms. Alice coughed and went back to winding Click.

"*The device requires an explosion to disperse the pollen over a wide area, and we apologize deeply for this. I hope no one was injured.*"

Alice kept winding Click. Nothing hurt that she could tell. "I'm fine. Where's Gavin?"

"*The Dragon Man? He wakes in the room next to yours. You may see him in a moment, if you wish.*" Lady Orchid fingered the silver pin that held her tunic shut. "*I know you find it difficult to trust us now. Perhaps it will be easier once we have explained.*"

"Who is *us*?" Alice put in. The maid started to comb Alice's tangled hair.

A hard look crossed Lady Orchid's face, as if she found Alice's interruption dreadful in some way. "*Prince Kung and me. We have saved your lives, you see. General Su Shun, the pretender who ascended the throne, wants you dead, Lady Michaels.*"

Alice gasped and fear tightened her insides. Gavin had been right. Still, she said, "Dead? But the reward—the emperor wanted me alive."

"*That was Emperor Xianfeng. As I said, he died recently.*"

Here, Phipps stopped translating. "How did he die, Lady Orchid?"

"The blessing of dragons fell on him, and he did not survive. It was exactly what he was afraid of."

"Then I'm too late," Alice whispered. She felt cold, and tears pricked at the edges of her eyes. "If the current emperor won't trade my cure for—oh good heavens, what will we do now?"

"Why did the new emperor continue the reward?" Phipps asked.

"The new emperor, General Su Shun, wants to personally ensure Lady Michaels's death. He does not dare invade Europe until he knows his men will not encounter the cure she carries."

"We were rather afraid that was what he might want," Alice said. "Still, we were hoping things might be otherwise."

"Wait—invade?" Phipps said. "Why does he want to invade?"

Orchid sighed. *"His hold on the throne is weak. But a war would ensure everyone is looking at battle instead of who occupies the Imperial Seat."*

The maid finished combing out Alice's hair and piled it high with Chinese combs. Light dawned in Alice's head. "And you want to put someone else on the throne. That's why you brought me here. Because I can help you in some way."

"You are very perceptive for a—you are very perceptive."

"Perceptive for a what?"

But Lady Orchid didn't answer. Instead, she said, *"I was once a concubine to the emperor, and—"*

"A concubine?" Shocked, Alice backed away on the bed, bumping the maid aside. Click made a noise of protest. For all her grace and beauty, this woman was nothing more than a common prostitute. Alice looked down at the coverlet. Had this very bed been used for—?

"Calm down, Alice," Phipps said. "It isn't catching."

"It's . . . repulsive," Alice replied. "I . . . this is . . ."

"Another culture," Phipps told her. "Here it's considered a perfectly honorable profession—"

"The oldest profession."

"And for many women, the only avenue to any kind of wealth or power."

"It's horrible! Selling oneself to a married man for the chance of—"

"Whereas you," Phipps interjected, "were only willing to sell yourself to an *un*married man."

"That was different," Alice snapped.

"Of course it was," Phipps said mildly. "This woman succeeded."

Alice snapped her mouth shut in a fury. Lady Orchid, who had been watching this exchange with polite interest, continued.

"As a concubine of the emperor, I bore him a son. His only son. The boy—we call him Cricket—is the true heir. We need to put him on the throne. He is only six years old, but Prince Kung and I will rule as regents until he is old enough to rule on his own."

"And why should we help you?" Alice asked, forcing herself back to the subject at hand.

Lady Orchid seemed taken aback. *"We saved your lives, Lady Alice."*

"Out of self-interest, Lady Orchid," Alice shot back. "If you didn't need me for something, you would have let this Su Shun have me without a second thought."

"Ah." Lady Orchid took a white handkerchief from her white sleeve without denying Alice's statement. *"Why did you come to China, Lady Alice? I can't imagine it was merely to claim the reward."*

Alice thought a long moment before replying. She didn't trust this Lady Orchid, and not just because of her . . . occupation. Lady Orchid was trying to make herself the power behind the throne of an empire, and such a person was automatically difficult to trust. Oh, she claimed she was trying to stop a war and rule the empire benevolently. And perhaps she would. But in the end, she was still a power-seeker, and in Alice's experience, such people would say or do anything to achieve their aims. It was only good luck that Lady Orchid's goals and Alice's goals seemed to correlate. Alice was quite confident that if this woman had wanted Alice dead, there would be no trace of a body, or even a drop of blood, to be found. The thought made Alice both nervous and more determined. She glanced at the other bed. The mute maid was now combing out Phipps's hair.

"What do you think, Lieutenant?" Alice said, deciding Cixi couldn't understand her. "Should we say why we're here?"

"We have to tell *someone*," Phipps said. "We can't just walk into the Forbidden City and look around for a cure. We need aid. And it sounds like this new emperor won't be very helpful, to say the least."

"I was thinking the same thing," Alice admitted. "But I don't trust her."

"No," Phipps said. "But that doesn't mean we can't all cooperate for the moment. Remember, we have something she desperately wants—your remaining alive and healthy."

"Very well. Translate again, if you would." She took a deep breath. "Lady Orchid, we have come to China to find a cure for clock—er, Dragon Men."

Phipps translated this. There was a long pause, and then Cixi said, *"Why?"*

The question took Alice aback. "The Dragon Man in the room next-door is my fiancé. He will die soon. I . . . want him to live."

"But being a Dragon Man is the greatest honor a commoner can achieve," Cixi said, clearly shocked. *"Regardless of how Su Shun feels about you, your fiancé could walk into the Forbidden City right now and they would treat him with honor and reverence."*

"Until he goes mad and dies," Alice said bitterly.

"His funeral would be enormous, and he would be buried in the Cemetery of Midnight Dragons. The eunuchs would burn incense on his grave every month, and his name would be added to the list of Dragon Men for recitation every New Year. No one would ever forget him."

"Look, I don't wish to debate this." Alice fumbled in her own sleeve and produced a rather grubby handkerchief, with which she dabbed her eyes. Her other hand still bore the corks. "I can cure the plague, or blessing, or whatever you to call it, among normal patients, but people who become Dragon Men change the organism somehow, and the disease becomes immune to my cure. I later learned that several cures in England have been invented and destroyed over the years, and China's reputation led me to believe a cure for Dragon Men may exist here. So we have come. That is the end of it."

"I see." Cixi sat down, and the maid pushed a stool under her. *"Then I regret to inform you that there is no cure for Dragon Men."*

The words struck Alice with all the impact of a physical blow, and the room rocked from side to side. Her vision dimmed. She saw Gavin chained to a wall in a straitjacket, howling and screaming, foaming at the mouth, biting at his lips until they bled. She saw his eyes, wild and terrible and filled with pain. It was the eventual fate of every clockworker.

She came back to herself. She tried to deny the words, tell herself Cixi was lying. But Cixi had no reason to lie about this. Slowly, she brought herself fully upright on the bed, forcing herself to face the awful truth. Phipps's face was iron. Click watched them both.

"How do you know this?" Alice said hoarsely.

"I was Imperial Concubine. I had my own eunuchs, my own maids, and my own spies. And I had the emperor's ear. I know—knew—everything that happened in the For-

bidden City. If someone had cured a Dragon Man, I would have heard of it before the emperor did. But if you don't believe me, think of this—why would we want to cure Dragon Men? The very idea is ridiculous! No one would even research such a thing."

"Clockworkers do as they wish," Alice replied weakly. "They—"

"Not here. The Jade Hand speaks in their ears, and they build what the emperor desires."

"The Jade Hand speaks? Is that the salamander Lieutenant Li implanted in Gavin's ear?"

"Indeed. No Dragon Man has ever researched a cure for the blessing of dragons, no matter what you may have heard. The blessing is a sacred thing. Emperor Xianfeng lived in fear of contracting it, but even he could not bring himself to order any of the Dragon Men to look into a cure of any kind."

"Oh God," Alice moaned. The world was falling apart around her. She had put herself and Gavin in mortal danger for a cure that didn't exist. "What will we do, then?"

"But . . . ," Lady Orchid continued.

Alice looked at her. "But?"

"There is no reason we could not look for a cure." Lady Orchid spoke slowly, as if the words were difficult to say. *"If my son were on the throne, and I were regent, I could order it done."*

"I don't understand," Alice said. "You just said—"

"The Dragon Men haven't found a cure in large part because the emperor has never ordered them to look for

one. If my son sat on the throne, I could tell him to order all the Dragon Men in the empire to look for a cure. Since China would not be at war, the Dragon Men would be . . . unoccupied. Imagine how much they might accomplish if the Jade Hand forced them all to work together."

"Oh. I—I don't think so," Alice said. "Frankly, I don't know that I can trust you, Lady Orchid, rude as that sounds."

"*I understand fully, but what other options do you have, Lady Michaels?*"

"Gavin is brilliant. He might find a cure on his own."

"*Perhaps.*" Lady Orchid's tone was languid now. "*Does he have a full laboratory on that ship of his? We didn't see one. Has he shown any expertise at working with the blessing of dragons? I don't recall hearing of any.*"

"No," Alice admitted. "But we could go look for someone who does have it. Unless you plan to keep us here."

"*Of course not. You are not prisoners. You are free to leave at any time.*" She paused. "*How much time does your fiancé have before the blessing takes him, more or less?*"

"I don't know. A month, we think. Two at most."

"*And in that time, you think you can find a Dragon Man, persuade him to begin research, and create this cure you seek.*" Lady Orchid examined her nails. "*That would be quite an accomplishment.*"

"She's toying with you," Phipps added after the translation.

"I'm aware of that. I don't like it."

"You won't find any such Dragon Man in China, of course," Lady Orchid continued as if there had been no interruption. *"No Chinese Dragon Man would work on a cure. So you must spend a certain amount of time traveling back the way you came. That may prove difficult. Your ship is rather conspicuous. You yourself do not blend in with Chinese. And you do not speak our language. I wonder how far such a lady could run before Su Shun found her, especially with so many people seeking her."*

Alice sighed. "Let's cut through the treacle."

"I don't know how to translate that," Phipps put in.

"You are saying that if I don't help you," Alice said, "then we have no chance of finding a cure before Gavin . . . succumbs, and I stand a good chance of being captured and killed. But if we *do* help you, you'll put all your resources toward creating a cure."

"I give you my sworn word as a member of the Imperial Court, Lady Michaels. I swear to you by the spirits of my ancestors and as a lady of the Yehenara clan that if you help me, I will fulfill this obligation to you."

And she bowed low before Alice.

"She is bowing as if before a lord," Phipps said. "Either she means every word, or she is the most skilled liar in all of China."

Alice still didn't trust Lady Orchid, but neither did she see an alternative. "All right," she said. "I agree to your terms."

A look of palpable relief crossed Lady Orchid's face. *"Thank you, honored lady."*

"I would like to see Gavin now."

Here, Lady Orchid hesitated. *"That may not be wise."*

Alice tensed. "What's wrong?" She bolted out of the bed and realized for the first time she wore no shoes or stockings. The maid bustled forward to slip her feet into a pair of soft white slippers. "You said—"

"It is possible to see him," Lady Orchid said quickly. *"I am just uncertain that you truly wish it."*

"Lady—"

"Very well." She said something to the mute maid, who scurried out. Moments later, the door opened again and a strange chair entered. Alice had seen wheelchairs before, but this one walked on delicate spider legs. White curtains shrouded the occupant. Alice strode forward and thrust them aside. Gavin sat within. In stark contrast to all the white clothing Alice had seen so far, Gavin wore plain black silk from neck to ankle. A round cap that flared out on all sides covered his hair. A day's worth of pale stubble covered his chin, and the ugly salamander still curled around his left ear. He didn't look up when Alice yanked the curtains away. His attention was rooted on a small painting in his lap. On the canvas, a woman with a white face and tiny ruby lips in a trailing red robe fanned herself near a shimmering brook. Chinese characters flowed down one side of the painting. Gavin stared at the painting as if he might fall into it.

"Gavin?" Alice touched his arm. "Gavin!"

He didn't respond. Alice's heart twisted and sank. It was his first fugue state in quite some time, and she had been hoping that the plague might have somehow left him. A foolish hope.

"The painting hung on the wall of his room," Lady Orchid supplied. *"If he is like other Dragon Men, he will eventually come out of this state and work on something fantastic."*

"And burn out his mind all the faster," Alice retorted. "Gavin! Darling, speak to me!"

But Gavin continued staring at the painting. Alice licked her lips. Clockworkers experienced two kinds of fugue states. The first, often triggered by an odd idea or a piece of machinery that needed repair or even a stray word, sent them into a frenzy of experimentation, designing, and building. The second, often triggered by something beautiful, usually something with a pattern to it, drew them into a trance. Music was a favorite trigger, but artwork or the spreading pattern in a droplet of blood could do the trick as well. Both fugues disturbed Alice greatly. During a building fugue, clockworkers turned into snarling monsters that treated even their closest loved ones like filth, and during a trance fugue, clockworkers stared and drooled. Alice always feared Gavin might not come back from whatever place he was visiting.

"Gavin," she repeated.

"He is speaking with dragons," Lady Orchid said through Phipps. *"It is very bad luck to disturb him."*

Alice ignored this. She shook Gavin's shoulder. "Gavin! Darling, listen to my voice. Come back to me. Please, Gavin. Follow my voice and come back to me."

Still no response. Disregarding the presence of Phipps and Lady Orchid, Alice leaned into the chair and kissed him. The kiss went delicate and deep. She felt like a single leaf landing on a pool to create tiny ripples that flowed out in all directions. Gavin jerked and gasped for breath. He blinked and looked around.

"What—?" he said. "Alice?"

Alice sighed with relief. "I'll explain in a moment. Can you stand up?"

"Yes." He started to glance down at the painting in his lap. "What is—?" Alice took the artwork away from him.

Lady Orchid's face was hard with disapproval, but she only said, *"It is not good to discuss powerful ideas with the door open."*

Gavin scrambled out of the chair, looking like his old self. He snatched the cap off his head and stared at it. "What happened? What's going on? Why am I wearing black pajamas and a hat indoors?"

Alice quickly explained the situation to him. When she finished, Gavin nodded. "We need to work with her, then. Where's my ship?"

"Prince Kung's men deflated your ship and brought it here under cover of darkness last night. It and all the automatons aboard it are safely hidden on the palace grounds."

"What about Lieutenant Li and his men?"

Alice had completely forgotten about them, and she felt a little guilty that she hadn't asked after them.

"They are safe."

"Safe? What does that mean?" Gavin asked.

Lady Orchid cocked her head. *"Is he important to you, Lord Ennock?"*

"I'm not a lord—"

"The blessing of dragons makes you a lord."

"Oh. Uh, Li is important to me, yes. I want to know what happened to him and his men. Did you turn them over to Su Shun for execution?"

"Certainly not!" Lady Orchid looked horrified at the idea. *"Su Shun would torture them to find out what they know, and we would be undone. At the moment, they are waiting in one of the outbuildings. The men who can read and write will be executed with honor so they cannot be forced to write what they know, and those who are illiterate will have their tongues cut out so they cannot betray us. We are merciful here."*

Phipps clearly had a hard time translating these words. Gavin looked as unhappy as Alice felt.

"No," Alice and Gavin said together.

"I beg your pardon?"

"No," Gavin repeated. "Li is a good man who did his duty, and his men don't deserve any of this. If you kill or maim them in any way, I won't help you. That's the end of it."

"But—"

"I won't discuss it." Gavin folded his arms. "I'd rather go mad from the plague."

"I . . . very well, Lord Ennock. We will keep them here until this is over."

Gavin bowed to her in a perfect imitation of the gesture Lady Orchid had made earlier. "Thank you, Lady Orchid. You are most kind."

His words seemed to placate her a little. *"We must discuss what to do next, then."*

"You don't know?" Phipps said. "I thought you had a plan."

"Your pardon. I have only recently arrived in Peking with my son after fleeing Jehol for our lives. There has been little time for planning."

"Well." Alice sat on the bed again, and Click moved into her lap. "It seems to me that there's only one quick, sure way to put your son on the throne, Lady Orchid."

"And what is that?"

"We must steal the Jade Hand."

Chapter Eleven

A faint tremble shook the table as Cixi set her teacup on it. Prince Kung paused over his own cup to glance at the ceiling, as if it were at fault.

"The war machines are stomping about," Kung said. "I wonder if Su Shun will invade even if he does not find Lady Michaels."

"He cannot hold the throne if he does not invade," Cixi said. "No emperor can be so disfigured as he. This war is a distraction from his disqualification."

"He is a warlord, and he intends to prove it to the world." Prince Kung drained his cup. They were sitting in his chambers, again with the spy holes closed. Zaichun was squirreled away in another room, still in disguise. So far as the servants were concerned, Kung was sheltering a recently widowed cousin, a casualty of the second war over opium. "One wonders what you thought of the conversation with the foreigners."

Cixi pursed her lips. "It is difficult to discuss anything with such people. They have no manners, and they ask direct questions that make a lady of any delicacy blush. One is forced to say things one would never normally say. It is quite shocking. No wonder they are called barbarians."

"They say the opposite of us, you know. They claim we never say what we mean and that our faces are inscrutable." He started to refill his cup from the pot, but Cixi quickly leaned forward to do it for him, automatically taking the role of concubine. "The philosophers remind us that everything must have its opposite. Nothing can exist by itself. Yin and yang."

"Perhaps," Cixi conceded. "But I do not see how philosophy is helpful."

"And there is a seed of each thing in its opposite. We know yin has a spot of yang, and the other way around. You yourself experienced it just now."

"This is difficult to understand."

Prince Kung hid a smile behind his hand. "After years of living in the Imperial Court, where one must watch every word and ensure every sentence has two, three, or even four meanings, was it not the tiniest bit refreshing to speak with people who expected you to say exactly what you meant and gave you the same thing in return?"

"Hm." Cixi toyed with a bit of fish in the bowl before her with her chopsticks and considered. He had a point. Talking to these foreigners had been shocking, but with that had also come a little daring thrill, and afterward she had to admit she found it . . . interesting even if their manners were distasteful. "Perhaps a tiny bit refreshing."

"I found it so as well, before Xianfeng sealed the borders. Another reason why our two worlds must cooperate. Everyone thinks the other side is dreadful, but once the sides begin talking to each other, we inevitably find the other side interesting and refreshing. They are more like us than we know."

"Lady Michaels is quite devoted to Lord Ennock," Cixi admitted. "I did not know Westerners felt that way about one another. One hears about . . . depravities in their bedchambers, but nothing about deep feeling."

"Another rumor they spread about us." Kung shifted on the floor pillow. He still looked strange and unkempt with his hair and beard growing out. "I will need to meet them soon to talk further. Where are they now?"

"On their ship in the third stable. Lord Ennock insisted on examining it, and it seemed to me a good place to hide them. We took them out in a spider palanquin with the curtains shut so the servants wouldn't see. They are eating. I think even you couldn't bear to watch that, my lord."

"I do have my limits. What do you think of Lady Michaels's idea to take the Jade Hand?"

"It makes me nervous." Cixi picked up an empty cup and ran her finger around the rim. Her ribs felt tight. "It *would* be the fastest way to unseat Su Shun."

"The difficulty is that Su Shun has returned to the Forbidden City and spends all his time within the red walls. My spies tell me he does not leave it for fear someone will seize the throne from him."

"Which is exactly what we are attempting to do," Cixi mused. "Can we lure him out?"

"That's a possibility, though he will surely be heavily guarded if he comes outside. His generals and the Dragon Men speak for him outside the Forbidden City. They are handling most of the day-to-day decisions now."

Cixi blinked. "Dragon Men?"

"Yes. Su Shun gives them basic orders, but they carry them out in their own fashion."

"So China is being run by *Dragon Men*? But they are . . . it is . . ."

"Yes," Kung repeated. "They are powerful but not fit to rule. Already in the southern provinces, peasants are being ordered to tear out rice fields and plant lotus instead because Lung Min finds the lotus more aesthetic."

"But Xianfeng was planning to expand those fields next year. This will cause food shortages!"

"It will. And Lung Chao is causing new roads to be built in characters that spell out mathematical equations. More peasant labor being taken from the fields."

"He will drain the treasury," Cixi said tightly. "Why is Su Shun allowing this?"

"Everything is a distraction from his weak position on the throne. And he is busy overseeing the new military. It is quite impressive, as we have already been feeling."

"China is ruled by lunatics. We must stop this quickly."

"And for that, we need the Jade Hand." Kung gestured at the Ebony Chamber, which sat on one corner of the table. The gold dragons chased one another like playful flames across the black wood. "Speaking of the treasury, I have discovered that my own resources are wearing thin. As I am out of favor with the new Imperial Court, I have lost several important contracts. It has also become more expensive to maintain good spies in the Forbidden City. It did not help that we unexpectedly had to dress everyone in the household in white for the emperor's mourning."

His hinting couldn't have been broader. Cixi felt on firmer ground here. She knew what was expected, and she knew what to do.

"Of course." Cixi slid the box to her. "I took many, many valuable jewels with me when I fled. I am sure even a handful will make up for your losses."

She spun the phoenix latch wheels to 018 and opened the Chamber.

It was empty.

Ice water ran down Cixi's back. "This is impossible," she whispered.

She felt around the box's interior, then tipped it upside down and shook it, a nonsensical move, but one she couldn't help. The dragons twisted under her fingertips. Nothing. A fortune in jewels, vanished, and all her hopes gone with them.

"What happened?" Kung asked.

"I do not understand," she said in horror. "The Chamber never left my sight except when I talked to the foreigners, and then it was locked away in my room. No one can open the phoenix latch. They would have to steal the entire box, and they clearly did not." Panic swept over her, and only a lifetime of training kept her from bursting into tears. "What will I do? What will *we* do?"

Kung puffed out his cheeks. His worried eyes looked even more worried now. "We will think." He paused to do just that. Cixi found her mind couldn't work at all, and she merely sat. Su Shun would now keep the throne, and eventually he would hunt her down and kill her and Zaichun.

"I will take a moment to be as blunt as a foreigner, since we are in extremis," Kung said at last. "I have enough money to keep my household running for another two weeks. That is not taking into account spies and bribes and everything else associated with trying to wrest the throne away from Su Shun. Without your jewels, I will have to sell property to remain solvent, and that is a dragon eating its own tail."

Cixi sat upright, her fingers gripping the table. Now was not the time to panic. Now was the time to act. "Very well, then. We need to do two things. We need to find out what happened to the jewels, and we need to talk to the foreigners. We need to make a plan."

"A plan," Kung said, "that does not involve money."

Gavin poked at the strange food with the two sticks he'd been given to eat with. Clockwork reflexes or no, he couldn't seem to get the trick of eating with them. Some of the food seemed to be little dumplings folded in half, and he had solved the problem of eating by simply stabbing them with one stick like a single-pronged fork, but anything with rice or bits of chopped vegetables in it were beyond him. Phipps, who was sitting at the table on deck across from him, used the chopsticks with ease, and Alice, though a bit clumsy, was already at least competent. Gloomily he stabbed another damp dumpling and wondered why Lady Orchid hadn't provided them with the eating spiders he'd seen Yeh and the Chinese ambassador use back in London.

"This is quite good," Alice said. "I could rapidly get used to this cuisine. What's in it, do you suppose?"

"I've learned the hard way," Phipps replied, "that it's best not to ask. Rather like sausage."

They were sitting on the *Lady*'s deck, but not outdoors. The ship currently lay hidden within an enormous storage building within Prince Kung's compound, and they had been given strict instructions not to show themselves outside for fear they'd be discovered. The large storage building around them was warm and stuffy in the August heat, and Gavin was glad for the light silk pajama-style outfit he'd been given, though he refused to wear the round cap indoors. Phosphorescent lanterns gave them light without additional heat.

Since Lieutenant Li's men already knew what was going on, Prince Kung had posted a handful of them at each of the exits, though whether to keep the foreigners safe or ensure they didn't escape, Gavin wasn't quite sure. They showed him a great deal of deference, however, and the salamander made strange weight around his ear. He tried not to think about the bit of machinery it had inserted into his brain or Cixi's revelation about the clockwork plague, but it was difficult. He found the chopsticks becoming heavy in his hand, and his appetite faded.

The *Lady of Liberty* herself was partly dismantled. Gavin had arrived in the building to find Kung's men had deflated her envelope and folded it neatly. The endoskeleton had been collapsed in on itself and rolled up, as it had been designed to do, and both endoskeleton and envelope lined the gunwale. The paraffin oil generator purred to itself and puffed steam. Gavin's wing harness was attached to it. Now that they weren't flying anywhere, he could use the generator to charge the battery. Not that he was going to fly anywhere in the near future. He saw a long line of devastating failures stretch out before him: Alice hadn't been able to spread her cure as they had hoped; he had finished a pair of wings but barely used them; and, not least, he was dying of the clockwork plague.

Damn it, he hated this. He hated feeling unhappy (though who enjoyed it?), and he hated feeling so out of balance. It wasn't normal. It wasn't *him*. It must be the clockwork plague. Or was it? Could he blame all his problems on the disease? It would certainly be convenient, a nice way of avoiding a depressing truth. He poked morosely at his food bowl, the chopsticks clumsy in his hands.

"Having trouble, darling? Here." Alice plucked a bit of something from her bowl and held it out to Gavin, who wryly accepted it. Click, who was sitting on a stool of his own, watched with vague interest, then licked a paw with his steel wool tongue.

"Delicious," Gavin pronounced.

"Feeding tidbits to your fiancé." Phipps set her own bowl aside. "I believe the term for that is *twee.*"

"What's the point of having a fiancé if one cannot indulge in his tweeness?" Alice said.

Gavin choked on the bit of food and coughed wildly. Phipps thumped his back with her brass arm. Alice sipped some tea with a perfectly straight face.

"What?" she said. "You know I've always admired your tweeness, Gavin. It's so noticeable."

Now even Phipps's face was turning red. Gavin slapped the table, making the lantern jump and dishes rattle, his face contorted with suppressed laughter.

"You . . . didn't just . . . say . . . ," he gasped.

"Of course. Why, every woman knows she can judge a man's worth by his tweeness."

Gavin lost it. The laughter burst from him in small explosions. His fists pounded the table. Phipps joined in, and at last Alice smiled, then giggled, then laughed. The sound rose on wings to the rafters and disturbed the pigeons roosting above. Gavin felt lighter for it, and he touched Alice's hand.

"This is quite the reversal," she said. "Usually you're the one who keeps my spirits up."

"The world is upside-down," he admitted. "Everything is backward."

One of Alice's little automatons, a whirligig, sputtered up from one of the hatchways carrying a brass spider. It flitted over to Alice and deposited the spider on the table in front of her. It twitched and tried to walk, but all four of its left legs weren't working. The whirligig backed away and chittered.

"Now what happened to you?" Alice asked, turning the spider over. "Click, would you bring my tools, please?"

Click regarded her for a moment, then jumped down and trotted away. A moment later, he came back with a black bag in his mouth. Alice accepted it from him with thanks and extracted from it a roll of black velvet, which she unrolled across the table, revealing a set of small, intricate tools. The velvet was embroidered with *Love, Aunt Edwina.* Alice tried to select a tool with her left hand, but the corks on her fingertips got in the way.

"Bugger this," she muttered, and pulled the corks off with little squeaking sounds. "No one will see in here."

Gavin glanced around and lowered his voice. "You could start spreading the cure here, you know. It wouldn't be difficult to pull one cork away and scratch a servant or two. The cure would spread fairly quickly through Peking after that."

"That's my intent." Alice set the corks aside. "Though I can't do it here. I'm sure any servant I scratch will let Prince Kung know immediately, and they'll cut off his head or something equally horrible. I will wait until I can get into the city."

"Doesn't Lady Orchid *want* you to spread the cure?" Gavin said.

"Lady Orchid wants the throne," Phipps corrected. "I don't know that she wants Alice to destroy the future of Dragon Men. Lady Orchid promised only to find a cure for Gavin, not reopen the borders or bring Alice's cure to China. Have you noticed she's guarding us with men who have already had the plague and can't spread the cure? Once she puts her son on the throne, she'll probably want a steady supply of Dragon Men to ensure he stays there. I would. And that means Alice is a potential threat to her regency. She and Prince Kung will either have to send Alice home before she cures anyone . . . or kill her."

"The thought had occurred," Alice agreed.

Gavin set his jaw against a wave of anger. "I'll kill them myself first."

"Thank you, darling," Alice said, "and I'm not saying you shouldn't, but let's hope that won't be necessary."

"That was . . . bloodthirsty for a baroness," Phipps opined.

"I long ago decided that it is better for me to live than for enemies to survive," Alice said primly. "In any case, I do think we've decided on the best course—help Lady Orchid get her son on the throne so she can order the Dragon Men to cure Gavin, as she swore to do. Then we'll flee as quickly as we can."

She picked up a tool and used it to unfasten a trapdoor on the spider's underside while the hovering whirligig looked on with concern.

"How *do* you do it?" Phipps asked. "I never had the chance to ask you, even when you were with the Ward."

"I honestly don't know, Lieutenant." The spider went still as Alice extracted a number of tiny parts from the spider and laid them on the black velvet, where they stood out like little brass stars. Her hands moved gracefully, fluidly, with soft precision. Gavin automatically noted each part, how they went into the spider, the wear marks, the size and shape and weight, how they pressed sensually into the cloth. His heart rate increased, and a coppery tang came into his mouth. It was exciting to see Alice pull apart the little machine, and he felt himself falling into a delightful fugue again.

"Some clockworker inventions can be recreated by normal people," Phipps was saying, oblivious to Gavin's interest. "Babbage engines that let machines 'think' on a basic level, tempered glass for lightbulbs and cutlasses, dirigible designs. But truly intricate work such as automatons that understand human speech or Gavin's wings or the Impossible Cube—only a clockworker can create them, even if the clockworker draws diagrams. The Third Ward tried for years even to made basic repairs on them, and we completely failed. But you—"

"Yes, Lieutenant." Alice was absorbed in her work. She pulled the flywheel out of the spider and held it up with a pair of tweezers. "Off-center. No wonder its legs were paralyzed, poor thing."

"How do you do it?" Phipps asked again. "You must have some idea."

"None." Alice ran her fingers deliciously over the flywheel, and Gavin felt it as if they were running over his own skin. Grasping the flywheel by the piston, she slid it back slowly into place with a click. The spider twitched and Gavin shuddered. "I look into a machine and just *know*."

"It's a singular talent." Phipps crossed her arms, brass

over flesh. Her monocle gleamed in the phosphorescent glow of the lanterns. "I've never seen anything like it."

"It makes me a little nervous, to tell the truth, Lieutenant." She replaced more gears and screws with slow, deft twists. Gavin was unable to take his eyes off the muscles and tendons in her hands. His chest ached. "When I was defusing Aunt Edwina's bomb in the basement of the Doomsday Vault, it occurred to me that my little talent is a version of the clockwork plague—not deadly enough to be plague zombie, not powerful enough to be clockworker. My entire family died of the plague—my mother and brother died of it right away, and it killed my father slowly. Aunt Edwina became a clockworker, of course. So it's rather difficult to believe that I didn't contract it."

"Do you think you contracted some different version?"

"I sometimes wonder," Alice said. "Aunt Edwina was the world's greatest expert on the clockwork plague. Did she try an early version of her cure on me when I was young? One that worked only partway? Is that the reason she chose me to carry her final cure?" She held up her spidery hand with its burbling tubules. The spider gauntlet had a surface temperature of ninety-six point five degrees, weighed three pounds, two ounces, and carried two drams of blood, Gavin noted. "It would explain a great deal, including why my talent won't let me take this spider off. Edwina might have known how to create something even I can't dissect."

"Do you *want* to take it off?" Phipps asked, surprised.

"Well, no," Alice admitted. "It's ... dug in. It moves as I do, and those tubules are like my own arteries and veins by now. I don't know what would happen if I tried to take it apart. And if I did, I wouldn't be able to cure anyone."

She finished putting the spider back together, gave it a few quick winds with the key on the chain around her neck, and set it back down again. It quivered, then leaped off the table and skittered away. The whirligig chirped in alarm and swooped after it. Gavin watched the air currents in its wake, how the propeller chopped them into tiny streams that twisted one around the other. He could feel their silky smoothness, see how they intertwined, sense the soft temperature differences between them. He looked closer, examining each eddy's individual particles. They vibrated and buzzed like invisible bees. The particles themselves were made of smaller particles that were both there and not there, puzzle pieces in shells that twisted through tiny pockets of the universe, refusing to exist, refusing to vanish, and those particles were made of even smaller particles that came in pairs or trios.

"Gavin!"

He tried to shut out the voice and concentrate on the fascinating parade. Each set of particles was carefully balanced. Even as Gavin watched, one particle sent a bit of energy to its partner. For the tiniest breath of time, a seed of the energy lived in both particles, and then they ... changed. He couldn't put his finger on how, but they did. It was as if two red flowers existed side by side until a bit of pollen blew from one to the other and both flowers became green. It happened with breathtaking precision, a trillion times a trillion times every microsecond, with no guiding hand to ensure it went right. It was entrancing. Exquisite!

But that wasn't the end of it. Those tiny particles were made of—

"Gavin!"

"The tiny bees exchange pollen and make the flowers change color," he muttered. "Red becomes green, and each has a piece of the other."

"No, darling, no. Please come back."

There was a sharp jerk. Gavin blinked. He was sitting at the table again. Alice was holding his face in both her hands, and her claws pricked his cheeks. Her brown eyes were both frightened and worried. He felt her breath on his chin.

"What?" he said. "What's wrong?"

"The plague pulled you under again." Alice let him go and returned to her own seat. "That's your second fugue today, darling."

He shook his head. The particles were important; he could feel it. If only he could look at them more closely, watch their patterns and come to an understanding. But when he looked at the path the whirligig had taken, all he saw was empty air.

"Gavin!"

"My second?" he said.

"The painting was your first."

"I don't remember," he said, still staring after the whirligig.

"The Chinese woman by the stream. She held a fan. There was Chinese writing."

Alice's voice sounded desperate, but Gavin, still hoping to catch the parade of particles again, couldn't bring himself to look in her direction. Still, her tone called for some response. "Oh. Right. Yes, now I remember," he said vaguely, lying. "She held a fan."

"It's getting worse," Phipps said. "You told me a month ago that Dr. Clef said he had two months, perhaps three. But that was an optimistic estimation. It looks like we need to be pessimistic."

"I refuse to believe we came all this way for nothing, Lieutenant." Alice pulled a handkerchief from her pocket, and when she did, the little silver nightingale encrusted with gems fell out. Alice picked it up and pressed one of the eyes. The little bird said in Gavin's voice, "I love you always."

This cleared Gavin's head of the half trance he was in. "I . . . Hello."

"Welcome back, darling," Alice said. "Where were you?"

He shook his head. "I don't think I can explain it in words. But I can see why Dr. Clef and the others went there. It's beautiful."

"Don't speak that way!" She grabbed his hand. "It frightens me when you do. I'm losing more and more of you every day."

He looked at her concerned, beautiful face, trying to etch every feature into his mind so he wouldn't forget her, no matter how much of his mind the plague burned away—her honey brown hair and her small nose and her pointed chin and her warm eyes. He couldn't possibly forget any of it. Could he? He fingered the salamander that circled his ear and felt a sorrow that threatened to crush him. He had learned of his status as a clockworker only a few months ago, but it felt as if a lifetime had passed, as if he couldn't remember a time before it. His back ached where the pirate's whip had left deep, ropy scars after the attack on the *Juniper*.

"I'm trying to stop," he said. "I am. It's very hard to stay aloft."

"Would you play, then?" She pointed at his fiddle case, which was lying on the deck near his wing harness. "Perhaps it'll keep you focused. Certainly it gives me pleasure."

"I wouldn't mind, either," Phipps said, "and I'm not in love with you."

Gavin flashed a smile at that. He set bow to strings and played "The Wild Hunt," letting the music slide and soar. The song rushed and roared about the deck, pushing at the ropes and rebounding from the envelope. Alice closed her eyes and Phipps tapped her feet. Gavin's smile widened. He loved getting a listener lost in the music, towing someone along and sharing the beauty. Provided he didn't make a mistake and spoil the loveliness. A faint hot draft wafted over him, whispering over black silk, and for a moment he was in another place.

Cobblestones, clopping horses, and the smell of open sewers. A man with pale hair played flawless fiddle, his fingers flying over the neck. He grinned down at Gavin and started to say something. Then the memory was gone. The song ended, and Gavin lowered the fiddle.

"You were thinking of your father again," Alice said, not quite accusingly.

"More and more often," Gavin admitted. His back still ached. For a moment, the spot where the mechanical nightingale had pecked him itched, and he scratched it idly. "When I'm not thinking of you."

"You know, I think that's the first time I've heard you use flattery, Gavin Ennock," Phipps said, and Alice laughed.

"All women like flattery," Alice said, "even when they're waiting to hear from—"

"Lady Orchid!" Phipps interrupted.

They all turned. Lady Orchid and a worried-looking man in a white cap were coming up the gangplank. Lieutenant Li preceded them, holding a phosphorescent lantern in one hand. In the other, he held a black box with dragons on it.

"We would like to speak," Lady Orchid said.

Chapter Twelve

Dragons embossed in gold twisted across the surface of the box, and they engaged Alice's eye. Hypnotic, really. Rather like the Impossible Cube, but pleasant, without inducing a headache.

Everyone got to his feet as the new trio boarded the ship. Gavin attempted a bow in the Oriental fashion. A smile quirked at the edges of Lady Orchid's mouth, though Alice couldn't tell whether it was a smile of approval or disdain. Since they were trying to be optimistic, she settled on approval.

Gavin scrambled about for chairs for everyone. Kung hesitated a moment, but Orchid settled into hers as if she had used them all her life, though Alice didn't remember seeing anything but a low stool in the grand house, and Yeh had sat on pillows back in Tehran. Did the Orientals even use chairs? Li was the only one who remained standing. He set the box on the table in front of Lady

Orchid. The dragons looked as though they were dancing. Gavin was avoiding looking directly at the box, and Alice wondered nervously if the dragons might draw him into one of those awful fugues.

"I am Prince Kung," the man said. "Emperor Xianfeng was my half brother."

"I am sorry to hear of your loss, sir," Alice said formally.

"Thank you." He took a breath. "It is . . . strange to speak with foreigners, but still interesting."

"In what way?" Phipps asked.

"You do not know our manners, just as we do not know yours, though it was good of Lord Ennock to make an attempt." He nodded at Gavin, who flushed slightly. "You speak too bluntly for us, too forthrightly. On the other hand, we have little time, and our usual ways to discuss will fail. So I will be . . . forthright. I have learned English because I feel our two worlds, East and West, would be better off in cooperation than at war. My half brother did not feel as I do, and General Su Shun definitely does not. He intends to invade the West as soon as he can confirm the death of Lady Michaels."

He repeated this in Chinese for Orchid's benefit.

"We know this," Gavin said. "We also know that Lady Orchid wants to put her son on the throne so she can rule as regent."

"That is so," Kung replied with a nod. "Normally, we would work out a careful, subtle plan to discredit Su Shun and push him off the throne, or even assassinate him through a careful campaign of poisons. But we simply do not have time."

"He is already partly discredited," Orchid said in Chinese, with Kung translating. *"The emperor cannot be one who is disfigured by the blessing of dragons. He must be unsullied so his body may accept the power of the Jade Hand."*

Phipps crossed her arms in a familiar gesture. "So the emperor must be physically perfect, but once he ascends the throne, he becomes disfigured. Interesting."

"Not disfigured," Kung replied. "Enhanced. The Jade Hand is a piece of heaven. Therefore, it does not mar. It improves."

"But my arm and my eye"—Phipps held out the former and tapped the latter—"are disfigurements?"

"They are not the Jade Hand."

"It makes as much sense as declaring a bit of glassy carbon valuable," Gavin said. "I think the point Prince Kung wants to make is that the fastest way to change power is to steal the Jade Hand and give it to Lady Orchid's son."

"Wouldn't that mean . . . cutting off the boy's hand?" Alice asked in a hesitant voice.

"Yes," Orchid said simply.

A moment of silence followed.

"Su Shun cut his own off when Xianfeng died," Kung said at last. "It's been that way since the time of Lung Fei."

"Wait," Alice said as something occurred to her. "If you are—were—Emperor Xianfeng's half brother, you must also be half brother to Jun Lung, the Chinese ambassador to England."

"Ah, yes." Kung nodded. "My brother shares my views on East-West cooperation, though he was more or less exiled for his pains."

"Was he a Dragon Man?" Gavin asked. "His family name was Lung."

Kung shook his head. "Coincidence. Lung was once common as a family name until it became customary for Dragon Men to take that name, but here and there you will still find a Lung who has not received the blessing of dragons. Xianfeng was a Lung before he took his Celestial name. My brother is even more aggressive about cooperation with the West than I, and the ambassador position was granted him to get him out of Peking, I am sorry to say."

"Along with his son, Feng," Alice said leadingly.

"Feng, yes." A vague look of distaste crossed Kung's face. "We do not speak of my nephew."

Alice leaned forward. "Because he was disgraced for not being able to follow into Jun Lung's profession."

"You know of this?" Kung looked startled.

"Feng was my friend," Gavin said. "I saved his life, and he saved mine. More than once."

"Where he is now?" Kung demanded.

Alice and Gavin exchanged glances. There was an uncomfortable pause, and then Gavin finally said, "Sir, I regret to inform you that Feng has died."

"Has he?" Kung didn't look distressed. Rather, he calmly steepled his fingers. "How?"

"It is a long and complicated story," Alice said. "And we will gladly give you every detail at a more opportune time. However, suffice it to say that Feng sacrificed his own life to save mine and Gavin's."

"Actually," Phipps said, "his sacrifice saved the entire world."

At this, Kung raised both eyebrows. "The world?"

"Perhaps even more," Phipps said. "Far from being ashamed of your nephew, sir, you should be proud of him."

"I see. Then I am most eager to hear this entire story." Kung resettled himself. "But as Lady Michaels has pointed out, first we must finish our current business."

"*We have a number of problems to overcome if we wish to steal the Jade Hand,*" Lady Orchid said. "*Su Shun has barricaded himself in the Forbidden City, and I don't think we can lure him out.*"

"What exactly is the Forbidden City?" Gavin asked. "I've heard of it but don't know anything about it."

"*The Forbidden City is the official palace compound of the emperor in Peking,*" Kung explained. "*It is located in the northeastern part of Peking and is surrounded by a moat and a high wall pierced by four gates. It covers many acres, including a river, and contains many buildings. A second wall surrounds the Palace of Heavenly Purity, where the emperor once lived, but after the great Emperor Yongzheng died, the emperor's residence moved just outside the second wall to the Hall of Mental Cultivation, which is fortunate for us. The difficulty is that only a handful of people are allowed to go in or out of the city itself. Concubines are not allowed to leave the Forbidden City without special permission, and only recognized con-*

cubines are allowed to go in. The same applies to general maidservants—everyone is scrutinized upon entering and leaving."

"What about men?" Gavin asked.

Lady Orchid looked shocked. "*The only men allowed into the Forbidden City are close friends or advisers to the emperor, and even they must leave after sundown. No man but the emperor passes the night in the Forbidden City.*"

"Why is that?" said Alice.

"To ensure proper succession, of course," Kung replied. "No one can doubt that Lady Orchid's son is anyone but the emperor's issue because no man has ever been allowed to spend time in Lady Orchid's presence. Until she fled, at any rate."

"But you mentioned eunuchs," Phipps put in.

"*Of course there are eunuchs.*" Lady Orchid pulled a fan from her belt and waved it. "*The Forbidden City couldn't function without them. They run everything. They guard the gates, they collect the taxes, they keep inventory, they cook, they clean, they entertain, they transcribe messages—everything.*"

Gavin shifted. "When you say *eunuch*, you mean a man who's been—"

"*Yes.*" Li spoke for the first time, and when Kung looked reluctant to translate for a mere lieutenant, Phipps stepped in to translate, though Alice was the only one at the table who couldn't understand him. It was growing frustrating, and she wished she understood the strange, singsong language. "*A male whose three pre-*

*ciouses have been removed. Usually in boyhood, at age
seven or eight, though a few have the procedure done in
adulthood. The eunuchs maintain a special chair with a
hole in the bottom for—"*

"Thank you," Gavin interrupted shortly. He looked
ill.

"Good heavens!" Alice felt sickened herself. "Why on
earth would parents do such a thing to their own child?"

Lady Orchid cocked her head. *"The Forbidden City
needs thousands of eunuchs, and they hire more than a
hundred every year. Any such boy—or man—who pres-
ents himself to the city gates is guaranteed a position. At
the beginning, that includes plenty of food, clothing, a
small amount of money, and a chance to attain real power.
It does not matter what family one is born into or what
one's father has done—all eunuchs have an equal chance.
What chance do you offer the poor in your country?"*

"Certainly not a chance at mutilation," Alice snapped.

"Your poor starve in the streets, from what I hear." Lady
Orchid waved her fan. *"Along with those who contract the
blessing of dragons. Here, we cherish such people."*

"You cherish the Dragon Men," Gavin corrected.
"What about zombies?"

*"They are rounded up and put in a place where they
can await their time. They certainly don't wander like lost
toddlers."*

"Now, look," Alice began.

"I think," Li put in, *"it might be best if we discussed
these things at another time. We need a plan for the Jade
Hand."*

Alice glanced at Gavin. He had grown up half starved in the streets himself. Would he willingly have traded that part of himself for the guarantee of a job? Given the chance, would his mother have allowed it? No, of course not. She was being ridiculous.

"You said the Forbidden City has thousands of people in it," Gavin was saying. "They have to eat. How does food get in? And messages?"

"Food, cloth, animals, and other market items are brought to the gates." Lady Orchid continued to fan herself. *"The eunuchs receive everything and make payments at the gate. Merchants and messengers never set foot inside the city. Not only are they male; they are not worthy. The only other way in is through the Passage of Silken Footsteps."*

Click jumped into Alice's lap. She idly touched his head. "And what might that be?"

"A secret passage that leads out of the Forbidden City. It was built in case the emperor needed a hasty emergency exit. But it is also heavily guarded by both eunuchs and machines. No one is allowed near it. I am one of the few people who even know it exists."

"The walls are also impregnable," Li said. "A number of Dragon Man inventions keep watch round the perimeter. Anyone who tries to climb over is instantly killed. The only weak points are the gates, and they are just as heavily guarded with machinery."*

Gavin cracked his knuckles. "Machinery is our specialty."

"But not if we have no chance to study it first," Alice mused.

"There is, of course, a much simpler way," Lady Orchid said.

Phipps raised an eyebrow, the one not covered by a monocle. "And?"

"Bribery. The eunuchs are quite corrupt. For the right price, anyone can gain entry to the Forbidden City."

"Why didn't you say that earlier?" Alice cried. "That makes everything much easier!"

Kung hesitated. "Sufficient funds are . . . not available."

"I have money," Alice replied promptly. "More than enough, I'm sure."

Here even Lady Orchid bolted upright. *"You have?"*

"Certainly." And she explained about the reward. The silver bonds would easily provide enough to bribe their way into the Forbidden City, perhaps even get them close to Su Shun, and then—

"Unfortunately I do not believe that will work," Kung said. His hands were clenched around a cup. He seemed to notice and made himself relax. "I have heard all about those reward bonds. They were issued outside China and can be used only outside China. The borders are sealed, as you may remember, and those bonds are actually illegal here. They are worthless."

Alice wanted to slump in her chair. Why was it every time they came up with an idea, something happened to destroy it? Sometimes it felt as if the world didn't want them to succeed. Even the clockwork plague had abandoned them—Gavin seemed to feel no urge to come up with a brilliant or outrageously creative plan.

And then something else occurred to her.

"Why did you bring up bribery at all," she asked, "if you have no money?"

"I had money, but it seems to have . . . vanished," said Lady Orchid.

"Does it have something to do with that box?"

Here Lady Orchid hesitated. *"It is called the Ebony Chamber."* And here she spun what seemed to Alice a very strange story about a box and a missing declaration for the heir to the throne and an equally missing lot of priceless jewelry.

"May I?" Alice said, and at Lady Orchid's nod, she pulled the box to herself and picked it up to examine it from all sides. Her brow furrowed as her hands wandered over it. Click put out a paw and batted at it.

"You're a dear," Alice told him, "but don't touch, please."

"What is she doing?" Li asked.

"Alice is talented with clockwor—Dragon Man inventions," Gavin supplied. "She's the only person we know of who can reassemble or repair them."

Kung looked impressed. "We must keep this fact from Su Shun, or he will add her as a concubine."

Alice decided she was too busy with the Chamber to react to this outrageous idea. She opened it and looked inside, then closed it again. There was much more to this box than a simple lock. Without knowing quite why, she brought the box up and lowered it over her own head. Instantly she became dizzy. Darkness swirled around her, but it was darkness with texture, like silk and sandpaper together. Layers of it slid over her, stealing her breath away. She felt hundreds of places all at once, and for a second she understood what a clockwork fugue was like for Gavin.

She jerked the box away, and the world abruptly returned to normal.

"Are you all right?" Gavin asked.

"Perfectly," Alice replied, trying not to pant. "Though I am not in a hurry to try that again." The dragons shimmered and twisted, laughing in their golden silence, and the phoenix latch glimmered enticingly. She ran her fingers over it. "Did you say the combination number was oh-one-eight?"

"*Yes.*"

"Because the latch is not set to oh-one-eight. The last number is set between seven and eight."

"*Why would that matter? The lock opened.*"

"It matters quite a bit," Gavin murmured. "Oh, how it matters."

As if in a dream, he moved his finger toward the phoenix latch and flicked the number fully to 018. Sudden weight pulled the Ebony Chamber down, and it dropped from Alice's hands to land with a thud on the table.

"Thank you, darling," Alice said with satisfaction. "And now . . ."

With a magician's flourish she opened the box. Everyone crowded around to look. The phosphorescent light gleamed off a pile of jewels.

Lady Orchid gasped and pulled the box to her. "*My jewels! Where did they come from?*"

"That may be difficult to explain." Gavin cleared his throat. "For a while, the Third Ward housed a clock-worker named Viktor von Rasmussen. He discovered that there are different universes that exist side by side with this one. We can't see or hear them, but they still exist. Dr. Rasmussen even found a way to bring different versions of himself from those universes into this one."

Phipps shuddered at this. "Took forever to persuade him to send them back." she said. "Caused no end of trouble, and a long line at the privy,"

"This box was created somehow like the Impossible Cube," Gavin said. "It bends time and space around it-self and creates . . . a gate into other universes. Though I don't understand how it works without a power source."

"Anything you put into the box doesn't actually exist in our universe anymore," Alice put in. "When you set it to oh-one-eight, anything you put inside goes into a . . . a piece of universe number eighteen, for want of a better way to put it. Change the lock to another number, and you're looking into a different universe. You have a thousand universes to choose from—more than that, if you count the half spins and quarter spins that seem to affect the box as well."

Gavin rose and said vaguely, "I'll be right back." And he went below.

"*I am not worthy to understand,*" Li said with a shake of his head. "*This is very confusing.*"

"Let me demonstrate." Alice picked up Click and dropped him into the box. He yowled with surprise and disappeared inside, even though he was a bit larger than the box and the box was already filled with jewelry. Alice shut the lid on him before he could jump back out, noted the latch—it was still set to 018—and spun it at random. The numbers landed on 365. The yowling ended. Alice opened the box again. It was empty of both cat and jewels. Lady Orchid made a sound of protest.

"It's all right," Alice told her. "Click is still here, but he's also gone elsewhere. You could say that he exists and does not exist at the same time."

"How much material will fit in there?" Kung asked.

"I'm not sure, though it looks to me like this box is the embodiment of an infinite set. You can add an infinite set to an infinite set any number of times and still have room for more infinite sets, so I think you could add an infinite amount of material to this box and still have room."

"Fascinating," said Lady Orchid tightly. *"Please bring back my jewelry."*

"Of course." Alice reached for the latch.

"When you do," Phipps put in, "point that thing away from me. I have a feeling your cat won't be very happy."

Alice reset the phoenix latch to 018. It belatedly came to her that she might be wrong and that she might have condemned Click to a terrible destruction. Her rash actions were almost like a clockworker's, and she didn't enjoy that thought in the slightest.

She opened the box. Click sprang out and rushed away with another yowl. He fled belowdecks past Gavin, who was coming up with the Impossible Cube, its lattices still dark. He set the Cube on the table opposite the Ebony Chamber. The Chamber was still filled with jewels. The Cube was filled with empty space.

"What are we to do with this?" Li said.

"I'm not sure," Gavin said. "I just . . . wanted it nearby." He paused a moment. "Who created the Ebony Chamber?"

"Lung Fei," answered Kung. *"The same Dragon Man who created the Jade Hand and the salamanders. They are all connected."*

Lady Orchid, meanwhile, carefully tipped the jewels out of the Ebony Chamber. They made a gleaming hoard of stiff beauty on the tabletop. She was setting the box down again when she froze. *"Connected. No."*

"What is wrong?" Kung asked, looking worried again.

"They are all connected. Kung, I know why the Chamber was empty, why there was no paper proclaiming the heir's name." She put her hand inside the box to feel around, then withdrew it with a sharp gasp. *"What—?"*

"It feels odd, yes." Alice leaned toward her. "What did you mean just now?"

"I have seen Xianfeng open the Ebony Chamber more than once. But whenever he did so, he placed the Jade Hand over the phoenix latch. Like so." She put her palm over the latch, covering it completely. *"I thought it was to hide the numbers from the eunuchs. But now . . . if the Chamber is connected to the Hand . . . I wonder."*

"The Hand creates another infinite set," Gavin said with a nod. "There's oh-one-eight and oh-one-eight-A."

Lady Orchid shut the box and tried other numbers—

009, 005, 000. Every time she opened the Chamber, it was empty. This only seemed to confirm what she was thinking. *"I believe he did declare an heir—my son—but we need the Jade Hand to open the Ebony Chamber to the correct . . . place."*

"All of which only reinforces our—your—need to lay hands on the Hand, so to speak," said Alice. "We became rather sidetracked."

"Yeah. An infinite set in an infinite set." Gavin slowly turned the Ebony Chamber open again and held the Impossible Cube over it. "So, what would happen . . ."

Electricity arced blue from the Chamber to the Cube. It snapped and hissed like a nest of snakes. Alice's hair rose, and she felt it prickle across her neck. A low rumble built swiftly into a high whine, and air moved through the stable.

"Gavin!" Alice cried. "Stop!"

But Gavin seemed caught in a trance. He lowered the Cube closer to the box. The whine grew louder and more shrill, a dragon screaming its own death. Power twisted and writhed around Gavin's hands and spilled onto the table. The cups and dishes shattered. Jewelry flew in all directions. Everyone, including Phipps, seemed stunned. Alice moved. She shoved the table hard. The Ebony Chamber went flying, and one of the table legs caught Gavin's thigh. His hands jerked, and the Impossible Cube bounced across the deck in the opposite direction. The whine faded and the electricity stopped. The Chamber remained dark except for the limned dragons dancing across it, and the Impossible Cube carried a soft blue glow except for a few dark places where the lattices crossed one another. A blanket of silence dropped over the deck.

"Goddamn it!" Phipps pounded the table with her brass fist. "And damn it again! Ennock, if you ever do that again, I shall rip your bollocks off and stuff them up your arse!"

Alice flushed at the dreadful vulgarity, the worst she'd heard in her life. "Lieutenant! There's no call for—"

"Not the time, Michaels." Phipps had lost her hat yet again and cast about for it. "Is everyone all right?"

Everyone reported that they were, including Gavin. Kung and Orchid gathered up the jewelry and piled it on the table again. Li scooped Phipps's hat from the deck where it had fallen and returned it to her with something in Chinese that no one bothered to translate for Alice. Phipps responded from her chair, and Li bowed to her. He stayed bowed for a little longer than strictly necessary, or so it seemed to Alice, and Phipps gave him a long look with an expression Alice had never seen before as she put her hat back into place. Then she caught Alice looking at her, and her expression went wooden again.

"I'm sorry," Gavin said. "The plague was . . . I'm sorry. I won't do that again."

He wouldn't meet Alice's eyes, and she knew they were both thinking the same thing—three fugues in one day now. Her stomach felt cold and sick, and more than anything she wanted his arms around her for just a moment, but not in front of all these people.

"What happened, then?" Alice asked.

"I don't fully know." Gavin gave the Impossible Cube an uneasy glance. "The two of them seem to share a connection."

"Two infinite sets," Alice agreed.

"Two sets of infinite." Gavin's voice was dreamlike. "One gives power; the other takes it. I can see it down to the matching particles. What one does, the other matches. When these two are one, they can split the particles in pieces, change gravity, tilt the world and slosh the oceans. It calls to water. Always water. Tilt the glass and slop it over, flood the land, flatten mountains, and we'll all be underwater."

"Flood and plague will destroy us if you don't cure the world." The words of Monsignor Adames echoed from the Church of Our Lady in Belgium and slammed through Alice with the force of twelve hammer blows.

"Gavin, you're frightening me." Her voice was shaking. "Snap out of it."

"Together they can flood the continents with their infinite. Tilt the world, slosh the glass. Tilt the axis, flood the—"

Phipps slapped him on the face with a *crack*. Gavin started, then blinked at them all with wide blue eyes.

"What's the matter?" He put a hand to his cheek. "What did—?"

"We shall keep the Cube and the Chamber separated until we can study the phenomenon further," Alice said briskly over the thickness in her throat. "Right now, we need to plan our way into the Forbidden City."

This remark was met with general assent, though

everyone found it difficult to keep their eyes off the Cube and Chamber, squatting like hungry lizards only a few paces away. Even the impressive pile of jewelry on the table couldn't compete.

"Flood and plague will destroy us if you don't cure the world," Alice thought. *But we'll never put them together, so that so-called prophecy won't come true, Monsignor Adames. Of that, you may be sure.*

"The secret passage goes under the moat and both walls," Lady Orchid said. *"One end is found in Jingshan Park, which is outside the northern wall of the Forbidden City. The other end emerges just behind the Hall of Mental Cultivation, the emperor's residence. Eunuchs guard several points along the entire passageway, and we will need to kill or bribe each one."*

"Can they all be bribed?" Alice asked doubtfully.

"I doubt it very much. Some will raise an alarm no matter what we do."

"I thought you said you were one of only a few people who even knew the passage existed." Gavin drew up a chair again. "What about all these eunuchs?"

Lady Orchid waved this aside with her fan. *"Their tongues have been cut out so they cannot reveal its existence, and neither can they read or write. This is why they are easy to bribe—many are unhappy with their situations."*

"I can imagine," Gavin growled.

"Once you have emerged from the passage, you will find more guards and servants," Kung said. *"They are*

everywhere. And then you will have to enter the palace, find Su Shun, and take the Hand from him."

"I can build us some weapons," Gavin said doubtfully, "but I don't think we can do this alone."

"The young lord is correct." Li had taken up a position behind Phipps's chair now. *"You will need men to fight when you are in the passage, and men to fight when you are in the Forbidden City. The fighting will serve as a distraction for the guards so you can find Su Shun and take the Hand. Once you have given the Hand to Prince Zaichun, he can end the battle."*

"Where would we find someone suicidal enough to—oh." Alice stopped herself. "Are you . . . volunteering, Lieutenant Li?"

He bowed to her. *"My men and I stand ready, Lady Michaels."*

She shook her head. "We can't ask you to do that."

"You saved our lives, Lady Michaels. I only ask that you do not disappoint us with refusal. My men and I only wish to serve you and, if necessary, die with honor."

"We accept, Lieutenant," Gavin said before Alice could object again. "And thank you. You and your men honor us with your service."

Yet another bow from the lieutenant. Alice abruptly found the air too close. She got up and stalked toward the front of the ship, picking her way around the rolled-up endoskeleton and the piles of silk. One of the whirligigs flitted up from below to land on her shoulder, and she touched it with an absent gesture. Thoughts swirled through her head. So much was happening so fast, and she couldn't take it all in.

And then Gavin was there. He put his arm around her waist. She started to pull away at first, then sighed and leaned against him. It was good to stand with someone strong.

"Penny?" His eyes were very blue, and the salamander made a brass circle around his ear. "Or maybe I should offer a nickel. Inflation, and all."

She managed a weak smile. "It just came over me all at once that our plan involves bringing a number of men into the Forbidden City so they can fight and die, and then we intend to kill a man, cut off the hand of a small boy, and graft one of the dead man's hands onto him. I don't know how we came to this point, and I don't know if it's right."

He nodded. "I think the fact that we're questioning what we're doing means we're on the right path. The only people who don't question themselves are tyrants and despots."

"And . . . clockworkers," Alice whispered.

His arm tightened around her waist. "And them. Look, we're risking our lives, too. Tyrants don't do that—they make other people risk their lives. Besides, thousands will die in Su Shun's war with the West if we don't stop him."

"I know." She sighed heavily. "I do know. I just don't like carrying this kind of responsibility. I never asked for it. I certainly don't want it."

"Another good sign, I think. Su Shun *does* want it, and

look where it's taking him." He paused. "But that's not the worst of what's bothering you."

"No." She stared into space. "They're asking you—*we* are asking you—to build weapons. That means you'd probably go into a fugue. It frightens me, Gavin." He started to protest, and she held up a hand. "I know all the reasons we're doing it, and I agree that we must. But the fear is still there. I'll just have to live with it."

There wasn't anything else to say, so he gently turned her around. "We should go back and see what they're planning."

At the table, Phipps was pointing to the map. "So your spies put piles of gunpowder and ammunition here and here and here."

"Indeed," Kung replied. *"The question is, what can we do with them?"*

"Did he say gunpowder?" Alice put in.

"He did," Phipps said.

"Hm." Alice studied the map. "I might have an idea, then."

"We have a few ourselves." Phipps drummed her brass fingers on the table. "Gavin, what kind of weapons can you build by tomorrow morning?"

He glanced at Alice, who kept an impassive look on her face. "Tomorrow morning?"

"In three days, the Jade Hand will have grafted itself permanently onto Su Shun's arm and give him a stronger hold on the throne," Li explained. *"It would therefore be best to go after him tomorrow night."*

"Oh." Gavin ran a finger over the salamander at his

ear. "If you bring me more copper, a steel bar, and some magnesium, I could probably build a pair of electromagnetic emission power pistols, and maybe a vibratory frequencation blade."

"I definitely can't translate that," Phipps complained.

"Two large pistols that make *zap* noises and a sword that will cut through almost anything until the power runs out," Alice supplied.

"Easily done," Kung said.

"What was the lady considering?" asked Li.

Alice touched the little whirligig on her shoulder and thought a moment. "My whirligigs can follow fairly complicated orders if they are worded properly, though Click has a distressing tendency to do as he wishes. If we avoid using him, I think we can create quite a display for our Forbidden City friends, though you two lieutenants would have to work out a few military details."

"I see." Phipps turned to her Oriental counterpart. "Can we do that, Lieutenant?"

Li made one more bow. *"It would be an honor, Lieutenant."*

Alice looked between them one more time.

Interlude

A pall of oily smoke and steam hung over the Outer Court of the Forbidden City. In the great space between the orderly clusters of red-tiled buildings gathered the machines. Dragons of iron and brass coiled around themselves, hissing and muttering. Copper tigers raked the cobblestones. Mechanical elephants stomped heavy feet and trumpeted to shake the air. Flocks of small birds with sharp, shiny claws, wheeled overhead. Black-clad Dragon Men moved among them with tools, making adjustments, adding weapons, improving engines. At the behest of one Dragon Man, a tiger opened its mouth and a pistol cracked three quick bullets at a wooden target, which vanished in a pile of splinters. Another Dragon Man gestured at a live cow standing to one side of the court, and a hundred brass birds descended on the animal. The cow had time to make a surprised grunt before it was reduced to a pile of wet meat and yellow bones.

General—no, *Emperor*—Su Shun stood on the snowy steps of the Hall of Supreme Harmony. Creamy clouds covered the summer sun and filtered the light drifting down on the hundreds of buildings, large and small, that made up the Forbidden City, safe behind scarlet walls and an azure moat. The city bustled with activity as it always did, but now a new intensity wove itself into the eunuchs and the maids. They kept their heads down and hurried more quickly about their tasks, trying not to draw attention to themselves. The concubines were especially worried—Su Shun might decide he didn't want "used" concubines and demand fresh ones, which would put all of them out on the street. Most of them would end their days in brothels, since no one wanted to marry a cast-off concubine.

Su Shun stood above them all in his new suit of yellow armor, yellow for the Celestial Throne, yellow for the emperor, and made a grim smile that covered only half his face. The other half of his face, the brass half, remained immobile. Behind him rose the Hall, with its magnificent scarlet pillars and its gold carvings and its two tiers of swooping tiled roofs, though eunuchs were even now taking away the jade treasures stored within and prying gold from the walls. Su Shun had no use for jade or gold, but both would fetch a high price, and war was costly, especially a war involving Dragon Men.

When Su Shun had given the order to begin the sale, two of the eunuchs had dared to voice mild protest. Su Shun had raised the Jade Hand and spoken to Lung Chao, Emperor Xianfeng's favorite Dragon Man. The

Hand had glowed, and Lung Chao, with his enhanced strength and reflexes, had broken one man's neck and crushed the other's windpipe before anyone could move. Now the eunuchs obeyed with alacrity.

Su Shun allowed himself a small smile. The Hall of Supreme Harmony belonged to him, as did the entire Forbidden City and the empire beyond it. A true ruler now ruled the one true empire. It was time to bring China back to the old ways, when emperors were heroic warlords who fought on the field, not opium addicts who simpered behind silk curtains.

He was well aware how tenuous his rule was. Although he came from a noble family, his rebuilt face precluded him from any hope of touching the throne. Only a physically perfect man was considered worthy to receive the Jade Hand; its power would overwhelm a lesser one. That word *lesser* had irked him for dozens of years. Xianfeng's father, Emperor Daoguong, had been physically perfect, but he had also been a complete fool. Su Shun had gritted his teeth while the emperor bungled attempt after attempt to keep control of the opium that continued to seep into China thanks to British merchants. But at the height of the old man's power, more than thirty thousand chests of the sticky black balls glided across the borders every year. Su Shun watched his own father succumb to the darkness, withdrawing from his sons and turning weak as a hollow reed, until one day he simply shuddered and died, the pipe he loved more than his family still in his mouth. Su Shun hated the smell of the smoke, hated the crackle of the little flame, hated the *ffffff* sound of the smoking going in, deadly as poisoned feathers. He swore he would rid China of the filth, both the opium and those who sold it.

It was clear Daoguong and his family weren't fit to rule. Daoguong had trouble thinking past China's borders and had no desire to expand China or put down the British once and for all. Su Shun knew better. And Su Shun had patience.

The Jade Hand twitched, and a twinge of pain threaded up Su Shun's arm. He kept his expression neutral. He would not show pain here, in the Outer Court. People might mistake pain as an admission that he wasn't fit to rule, and he hadn't coddled that spoiled brat Xianfeng for eleven years—eleven years!—to watch it all drift away like so much opium smoke. When the boy had shown an interest in common whorehouses and even the opium dens, Su Shun had encouraged him, helped him disguise himself and move among the lice-ridden prostitutes and smoky drug dens, hoping the little idiot would catch something and die. But the ancestors had smiled on Xianfeng, or perhaps they had frowned on Su Shun. Either way, the limp little prince had minced up to the throne after Daoguong's death and, after inhaling copious amounts of opium, accepted the Jade Hand while Su Shun gave his false half smile. But still Su Shun waited.

And then the English came, with their ships and their cannons and their clanking clockwork monstrosities, nothing like the elegant masterpieces created by fine Dragon Men. They came with their treaty that allowed them to thrust even more opium down the throats of good Chinese, along with their cheaply made factory goods that put Chinese merchants out of business. The supercilious sneer they gave Su Shun over the treaty table was nearly enough to make him draw sword and pistol to attack right then. But he held himself in check, and that had been for the good. What little will Xianfeng had left seemed to drain out of him after that treaty, and he spent more and more time with his opium pipe and that concubine cow of his, the one who mooed so prettily in his ear and who actually managed to drop a son. How she coaxed a boy child out his opium-laced loins, Su Shun still didn't understand. He clenched his teeth and spent hours ensuring the emperor had all the opium silver could buy. He encouraged him to smoke more and more of it because opium was of the feminine yin, and it drained away the male yang. He also talked him into using the Passage of Silken Footsteps out of the Forbidden City to spend himself on Peking prostitutes, both male and female, so that none of his seed would reach the concubines or his breathless empress. Both schemes had worked for a while—none of the other concubines had become pregnant, and Su Shun had seen to it that any whore who had thrown babies nine months after a celestial visit had quietly disappeared with their litters. Su Shun would have liked to accuse Cixi of infidelity; he had even dropped a few hints into the Xianfeng's ear, but the emperor waved them aside as ridiculous. The only thing Su Shun had managed to do was delay Xianfeng in writing the name of his heir for the Ebony Chamber to swallow.

And then fate had played straight into Su Shun's hands. The English had attacked again, making it all the way to Peking. An idea had come to Su Shun, and he arranged for a decently pretty woman to be infected with the dragon's blessing and put into a concubine's guise. The woman was willing enough to die, for the amount of money Su Shun paid her would take care of her entire family for the rest of their lives, and it was easy enough for her to join the evacuation train during the confusion. Su Shun couldn't even remember her name, but she had done the job admirably. The emperor was dead, and after a bit of scuffling, Su Shun had the Jade Hand.

He held it out before him, as he had done many times before in the last few days. His right arm still hurt, and sometimes the pain flared as if it had been dipped in molten brass. But the spikes at the top of the Hand had snapped into his flesh, and the brass-bound green fingers twitched. Most of the time he felt nothing in it, but occasionally it seemed he could feel an ache in his missing palm. He could no longer hold a sword or fire a pistol, but perhaps he would learn to do so with his left. The pain flared again. Su Shun gestured, and one of the eunuchs kneeling around him held out a bowl. Xianfeng had used opium to dull the affliction, but Su Shun was not so foolish. Su Shun tapped the bowl, and the eunuch drank half of it. Su Shun waited a moment, and when the eunuch didn't topple over dead, he accepted the bowl and drained it dry.

Another eunuch hurried up to the bottom of the stairs, dropped to his knees, and knocked his forehead on the stones. Su Shun snapped his fingers, and the eunuch rose again. His head was fuzzy from lack of proper shaving, and his robe was still white. The hundred days of mourning for Xianfeng were still in effect, and Su Shun didn't dare shorten that time period, though it grated—he would have preferred to stuff Xianfeng into his tomb and pretend the idiot had never existed. People had short memories, and the faster he could shove Xianfeng aside, the more entrenched Su Shun's rule would become. Even now he could feel the Jade Hand sinking deeper into his flesh, becoming one with him. Soon nothing would release it.

"What is it?" he asked the eunuch. "Tell me you've found Cixi and that whelp of hers."

The eunuch hesitated, which told Su Shun the answer. "I bring news of a different kind, Imperial Majesty," he said in his high, fluting voice. "Rumors are circulating around the city about Lady Michaels and Lord Ennock."

A bit of excitement flicked through Su Shun, tinged with a bit of fear, though he kept both away from his face. Alice Michaels—the woman with the cure. He glanced at the war machines in the Outer Court. The only reason they and the army and the rest of the machines waiting outside the Forbidden City weren't marching west was that Su Shun was afraid of the men encountering her and her infamous cure. It had all but died out on its own since she had vanished three years ago. Lung Hun, who specialized in the blessing of dragons, said it was a strange paradox—the cure destroyed the disease, but the cure eventually died out without the disease to play host to it. If he could destroy Alice Michaels, he could destroy the cure and keep the Dragon Men safe for his invasion.

"Proceed," he said tightly.

"Your Imperial Majesty knows that Michaels and Ennock were captured at the border and were on their way here, as your Imperial Majesty ordered, and Ennock was fitted with a salamander to make him a Dragon Man, but both of them vanished before they reached the city, with no sign of where they—or our troops—went."

"Yes, yes, get on with it."

The eunuch prostrated himself again. "As your Imperial Majesty demands," he quavered. "I am only a messenger, and I pray you will not have this humble servant whipped or burned or—"

"I will not have you beaten," Su Shun growled, "if you just tell me what you learned."

"They hide somewhere in Peking," the eunuch said to the ground. "We do not yet know where."

Su Shun's eyes went wide. He strode down the steps and hauled the shaking eunuch to his feet by the collar of his white mourning robe. The eunuch squealed. *"What about the cure?"* he snarled. The other eunuchs tried to shuffle farther away without seeming to. Far below, the Dragon Men paused in their work. A copper tiger roared.

"M-m-m-majesty . . ."

"Speak!" Su Shun bellowed. "Or I will tie your entrails to a rock and throw them down a well!"

The eunuch's eyes were wild with fear, and a smell of fresh urine permeated the air. "Th-there is no sign of the cure in Peking, M-majesty."

"Do not lie to save your skin," Su Shun hissed into the man's face, "for I will nail it above my bed if you are."

"It is the truth, Celestial One."

Su Shun released the eunuch so abruptly, he fell and tumbled partway down the stone steps. Facedown, he lay there, still quivering.

"Send the army into the city," Su Shun ordered. "Begin house-to-house searches. I want her found and brought to me immediately. Alive. The reward of four hundred pounds of silver for her still stands. And I want Cixi and her little bastard brought with her. Go!"

The eunuch scrambled away, barely remembering to knock his head at the bottom of the stairs. Su Shun raised the Jade Hand. A tingle ran down his arm, and power flared across the brass inlays. The salamanders, curled around the ear of every Dragon Man, made an answering glow, and they stopped working.

"Lung Chao!" Su Shun boomed in the voice he used when addressing legions of troops. "Bring your birds!"

Below, Lung Chao turned away from the mess of cow he had been examining and ran lightly toward the steps. He bounded up the white marble without pausing, and Su Shun wanted to kick him back down the stairs, even strike off his head, for not kowtowing properly. But Lung Chao was a Dragon Man, and immune to Imperial protocol. Su Shun needed every Dragon Man he could get, and it would be foolish to execute one for forgetting to bow. He might as well as throw a magic sword into a volcano. At least Lung Chao remembered to kneel when he reached the emperor.

"Majesty," Lung Chao said. His deadly flock of birds clattered to a noisy landing on the Hall steps, and they peered up at Su Shun with eerie, blank eyes.

"Can your birds search the city from above?"

"They can, Imperial Majesty. They are very much like my border guards."

"Then take them out to search for Alice Michaels and Gavin Ennock and Lady Cixi."

Lung Chao paused. "Are you positive you want this?"

The direct address caught Su Shun off guard. "What are you talking about?"

"They will come to you. Like worms. Like serpents. Like rabbits and moles wearing silken slippers, they will come. The balance is wrong, and it will correct itself."

"The balance?"

"Yin and yang, you and she. You and Cixi, hand in hand." Lung Chao gestured toward the Jade Hand. "The right is wrong and must be righted."

If one of his commanders had spoken to him this way, Su Shun would have smashed him across the face and had him beaten with thin rods. But he needed to think less like a general and more like a ruler. And this was a Dragon Man. Instead, Su Shun held up his right hand, the Jade Hand, and said, "Silence."

The Hand glowed, as did the salamander in Lung Chao's ear. Lung Chao's words ended.

"Do as I bid you. And kowtow when you leave."

Lung Chao obeyed. His little flock of birds followed him, and suddenly this gesture seemed too small, so unworthy of an emperor. Once again he held up the Jade Hand, and the familiar tingle came with the glow. The Dragon Men turned to face him. Su Shun only wished the Jade Hand's range reached farther than a long bowshot; the Hand could summon any Dragon Man within its range, and it gave Su Shun the power to command any Dragon Man who could hear his voice, but this Ennock boy was beyond the reach of both. For the moment.

"Dragon Men of China," Su Shun boomed, "take your inventions and go forth into the city. Find Alice Michaels. Find Gavin Ennock. Find Lady Cixi. And bring them to me!"

A hundred salamanders glowed all around the Outer Court, and then, one by one, the Dragon Men turned to their inventions. With yips and yaps and wild shouts, they clambered atop stomping elephants, unleashed tigers, mounted dragons, and swarmed toward the five arches of the Meridian Gate. The eunuchs on duty hurried to open four of them—the center arch was reserved for the emperor alone—and the mass of Dragon Men plunged through to the city beyond.

Chapter Thirteen

Gavin wrenched awake. The scars on his back burned like fiery ropes, and he still felt the cold hands of Madoc Blue, the pirate, tugging at him and tearing at his clothes. He still heard the sound of the knife going into Blue's neck and smelled the coppery blood washing over his hands. Gavin had killed Blue more than three years ago, and the other pirates had whipped scars into Gavin's back for laying hands on one of their own, even to defend himself from rape. But in Gavin's dreams, Blue lurched back to life and pawed at Gavin even as the first mate's lash descended. Ever since that terrible day, deep sleep eluded Gavin, and he always bolted awake in a thin veneer of night sweat. As a result, he avoided sleep for as long as he could—one of the few advantages of being a clockworker was that he could go for days without a wink. Apparently the lack had finally caught up with him.

He groaned and sat up. His back protested, and his head thumped with pain. The salamander circling his ear felt heavy. It came to him that he was slumped in one corner of his little laboratory aboard the *Lady of Liberty*. He staggered stiffly to his feet. The room was hot and stuffy. The little glow forge, the one that heated without an open flame, ticked softly as it cooled down. Tools lay scattered everywhere, along with scraps of metal and bits of wire. Click was sitting on a fold-down shelf amid the detritus, watching with interested eyes.

"What do you want, cat?" Gavin muttered.

Click cocked his head, the mechanical equivalent of a shrug. Gavin managed a stretch and felt his back pop. He winced, then leaned against the worktable with a sigh. Four fugues in twenty-four hours. The plague was catching up with him.

His hand touched warm metal, and he drew back. Laying on the table were four large pistols, fat and gleaming. Both were made of brass and copper, with glass coiling around the barrels like transparent snakes. Next to them lay a sword hilt. Gavin could just make out a stiff wire sticking out of it. Cables snaked under the table to a set of heavy-looking rucksacks—batteries for all five weapons. Gavin picked up the sword hilt and pressed a switch on the bottom. The wire glowed blue—it was made of the same alloy as the ship's endoskeleton—and it made an eerie hum that wasn't quite any note Gavin could name. It set Gavin's teeth on edge. He whipped it around, and with a *vvvvvip* noise it sliced through a piece of scrap metal as if it was wet silk. With a nod, he switched it off. The pistols crackled when Gavin tried them, though he didn't fire. All the weapons were simple improvements on ones he had already seen — the pistols were like al-Noor's, and the sword was a thinner version of the one wielded by Ivana Gonta, the clock-worker, back in Ukraine. He remembered working on them, but only halfway, as if he were recalling a dream from several nights ago, or a story he had once heard.

Click jumped down from the table and strolled over to a corner, where a sheet was covering something that stood upright. He batted at the dirty white cloth. Gavin whipped it aside. It was a metallic body for a mechanical. Spindly arms, jointed fingers. No head. Wires, pistons, and a few springs stuck out of the neck opening.

Gavin recognized the body immediately. It was a duplicate of Kemp. He went to one of the cupboards, took out the broken, powered-down mechanical head stored there, and inserted a screwdriver into one of the holes in back. The single unbroken eye lit back up.

"Madam. Madam. Madam," the head said. "Madam. Madam. Madam."

The voice brought back memories of the fight with the Gontas and the Zalizniaks back in Kiev, when Kemp's body had been destroyed and his head damaged. Gavin, ready to die for Alice in that fight, had already given himself up, but Alice had refused to let him go. In the end, she had saved him, and a little girl had perished in his place.

"Madam. Madam. Madam."

Gavin switched Kemp's head back off and tried it on

the body. It fit, though it would take a little work, and the head still needed repairs. Still, Alice would be glad to have him back again.

A knock came at the door. Gavin whipped the sheet back over Kemp before calling, "Come in."

Alice entered with a basket. Food smells emerged from it, and suddenly Gavin was ravenous. For a moment, he didn't know which he was happier to see—his fiancée or the food. But his better nature overcame him, and he kissed her before taking the basket. He noticed she hadn't replaced the corks on her iron fingertips.

"Goodness, you're all rumpled," she said, smoothing his hair. She didn't touch the salamander. "You need a bath. And a shave."

"How long have I been . . . away?" he asked. The basket contained a number of small bamboo containers, each containing a number of dumplings or buns, each filled with tiny bits of sweet bean paste or chopped vegetables. Pieces within pieces within pieces. Fascinated, he started to spiral down into the plague again, but Alice's voice snapped him back.

"Last night and today," she said. "The sun is setting. I came in to check on you once, but . . ." She trailed off.

"I didn't hurt you, did I?" he asked, horrified.

"Certainly not!" she shot back. "But you were dreadfully . . . rude. I know it isn't your fault," she added hastily. "The plague takes over, and you aren't yourself."

"I'm sorry," he said.

"I blame the plague, not you," she replied briskly. "Soon we'll get that taken care of."

Would they? Gavin was starting to wonder. Lady Orchid said China had no cure for clockworkers, and even with all the Dragon Men working together, how could they possibly find one before he went completely mad? Gavin had met any number of clockworkers during his time as an agent for the Third Ward, and the ones who had multiple fugues in a single day were nearing the end of their sanity, and their lives.

"But," Alice continued, "it did mean I didn't check on you for quite some time. You look as though you slept in here."

He stuffed a bun into his mouth without regard to manners. Click wound around his legs as if begging, though he never ate. "I did. I don't know how long. We have some weapons now, but they're untested."

"Your weapons always work, darling. What do we have?"

He showed her while he ate, and she was suitably impressed, especially with the sword. She gave it a cautious wave, and it left a growling blue trail in the air. Click backed away.

"This might catch on," she said. "I've never seen the like."

"Thanks. I think I built it for you."

She gave a little laugh. "Most men bring flowers, you know. But I'll take it." She set it down and suddenly touched his face with the back of her right hand, the one without the spider. He closed his eyes and took her hand with his own. They both stood like that, without speaking, for a long moment. It was all Gavin needed right then. He wanted to capture that moment and hold it forever, make it a single, perfect note that never stopped, more powerful than any mere symphony.

"How," he said at last, "does a cabin boy on a merchant airship end up in China, in love with a beautiful baroness? Are we nothing but game pieces on a board?"

"If it meant being with you, Gavin, I would happily make myself a pawn of fate."

He kissed her, softly and on the mouth, then again with hunger. He pressed his forehead to hers. "I'll make you my queen one day, my lady."

"And you, my lord, will be my knight in black pajamas."

Another laugh. "Let's take all these up top. Where are the others?"

"Phipps and Li are still here. Lady Orchid and Prince Kung have left, but they should be returning any moment." Alice paused. "I'm afraid we do have some bad news, darling."

"What is it?" He grew tense.

"Let's discuss it up there."

They carried the weapons and battery packs up top. Click followed. On the way, Gavin said to Alice, "Why haven't you put the corks back on?"

"I don't like them." She flexed her left hand, and the iron spider creaked softly. "Actually, I'm planning to 'accidentally' scratch a few people, no matter what Lady Orchid might think. It would be foolish not to."

"And you're anything but foolish."

"Let's see. I'm sneaking into a heavily fortified palace

to attack the most powerful despot in the world and cut his hand off on the small chance that his successor will find a way to heal an incurable disease. No, not at all foolish."

"Well, when you stack it all up like that . . ." The bird poke on his neck itched again, and he unsuccessfully tried to juggle battery packs to get to it. "Besides, I have total faith in your ability to destroy empires. If this works, you should see if Queen Victoria will hire you to handle Tsar Alexander in Russia. Make a fortune."

Alice made an unladylike noise.

Up top, things were much as Gavin remembered them—dim light from a setting sun filtered in through the high stable walls, and the *Lady* sat motionless on the floor. Lanterns provided a bit more light. It was like living in a hot, stuffy cave. Phipps and Li were drinking tea and talking in low voices. At first Gavin thought they were discussing strategy, but then Phipps actually gave a low laugh and covered her mouth with her hand in a feminine gesture Gavin had never in his life imagined she would make. They both caught sight of Gavin and Alice, and cut themselves off, looking a little guilty. Alice cut Gavin a sidelong look.

"Gavin's out of his fugue, so it's safe to talk to him," she announced. "He did a wonderful job on the weapons."

"Let's see them," Phipps said. "Hing—Lieutenant Li—says things in Peking are getting worse and worse."

"What things?" Gavin set the battery packs on the deck next to the Impossible Cube and the Ebony Chamber while Alice set the pistols and the sword on the table. "Alice said something was—"

"They're looking for us, darling," Alice interrupted.

"Who?"

"The Dragon Men."

Gavin looked at her, puzzled. "Well, we knew that."

"No, I mean they're *looking* for us. In the city. They know we're here somewhere, and they're out with their automatons and mechanicals. They're climbing over walls and knocking down doors. A section of the city caught fire after one of their dragons breathed fire on someone, and they still haven't managed to put it out."

"Then we need to move on Su Shun," Gavin said instantly. "Tonight." He picked up his wings, shrugged into the harness, and set about buckling and buttoning. "The sun's almost set. Can your men be ready to leave when it's fully dark, Lieutenant Li?"

"They are ready on a moment's notice, Lord Ennock," Li replied.

"What are you doing?" Phipps asked.

"I'm not going into the Forbidden City without these." Gavin finished the final buckle and shrugged his shoulders for a test furl. The wings opened with a soft metallic clink. It felt good to wear them again, as though he had reattached a missing leg. The battery was fully charged, too, thanks to the *Lady*'s generator. "We might need a scout or an escape route. And they're handy in other ways."

He yanked on a pulley, and his left wing snapped outward. It caught a deck chair and sent it spinning. Click jumped back with a sharp hiss.

"Prince Kung and the lady will be here soon," Li said. *"And then—"*

From high up came a crash of splintering wood. Gavin tensed. Alice snatched up the wire sword, though it wasn't connected to its battery pack. Phipps and Li leaped to their feet, Phipps with a glass cutlass and Li with a pistol.

Bits of wood showered from the rafters, and a brass nightingale flashed downward. Gavin snapped out a hand and caught it without thinking, and only after his fist closed around the tiny automaton did it occur to him that the bird might be dangerous. Sawdust clung to the nightingale's head where it had smashed through the wooden wall. The tip of its beak was stained red.

"Good catch," Phipps breathed. "Is it a spy?"

"I don't know," Gavin told her. "I'll have to take it apart and see what—"

I see the moon, the moon sees me.
It turns all the forest soft and silvery.
The moon picked you from all the rest,
For I loved you best.

Gavin stared. His hand froze around the little bird. The voice that emerged from its red-stained beak was like Gavin's, but not quite. It was deeper, with a different tone. And it sang the song in A-flat, which Gavin had never done in his life.

I have a ship, my ship must flee,
Sailing o'er the clouds and on the silver sea.

The moon picked you from all the rest,
For I loved you best.

The voice touched his soul with a ghostly hand, warm and cool at the same time. It called up chilly summer nights and soft music bouncing off hard cobbles. His hand trembled with the effort not to crush the bird in his plague-strong hand.

"How does it know that song?" Alice demanded beside him. "Gavin, what's going on?"

"I—I . . ." Gavin's mouth was filled with sandpaper and joy and fear. The clockwork plague flared back to life. "I have to go. I have to go right now."

"What?" Phipps lowered the cutlass. "Gavin, you can't just—"

But Gavin was already moving. He tossed the little bird into the air and, for reasons he couldn't articulate, snatched up the Impossible Cube and ran toward the gangplank. The nightingale flew ahead of him. The plague pulled him along, wiping out rational judgment. His only thought was to follow the fascinating nightingale back to its source. Nothing else mattered. Nothing else existed.

"Gavin!" A honey-haired woman moved to block his way. "You can't just leave!"

His wings glowed. He vaulted over her head and glided to one of the stable doors. Ignoring the shouts behind him, he yanked it open onto an evening courtyard. The two surprised soldiers standing guard outside didn't have time to react as the nightingale shot through the opening and Gavin followed. He dashed over the stones. Power coruscated over his wings. They chimed softly and propelled him into the darkening sky. The woman's cries thinned and vanished beneath him, and he was only vaguely aware of her distress. He had to follow the bird.

Peking stretched out below him in a blocky series of red and brown tile roofs with upturned corners. A few scattered torches and lanterns were lit, and he smelled smoke. In the distance, flames flickered hungrily around some of the buildings. The streets below him were mostly empty, and though it was growing dark, Gavin didn't quite understand why this was, until he saw the elephant. And the tiger. And the dragon. They and other automatons were stomping through the city, each accompanied by a Dragon Man and soldiers. Even as Gavin watched from above, an elephant smashed through a wooden gateway. Four soldiers and the Dragon Man boiled into the courtyard beyond it. Gavin couldn't hear the shouts and screams of the inhabitants, but he knew they were there, nonetheless. The salamander circling his ear grew chilly in the evening air. None of the people below looked up. He took all this in with a glance, however, and didn't pause to consider any of it. The brass nightingale was flying, and he had to follow.

The little bird sped up, but Gavin kept pace with easy sweeps of his wings. Even with the Impossible Cube, flying was as easy as thought. They passed over the borders of the city, and the houses faded into farmland. The sun set fully, but a full moon rose, turning the nightingale's brass body to liquid gold and changing the red stain on its beak to black. Still Gavin flew, trailing blue power behind him. They were going northwest. Occasionally it occurred to Gavin that he had fled something—some*one*—important, but the clockwork plague pulled him forward, drew him on through the cool night air.

The moon spilled silver over cattle pastures and rice fields that eventually gave way to hills and paper-leaved forests. Roads threaded through the trees, then faded and vanished. Mountains rose up, some green, some frosted with ice. And then the little bird dove. Gavin followed, in a terror he would lose it. It flew toward a valley dotted with pinpricks of light. As he drew closer, he made out buildings cut into the side of one of the mountains, creating strange steps up to the sky. Graceful bridges and walkways arched between them, and trees clung ferociously among the rocks. And all of it was overrun by water. A hundred rivulets started in the forests at the mountaintop, streamed down the face of the mountain, ribboned through the network of buildings, and joined up in a serpentine river at the bottom of the valley. No building was more than a few steps from running water. Gavin's eye wanted to trace all the rivulets, find the patterns and permutations, but he also needed to follow the bird. He tore himself away from the lovely waters and followed the bird down to one of the buildings. It lay exactly halfway up the mountain, between two streams. An overhanging tiled roof jutted out a little way like a porch. The bird fluttered down somewhere under the roof, and Gavin landed on the smooth stone beneath it. A pair of round paper lanterns hung on the two pillars that supported the overhang, and Gavin's eyes took a moment to adjust to their yellow light amid the pearly sound of rushing water. He clutched the Cube to his chest as his wings powered down and folded back over his shoulders.

"So it found you. That's . . . fantastic."

The voice was the same one that had come from the nightingale. Gavin's body went weak, and for a moment he couldn't find his voice. The Impossible Cube dropped to the ground.

"Dad?" he said.

Chapter Fourteen

The ghost parade floated through the empty city streets. Men and even a few women dressed in white robes and wide white hats beat solemn drums and carried white lanterns to light the way. A white-clad little boy with a candle led the way. A pretty woman walked a few paces behind him, giving quiet directions. She held a box wrapped in white cloth. Everyone else in the parade howled and cried and pulled at their faces. They groaned the dead emperor's name and begged the spirits of the ancestors to welcome him and keep him safe. Their moans twisted down the streets and sent shivers down Alice's back, even though she was among mourners. Her white robe swirled around her arms and legs, and she kept her head down so her hat would hide her face. The unfamiliar presence of the wire sword bumped at her side, and the battery pack pulled at her back and shoulders. The muddy streets had already stained the hem of her robe and splattered the cloth. Thank heavens she was wearing sturdy shoes. She desperately wanted to scan the skies for signs of Gavin, but she dared not look up and expose her foreign features.

"I don't like doing this without Gavin," she muttered to Phipps, who was walking beside her.

"So you've said a number of times," Phipps replied from the depths of her own white robe. They were both walking in the middle of the group to hide themselves better. "But we can't wait for him. If we're going after the Jade Hand, we have to do it tonight."

A crash, a small explosion, and a scream from a side street overpowered the groaning for a moment. Alice automatically turned, wanting to run and help, but Phipps put a firm brass hand on her arm. "Don't."

"But—"

"I said don't. We can't afford—"

A brass tiger pulling a two-wheeled cart with a black-clad Dragon Man in the driver's seat galloped out of the side street. The tiger was carrying a doll in its mouth, and the Dragon Man—a woman, actually—was laughing uproariously. Alice shrank back, ready to run. The cart rocketed toward the ghost parade until the Dragon Man caught sight of the white-clad people. With a shout, she—he?—turned the tiger aside and rushed off down another street.

"Don't," Phipps said one more time. "The Dragon Men are still looking for us, but if they think we're a mourning parade for the—"

"I know, I know," Alice said. "But what kind of monster lets loose a bunch of lunatics on his own people?"

"The kind of monster we're going to stop," Phipps replied shortly.

Alice gave the little boy—Lady Orchid's son, Cricket—an unhappy look. "Even if it means cutting off a child's hand?"

"You're doing your best to topple your second empire in a year, yet you balk at cutting off a child's hand so he can become emperor." Phipps gave a short bark of a laugh that meshed strangely with the cries of the men that surrounded her. "How do you live with all your contradictions, Lady Michaels?"

The parade continued. The mourners, Lieutenant Li and his troops in disguise, made a good job of it. The crying hid the occasional clank of sword or pistol or metal limb. Phipps herself kept her head down to keep both her Western features and her monocle out of sight. Occasionally people looked out of windows over courtyard walls or threw small packages of food and tiny coins wrapped in white or yellow cloth. The soldiers picked these up and ate the food and pocketed the coins. Alice worked out that in religious terms the packets were meant to be an offering to the spirit world, though in practical terms they fed and paid the mourners, much like offerings at church on Sunday were supposed to be for God but ended up buying food for the minister.

It was a long and nerve-wracking walk to Jingshan Park, which bordered the Forbidden City on the north and where one end of the Passage of Silken Footsteps was hidden. It seemed a strange way to hide, wearing white in plain sight and making as much noise as they

could, but they moved unmolested. Three other times
they encountered Dragon Men with animal-shaped automatons, and each time Alice's heart stopped. But each
time, the Dragon Man caught sight of the white robes
and turned aside. Lady Orchid, with her white-wrapped
box, remained a paragon of calm, while Alice was sweating inside her increasingly filthy white robe, and her
mouth was dry as an iron pan on a hot stove from the
constant tension. She wished for Click and her other automatons, but the little ones had their own part to play
in this, and Click, who was obviously of Western design,
had no way to remain inconspicuous in a Chinese mourning parade. So she had left him behind on the *Lady*.

The summer air was both hot and sticky, and Alice
felt like boiled rice in the heavy clothing. Her legs ached,
and she wanted nothing more than to lie down with
something cool to drink. Then she saw a ragged shadow
lurching along a red-painted wall. It was a plague zombie, the first she had seen since arriving in China. Lady
Orchid had told her plague zombies were routinely
rounded up and hidden away here. This one must have
escaped, or perhaps the poor soul was a new victim of
the disease. In any case, Alice worked her way to the
outer edge of the false parade and made a dash for the
zombie as it shambled around a corner. Phipps hissed
something at her, but Alice ignored it. She followed the
zombie, a dirty snowflake swirling after a bit of coal, and
easily caught up with it on the empty street. Not it—him.
The creature was a young man. Like every other zombie
Alice had encountered, his clothes were rags. A foul

smell hung about him. Sores wept pus and blood, and tattered red muscle showed through splits in his skin. Alice had lost count of the number of people she had cured of the plague, but the heartrending sympathy for its victims remained strong as ever. The young man stared at her with fever-yellow as she rolled up her sleeve to expose the iron spider. Its eyes glowed a hungry red. This would be her first cure in China.

"Spread this," she told the uncomprehending young man. "Spread it far and w—"

A loud mechanical hiss interrupted her. Alice spun and found herself face-to-face with a multilegged, serpentine brass dragon the size of a horse. Perched behind its head at a control panel was a lithe, older man dressed all in black. White whiskers trailed from his chin, matching the brass ones on the dragon. The Dragon Man said something in Chinese, and the dragon hissed again. Damp steam issued from its nostrils. Alice squeaked and backed up, nearly bumping into the zombie. Her heart all but jumped from her chest. She fumbled for the wire sword, but it was under her robe and she couldn't get at it.

The Dragon Man grinned and worked the controls. The dragon lifted its front leg, and with a delicate claw under Alice's chin, pushed her face up so the moonlight spilled across it. The Dragon Man began to laugh with glee. He had recognized her—or figured out who she was. It didn't really matter. Alice jerked the stupid robe up, still trying to get to the sword. The dragon reached for her with another foot, one easily big enough to get around her waist. Alice wanted to scream in both fear and frustration. After coming all this way, it was going to end here.

A metal wire whipped through the air and wrapped around the Dragon Man's neck. With a *hoik* sound, he was yanked backward off the brass dragon. Without someone to guide it, the dragon froze. Alice squirmed free and dashed around it. Behind the automaton was Susan Phipps. The wire snaked from her brass palm, and the Dragon Man lay at her feet, gasping and clawing at his neck. Phipps wrapped the wire around both wrists and braced a foot on the Dragon Man's chest.

"Susan!" Alice cried. "Don't!"

Phipps yanked hard. There was a wet *crack*. The Dragon Man twitched once and went still.

"Oh God," Alice whispered. "I wish you hadn't."

"You left me little choice." Phipps coiled the wire back into her hand. "He was under orders from the salamander in his ear, and we couldn't have done anything else to stop him. The night will be bloodier before long, Alice. You'd best accept that."

Alice nodded once, her jaw set. Phipps was right, but Alice didn't have to like it. She found the plague zombie still huddled near the wall. Before anything else could happen, Alice swiped his arm with her claws and sprayed the wound with her own blood.

"Be well," she said quietly as he limped away, taking the cure with him.

"Can you drive this thing?" Phipps asked pleasantly from the seat behind the dragon's head. "I don't see any point in wasting it."

The parade continued on its way, with the addition of the brass dragon. Alice's talent with automatons let her figure out the controls quickly, and the few people on the street assumed the machine was merely part of the mourning. Riding was easier than walking, at any rate. Alice offered Lady Orchid a seat, and the woman gratefully accepted—clearly she wasn't used to physical labor. She held Cricket on her lap, making it a tight fit behind the dragon's head. Phipps and the soldiers continued on, unbothered.

They passed the Forbidden City on their way. Pagoda-style buildings with multiple roofs poked above the high walls, and the moonlight turned the wide moat around it to mercury. It looked as remote and untouchable as a celestial temple, which, Alice supposed, was the entire idea.

Jingshan Park pushed down against the Forbidden City's northern border. It was a pleasant sprawl of hills and trees, meadows and ponds, shrines and pagodas. According to Lieutenant Li, who walked beside the brass dragon, the hills were artificial, built up one bucketful at a time to approximate the axis of Peking and to accommodate the principles of something he called *feng shui*, which neither he nor Phipps could translate.

"The five hills are placed so energy can flow properly," Li said. "It is difficult to explain in English."

"As long as the secret passage works, the energy may flow as it likes," Alice replied.

The soldiers stopped their mournful crying and howling the moment they entered the park, which was deserted after sunset. Everyone stripped off their white robes, revealing armor and brass limbs and swords and pistols, and Lady Orchid unwrapped the Ebony Chamber. The robes they left in a cobweb pile near a fishpond.

"Some gardener will think himself rich in the morning," Li observed.

Lady Orchid climbed down from the brass dragon, taking Cricket with her. *"This way,"* she said.

She took them to an enormous tree, easily as wide as four men, and did something to it. A section of bark swung outward, and Alice realized the tree was artificial, cunningly constructed from plaster or resin or stone to look real. The artistry was perfect. Even the leaves looked real.

Behind the section of bark, a stone staircase spiraled downward. At the top stood a pair of surprised-looking men in the round, peaked hats Alice had learned were the uniform of imperial eunuchs. The men smelled faintly of urine, even from the back of the dragon, and Alice wondered whether Lady Orchid and the soldiers had startled them badly. Neither spoke, and Alice remembered their tongues had been cut out.

One of the men reached for a bellpull, but Lieutenant Li's sword sliced the rope above his head. For a dreadful moment, Alice thought Li intended to kill the eunuch as well, but Lady Orchid stepped forward and spoke to them both at length.

"She's telling them what's happening," Li murmured to Phipps and Alice, even though Phipps understood Chinese. Even from the dragon's back, Alice noticed that Li stood quite close to Phipps. "She says we're trying to put the true emperor on the throne and they can help. Most of the eunuchs are unhappy with Su Shun and the way he is spending money on the army—far less silver for them—and will be pleased with the idea of a change. And these eunuchs have a wretched appointment, guarding a door no one uses. So they probably won't ...Ah, there we are."

From the Ebony Chamber, Lady Orchid took two pieces of jewelry, a jade fish and a gold bracelet set with sapphires. The eunuchs accepted these with newly solemn faces and stepped aside.

"I'm glad you didn't kill those men," Alice said, "but I have to admit that I'm rather surprised you didn't."

"Someone might find the bodies if we left them in the park," Li said. "And I cannot send them tumbling down the staircase. It contains several traps, as Lady Orchid is explaining. On the way down, you must step on the stones with the characters for *Long life and eternal health to the celestial son of heaven, may he live forever under—*"

"Wait, wait." Alice held up her hands. "I couldn't remember all that, even if I could read Chinese."

"Just step where everyone else steps," Phipps said, "and don't make a mistake."

"What happens to those who make a mistake?"

"I'm not completely sure." Phipps cocked an ear toward Lady Orchid, who was still speaking. "But it seems to involve a great number of spikes and slow-acting poisons."

"You go first," Alice said.

"What are you going to do about that dragon?" Phipps asked.

Alice got down from the dragon and stared at the steps for a long moment. She spotted the dozens of clever little holes for the spikes Phipps had mentioned, and her mind traced pathways, running automatic calculations. "I think there's a way to bring it with. I hate to let it go to waste."

Meanwhile, the eunuchs, who didn't seem so sure of their lives now that they had given up the secret of the staircase, fled into the night. Cricket peered at the spiral stairs with interest. Alice had had limited interactions with the boy, but he had so far seemed bright and intelligent, and he hadn't once complained about the long walk to the park. She wondered if he understood that they were planning to make him a straw emperor, or if he knew that by evening's end he would have lost either his hand or his life. Doubt dragged at her like a wet cloak. Were they doing the right thing? But if they turned back, how many thousands of others would die in a war between Britain and China? How many young men were even now asleep in their beds, awaiting a death sentence they didn't even know was coming? How many children would be orphaned?

She remembered the final moments of her aunt's life, how Edwina had been forced to die in order to unleash the plague cure on the world. Alice had demanded to know why the world seemed to work on all or nothing, why there was no way to win without so much sacrifice.

Aunt Edwina had promised to ask God. Alice herself intended to have a few choice words with the Almighty about the rightness of a world that endangered the lives of children in order to save everyone else.

Lady Orchid studied the stairs. They were marble inlaid with Chinese characters in jade, and they meant nothing to Alice, though the workmanship was absolutely stunning. It seemed a terrible shame to hide such lovely art in the dark on the chance that a single man might tread on it. Gavin would have thoroughly appreciated it.

Gavin. Alice climbed back onto the dragon and glanced upward. Where on earth was Gavin? She had been concentrating on the current plan so she wouldn't have to think about him haring off—flying off—and leaving her. A strange mixture of anger and worry mingled inside her. She had no idea why he had left after that brass nightingale had sung that song—their song—to him. The voice had been eerily similar to Gavin's, but it wasn't his. Perhaps it was a trap, designed to send him into a clockwork fugue and lure him away. But a trap set by whom? And if it were, why hadn't the person come after Alice as well? She carried the cure. She was the enemy to China. Who here was looking for him?

It couldn't be his *father*. Could it?

She turned the idea over in her mind. It made a certain amount of sense. Gavin's voice was similar to the one recorded in the bird, the way a son's voice might be like his father's. Gavin's father had been an airman, and airmen traveled far and wide, so there was no reason the man shouldn't be somewhere near a large city. If he were alive, he had to be somewhere, and why not Peking? More than one person had prophesied that Gavin would meet his father again, and although Alice had dismissed such things as superstition, some of them had mentioned a science that she hadn't been able to follow. Perhaps they had been right after all.

Still, all the explanations in the world didn't diminish their need for his help.

From her pocket she took the silver nightingale, the one she had thought unique in the world and only recently come to understand was only one of many. She pressed the left eye and murmured to it, "Gavin, where did you go? We need you." That was stupid. Why was she holding back? She added, "*I* need you."

She tossed the nightingale into the air. It sprang to life in the moonlight and fluttered away as Lady Orchid began a careful descent down the deadly stairs.

Still clutching the Ebony Chamber, Cixi finished the phrase to herself: *"Under the blessing of dragons."* She reached the bottom, paused, and allowed herself a small sigh of relief. She hadn't been sure of herself. She had teased the code for the staircase out of Xianfeng more than two years ago after some pillow time together, but she hadn't been able to write it down and she hadn't been completely certain of her memory.

She checked behind her. Zaichun was coming down. She wasn't worried about him—his memory was excellent and he understood the consequences of making an error. The foreigners, on the other hand, were another matter entirely. Lieutenant Li and his soldiers, whom Cixi desperately needed on her side, were loyal only to the foreigners, so she couldn't afford for any of them to die. It grated on her to work with barbarians; yet it was also fitting, using foreigners to further the ends of the Chinese Empire. And she did have to admit they had figured out the secret of the Ebony Chamber whereas she had not. Clearly Western thought had *some* merit to it. Kung was right—when Zaichun controlled the Jade Hand, she would have to open wider relations with the West. It wouldn't mean abandoning everything Chinese for everything English—the very idea nauseated her—but there would be no harm in picking and choosing a few good concepts. This idea of encouraging girls to read, for example, had merit. Cixi's mother had fought long and hard to teach her the characters, and if she had not known them, she would never have reached her current position. Reading opened doors. Perhaps Lady Michaels would be willing to stay on as an adviser. No, it would have to be Lieutenant Phipps—she spoke a proper language. And there was another intriguing idea: women with military titles. Reading might open doors, but the army smashed them down.

Li arrived at the bottom of the steps, followed by Phipps. Cixi noticed the way Lieutenant Li hovered over Phipps the same way a windup hummingbird hovered about a steel flower. Was either of them aware of it?

With a dreadful crunching sound, the dragon spiraled around the final turn of the staircase. Spikes leaped out of the staircase to snap and ping off the dragon's feet and underbelly. Alice, her arms and legs tucked in close, sat in the precise center of the seat behind the dragon's head. It came to a halt at the bottom of the stairs. Cixi backed away, holding the Ebony Chamber like a shield.

"There," Alice said through Lieutenant Li. *"And now we don't have to worry about one of the soldiers making a mistake."*

"Lady Michaels can be . . . direct," Lieutenant Phipps added.

"I see." Cixi's fingers were white around the Ebony Chamber's dark wood. "Is she aware that it will take one of the Dragon Men most of a week to repair all that? Not to mention the cost in silver?"

"I doubt she'll much care." Phipps touched her monocle. "I imagine she would say something about taking the throne requiring a few sacrifices."

"That was funny." Zaichun giggled. "She's a dragon *lady*."

"Indeed," Cixi said as Alice moved the dragon aside for the soldiers.

"Are we going back home now, Mother?" Zaichun asked.

"We are, Little Cricket," she told him, tearing her eyes away from the damage. "You will destroy the cruel man who has stolen your father's throne and take your rightful place upon it."

"Does that mean I'll have to chop off my hand?"

Cixi hesitated. "You won't have to do it yourself, my lucky cricket. It will happen with such speed, you won't even feel it. And then you will wear the Jade Hand and be emperor of all China."

"But . . . I don't want my hand to be chopped off."

Anger flashed through Cixi, but she held herself in check. "I know you don't. But I also know you are brave and that you are willing to make this sacrifice for the good of the empire."

Zaichun bit his lip, but he nodded once.

"And," Cixi added, "remember that the Jade Hand will allow you to command the Dragon Men. You can make them do whatever you want."

"Anything at all?"

"Anything at all."

"Can I make them sing the yellow duck song and then jump into the moat?"

While they were speaking, the rest of Lieutenant Li's men came down the staircase. Nothing had gone truly wrong so far. If the Dao's lessons were at all correct, that meant something would go terribly wrong later. Cixi shuddered to think what it might be.

The tunnel was high and wide, big enough to accommodate a train. Phosphorescent lanterns glowed at regular intervals, casting a bright white and blue light that made a kind of daylight underground. The floor bricks were red and gold, and landscapes painted on the walls and ceiling changed the claustrophobic underground feel into a pleasant garden stroll. The colors looked perfectly normal despite the strangely colored lighting, and Cixi happened to know it had taken months of experimentation with pigment to figure out how to make a tree

appear the proper shade of green when lit by phosphorescent blue. Under normal light, leaves would appear a
sickly yellow.

The group proceeded ahead. Cixi and the dragon remained in the lead, with Phipps and Li as translators.
Cixi was already resolving to learn the dreadful-sounding
English language. It couldn't be hard, and it would certainly be convenient. Such thoughts were, she knew, de-
liberate distractions from fear of the task ahead. But that
was the Chinese way—avoid, distract, delay. Confronta-
tion was rare and difficult to deal with, and Su Shun's gift
for it had given him the upper hand. Cixi had found new
allies, however, who were talented with it as well.

They moved quickly down the damp tunnel. Alice still
rode the dragon, though now she also brandished the
wiry sword Gavin had made for her, while Li carried one
of Gavin's new pistols. Cixi carried only the Ebony
Chamber. A moment later, about when Cixi judged they
were under the moat, four tongueless eunuchs in pale
robes and wide conical hats appeared. Cixi quickly
snatched four more jewels from the Chamber, one for
each, and explained the situation again.

"These are my gift to you," she finished, "and if—
when—we succeed in our mission, you will be granted
places of honor in the new court, and we will see if the
Dragon Men can fashion new tongues of silver for you
so that you may speak once again."

That last was a lie. As long as they knew of passage,
they couldn't be allowed to speak of it. Still, three of the
eunuchs bowed their acceptance. The fourth began to

make a bow, then changed his movements partway through and lunged for a bellpull.

Li fired his new pistol. It spat a bolt of orange energy that caught the eunuch in the chest. It flung him backward, but not before he managed to grab the rope. He flew through the air, yanking the bellpull as he went, his chest a smoky mess. A gong sounded, and the smell of cooked meat sizzled in the tunnel. The other three eunuchs sprinted off down the tunnel.

"Uh-oh," Phipps said. "What did that alarm do?"

"I don't know," Cixi said in a hushed voice.

A section of wall rumbled aside, and from it stepped a metal creature the size of an elephant. It had the body of a tiger, the claws of a crocodile, the tail of an ox, the antlers of a deer, the beard and teeth of a dragon, and the scales of a fish. Many different kinds of metal came together to create it—bronze, brass, copper, steel, and even gold. Atop its head was a small glass dome, and inside was a pink mass of human brain.

"Qilin!" Cixi cried.

The Qilin prowled forward, moving with agility that belied its size. It barred their way ahead of the tunnel. The soldiers fell flat on their faces in terror. Cixi herself quivered, and Zaichun huddled against her. Cixi's mother had told her a number of stories about the Qilin, a creature of power and grace that punished the wicked by roasting them in its fiery breath. The gods themselves smiled upon the Qilin, and only the dragon and the phoenix were more powerful.

"Holy God," Phipps said. Cixi didn't know the language, but from her tone she guessed they were words of fear.

Li fired his pistol at it. The orange bolt bounced off the Qilin's metal hide and gouged a piece out of the painted tunnel wall. The Qilin turned and exhaled at him. Cixi smelled a terrible stench, then heard the *click* of a spark. Flame burst from the Qilin's mouth.

"*No!*" Phipps screamed.

But Li was already moving. He dove straight toward the Qilin and slid under the flames on his belly to fetch up between the creature's forelegs. Phipps snapped out her brass hand, and a coil of wire snaked from the palm. To Cixi's amazement, it wrapped round the Qilin's mouth. Phipps yanked, and the Qilin's jaws snapped shut. Li scrambled to his feet, his movements slowed by the battery pack on his back. The Qilin reared back, and Phipps was pulled bodily into the air.

Alice barked something directly behind Cixi. She jumped aside as the dragon with Alice behind its head galloped forward. The dragon was barely half the Qilin's size, but that didn't seem to faze Alice in the slightest. The wire sword, now glowing blue, was raised high above her head, and she shouted in English. Cixi didn't know what to make of such a sight.

Phipps slammed into a wall, but she managed to twist so her brass arm took the brunt of it. Still, she was clearly dazed. The Qilin wrenched its mouth open, snapping the wire. Li scrambled around underneath it in a desperate dance to avoid being crushed by its pounding feet. The dragon reared up. Alice swung the sword, and it described an azure arc. With a *crack* it intersected the Qilin's shoulder. A chunk of metal fell out and crashed to the floor. The Qilin bellowed, the first sound Cixi had heard it make. It turned on Alice, who waved the sword and shouted again.

The Qilin lashed out with a heavy paw. Alice tried to make the dragon dodge, but the Qilin was faster. Caught by the blow, the dragon crumpled like a paper lantern. Alice gave a scream as her automaton crashed to the floor. Cixi put her hands over her mouth, frightened to death. Zaichun trembled behind her, and the soldiers remained motionless on the floor. The Qilin was overpowering. There was no way to defeat it. Lieutenant Li suddenly appeared again. He had abandoned his pistol and was climbing up the Qilin's side, using the scales as handholds. He gained a position above the glass dome that housed the creature's brain and raised both hands in a double fist. Cixi held her breath as he brought them crashing down on the glass.

They bounced aside without even a scratch to show for it. The Qilin shook itself like a dog, tossing Li off like a flea. Cixi heard the hissing sound of its breath. The Qilin would incinerate them all, as it incinerated all sinners and doers of evil.

Sinners. The Qilin—the creature from the fairy tales—punished only sinners. This one had been created by a Dragon Man and was controlled by a human brain, but—

Cixi ran forward. "Wait, holy one!" She flung herself to the ground before the Qilin and knocked her head on the floor as if she were approaching the emperor. The stench of the gas made her dizzy. She held her breath and waited for the *click* and the terrible pain of the flames.

Nothing happened. She risked a peek between the fingers that covered her face and saw the Qilin had stopped.

"Holy one," Cixi said, her heart knocking at the back of her throat, "we are not the sinners you seek. I am Lady Yehenara, Imperial Concubine to Emperor Xianfeng. Behind me stands Zaichun, his son, who was deposed by the evil Su Shun. We only wish passage into the Forbidden City so we may right a great wrong and put the rightful emperor on the Celestial Throne. I beseech you, holy one, forgive us our deeds here and grant the blameless young emperor permission to pass."

The dreadful stench continued. Cixi kept her face down and tried not to tremble. She was risking not only her life, but her son's. Suddenly she wanted to hold him, embrace him as she hadn't done since he was a baby. The Imperial Concubine did not show such affection to her son. Affection was a weakness that her enemies might exploit, and the only solution was to enforce a strict distance. But she felt it nonetheless, and right then she prayed hard to all her ancestors and any spirits that might be listening that the Qilin—or whatever brain that *believed* itself to be a Qilin—would see Zaichun as an innocent, someone who could not be harmed. Or, if they would not answer her prayer, at least take her life instead of his.

The Qilin exhaled more gas. The stones rocked beneath Cixi's head. She gave a soft moan and waited for the inevitable end. Then there was a creak of moving metal, followed by silence. Cixi peeked again. The Qilin had backed away and was now sitting to one side on its haunches.

Cixi slowly got to her feet. The Qilin didn't move. She ran to Zaichun, who was still standing paralyzed by the tunnel wall. For a moment she hesitated. Then she embraced him as a mother.

"My Cricket," she whispered.

"Mother?" he said into her robe.

She drew back. And how would she cut off his hand now? "We must see to the others."

The soldiers were all unharmed, of course, though somewhat embarrassed by their superstitious response. Alice struggled to free herself from the wreckage of the brass dragon. Two of the soldiers hurried to help. She was limping slightly and favored one arm, but her sword seemed undamaged. The dragon was a total loss. Other soldiers were rushing over to Lieutenant Li and Lieutenant Phipps. Li was completely unharmed, but Phipps staggered about, and Li insisted she lean on him. Her brass arm trailed the broken wire. Once she recovered herself, she held it out to Alice, who cut the wire off with the sword. Throughout it all, the Qilin didn't move. It may as well have been a statue in the imperial gardens.

"How did you convince it to do that?" Phipps asked.

Cixi threw the Qilin a glance. "Go farther down the hall."

Everyone quickly marched past the creature. Its pink

brain seemed to stare at them from within the little dome, and Cixi wondered to whom it had belonged. Once the creature was out of hearing range, Cixi said, "It seemed to me that any human brain put into a creature like that would either go mad or survive by making itself believe it truly was a Qilin. And the true Qilin punishes only sinners or doers of evil. I convinced it that we were neither one."

"That was quite a risk," Alice said, flexing her wounded arm. *"I have to say I am impressed, Lady Orchid."*

"No more than I am impressed by the way you attacked it," Cixi replied. "Tell me, do all Western women act like you and Lieutenant Phipps?"

Alice gave a laugh at that, the first Cixi had heard from her—or any other foreigner, for that matter. How strange to hear, and to realize that foreigners could laugh, too. *"Hardly. Though I wish more of us would."*

From overhead came a thudding noise, as if a giant were stomping about. The vibrations traveled through the tunnel stones up through Cixi's feet. She exchanged looks with Lieutenant Li and knew he was thinking the same thing—Su Shun was making the Dragon Men work long and hard into the night on the machines of war.

They encountered two more sets of eunuchs, but all of them were amenable to the bribes Cixi offered them. In the end, they arrived at a pair of wide lacquered doors guarded by eight robed eunuchs. The doors, Cixi knew, opened into a false storage building not far from the Hall of Mental Cultivation, where the emperor lived. At this time of night, the streets of the Forbidden City would be largely deserted, but anyone who saw them would assume they had a right to be there.

Before the eunuchs could raise the alarm, Cixi identified herself one more time, and each one accepted a priceless piece of jewelry.

"I thought you said no one knew about this secret passage," Alice said as Cixi closed the Chamber again. *"At my count, at least twenty-two eunuchs know of it, not to mention whoever designed it, and the people who built it. Even people who can't speak can communicate."*

"Eunuchs hardly count," Cixi said dismissively. "And the workers who built the passage are long dead. No one of importance knows of its existence."

The eunuchs grabbed the handles, and the doors creaked open. Standing in the opening was a platoon of soldiers with a variety of weapons drawn. At the head, his half-brass face gleaming in the light, stood Su Shun.

Chapter Fifteen

The man carried a small book and wore a long blue tunic over loose white trousers. He laid the book on a small table set with Oriental tea things next to the door and picked up a cup. The brass nightingale fluttered down to perch on his shoulder. "I was reading when you arrived, but now I think it's time for tea. It's a nice night to sit outside."

Gavin took a step forward, then another. He couldn't stop staring. He stared so hard, his vision seemed to double, creating two men, one surrounded by water, the other reading by candlelight. The man was taller, but he and Gavin had the same white-blond hair, the same sky blue eyes. The nose and chin were different, and the man was broader in the chest and shoulders. His face was unlined, and he didn't look more than thirty. Still, Gavin knew without a doubt this was his father.

The soft rush of the streams flowed all around them.

Gavin abruptly thought of the tarot card at the circus in Kiev. The card had shown a pale-haired man surrounded by water. The man on the card wore blue robes, and in one hand he held a chalice.

"The King of Cups," Gavin said. "You're the King of Cups. From the card. Linda flipped you over like a paired particle, and now the pathways cross."

The man nodded, understanding. "I can see the clockwork plague got you. So yeah, we're connected like pairs of particles. What slaps you slaps me, yep, yep. Nice to see you, kid. I guess I should say all the father things—how you've grown, how much a man you've become, how—"

Gavin hit him. Or he tried to. His fist flicked out of its own accord, and the man moved aside just enough for the blow to miss. The little bird clung tightly to his shoulder. Fully angry now, Gavin punched again, a hammer blow to the chest, but the man blocked it with his forearm, again with just enough speed and movement. His cup shattered on the stones. Gavin followed with more blows—left, right, hook, chop. The man dodged or blocked each one. His face remained expressionless. The balanced fight went on for some time, until Gavin backed away, panting. The cloak that was his wings dragged at his back.

"Sorry," the man said. His voice was low and serene.

"Damn you," Gavin said, and his voice was equal parts rage and anger.

"You're pissed at me. You should be, kid. But maybe when you understand—"

"You're a *fuck*." Gavin was spewing venom he hadn't known he was carrying. "You abandoned me and everyone else, and why? So you could be a monk in China? I grew up missing you and hating and wondering what I did to make you leave. I don't even know your name because Mom wouldn't even say it. Understand? I understand. You're lower than shit on a sewer snail."

He nodded. "Maybe we can grab a seat. The edge of the porch here is real nice for sittin' and drinkin' a little tea at night."

"What for?" He turned his back and looked out across the dark valley. Stars hard as jewels shone in a black ocean that threatened to swallow them. "Maybe I should just leave. I don't think anything you say could make me happy."

"I'm sorry. Really." The man came up behind Gavin and put a hand on his shoulder. At his touch, liquid gold flowed through Gavin. Warmth bathed him in a delicate river, carrying away fear and anger like so much flotsam and leaving his soul clear as glass. The man dropped his hand, and the feeling receded. The stones came back under his feet and the darkness pressed in, carrying the breath of trees and water. Gavin faced the man again. His wings flared.

"What was that?" he asked, his voice low.

"Qin Lung," said the man.

"I don't understand."

"My name here is Qin Lung. Means—"

"Azure dragon." Here Gavin did sit down, though it was because his legs went weak. The wings clinked,

hanging over the edge of the porch. "All the Dragon Men are named Lung."

"Yep, yep. They—we—ain't members of our own families anymore and get the family name Lung. Dragon. The people here don't see a lot o' blue eyes, and I came from across the water before I found my balance, so they called me Azure Dragon. My name in America"—he said the word as if he hadn't spoken it in a long time— "was Henry Uriel Ennock. But I don't go by Henry. Call me Uri. Or Dad. Whatever floats your airship."

"Uriel? Your name is Uri?" The revelations were coming thick and fast, which was probably why Gavin couldn't help but focus on small, foolish details.

"Yep."

"All right."

Heavy silence dropped over them. There was so much to say, so much to ask, and Gavin didn't know where to start. His entire life was a tangle of threads, and he couldn't find an end to pull. He felt tense and strange. Uri, on the other hand, seemed perfectly at ease. The quiet, serene expression never left his face.

"So," Uri said, "I've sorta lost track of time. How old are you now?"

"I turned nineteen this last summer." Gavin held up the Impossible Cube. "Though if you look at it another way, you could say I'm twenty-two."

Uri let that pass. "How's your ma? And your brothers and sisters?"

This raised some hackles again. "I haven't heard from them in a while. Jenny's married and probably has a kid by now. Harry works as a drover, but he drinks. Ma was able to send Patrick to school some with the money I sent her after I joined the Third Ward, but that was a while ago, so I don't know what he's up to now. Violet's working in a factory, I think. You'd know all this if you were home."

"But I ain't home, so I don't know. That's the way it is."

It was on the tip of Gavin's tongue to ask why, but the words wouldn't come. He wasn't sure he wanted to know the answer.

Uri set his hands on his knees. "Your feelings are jumbled up. You wanna talk to me, but you don't know how."

"How do I talk to a father who was never there?" Gavin shot back.

"I'm here now. Or maybe *you're* here now." Uri stroked the bird on his shoulder. "It wasn't easy to make that happen, kid."

"Yeah? How did you make it happen?"

"Those birds. I invented them a long time ago, when I first got to China," Uri said in his quiet, absent voice. "They grabbed the emperor's attention, and he wanted a whole flock of them for a weapon. The Jade Hand ordered me to make them, so I did."

Uri pointed to his ear, and for the first time, Gavin noticed the salamander curled around it. A strange hope swirled inside him.

"You've lived a long time as a Dragon Man," he said in a tight voice. "I don't understand how."

"Nah. You wouldn't. Not yet." Uri rose and got two cups of tea from the table. He gave one to Gavin. "But

I'm telling this story out of order, aren't I? It's because time means somethin' . . . different in this place."

Gavin accepted the cup but twisted it in his fingers, too distracted to think of drinking. Everything was so damned strange. He wanted to hate his father, but he also wanted to please him. He was caught on the edge of a square, unable to tell which way he would tip.

"I was an airman, you know," Uri said.

"Yeah. Me, too." He paused, still hanging on the edge of the square. "Are you glad?" *Proud?*

Uri waved a hand. "Doesn't matter. Your own path has to make you glad or not. Another guy's opinion matters much as wind matters to a mountain. But," he added thoughtfully, "being an airman is a damned good path."

It was the right thing to say, and Gavin felt himself relax a bit. "So how did you end up in China?"

"I was on a run to San Francisco, and I pulled down the clockwork plague."

Gavin breathed out. He knew this was the case, but it was hard to hear it said aloud. "And?"

"I thought I was going to die. I was sick bad, but no one would help me or even let me come close to them. One night I fell asleep in a stinking alley, and my fever broke. I still remember how it felt, like something snapped inside me. It jerked me awake, and the entire universe swallowed me. It was incredible. I was a clock-worker, and I wasn't sick anymore."

"Why didn't you tell us?" Gavin demanded, angry again. "Why didn't you write or telegram? Or come home?"

Uri remained serene. "I was a different man then, Gav. I didn't always think right. That's not an excuse. It just is. Maybe I thought I was sparing you the pain of hearing I was sick. And later, I was sparing you the pain of having a clockworker in the family."

"Yeah, well, you were wrong."

"Can't argue with you. There's no way to make up for it. I would if I could. All I can do is say I'm sorry."

Gavin shifted on the hard stone. Suddenly he realized that he hadn't touched this man, his father, except to hit him. He set the cold cup down and reached out to put a hand on Uri's shoulder. It was heavy and warm. Gavin's throat thickened, and he dropped his hand.

"Anyway," Uri said, "I woke up in Peking after a fugue. Looked like I'd stolen a boat, fitted it with a new engine I built, and zipped all the way across the Pacific just for the hell of it. The Chinese realized I was a clockworker— Dragon Man—and they brought me to the Forbidden City. In there, the eunuchs stuck me with a salamander like yours, and for months I invented for the emperor. I built birds. Wings. I was always good at wings."

Gavin flexed his own. "It runs in the family."

"Those," Uri said, "are fucking genius, and I want to look at them. I was never able to fly myself."

"Not enough lift, right?"

"Yep, yep. Even Chinese kites don't give enough."

"It's the alloy. The wings push against—" He stopped. "No. I want to hear about you. What happened then?"

"I invented birds that recorded messages and flew to the last person they touched. The emperor loved them, and he gave them to his family. Later, they became the big thing for running messages between lovers."

Dad had built the silver nightingale that recorded voices? Gavin felt in his pocket, but it was empty. Alice still had theirs.

"Then the emperor told me to make my birds into weapons because he wanted something that would patrol the borders. I didn't want to, but when the Jade Hand talks, you listen. I made two, just enough to shut the Hand up. But what the emperor didn't know was that I also had added somethin' to the design. Somethin' the Hand didn't ask for. It didn't say I couldn't, you know? See, I added a bit that put the birds on the lookout for my kids. They all look for you kids, just in case you might come to China."

"How the hell would they do that?"

"We're all made up of tiny bits that copy themselves over and over, and half of those bits come from our moms and half from our dads. Maybe one day we'll be able to tell exactly who is born to who, and the emperor won't need to hide his concubines behind red walls. But my birds look for people who are half like me. My kids. My son."

"Why?"

His gaze went far away again. "Time is all one piece, Gavin. It's a river with a beginning and an end, but it's still all one piece, and everything happens all at once. You can be sucked into it, or you can stand outside it, but it all stays one piece."

"So you're saying you saw that I was going to come,

and you arranged for the bird to tell you when I crossed the border."

"Kind of. I knew about you because it was also happening when I first arrived. And it's still happening now. I couldn't avoid creating the bird to find you, and you can't avoid singing the moon song. It had already happened, and it was happening, and it will happen again. That's why you came, you know. You couldn't avoid it any more than I could avoid sending the bird. Yep, yep."

"So we have no choice?" Gavin interrupted. "We're little automatons that follow the rules?"

"Not what I said. You've already made all the choices, the ones that make the river's course. Us guys who step outside the river can see them; that's all. It's better to accept what has happened and what will happen."

Gavin's head was beginning to swim. "How does it all end, then? Can you see that?"

Uri ignored the question. "Once I finished the emperor's command, I was . . . unhappy. I didn't want to create more weapons, no sir. But I heard rumors about a place where Dragon Men could go, a place where they could invent and study in peace until their time came. A place called the Blessed Monastery of the Azure Water. When I finished the two birds, the Jade Hand stopped commanding me, so I created a spinning device that mesmerized the eunuchs. That let me sneak out of the Forbidden City. Took me a few weeks of searching, but I found this place. It looks like an ordinary monastery, and the emperor leaves it alone, but there's a lot more to it than he knows."

"That must have been years ago. How are you still alive?" Gavin leaned forward. A hope he had been hiding, not daring to show, slipped out into the moonlight. His voice was small. "Dad, do you have a cure?"

"Ah. That's the problem, isn't it?" Uri touched his salamander again. "There's a cure, but it's not the one you're thinking of."

Gavin's breath caught with excitement. "Can you cure me?"

"No."

The hope died, and he felt the wings dragging at his back again, pulling at the scar tissue under his black shirt. He looked away, not wanting Uri to see him upset.

"But," Uri continued, "you can damned well cure yourself."

"I don't understand."

"Yeah. That's why you still carry the plague." Uri set his cup on the stones with a soft click. "See, the reason we clockworkers die so fast is that the plague makes us look the universe straight in the eye. Trouble is, we have a strong sense of self, so we try to stay separate from the universe even when the plague makes us look at the whole damn thing. We're *part* of the universe, not separate from it. Means we can't hold ourselves apart while we're looking at the whole. The paradox burns your mind out, like a candle dropped into a bonfire."

"Then how—?"

"The candle can't hold its shape in the bonfire. It has to become *one* with the fire. If it does that, it still exists, but in a new form. You gotta accept yourself as a clockworker, accept everything the universe is trying to show you, become one with it. The universe can't harm itself, you see. Become one with it, and you become immune to it. Serene. Balanced."

"That's ridiculous," Gavin scoffed. "It's a disease. You can't become 'one' with it or cure it by . . . by *thinking* hard."

"But here I am, kid," Uri replied with a quiet smile. "You felt it when I touched you. And there are more than a dozen like me. Almost ageless, like the dragons."

"Ageless? That's why you look so young?"

"We age slowly. I figure I'll live another three hundred years. You can find it, too, Gavin."

"Find what?"

"I told you: acceptance. Serenity. It's all part of the balance."

"Now I'm confused again."

"Yeah, it's hard to explain. The balance is all one piece, like time. You need to understand it, all at once. And when you do, nothing else will matter."

Nothing else will matter. Gavin remembered his first flight, how nearly perfect everything had felt, and how nothing else had mattered—until the giant squid had come for Alice.

Uri nodded at the Impossible Cube. "That's a real piece of work. What is it?"

"Dr. Clef—a friend of mine—made it. I don't understand it completely. I brought it along because . . . I don't know why, actually."

"What's it do?"

"It twists the universe around itself. It transforms energy from one form into another and fires it. And it probably has a few dozen other uses we haven't figured out yet."

"How's it do that?"

"It's unique in all the universes," Gavin said. "It—"

"No." Uri held up a finger to interrupt. "It ain't. Nothing's unique. Nothing. The Dao teaches that everything has to balance. Everything has an opposite, and the opposite holds a seed of the original."

"Why are we talking about this?"

"It's *important*, Gavin. You gotta understand." From beneath his tunic he extracted a medallion. Two fishlike designs swirled around it in black and white. The white half had a black dot in it, and the black half had a white dot in it. When Gavin looked closer, he realized the two dots were actually the overall design done in miniature. He had never seen the design before, but it was compelling. He felt another fugue coming on, and he pushed hard to keep it at bay.

"The yin and the yang," Uri said. "Female and male, water and fire, light and dark, mountain and valley, death and life, plague and cure. They can't exist without each other. Sometimes one gets to be more powerful than the other for a while, but eventually the universe finds the balance. Plop a stone in a pool, and you create waves, highs and lows, but finally the pond becomes calm and smooth like the silk on an envelope."

Gavin tore his eyes away from the medallion. "What does this have to do with Impossible Cube?"

"That Cube of yours can't exist on its own any more than light can exist without darkness or joy can exist without sorrow. You said the Cube fires energy and twists the universe in weird ways. It's unstable. So its opposite must absorb, take things in and hold them, make everything *more* stable. Those two things will find each other, pull together eventually to create a balance."

Gavin almost protested again—Uri almost seemed to be attacking the uniqueness of Dr. Clef's work, and even after everything the man had done, Gavin still felt a loyalty to Dr. Clef—but then he knew what the answer was, and it sent a little thrill through him.

"The Ebony Chamber," he breathed. "It's an infinite set that opens into an infinite number of universes. The Cube is a fixed point across the universe. They're opposites. Why didn't I see that when I started to put the two of them together?"

"You did *what*?" A tremor crossed the serenity on Uri's face. "God's balls, Gavin! What possessed you to do something like that? Yin and yang need each other, but they're still separate. Together, they destroy each other completely."

"I was in a clockwork fugue." For a moment Gavin felt like a little boy who had been caught throwing rocks at windows. "I wasn't thinking right. But Alice stopped me."

"Alice?"

"Oh." He felt flustered again. "She's my . . . we're getting married."

"She a clockworker?"

It wasn't the reaction Gavin had been expecting. This

entire conversation wasn't anything he'd been expecting. "What? No. She cures the plague. But not in clockworkers."

"Yin and yang," Uri said with a nod. "One is earth and water, the other air and fire. They always find each other."

"That's not—I don't—"

"Listen, Gavin, does the universe speak to you? Do you see what no one else does? What not even other clockworkers see? Tiny things?"

Here Gavin stared at him again. "Yes. Particles that move one another. I've never been able to explain it." He began to grow excited. It was the first time someone else seemed to have experienced such things. "They have colors and . . . flavors. Sort of. No, that isn't right, but we don't have words for what they are or what they look like. Maybe you can't even give a name to something so small. Some of them affect each other without touching, in pairs . . ."

He stopped. Uri's serene expression remained.

"You're going to say yin and yang, aren't you?" Gavin said.

"I don't need to."

"But what does it all *mean*?"

"Why don't you know how they all work?" Uri countered. He held up the medallion, swirling and enticing. Gavin couldn't take his eyes from it, and he found answers sliding out of him like water from a sieve. "Why don't you understand these tiny particles of yours?"

"I've tried, but something always seems to get in the way."

"What, exactly, gets in the way?"

"Alice," Gavin replied without thinking.

"How does she stop you?"

"She calls me back every time I go too deep."

"Why does she do that?"

"I don't know."

"Yes, you do. Why?"

"Because she loves me."

"But if she loved you, she'd want you to be happy and find what you need to find."

"She's afraid I won't come back. She won't . . ." He trailed off, and the rhythm faded.

"Won't what?"

"She won't let me go," he whispered.

"Is that important?"

"Very." He sat up straighter, and his wings clinked. "Those particles are the key to understanding everything, aren't they?"

Uri merely gave the serene smile. He set the medallion aside, breaking the half fugue.

"If I understand the particles," Gavin said slowly, "I'll understand the universe. Become 'one' with it. And that'll cure me because the secrets won't burn out my mind anymore."

"Yep, yep."

Gavin blinked, surprised. "No mysterious questions? No strange double-talk?"

"Nope. You nailed it."

"Let me see that amulet again." Gavin took it from Uri's proffered hand. The design was a snowflake frozen in metal and paint. The two dots of black and white that were themselves designs contained two dots of black and white that were designs, which contained two dots of black and white. They pulled him in and down, farther and farther down. The crystalline lattice that made up the medallion's structure repeated itself, shapes within shapes, patterns within patterns. The tiniest particles hovered there, dancing in pairs. And what were they made out of? He reached for one of them, and it turned. So did its partner. Incredible. He could go farther down, pry the particle apart, and peer inside. Secrets whispered inside his head, scratching at his mind like an infinite number of cats in their infinite boxes. An overwhelming, endless field of infinitesimal boxes lay before him. It was too much, too powerful. The little bits pulled him in an infinite number of directions, and he had to keep himself together, had to . . .

But that wasn't it. Dad had said he needed to let go, let it flow, accept it. His heart pounded. He was facing his own obliteration. If he let himself fall apart, he would never find himself. Was this what Dad had seen?

The thought of his father brought a slash of anger. He was putting his trust in the man who had turned his back on his family. Sure, the plague had made Gavin do strange things, but he was fine now. Nothing was stopping him from writing—or even coming home. The anger tightened his chest, and Gavin became aware of his breathing, of the cold stones under his backside, of the wing harness dragging at his back, and then he was sitting in front of Uri, the medallion clenched in his fist.

"I can't do this," he said.

"I think you were close," Uri observed.

"No."

"You're angry again."

"I haven't *stopped* being angry. I've just been hiding it."

"Your anger is your own." Uri shrugged. "You can let it go, or let it run your life. That's your choice, kid."

"I'm supposed to be helping Alice sneak into the Forbidden City. I shouldn't even be here." Gavin rose, stood with one foot over the edge of the porch with darkness below him. "Your bird put me in a fugue, or I wouldn't have come."

"So why don't you leave?"

"I should." But he hung there.

"Maybe you need to learn something here," Uri said. "And once you learn it, you'll be able to help Alice the way you want to." He held up the medallion again. It was compelling, almost hypnotic.

Gavin sat back down again. "I don't know what I'm doing."

"You don't need to know. Let the universe tell you." He paused, then reached into a shadow and came up with, of all things, a fiddle case. He opened it. "Do you still play?"

The unexpected question made Gavin feel self-conscious. "Of course I play. I earned money on street corners, bought bread with it because *you* weren't there."

"Play for me."

"No."

"If you didn't want to play, why did you say you still know how? This is a great fiddle. I bought it in San Francisco. Or maybe I stole it. My memory of that time isn't very good." He ran the bow over the strings in liquid notes that shot old memories down Gavin's back. "My old fiddle was better, though."

"The old one isn't your fiddle anymore. It's mine. You left it behind, just as you left everything else behind."

"Yeah." His eyes took on a faraway look. "Still, it sure would be nice to hear you play again. It's been so long. Yep, sure would be nice."

Gavin hesitated, then relented. He took the fiddle from his father and, still seated, began to play with the moon hanging over his shoulder and turning his wings to mercury.

> *I see the moon, the moon sees me.*
> *It turns all the forest soft and silvery.*
> *The moon picked you from all the rest,*
> *For I loved you best.*

His hands shook as he played. He couldn't make a mistake, not in front of his father on his father's instrument. It had never occurred to him that he might one day play for Dad, the man who had admonished him not to make mistakes. He slowed the song, but that only made things more difficult.

> *I have a ship, my ship must flee,*
> *Sailing o'er the clouds and on the silver sea.*
> *The moon picked you from all the rest,*
> *For I loved you—*

His left hand twitched on the final note. The fiddle squawked, and there was no way to recover. Gavin corrected and replayed the note, but the damage was done. He stopped playing and felt the heat rise to his face. He wanted to fall backward off the edge of the porch and let himself crash to the rocks below. But he sat with his head bowed instead, waiting for the inevitable harsh words.

Uri sighed. Of course. The terrible playing deserved that exact reaction.

"I remember that song so well," he said. "Your mother loved it."

Gavin's head came up. "I messed it up at the end. It was awful."

"Perfection doesn't exist, kid. One mistake doesn't ruin the whole song any more than a single ripple ruins an entire stream." Uri touched Gavin's arm. "You play it better than I ever did. No wonder that Alice girl fell in love with you."

Something broke inside Gavin at those words, something he couldn't define. Chains he hadn't known he was carrying fell away, and he wanted to weep for the lightness.

"Maybe I should try again," he said hoarsely. "Where's that medallion?"

But as he was reaching for it, a familiar silver nightingale encrusted with jewels zipped under the overhang. It landed on Gavin's shoulder. He clapped a hand over it, and it was as if Alice were standing next to him. He missed her with a deep intensity that made this place feel all the more foreign. Uri cocked his head and touched the brass bird on his own shoulder.

"Is that one of mine?" he said.

"Probably. It belonged to the emperor's nephew." He pressed the bird's right eye.

"Gavin, where did you go? We need you!" Short pause. *"I need you."*

The nightingale fell silent.

"She has a pretty voice," Uri said. "Reminds me of your—"

"Don't finish that sentence," Gavin warned. "Not even in your head. I need to go."

"You coming back?"

Gavin, who had already gotten to his feet with the Impossible Cube, paused and said, "Do you want me to come back?"

"The Dao teaches us that once you become one with the universe, there are no needs, no wants, no desires. Everyone has to follow his own path, and it doesn't always travel where we—"

"Fuck the Dao, Dad. Do you want me to come back or not?"

Uri fell silent. He took the fiddle into his lap. Gavin watched him, trying to stay dispassionate. The two Dragon Men stood on the mountainside, surrounded by flowing water; one with wings and one without; one with a fiddle, one with the Impossible Cube; one older, one younger. The universe hung balanced between them. Gavin held his breath, and even the water seemed to slow.

At last Uri said, "You need to find your own self, Son, wherever that is."

"Fine, Dad," Gavin said tiredly. "You have your life, and I have—"

"But," Uri interrupted, "I think the universe would smile if your path and mine traveled side by side again."

Gavin gave a short bark of a laugh at that. "And maybe that's the best I can hope for. All right, Dad. Maybe I'll come back. But think about this—maybe *you'll* come back."

They embraced, a gesture made clumsy by Gavin's wing harness, and for a small moment Gavin let himself be a small boy again. Then he turned and leaped off the edge of the porch. His wings left a blue trail as he followed the silver nightingale back to Alice, the Impossible Cube clutched in his hands.

Chapter Sixteen

"Li and his men will be beheaded in the courtyard," Phipps muttered to Alice. "Su Shun has other plans for us. They won't be pleasant."

"No doubt," Alice replied tightly. Su Shun's men had taken her wire sword away, of course, along with the new pistols and the weapons Li's soldiers carried. They couldn't take away the metallic hands and arms, at least. Or rather, Alice amended privately, they hadn't done so yet.

Su Shun's men herded them out of the false storage building and into the streets of the Forbidden City proper. It truly was a city, with walkways and buildings and parks, and Alice wondered whether she was the first Westerner ever to see it. She also wondered if she would survive to tell about it. The buildings all had the odd peaked roofs that swooped up at the eaves. Lanterns on poles burned everywhere to provide light. The air smelled of gunpowder and hot metal. The thudding and thumping Alice had felt underground were more prominent up here.

Imperial soldiers surrounded them on all sides, weapons drawn and ready. Su Shun himself, dressed in a suit of yellow lacquered armor, walked at the head of the procession with a single soldier between him and Alice. He had taken personal possession of Alice's wire sword and wore the battery pack, though he had to wield the weapon with his left hand. The Jade Hand glowed softly at his right. Alice stared at it. The thing they had come for was so close she could almost touch it. She tried to keep the fear under control, but every step took them closer to torture and death. The iron spider on her left hand felt chilly despite the heat of the August night.

"I thought there were no men in the Forbidden City after sunset," she murmured to Lieutenant Li. "Are all these soldiers eunuchs now?"

"No," Li murmured back. "The emperor would appear to have made some changes."

A soldier snapped something at them, presumably an order to be quiet, and Alice fell silent. Her mouth was dry, and she desperately wanted a drink. As they marched through the streets, the machinery sounds grew louder and were punctuated with the occasional explosion. They passed an enormous well with a freestanding windlass over it, and Alice noticed a sad look pass over Lady Orchid's face. Alice wanted to ask about it, but she didn't dare.

Lady Orchid still held the Ebony Chamber, and

Cricket walked next to her. The boy looked frightened and was trying not to show it, a feeling Alice understood. She scanned the skies. Empty.

Not far from the well, they reached what had once been a wide expanse of lawn. The grass was chewed up, and divots of earth lay everywhere. Many of the stone walkways had been shattered into rubble. Dragon Men, their salamanders glowing in their ears, worked like mad among dozens of animal-shaped machines that stomped and roared and clawed and breathed fire and shot rockets into the air. Piles of ammunition stood with enormous kegs of gunpowder near stacks and stacks of raw metal, and forges glowed like scattered demons. Lady Orchid put a hand over her mouth at the sight, and Alice understood that this had once been a place of tranquility and beauty. Heaven had become hell.

At one end of the lawn stood a wide marble three-sided staircase that led up to a tall, multiroofed building—a pavilion of some sort. Large chunks of the pavilion had been carved out, either blasted away or pried loose. Two stone dragon statues guarded the top of the stairs. Their jade eyes and teeth had been pried out. Su Shun led them to the front staircase, which faced the ruined lawn. Su Shun mounted the steps partway to the top, turned to face them, and held out the Jade Hand. Instantly, the soldiers forced everyone down to their knees and pressed their faces to the stones at the bottom of the stairs. The soldier who forced Alice down was none too gentle about it. He rapped her forehead against the ground hard enough to make her dizzy, and she couldn't help crying out in pain. The soldier pulled her upright, though she was kept on her knees. Her face burned. Su Shun stood on the fifth step, his half-brass face a hard mask. He said something sharp, and two soldiers hauled Lady Orchid up the steps to him, Ebony Chamber in her grip. The gold dragons crawled across it. Cricket shouted something and tried to run after her. Su Shun snarled, and one of the soldiers twisted Cricket's arm behind him. He howled and struggled. Alice wanted to snatch him up and run, but there was nowhere to flee to. Then Lady Orchid spoke to him, and he stopped. Su Shun flicked out the Jade Hand and cracked her across the face, sending her to her knees. Cricket yelled again, but the soldier easily put him on the ground, too. Alice trembled with outrage but kept her wits about her. Nothing would be gained by protest. Not yet.

Su Shun reached down and plucked the Ebony Chamber from Lady Orchid with the Jade Hand and set it on the stairs above him, then said something to the assembled soldiers and Westerners.

"He's telling us to translate for anyone who can't understand a proper language," Phipps said in a tight voice. "He wants everyone to understand what is happening here."

"The weak and corrupt dynasty is at an end," Su Shun boomed, with Phipps translating a moment behind him. *"The final remnants of the dogs we called the Qing kneel before a true emperor, not an opium smoker who kowtows to the West, but a warrior who conquers it."*

"You are not the emperor, Su Shun." Lady Orchid was

kneeling on the stairs, but her back was straight and her demeanor was proud. *"You can kill me and you can kill the son of Xianfeng, but that will not make you emperor."*

Su Shun flipped the switch on Alice's sword, and it growled to life. He moved the wire blade within an inch of Lady Orchid's throat. The Imperial Concubine didn't turn a hair, and Alice was impressed despite herself.

"Let us find out," Su Shun said.

But Lady Orchid couldn't be stopped. Her voice rang throughout the courtyard, and even the Dragon Men paused in their work to listen. *"Sitting at the emperor's table and eating from his dishes does not make a good emperor, Su Shun. It only makes a fat general. We all know that the Ebony Chamber guards the name of the true heir to the throne. It does not guard your name."*

The flesh half of Su Shun's face flushed a deep red at Lady Orchid's words. Alice didn't understand the reason for it—the insult about eating at the table seemed mild to her. Perhaps it was worse in Chinese than it was in English.

"And now your head will bounce to the stones while your son watches." Su Shun drew back the sword. Cricket continued to struggle in the soldier's grip.

"And now you will be nothing but an empty suit of lacquer," Orchid retorted. *"Before all these witnesses, all these soldiers, all these Dragon Men, I say you are afraid to open the Ebony Chamber with the Jade Hand."*

The trap snapped shut. Alice could see the understanding on Su Shun's face. He himself had arranged for many witnesses for the proceedings here, and those witnesses would spread far and wide what Su Shun did next. If he refused to open the Ebony Chamber with the Jade Hand, everyone would whisper behind his back about it, and his shaky hold on the throne would erode and vanish like farmland in a desert. If he did open it, there was every reason to believe the paper inside would bear Cricket's name. Su Shun had lost. Lady Orchid raised her chin in triumph despite the sword vibrating beneath it.

Alice held her breath. Su Shun held the humming sword. A flicker of movement would send Lady Orchid's head tumbling down the steps. The tendons in Su Shun's hand stood out like wires. Abruptly he swept the sword away.

"*We will . . . open the Ebony Chamber,*" he said.

Wisely, Lady Orchid said nothing, though Alice could read the exultation in her eyes. Alice herself felt as if she might float away with the sudden release of tension. Su Shun slowly turned to the Chamber on the steps above him. The gold dragons on its glossy surface glimmered and shifted in the bright lantern light, and the phoenix latch seemed to flicker and dance with a life of its own.

"*I believe the combination is eighteen,*" Lady Orchid supplied helpfully. "*It is already set. Naturally, the general would not dream of changing the numbers.*"

A thundercloud crossed Su Shun's face, and for a moment Alice wondered if Lady Orchid had gone too far in addressing him as *general* and obliquely saying he might try to lie. But Su Shun pressed the Jade Hand to the phoenix latch. A clear *click* sounded across the courtyard. The Dragon Men and the soldiers gave up all pretense of politeness and craned their necks to see. The lid of the Ebony Chamber popped open. Su Shun's jaw moved back and forth as he ground his teeth, but he reached inside. Alice felt as if she might fly apart.

There was a long pause. Then Su Shun laughed. He laughed and laughed and laughed some more. He pulled the Jade Hand—empty—from the box and knocked the container sideways so everyone could see inside.

The Ebony Chamber was empty.

A sigh went through the assembled people. All the fear came rushing back. Alice's stomach churned, and she nearly vomited on the stones.

"Before these witnesses, I proclaim the emperor declared no heir." Su Shun raised the growling sword to the sky, and his voice was rich with reclaimed luster. *"Since I bear the Jade Hand—"*

"No!" Lady Orchid rushed at Su Shun, her fingers formed into claws. She swiped at the fleshy side of his face and scored furrows. But he caught her wrist with the Jade Hand and twisted. She dropped to one knee.

"Your filthy hand struck the emperor!" he howled. *"Let it pay the price before you die!"*

He swung the wire sword around. The snarling blade sliced through Lady Orchid's right wrist as if it were paper. Lady Orchid screamed. Her hand dropped to the staircase with a horrible *plop*. Su Shun released her, and she held the stump before her eyes, too shocked to believe what she was seeing. The blade had cauterized the wound as it cut, leaving no blood. Threads of smoke drifted up from the half-cooked meat. This time Alice did throw up.

Vomit spattered across the cracked cobblestones and left burning acid in her mouth and nose. Phipps looked green. Cricket was crying openly now, not caring who saw.

Alice thought she heard a faint, familiar clicking sound from overhead, and a bit of whirling brass caught the tail of her eye. She didn't dare look directly at it.

"Enjoy your perfect beauty now, Imperial Concubine," Su Shun said. *"Captain! Throw this pig filth down the well like her dogs and send her illegitimate brat after her."*

The captain bodily lifted Lady Orchid and carried her toward the well Alice had noticed earlier. The soldier with Cricket followed. Both Orchid and Cricket fought and yelled. Alice cast about for something to do, but she couldn't think of a thing. A dozen weapons were pointed at her, and if she got up or even protested, she would die in an instant. In cold horror she watched as the captain lifted the screaming Lady Orchid over his head and dropped her into the dark pit. The earth swallowed her screams. Seconds later, the soldier dropped Cricket in after, and his cries likewise vanished. Alice wept. She couldn't even hear the splash.

"Monster!" she cried at Su Shun, tears streaming down her face. "May you rot in hell!"

"I won't translate," Phipps said hoarsely. "Though I think he understood the general idea."

That seemed to be the case. Su Shun made a sharp gesture, and one of the soldiers grabbed Alice's arms with a steel grip that left bruises. He dragged her up to the stairs to the new emperor's feet. The eyes on her spider gauntlet glowed green—no one near her carried the clockwork plague. She looked up at Su Shun and his yellow armor and his half-brass face and his metal neck all ringed in rivets. There was a fury in his eyes, but fear, too. In that moment, she saw that he was little more than a boy surrounding himself with a wall of metal and creating toys that would fight for him. Under other circumstances she might have found him pathetic or even pitiable, but right now a woman and a child were, at his order, drowning in fear and darkness. The snippet of whirling brass tugged at the tail of her eye again, but she kept her eyes on him.

"Do not look the emperor in the eye, pig spawn," Su Shun snapped.

"You're nothing but a tin bully," Alice snapped back, and spat at his feet.

At those particular words, Phipps, Li, and all of Li's men put their hands over their ears. So did Alice. The imperial soldiers had time to look puzzled. In a rage, Su Shun drew back the vibrating sword, and at that moment, an explosion rocked the Forbidden City. Heat blasted through the courtyard, and a shock wave knocked flat everyone who wasn't kneeling, including Su Shun. A second blast followed the first. Several of the Dragon Men's mechanical animals were knocked over. The gunpowder and ammunition stores—the source of the explosion—roiled up to the sky in a choking cloud of black smoke. Alice, who was braced for the event, recovered first. She leaped past Su Shun and snatched up the Ebony Chamber. With shaking fingers, she spun the phoenix latch to 000 and opened the lid. Out of the impossibly small space, Alice drew one of Gavin's new pistols, trailing its battery pack by a cable, and threw it to Phipps. Alice tossed a second pistol to Li and kept the third for herself. She started to shrug herself into the battery pack, but the well caught her eye. How long had Lady Orchid and Cricket been down there?

Chaos erupted in all directions. Phipps turned and fired at the Dragon Men's automatons without bothering to put the battery pack on first. Her pistol spat crackling orange bolts that hissed and sparked over the mechanical animals, blowing holes in them or melting them. Li joined her. The black-clad Dragon Men scattered like shadows before the light, howling as they went. Li's men shot to their feet and leaped for their imperial counterparts, wrestling the stunned guards to get their weapons back. Su Shun was staggering to his feet, shaking his head. Alice tried fumbling with the battery pack, but her fingers were numb. And the well—always the well.

Su Shun raised the Jade Hand and shouted something. The Hand glowed, and all about the courtyard, tiny points of light showed a gleaming salamander where a Dragon Man heard his voice and halted dead in his tracks.

"Alice!" Phipps yelled, still firing at automatons. "He's telling the Dragon Men to defend him! Shoot him! Shut him up!"

The Dragon Men were running toward their inventions now, the fifteen or twenty that still worked. The Dragon Men whose automatons had been destroyed ran toward Su Shun, apparently ready to fight with their bare hands. It might have been funny but for the heightened strength and reflexes granted them by the plague. Two of the Dragon Men, in fact, leaped forward like baboons, covering half the distance to Su Shun in a single jump. Li caught one in the chest with a pistol shot, and he vanished in a fiery scream.

Alice glanced at the well in which Cricket and Lady Orchid were drowning, then raised the heavy pistol and aimed it at Su Shun. The cable dragged her arm toward the battery pack, which lay at her feet. Her hands were shaking. She had never shot anyone before. Su Shun turned to look at her. The fear had left his eyes. Flames from the fires behind Alice reflected in them, giving him a dragon's gaze. He had just murdered two people and planned to kill thousands more. Why was she hesitating? Her finger tightened on the trigger.

The wire sword in Su Shun's other hand lashed out. With a *vvvvvip* it sliced through the power cable. It dropped to the stairs at Alice's feet, spitting orange sparks.

"Oh bugger," Alice said, and wondered if those would be her last words ever.

Su Shun drew back the sword. Alice tensed to dodge away, but knew she wouldn't make it. Dragon Men were beginning to swarm the steps. She had come so far, only to die.

Another blast rocked the stairs. This time Alice did lose her balance. She fell backward and landed on her posterior. Su Shun was flung down, and even the Dragon Men lost their balance. The sound of the blast had a strangely musical quality to it, and the realization made

Alice's heart sing. She looked up. Gavin, blue wings spread wide, rushed down from the sky with the Impossible Cube in his hands and the silver nightingale on his shoulder. Alice couldn't have been happier. He landed beside her as she scrambled to her feet. Two of Alice's whirligig automatons joined him, one of them still trailing the bit of fuse it had used to light the powder stores.

"I'm so glad to see you," she said. "All three of you."

The automatons squeaked, and Gavin grinned.

"Sorry I took off like that," he said in that wonderful voice of his. He aimed the Cube at Su Shun. "I'll handle him. Where's Lady Orchid?"

"The well!" Without another word Alice sprinted across the lawn, dodging cinders and burning patches of grass. Her automatons followed. The soldiers had kicked the cover open, though the large freestanding windlass remained in place. Next to the windlass stood a mechanical lizard of some sort. It wasn't bearded like the dragons Alice had seen. Both its front feet were placed on the windlass. Cricket and Lady Orchid had been down there only a few minutes. They could still be alive. Unless they had hit their heads on the way down or broken something or if they couldn't swim or . . .

Alice called down. "Lady Orchid! Cricket! Can you hear me?"

Nothing. Alice felt sick. Then a faint voice called back, "Alice?"

It was Lady Orchid. Alice breathed relief.

"I'll help you!" she called, hoping Lady Orchid could understand the idea, if not the words. "Hang on!"

She tried to think. The two whirligigs couldn't maneuver down in the well, and it took four of them to lift a person anyway. Alice examined the mechanical lizard. It had controls on it, levers and buttons hidden among the scales. Over at the steps, Su Shun had switched off the sword to thrust it into his belt and was now brandishing the Ebony Chamber. Gavin blasted another shot of energy, this time at Su Shun, but Su Shun caught the power in the open Chamber, which swallowed it. Heart pounding, Alice let her talent go to work. In moments she worked out how the controls operated, and she slapped a button. The lizard sprang to life. It cranked the windlass, and a bucket more than three feet across dropped into the well. The Dragon Men on the steps had recovered from Gavin's first blast and were moving in toward him. Gavin flared his wings, knocking two aside. The other Dragon Men had reached their automatons, but Phipps and Li continued to keep them busy with suppressive fire while the soldiers fought with one another, roaring like tigers and shedding scarlet blood.

A faint splash as well as a shout from Lady Orchid came from below. Alice hoped it meant she was ready. She was reaching for another control on the lizard when a hard hand spun her round. A Dragon Man, salamander glowing around his ear, stared at her. He licked his lips with quick, darting motions and said something Alice didn't understand, though her skin went cold at his tone. He held up a serrated knife. A strange calm came over Alice. She had hesitated on the steps with Su Shun, and it had cost so much. Now she wouldn't hesitate. Everything seemed to move slowly, as if wrapped in honey. She smiled at the Dragon Man and put out a slow hand to caress his cheek. He smiled, then shifted his grip on the knife, ready to stab. With a quick twist, Alice wrapped her fingers around the salamander at his ear and *yanked*.

The little machine came free with a wet, tearing sound. A trail of blood arced through the air. The Dragon Man's face went blank. He collapsed to the ground in convulsions, leaping and twitching like a landed fish. At last he gave one final spasm and went still. Alice didn't stop to examine him. She dropped the salamander and slapped the control on the lizard. It reversed itself, drawing the large bucket up with easy strength. In moments Orchid and Cricket appeared at the top of the well, drenched but unharmed. Lady Orchid's beautiful face was pinched with fear and pain. Cricket clung to her as they both sat in the bucket, and she held the rope with her good hand. Her stump trailed water, cleansed and strangely purified. Unfortunately, Alice could stay only long enough to make sure they were all right before she turned and ran back to the triple stairs. The staircase nearest her climbed toward the side of the big pavilion, which would send her up along Su Shun's right and, hopefully, out of his range of vision.

"You two," she said to the whirligigs, "go find Prince Kung and tell him to send reinforcements."

The whirligigs zipped off into the night sky.

Gavin, meanwhile, had taken to the air again to avoid the advancing Dragon Men, half a dozen of whom had crowded around Su Shun and the Ebony Chamber. The

Impossible Cube was barely glowing now, nearly out of power, and Gavin seemed reluctant to use it. Alice thought about the Dragon Man she had just killed and tasted nausea again. She understood Gavin's disinclination to kill.

But when Alice arrived at the side steps and started to climb, she saw things were changing. Li's men had turned the tide and had defeated or killed most of the Imperial Guards. Li and Phipps had destroyed nearly all the Chinese automatons, and even now Phipps was turning to focus her pistol on Su Shun and the Dragon Men around them. Phipps had no compunctions about killing.

"Surrender, Su Shun!" Phipps barked, or so Alice assumed—Phipps didn't translate.

Su Shun looked down at Phipps and her enormous pistol, at Li, who was finishing off the last of the automatons, at his soldiers, who were dead or defeated. His gaze lingered on Gavin, who hovered above them all with the Impossible Cube, and then he laughed again. Alice was truly beginning to hate this man and his grating laugh. Phipps aimed her pistol at him, but before she could do more, Su Shun raised the Jade Hand one more time and shouted. His voice reached Gavin, who still hovered above the carnage, and the salamander glowed in his ear.

For a wild moment, Alice thought there was no way for anything to happen because Su Shun was giving the order in Chinese, but of course Gavin understood that language now. Gavin twitched once. Phipps's pistol whined, and the tip glowed orange.

"Susan!" Alice screamed. "Look out!"

Gavin sang. As it always did, the Impossible Cube twisted the crystalline note into something terrible, and a dreadful power thundered down. It swept Phipps and Li and the rest of the soldiers aside like rag dolls. Even off to one side as she was, Alice was crushed to the stairs, and a hot wind blasted her hair and skirts. Sand and small stones stung her skin. She tried to push herself upright, but the forces pushing her down were too strong. The noise and pain went on and on, and she huddled against the steps in a hell of Gavin's devising.

And then it ended. Just stopped. Alice's ears rang in the sudden silence. She sat up. Her skin was scoured and raw. With wings outstretched, Gavin touched down on the stairs before Su Shun and knelt before him with the dark Impossible Cube. Everyone else in the courtyard lay scattered in broken dollhouse piles.

"Gavin." Alice's throat was choked with dust, and she had to cough to get the word out. "Gavin! Fight him!"

But her words were too quiet. If Gavin or Su Shun heard her, neither paid the slightest bit of attention. Su Shun snapped a question at Gavin.

"It's out of power," Gavin replied in a dull voice. "The water flowed away. The Ebony Chamber can recharge it, but putting the two closer together would make a dragon weapon so powerful that mere floods and volcanoes would be like teacups and lanterns in a mourning parade."

Su Shun backhanded Gavin with the Jade Hand and gave him another order. Gavin's head snapped back, but he spoke again, this time in Chinese. Alice assumed he was translating what he had already said, and ice ran through her veins at the smile that crossed Su Shun's face. Alice forced herself to her feet. Her legs were shaking.

Su Shun slapped the hollow Ebony Chamber open with the Jade Hand. Like a puppet on strings, Gavin turned on one knee and held the solid Impossible Cube over it.

"No." Alice tried to shout, but it came out in a whisper.

Electricity spat and arced from the Chamber to the Cube. A rumble shook the earth, and air moved across Alice's cheek. Sparks danced around the spider gauntlet on Alice's left hand, and the metal tingled. Gavin lowered the Cube. The sharp smell of ozone permeated the air, mingling with a tight tension. Thunder rumbled overhead. Fingers of lightning crackled in all directions, and matching flickers of it danced in the clouds above. Gavin's hair stood out, and a manic expression descended over his face. His wings quivered and glowed so brightly, they were hard to look at. The Impossible Cube was a thing of solid light, the Ebony Chamber an utter black void. Hungry cracks ran up all three staircases and the two dragon statues at the top shattered with ear-crushing explosions. Power swirled and dripped from Gavin's hands. Su Shun spoke again, and Gavin pushed the Cube fully into the maw of the Chamber.

A whirlpool of light and dark swirled around the two objects become one. It rushed outward, engulfing everyone in the courtyard. Phipps and Li and the surviving soldiers and Dragon Men convulsed hard as the energy swept over them, and overhead a thunderbolt boomed through the sky. The whirlpool sucked itself back into the Cube and Chamber, leaving an abrupt silence. Alice staggered up to the top of the cracking threefold staircase and realized her footsteps made no sound. Her clothes didn't rustle; her breathing was completely silent. Even her heart, frantic and fast within her chest, made no noise. Lightning tore the sky again, but no thunder came. The open box at Su Shun's feet glowed bloodred. Alice moved around until Su Shun was below her on the staircase and picked up a rocky bit of rubble from one of the dragon statues. She crept down the steps.

Sound returned in a rush. Thunder exploded overhead and wind rustled. The semiconscious people at the bottom of the staircase groaned and tried to stand up. Gavin's wings chimed their single soft note. And Su Shun's voice cut through it all. At his order, Gavin pulled the Impossible Cube out of the Ebony Chamber. The red radiance came with it. He tried to back away with it, but Su Shun barked another order. The Jade Hand glowed, and Gavin froze into a statue.

Alice struck. The rock smacked Su Shun's head. It made a sound very much like a muffled bell. Alice had hit the metal part of his skull. Su Shun turned, an expression of surprise and anger on his half-brass face. With quick reflexes he caught her wrist and wrenched the rock away before she could hit again. Pain bit her arm, and she dropped to the rock. Frantic, Alice tried to scratch his eyes with her spider gauntlet's claws, but he was a soldier and moved easily out of the way. He was laughing again, toying with her. How was it that he always gained the upper hand? She raged and fought, but he held her wrist and moved with her. It was like dancing with a snake. He was enjoying this. Behind him, Gavin stood motionless, holding the Impossible Cube. It had shifted from red to orange, and a low thrumming pushed against the air. At once Alice knew what was happening. She had seen the Impossible Cube run through the spectrum of colors before, from red to orange to yellow on up, and when it reached violet at the top, it would do something dreadful. It had torn time itself twice before. Now it held all the power of its infinite opposite.

"Flood and plague will destroy us if you don't cure the world."

The clockwork plague had created the Impossible Cube and the Ebony Chamber. Together, they could warp the forces that held the world in place, crack continents, and send floods all over the world. And it would happen in a very few moments.

Su Shun twisted Alice's wrist, forcing her to her knees. Clearly he'd had enough. His other hand locked around the back of her neck, and she didn't doubt he had the strength to snap the bones. His grip cut off her air. She gasped, trying to breathe.

And then Alice reached up to the wire sword at Su Shun's belt. Her fingers found the switch on the hilt and flicked it on. Before Su Shun quite knew what she was doing, she yanked. The vibrating blade slipped free, scoring Su Shun's side. He screamed with the unexpected pain and let go. From her knees, Alice punched him in the groin with her gauntlet. Iron crunched through lacquer, and she felt the impact of metal on flesh all the way up her arm. Su Shun stiffened and dropped without a sound.

Alice found herself standing above him, holding the vibrating sword and staring at the shallow gash she had opened up along his side. The cable from the hilt of the sword still led to the battery pack on Su Shun's back. Su Shun made a feeble attempt to grab at Alice. With a snarl of anger that surprised even her, she kicked him in the meat half of his face. He went still. She stood over him, panting.

Gavin remained where he was on the steps with the Impossible Cube. It glowed yellow now. Power radiated off it in waves, and the stones beneath Alice's feet shuddered. A section of the red wall surrounding the Forbidden City crumbled and splashed into the moat. Alice looked at the Jade Hand at the end of Su Shun's arm and then at Gavin. He wanted to move, but Su Shun's last orders stopped him, though he panted with the effort of trying to defy it. His eyes flicked a glance at the Cube, then at the sky.

Alice understood. He could take the Cube away from the earth. Up there, he could deal with it, detonate it or destroy it or—

The words Monsignor Adames had spoken to Gavin came back to her. *"You will cure the world, and Alice . . . Alice must let go."*

She met Gavin's eyes. She knew, and he knew. If she

let him go, if she released him from the Jade Hand, he could take the Cube away, stop it from destroying the world. But releasing all that power would kill him. The sword became a heavy weight in her hand. She tried to think. There had to be a way around this.

"Gavin," she said softly.

He managed a tiny nod. Emotion swelled, and tears pricked at her eyes. She remembered the moment she'd met him, when he'd given her a cheerful wave from high up in the tower where Aunt Edwina had imprisoned him. He was always bright and merry, and his music and his voice made her heart soar. How could she ever let him go? He was the one person who loved her as deeply as she loved him. The thought of a world without him made her want to lie down and die herself.

"I can't," she said. "Gavin, I just can't."

The Cube deepened from yellow to green. The tremors strengthened. More cracks began to appear in the walls around the Forbidden City. Alice felt the tension in her feet. Lightning blasted the air above them both. Phipps tried to get to her feet and fell back again. Li lay beside her.

"Please . . ." The sound of Gavin's voice was barely audible. He was fighting the Jade Hand's control. "Alice . . ."

It would be so easy, so simple to refuse. Gavin was going to die no matter what. What would it matter if she and everything else vanished as well? No one would know she had failed, because they'd all be dead, too. How many times had doomsday weapons come close to destroying the world? Maybe it was time for one to succeed.

The Cube shifted to bright blue. A great crack opened up in the courtyard. Some of the smaller buildings in the Imperial City collapsed, and the great pavilion behind Alice swayed noticeably. Over the noise, Alice heard screams and cries rising from Peking.

What was she doing? She couldn't condemn millions to death, no matter how much pain it might cause her. With a scream of her own, Alice, Lady Michaels, lashed down with her sword and sliced off the Jade Hand.

Chapter Seventeen

Gavin's muscles unlocked and he nearly stumbled. The Impossible Cube, bright blue in his hands, glowed with so much power, it felt both hot as the sun and cold as the void of space. He could feel it lashing out, gripping gravity and pulling at it, tearing at the roots of the planet itself. It would tilt the planet and bring the water. Su Shun had ordered him to push it into the Ebony Chamber and create the ultimate weapon, one that would let him command China, conquer Britain, control the world. But nothing could command, conquer, or control this.

The Jade Hand lay limp on the cracked stairs. More beautiful than a warrior queen, Alice Michaels stood over Su Shun's unconscious form, the quivering sword in one hand, gauntlet shielding the other. Tearing wind blew her hair around her head. The Impossible Cube lay in his hands between them. His world moved around her, but he had to leave her to save it. Fatigue pulled at him, and the Cube was oddly heavy. His wings pulled at his aching back. He couldn't do it. He couldn't leave her alone again. What was the point? He wanted nothing more than to hold Alice and wait for it all to end.

"Go!" Alice shouted. "It's your time, Gavin! Go now!"

He shook his head. "I left you once, Alice. I won't do it again. I'm *tired*, Alice. I'm tired of fighting the plague and fighting for the world. Eventually one of these stupid weapons we make will succeed. Why not let this one do it and get it over with so we can be together?"

Alice looked stricken. Tears stood in her eyes. "You can't, Gavin. You have to go. Take the Cube away."

He kissed her. "No. I'm finished, Alice. I've gone through hell once. I'm not doing it again."

"Oh, Gavin." She dropped the sword and put her hands on his wrists. More lightning sundered the sky. "Gavin, please. I don't want to do this. Don't make me do this."

"Do what?"

Her voice was measured, but there was a catch in it. "Don't you see it, darling? Look at the sky. Look at the clouds, the mist, the air." She was crying now, tears flowing in twin streams down her face. "And the Cube. The patterns on its back, its middle, its front. The patterns move and shift, move and glow. Aren't they fascinating? It's a pattern inside a pattern inside a pattern. Regularity inside regularity, infinite inside infinite."

Her voice, still audible over the shaking earth and growling thunder, reached inside him. He knew what she was doing, but still he couldn't stop it. The plague roared to life. The patterns she had mentioned were obvious now. He could see fractals in the clouds, patterns made of smaller patterns that repeated endlessly downward. The Cube was doing the same thing, creating more and more patterns. He couldn't stop looking at them. Now that she had pointed them out, he didn't want to.

"You want to have a closer look," she said. "You can fly, glide, soar, and examine, scrutinize, inspect."

"Alice . . . ," he whispered, and then took off with great sweeps of his mechanical wings. She spiraled down beneath him, and he caught *"I love you always"* as he flew away.

The Impossible Cube glowed a deep indigo as he clawed for altitude. The battery indicator on his wrist said he was running low, but that didn't matter. What mattered was that he had plenty of height, that he could reach the clouds. His ears popped, and he swallowed. An enormous lightning bolt zipped past him, missing him by only a hundred yards and filling his nose with ozone. Thunder boomed. Then the air grew cold and quiet, and damp mist closed in all about him, though it also felt heavy. The perfect crystalline chime kept him aloft and free, nothing holding him down, nothing holding him back. He rose above the cloud layer, trailing bits of mist. The clouds spread in all directions beneath a perfect silver moon. Flashes of red and blue light rushed about beneath his feet, and the Impossible Cube sent out its terrible, beautiful indigo glow. The patterns were so enticing. He stared at them, lost and thrilled. This was what he had been born for, and Alice had let him go.

He stared down at the Cube, rushing in and down now as he had rushed out and up before, finding the designs that made up designs, tiny particles made of particles made up of particles. And there they were, caught in the dance — the little pairs. The Impossible Cube had them, too. They turned and moved together. What one did, the other did. They were all connected. Particle and particle. Void and solid. Water and fire. Air and earth. China and England. Clockworker and Dragon Man. Cube and Chamber.

The Cube's countless particles had all changed color. He could see it now. They were supposed to be paired with the particles in the Ebony Chamber, but they weren't. They were pairing with particles in the earth, with particles that stabilized matter and made up gravity and affected time. When the Cube's particles turned, so did the ones in the earth, and when enough of them turned, the planet would tilt.

But Gavin could see it now. If the Cube's particles paired with something else, the Cube's grip on the earth would relax, and nothing would happen. All he had to do was redirect the pairing. He could do that if he understood the particles and became *one* with them so they answered his touch. He had to go down farther again, as he had almost done before.

The Cube's glow shifted again. It was a deep violet now, and the storm below Gavin's feet was growing more intense. The battery gauge on his wrist gave him only a few minutes more power as well. All this he was aware of even as he examined particles so small and so fast, they barely seemed to exist at all.

He reached down and in with his clumsy musician's fingers. The particles scattered before him. He had to do this, find the balance. He *could* do it. He had only to achieve perfection and the balance would be his. Perfection was the key to—

Uri's voice came to him as if from a book of wisdom. *"Perfection doesn't exist, kid. One mistake doesn't ruin the entire song any more than a single ripple ruins an entire stream."*

But that wasn't true. It was entirely possible to play the perfect song, build the perfect ship.

Be the perfect husband.

Perfect lover.

Perfect son.

But perfection was impossible, and anything that was impossible was therefore flawed. Perfection was therefore imperfect. It was a strange symmetry, an odd balance. Gavin shook with the implications.

Secrets whispered at him, pulled his mind in a thousand directions, pulled him away from the particles. But away was also toward. Out was in. No matter which direction he went, it would be the right one. He let himself go, released his hold on everything, and let a universe of particles and atoms and molecules and lattices and planets and quarks and stars and galaxies all rush through him all at once. He was a river, one piece that nonetheless flowed from beginning to end. He let go of Gavin Ennock.

An explosion rushed through him. He felt himself everywhere and nowhere, light and darkness, separate and together. He was himself and he was the universe because they were both the same thing. A calm ecstasy filled him. There was nothing more he needed now.

He found himself pulled toward a single particle. With negligent ease, he pulled himself toward it and looked inside, even though he already knew what was in it. He found himself looking at the entire universe again from the top down. And within that universe was a galaxy, and within that galaxy was a star, and around that star orbited a planet, and above that planet hovered a young man who didn't need a name anymore, for a name only served to separate him.

The Impossible Cube was fading, shifting into a spectrum of light not visible to the naked eye. But the young man could still feel the Cube in his hands. In fact, he could feel his entire body, every organ and cell and neuron and protein and molecule of water. He saw the microscopic plants clinging to his brain cells, and he saw another balance—plague and cure. Yes.

The Impossible Cube had warped time and sent the clockwork plague from the tortured present into the innocent past. The plague had then created clockworkers and a society that loved and feared them. One of those early clockworkers had created the Ebony Chamber, a balance for the future Impossible Cube. Or perhaps the Ebony Chamber had forced the creation of the Impossible Cube as a balance for itself. And then one day, a clockworker had created the Impossible Cube, which had warped time and sent the plague into the past.

The plague itself was destroying the world because

the plague had no balance. Alice's cure wasn't powerful enough. The world—the universe—needed something bigger to correct itself.

The young man reached into the disappearing Cube. There was the energy, and there were the particles pairing up with the wrong partners. The battery indicator on his wrist gave him only a minute of wing power, but he wasn't watching that. He reached down and felt a single person, a man walking through the streets of Peking below with newfound strength. The young man above looked into the older man below and saw Alice's touch there; he noted how the cure devoured the plague, how the particles spun and danced. He saw the vibrations; he used his perfect pitch to match the frequency. Thanks to her, he could see exactly what needed to be done. He took a deep breath, filling every sac in his lungs, and—

He.

SANG.

The long note rang like a trumpet, a thousand orchestras of brass, so powerful and sweet, it reached every corner of the world. It slid over mountains and caressed the forests. It stilled oceans and hushed deserts. Everywhere on Earth, people stopped what they were doing and looked up at the sky, entranced by the force and beauty of that one note. Later, no one was able to agree on what the sound was or where it came from, only that it made the heart ache with longing. People wept in houses and streets and factories and farms and fields as if they had awoken from the sweetest dream and only now realized what they had lost.

The Cube took the sound and twisted it. The note, sung with the absolute precision of one who understood the universe from the ground up and the stars down, changed the Cube. Its particles *changed*. They paired with countless trillions of particles hidden away in millions of human bodies all across the planet.

They paired with the particles that made up the clockwork plague.

The little particles ... shifted. As one, they made a quarter turn and changed color. A fundamental change took place. All across the world, the microscopic plants that clung to human tissue and created the clockwork plague cracked and fell into their component parts. The young man saw it happen in his own brain; he watched the disease dissolve and disappear.

Power streamed out of the Cube as the young man sang the plague away. The Cube's glow faded. It turned dark, and still the young man sang. There were still pockets of plague here and there in the world, and he tracked them down, singing them into oblivion with the voice of creation. The Cube cracked. The lattices Dr. Clef had painstakingly constructed fell apart as the young man drained the power that held them together. The Cube crumbled, and still the young man sang, directing the power safely away from the Cube and into the plague. As the last bit of the disease vanished and died, the Cube dissolved into a fine dust that blew away on the wind. The salamander in his ear pulled painlessly away and fell into the dark cloud.

The young man hung there a moment. It was over.

The plague was gone. The world was cured. *He* was cured. And he was still alive and well. The prophecy had been wrong. The storm at his feet rumbled and flickered. He glanced at the battery dial. A few seconds left. He could make it back to Earth if he hurried. The young man dove through the clouds.

A lightning bolt struck him full on. It cracked through his body and sizzled and scorched. The wing harness shattered, scattering glowing blue rings in all directions. Energized by the electricity and still defying gravity, they hung like water droplets while the young man plunged to the ground.

Chapter Eighteen

Alice watched Gavin vanish into the sky, trailing blue light as he went. It was the last she would ever see of him. The trembling Earth dragged at her, weighing down every bone and muscle. Her heart was an aching black hole in her chest. He was gone. Gavin was gone, and she would never see him, never touch him, never hear his musical voice. How could she go on without him? The world was dead.

Lady Orchid and Cricket, still dripping wet, arrived at the bottom of the steps. Phipps and Li also finally regained their feet. They all climbed up to Alice.

"What happened?" Phipps said, but Alice couldn't speak. She could only look to the sky. Phipps followed her gaze and then looked at Su Shun and the Jade Hand and the Ebony Chamber and seemed to work out what was going on.

"I'm so sorry, Alice," she said softly. "We'll see that he's remembered forever."

It all crashed in at once—months of travel, weeks of stress, days of holding herself together, and all for nothing. After a lifetime of foiling the impossible, Alice did one thing it never occurred to her she might do: She collapsed, weeping, into the arms of Lieutenant Susan Phipps. Startled, Phipps froze a moment, then held her tight, patting her back and making soothing sounds.

"He's gone, Susan," Alice cried. "I pushed him away, and now he's gone."

"You had to do it. He knows you had to do it," she murmured. "He loves you, and he knows."

Lady Orchid, meanwhile, was cradling her wrist stump and examining the Jade Hand without touching it. Su Shun still lay unconscious on the steps next to it in his lacquered armor. More tremors shook the courtyard, forcing everyone to stagger for balance. Cricket clung to his mother.

Alice stood upright again. Her eyes felt hot and puffy. She had no handkerchief and was forced to wipe her face on her filthy sleeve. "What next?"

"I don't know," Phipps replied. "This didn't come out anything like we'd planned. If only—"

The sound silenced them all. The purest, most beautiful sound Alice had ever heard reached through her, stilling all her fears like a gentle hand calming stormy water. The sweetness of it made her heart ache to bursting. It touched every part of her and filled her with love and peace and serenity. And most of all, the sound was utterly familiar.

"Gavin," she whispered.

He had done this once before, but on a smaller scale, beneath the headquarters of the Third Ward. His voice and the Impossible Cube had lifted her and cleansed her, washed her clean. Now it was happening everywhere, to everyone.

The entrancing sound rang on and on. Looks of peace and happiness crossed the faces of Susan and Li and Lady Orchid and Cricket and the soldiers and the Dragon Men. The sound continued for countless moments, filling the entire world, and Alice couldn't imagine how anything so wonderful could possibly end. But then it did, and she wept again, feeling the deep loss of love and beauty.

"Oh, Gavin," she called to the sky, "what did you do?"

There was a soft meow. Click was sitting next to the Ebony Chamber, looking at Alice with quizzical green eyes.

"Click?" Alice said. "Where did you—?"

Lightning flicked across the sky and thunder crashed. A strange feeling went through her left forearm and her hand. With a series of soft clinks, the iron spider that had burrowed into her flesh and drunk her blood all those months ago released itself. Quietly, and without pain, it slid off her arm and thumped to the ground next to the Jade Hand. The glowing eyes went dark.

Alice held up her lightened arm and hand in wonder. It felt as if the limb might float away.

"Are you all right?" Phipps asked. "Are you hurt?"

"I'm fine," she said. "It's so strange. Why did it let go now?"

All around the courtyard, the Dragon Men put their hands to their ears. The salamanders came away. They flung them aside or dropped them or crushed them in their hands with yells of joy.

"They are cured," said Lady Orchid, with Li translating a moment later. *"I think the blessing of dragons is gone."*

Su Shun groaned softly.

"What must we do about the Jade Hand?" Li said in both Chinese and English. "Young Lord Zaichun is here. We could—"

A few paces away, something clunked to the ground and clattered away. Startled, Alice picked the object up. It was a Dragon Man's salamander, bent and broken from the impact. What on earth?

Trying to understand, she peered upward. A figure was falling toward the courtyard. As it grew closer, she could make out the tattered remnants of wings. Her heart jerked. Gavin! He plummeted straight toward the stones near her feet. His arms pinwheeled—he was still alive.

Alice made a wordless scream. She had already let him go. She couldn't watch him die. But there was nothing she could do. She couldn't fly. She couldn't catch him. There was nothing for him to land—

Click meowed again from his spot near the Ebony Chamber. With chilly fingers, Alice snatched it up. The lid was still open from when Su Shun had opened it so Gavin could put the Cube inside. Not quite believing her own audacity, she ran forward with it. This had to work, this had to work, this *had* to work.

"Ennock!" Phipps barked. "Dive! *Dive*, you fool!"

Somehow, Gavin heard and understood. Perhaps it was the last of the clockwork plague still at work augmenting his mind, or perhaps it was sheer luck operating in their favor at last. He twisted round and came down, hands first, straight as an arrow. Alice maneuvered the Ebony Chamber directly beneath him and held her breath. Gavin slammed headfirst into the Chamber. White light and a terrible noise exploded in all directions. Blind, Alice staggered but managed to stay upright. The lid crashed shut in her hands, and Alice blinked her vision clear. She found herself standing alone in the courtyard and holding the Ebony Chamber. The remnants of Gavin's shattered wings lay in pieces all about her. They had been sheared clean off. Of Gavin himself there was no sign. The Chamber felt the same—no heavier or lighter than before.

Trembling with fear and uncertainty, Alice set the Chamber down.

"What happened?" Phipps asked beside her. Click had followed her down the steps. "Is he alive or is he dead?"

"I can't tell." Alice clenched her hands. Dread and doubt made cold lumps inside. Her words came out in tiny bursts. "Oh God, I have no idea. I'm scared to open it and find out. It's safer not to know."

"Just do it," Phipps said tightly.

The phoenix latch still read 000. Her breath quick and frightened, Alice unlocked the latch and opened the Chamber. Its hinges creaked like quiet laughter or a soft scream, Alice couldn't tell which. She held her breath and peered inside.

The box was empty.

"No," she whispered. "No. Please."

She reached into the box and felt around, as if that might change something. But all she touched was unyielding wood. Gavin was gone.

Sorrow crushed Alice to the ground. She knelt amid the shattered remains of Gavin's wings and pounded the stones on either side of the Ebony Chamber with her bare fists, not feeling the pain in her hands, only the pain in her heart. The solid stones refused to swallow her up. They left her there, cold and alone. Susan finally drew her up and away.

"Come along," she said. "We set out to stop a war, and we saved the world instead. Thanks to him and thanks to you."

Alice shook her head and choked out, "What kind of world takes away the one who saves it?"

But Phipps had no answer.

Lady Orchid, meanwhile, removed the battery pack from Su Shun's back, set it on the ground, and raised the wire sword high with her good hand. Her son stood next to her on the steps, looking pale. Both were still wet from the well. By now, eunuchs and maids were moving into the courtyard from other parts of the Forbidden City.

Most had fled the buildings when the tremors began and were now coming to a more central area for news. Surprise rippled through them when they saw the emperor half conscious on the stone steps and the Jade Hand in the grip of the Imperial Concubine. Alice saw Prince Kung, and with him were a great many soldiers. Her two whirligig automatons zipped in to land on her shoulders.

"I declare Su Shun a traitor to the people of China," Lady Orchid called over the nighttime crowd, and Phipps hastened to translate. *"Proof lies here, in the way the Jade Hand has rejected him."*

Zaichun picked up the Jade Hand. The bit of Su Shun's wrist left inside the Jade Hand chose that moment to slide out and flop to the steps at Lady Orchid's feet. The crowd murmured.

"No." Su Shun got to his hands and knees, shaking his head.

"See how he kneels before the true emperor," Lady Orchid continued. *"See how he confesses his guilt. And there is but one punishment for treason."*

Su Shun started to rise farther, but Lady Orchid was quick. She flicked the sword down. Although Su Shun saw it coming, he couldn't move out of the way. His eyes went wide as the vibrating blade sliced through his brass-bound neck, leaving no blood. His head tumbled down the steps, crunching and clattering, to fetch up at Li's feet. His empty eyes stared upward; his brass jaw gaped. Li shoved the head aside with his foot, and it rolled away like a piece of trash. Alice thought she should feel ill or upset, but she could only think of Gavin and the awful hole in her life. There was a brief silence, and then the crowd of maids and eunuchs cheered.

"The reign of the despot is over," Lady Orchid continued. *"The true emperor stands before you now."*

Zaichun gulped, set his face, and took a step forward. But Lady Orchid shut the sword off, dropped it, and took the Jade Hand from Zaichun. To the amazement of Alice and everyone else in the assembled crowd, Lady Orchid slid the Jade Hand over the stump of her right wrist. The hand jerked. It moved and clicked and inserted wires and metal strips. When it finished, Lady Orchid, in obvious pain but doing her best to hide it, raised the Jade Hand high. It glowed green.

"The hand has accepted a new emperor," she boomed. *"One who will govern all of China with a firm and just rule."*

The stunned crowd remained silent. Alice understood. The idea of a female emperor was unthinkable, impossible. The Jade Hand lent her some credibility, but—

"Bring forth the Ebony Chamber!" Lady Orchid commanded.

Before Alice could quite comprehend what was going on, Lieutenant Li brought the dark box with its gold dragons up the steps to Lady Orchid. Zaichun stared uncertainly. Li knelt at Lady Orchid's feet and knocked his head on the stones just as a soldier would for an emperor. The crowd murmured again.

"Rise, General," Lady Orchid said, and the promotion wasn't lost on Li—or Phipps. He handed her the Ebony Chamber. Lady Orchid showed it to the crowd with the

grace and style of a magician and then pressed the Jade Hand to the phoenix latch. The Hand glowed green. Understanding swept over Alice a second before the next event happened. The Ebony Chamber exploded open, and Gavin tumbled out onto the steps. His pale hair was disheveled and his clothes were torn, but he was alive.

"Gavin!" The greatest joy of her life overtook Alice. She rushed up the steps and swept him into her arms, or perhaps he swept her into his. Her automatons squeaked and leaped away, propellers whirling madly. And then Gavin was kissing her, and she didn't care who was watching or how many people saw. Her Gavin was here, and she would never be apart from him again.

"I love you always," he whispered.

"I love you always," she whispered back.

"Long live Emperor Cixi!" Prince Kung bellowed. *"Long live Emperor Cixi!"*

Kung's soldiers quickly joined in, which encouraged the others. Shouts and chants swirled around Alice, who was lost in Gavin's embrace. And then everyone fell slowly silent. Alice and Gavin parted, and she saw that the hundreds and hundreds of people—soldiers, eunuchs, maids, and even Dragon Men—in the courtyard had stopped chanting to kneel and knock their foreheads on the ground, formally acknowledging Cixi as emperor. Even Zaichun was on his knees. Gavin hesitated, then bowed deeply to her, and Alice sank into a curtsy. It wasn't strictly correct to make such obeisance to a foreign monarch, but the gesture would only solidify Cixi's hold on the throne, and after everything the woman had been through, Alice would be the last person to stand in her way.

Gavin came awake, slowly and luxuriously. Drowsiness slid away like a silken coverlet, and he essayed a stretch. The muscles in his back moved with easy smoothness. Soft fingers brushed his forehead, and he opened his eyes. Alice smiled gently down at him. He smiled lazily back and pushed himself upright.

"What are you doing in here?" he asked lightly. "This is my room."

Alice, who was perched on the edge of his bed, ran her hand down his arm. She wore a new outfit in the Manchu style—wide trousers and a long coat over it in embroidered blue silk. A whirligig sat on her shoulder. "Just watching you sleep, darling. You looked so peaceful, I couldn't bear to wake you."

"It was just a nap. Besides, you can always wake me, Alice. Any time."

"A nap?" She laughed. "Gavin, you slept all day and all night."

"Did I? It felt like only a few minutes. I haven't slept that long since I contracted—"

"I know. I *know*!" Alice was beaming now, and joyful tears stood in her eyes. "Oh, Gavin! I can't believe you did it."

"*We* did it," he said, trying himself not to tear up. "Both of us."

He kissed her, and now he felt the joy and relief carrying him up into pure sunshine. Fear and sadness melted into the ground, leaving only exultation and anticipation. An entire life stretched ahead of him, an entire life with Alice, and it started here. He ran his hands over her face and her shoulders, wanting to merge with her like two droplets of water. Nothing would separate them again, and the thrill was so powerful, it stole his breath.

But at last they separated. "That," Alice said, "was a wonderful kiss."

"I've got lots more," he said with mock seriousness. He started to stretch again, then halted. "Oh! Oh my God."

"What is it? What's wrong?"

He grinned, surprised that he could feel even more wonderful. "I just realized—I slept and woke up. Like a normal person. First time since that day the pirates captured the *Juniper*. No nightmares, no jerking awake. I'd forgotten what it was like."

She grinned back. "That's fantastic! I'm so glad for you. No, that sounds tepid. I'm thrilled, darling, absolutely thrilled!"

They embraced again, and he sighed as her arms went back around him. It felt so good to be alone with her here in Prince Kung's palace, far away from the chaos of the Forbidden City. The rooms Kung had set aside for Gavin were large and luxurious. A set of sliding doors opened onto a tranquil courtyard, where the sun was peeping over the compound walls. Soft summer breezes slid idly through the room, carrying the scent of flowers and running water.

"What's Lady Orchid doing now?" Gavin asked when at last they parted.

"Her name is actually Cixi, I've learned, and she's very busy consolidating her new empire," Alice told him. "She's grateful to her new friends from England. I also hear she was quite upset that she wasn't able to fulfill her promise of finding a cure for the clockwork plague."

"Well, that was only because I . . . it doesn't really matter," Gavin finished lamely.

"It does to her. The Chinese take these debts seriously. At any rate, she persuaded the Dragon Men to do some final work."

"Persuaded?"

"The Jade Hand doesn't control them anymore. She has to persuade them like anyone else must. I expect it must be *very* trying."

He laughed. "I'm sure. But the plague is gone. How are there still Dragon Men?"

"Your . . . cure affects different people differently, darling. Some Dragon Men—and, I assume, clockworkers— became normal men and women right away. For others, their intelligence seems to be fading gradually over time. It appears that a tiny minority may even retain their powerful intellect, though whether they'll go mad or not remains to be seen." She paused. "How do *you* feel?"

"I'm not sure." He thought a moment, trying to find the patterns and the particles. But all he saw was an airy room. And Alice. Always Alice. "I'm not very . . . I don't think I'm a clockworker anymore."

She breathed out heavily. "Oh, darling. That relieves me more than I can say."

He took her hand. It was a great relief not to feel the impinging madness all the time. But he also had to admit it was hard giving up everything he had seen and learned. The clockwork plague was gone, and now he was just himself. It would have to be enough.

"So, what did Lady Orchid—Cixi—ask the Dragon Men to do?" Gavin asked.

"They repaired the *Lady of Liberty* from stem to stern, and while they were working, they uncovered one of your projects and arranged for its completion."

"Project? What project?"

Alice raised her voice. "You can come in now."

The door slid farther open and a mechanical man entered. He was painted black and white, in a sort of butler's uniform, but with a distinctly Oriental sensibility, and he was carrying a fiddle case. Gavin clambered to his feet with a little shout. "Kemp!"

He almost hugged the automaton, then stopped, considering the gesture silly. Instead, he shook the mechanical man's free hand. Even that much seemed to put Kemp off a bit.

"It is good to see Sir again," he said. "Very good indeed. Thank you, Sir."

"How do you feel, Kemp?" Gavin asked. He looked the automaton up and down, half expecting his mind to analyze how he was put together, but nothing came to him. It was both odd and exhilarating.

"I am much improved, Sir," Kemp replied. "The Chinese Dragon Men finished the body you started and were able to reattach my head very nicely. I am quite ready to resume my duties. As a start, I have brought Sir his fiddle from the ship."

Gavin accepted it gratefully, checked it, and set it on the bed. "Thank you, Kemp. You always remember."

"Would Madam or Sir like something to eat? I have learned Chinese and can communicate with the kitchen staff quite readily."

"We would, Kemp." Alice said, and Kemp bustled off. "Thank you for that, darling. I missed him so."

"The Dragon Men—"

"Only finished what you started. And you started it when you were in that fugue state, didn't you? It means a lot that you were thinking of me, even when the plague had you."

Moments later, Kemp returned with a tray of tea and food. To Gavin's relief, it had no feeding spiders on it—just chopsticks. Click followed Kemp in and sat at Alice's feet while they ate. It was the most relaxing and wonderful thing in the world to simply share a meal with her, and what made it even better was knowing that he could do it over and over again for the rest of their lives.

"What are you smiling about, you devil?" Alice asked over her cup.

He rested his chin in his palm. "How beautiful you are. And how it must be a relief for you to be rid of that spider on your hand."

"Thank you. You're a dear." She held up her bare left hand. "It does feel nice. As far as we can tell, the clockwork plague is completely gone. The people who have it are recovering. The zombies will still be scarred—there's nothing for that—but no new cases, no new deaths."

"Humans can be what they were supposed to be," Gavin said. "No more, no less."

"Here's to no more." Alice raised her cup, and they clinked in a toast.

"Where's Phipps, by the way?" Gavin asked. "We need to talk to her about leaving, since the ship is finished."

"Oh. Susan. Yes." Alice cleared her throat. "Susan is staying on. As the new cultural attaché. I believe she and Lieutenant—that is *General*—Li have formed an ... understanding, and Susan wishes to explore it."

"You noticed that, too, did you? Huh. I never thought I'd see Susan Phipps with a gentleman caller, and definitely not one from China."

"Yes, well, I never thought I'd fall for a cabin boy from Boston."

"Street musician. I was a street musician. Starving artists have a lot more cachet, you know." He devoured a bean bun. "There's something I'm forgetting, though. It's important, but it won't come."

"Well, we do need to talk about where we'll go."

Gavin set down the chopsticks. "You know, I hadn't thought of that at all. I'd been so focused on China and the cure that I didn't think of afterward."

"We could stay in China," Alice said. "Cixi would keep us as honored guests forever."

"That's a kind offer, but I want to be closer to home when we raise our children."

At the word *children*, Alice wordlessly took both her hands in his across the table. "I agree."

"Should we head for Boston, then? You haven't met my family."

"Your pardon, Sir." Kemp poked his head into the room. A brass nightingale fluttered around his head. "You have a visitor."

"Hello, hello!" called a new voice. "You there, Gavin?"

The doors to the courtyard slid completely open and Uri Ennock strode into the room, his white-blond hair shining in the morning sunlight. Alice stared, mouth agape.

"That's what I forgot," Gavin said sheepishly. "Alice, I'd like you to meet my dad."

Epilogue

The rickety stairs creaked under Gavin's shoes as he and Alice climbed the steps of the old tenement building. The place was dirtier and dingier than he remembered, and smaller, too. But the stairwell and hallway still smelled the same—boiled cabbage, urine, unwashed bodies. Doors cracked open, and eyes stared at him and Alice. Their clothes stood out as richer and finer than anything the people here might own, though Gavin had taken care to wear simple twill and flannel while Alice wore a plain blouse and skirt. He swallowed and kept climbing.

"Don't be nervous, darling," Alice murmured. "I'm not."

Gavin didn't respond to this. Any number of things could go wrong. The worst was that Ma or Gramps might be dead. Or Ma might be angry with him for not writing in so long, or for not sending money. Or worse, she might just be disappointed.

They reached the fourth floor, and Gavin automatically turned right, just as he had done every day when he was a child, though the hallway was narrower than he remembered. The only light came from a high paper-covered window at the end of the hall. The place was scorching in summer and freezing in winter. Right now, in early autumn, it was tolerable, at least. He went to the first door, and for a moment he was six. He even had his fiddle with him.

"I haven't been here in years," he whispered. "Do I knock or just go in?"

"Oh good heavens." Alice reached around him and rapped smartly on the wood.

"Who is it?" came a voice from inside. The familiarity of it stung Gavin's eyes.

"Ma?" he said hoarsely. "I'm home."

The door banged open. Carrie Ennock, a short, thin woman with work-reddened hands and graying brown hair pulled into a bun, popped into the hall. "Good God! My Gavin! It's Gavin!"

She reached up with both hands to pull him down for a kiss, then hugged him hard. The top of her head barely came up to his chin.

"I knew you were coming. I knew it!" Her low voice was filled with emotion. "After that long note that everyone heard. It was *you*. I heard *you*. Oh, I'm so glad you're back!"

"I'm here, Ma." Gavin's own eyes were wet. "I'm sorry I didn't write. It got complicated."

"You're here. You're safe. That's all I care about." She hugged him again. "You're so *tall* now. A man."

"I never noticed you were so short, Ma," he said, trying to lighten the mood.

She tapped his chest with her hand. "That's enough from you, young man. And who's this?"

He stepped aside. "Ma, this is Alice, my fiancée. Alice, my mother, Carrie Ennock."

"How do you do?" Alice extended her hand.

"Well, that's wonderful!" Carrie shook Alice's hand, then embraced her, too. "Alice. I have a daughter named Alice. But I'm being stupid. Come in! Come in! This is your home, after all."

The little two-room flat was just as Gavin remembered it—cramped and bare and cold. Carrie kept it clean, but sewing was spread out everywhere. Clearly she was still doing piecework for seamstresses and tailors, and Gavin wondered about her eyesight.

"Where is everyone?" he asked.

Carrie rushed about, clearing cloth off two ancient ladder-back chairs and offering one to Alice, who took it as if it were an easy chair in a high-class tearoom. She seemed not to notice the lack of light or heat or the cracks in the floorboards or the smoke streaks on the plaster, and for that Gavin was grateful.

"Well, let's see," Carrie said. "Jenny is with her Elmer, of course. They have two little ones now—Benjamin and Louise. You're an uncle! Harry is ... well, he's out looking for work, I imagine."

Drinking, Gavin mentally filled in.

"Patrick found work down at the docks, which is helpful, but he hasn't found a girl yet." Carrie picked up needle and thread and started sewing again, an automatic gesture. She had to sew, Gavin knew, until the sun went down. Even her wayward son's return wasn't reason to stop, since she was paid by the piece. "And Violet's at the factory. She'll be off in a few hours. We can all have dinner together!"

Gavin could see she was calculating how to feed two more people on whatever was—or wasn't—in the little cupboards. He reached out and stilled her hands with his own.

"Ma," he said, "you don't have to do this anymore."

"What do you mean, honey?" She pulled away and went back to sewing. "I'm nearly done with this piece, and I can just get in another before dark. And what have *you* been doing? Talk to me while I work."

"I mean, Ma, that you don't have to sew anymore. Or work. Or live here."

Her needle never stopped moving. "How's that?"

From his pocket, Gavin took a thick stack of bank notes. He laid it on the table where Carrie could see it. She glanced at it but kept sewing.

"What is it?"

"It's yours, Ma," he said.

"Just like your father," she replied, still sewing.

At one time, that remark would have made him angry. Now he was just curious. "How so, Ma?"

"You vanish, and you think money makes it all right."

"Did Dad ever send money?" Gavin asked, surprised.

"For a while. Then it stopped. Just like—well, it stopped."

"I talked to him, Ma. I *found* him."

Now she did stop sewing. "Gavin Eric Ennock, don't you dare come back into my life with wild stories that—"

"It's true, Ma. He's alive. I found him. In China. He's not coming back, but he wrote a letter that explains everything." From his pocket he took a handkerchief and unwrapped the silver nightingale. "I don't blame you for being angry at him, or at me. Not all of it was his fault or mine. Part of it was the clockwork plague, though the plague was more our fault—mankind's fault—than we knew."

"What's that supposed to mean?" Carrie held the nightingale up to the light.

"It's hard to describe. I'll try, but after we've all had something to eat. At a nice hotel with a fine restaurant."

"With that?" Carrie said, gesturing at the bank notes. "It's a little hard to believe. Where did it come from?"

"I'm a baroness, Mrs. Ennock," Alice put in. "And, not to put too fine a point on it, I'm quite wealthy. Filthy rich, I believe you Americans say, and I've given a portion of my fortune over to Gavin. That money is his quite legally, and he has a suite of rooms reserved for you and your family at the Revere House."

"Oh!" Carrie looked overwhelmed. "I—I wouldn't know how to behave at such a fancy place."

"Mrs. Ennock." Alice leaned forward to touch her hand conspiratorially. "When you have pots of money, no one cares one bit how you behave. It's a *lot* of fun, believe me."

At that, Carrie laughed. "All right, then. Please call me Ma. And I want to know how my son ended up with a baroness."

"You'll hear all about it," Gavin said, relieved. "But Ma—what about Gramps? You didn't mention him."

Carrie hesitated, and Gavin's heart jerked. "Your grandfather . . . isn't quite the same, honey. He doesn't eat much, and he sleeps a lot."

"Where is he?"

"In the sleeping room. Go on, then."

Gavin took up his fiddle and went into the back room. Alice followed. Just as he remembered, there were no beds, just narrow pallets of threadbare blankets on the floor. A narrow window let in grudging light. His grandfather lay on one of the pallets. His hair was all but gone, his skin deeply wrinkled and mottled, his eyes closed.

"Gramps?" Gavin knelt beside him. "Gramps, it's me, Gavin. I'm back."

At first Gramps didn't move. Then he stirred slightly and his eyes opened. They were the same blue as Gavin's, though filmy with age.

"Boy?" he said gruffly. "That you?"

Gavin took his hand. "I'm here, Gramps. I'm back."

"Well, where the hell have you been all this time?"

Alice put a hand to her mouth to smother a laugh, and Gavin smiled. "It's a long story, Gramps."

"Don't tell me now, boy. I don't have time. Just do one thing for me, will you?"

"Anything, Gramps. You know that."

"Play."

Alice gave Gavin his fiddle. Carrie appeared in the doorway, holding the nightingale as Gavin tuned up. He sang:

I see the moon, the moon sees me.
It turns all the forest soft and silvery.
The moon picked you from all the rest,
For I loved you best.

Gramps gave Gavin a proud smile, exhaled once, and died.

They held the wedding a month later on the deck of the *Lady of Liberty*. Alice wore a white gown, which was still the rage for brides, and her spiders and whirligigs accompanied her down the aisle to the helm. Gavin awaited her in a new set of white leathers of his own, and he couldn't stop smiling. Click flatly refused to carry the rings, though he did deign to sit on the generator and watch. The priest, hired from a local parish, seemed a bit overwhelmed at marrying a baroness aboard an airship high above the city, but he performed the ceremony without a hitch. Carrie Ennock, her hands no longer reddened with work, looked ready to burst with pride and happiness, and Gavin's brothers and sisters cheered when Gavin lifted Alice's veil to give her a long, lingering kiss.

They held a reception directly afterward, with a great deal of drinking and music from hired musicians. Gavin thought it strange to have music played for him instead of by him, but it was his wedding day, so nothing was likely to be normal.

After the sun went down and Alice's whirligigs shuttled the guests back to the ground, they abruptly found themselves on an empty deck. The lights of Boston spread out below them like snowflakes scattered across velvet.

"Alone at last with my wife," Gavin said, trying out the phrase.

"Alone at last with my husband," she replied, doing the same.

"So why are we up here instead of in our stateroom?" He held out his arm to her. "Madam?"

She took it. "Sir."

He paused to kiss her one more time. "I love you—"

"Always," she finished. "Yes. Yes, indeed."

They strolled below, and Gavin couldn't stop himself singing. Alice joined in.

The moon picked you from all the rest,
For I loved you best.

AFTERWORD

Empress Dowager Cixi is one of the most enigmatic people in recent history. Strangely little is known about the woman who ruled China from behind a silk curtain in her son's throne room. Historical accounts tend to portray her as either a scheming, murderous vixen out to rule an empire or as an intelligent, capable woman who rose to a difficult occasion. I rather think she was a little of both.

Most of the characters in my fictional China did exist, and they play fictional roles quite similar to the ones they played in history. General Su Shun did trot the young Emperor Xianfeng out to brothels and opium dens as part of a long-term scheme to take the throne for himself, and Cixi did have him beheaded for his trouble. Prince Kung advocated for a more open relationship with the West, though historically he completely failed. Bu Yeh was a dreadfully overweight man who was supposed to be a gatekeeper between China and the West but who actually hated foreigners. The Qilin is a powerful force in Chinese mythology. However, Lieutenant Li lives only in these pages, and the Passage of Silken Footsteps is, as far as I know, completely my own invention.

—Steven Harper

ABOUT THE AUTHOR

Steven Harper Piziks was born in Saginaw, Michigan, but he moved around a lot and has lived in Wisconsin, in Germany, and briefly in the Ukraine. Currently he lives with his three sons in southeast Michigan.

His novels include *In the Company of Mind* and *Corporate Mentality*, both science fiction published by Baen Books. He has produced the Silent Empire series for Roc and *Writing the Paranormal Novel* for Writer's Digest. He's also written novels based on *Star Trek*, *Battlestar Galactica*, and *The Ghost Whisperer*.

Mr. Piziks currently teaches high school English in southeast Michigan. His students think he's hysterical, which isn't the same as thinking he's hilarious. When not writing, he plays the folk harp, dabbles in oral storytelling, and spends more time online than is probably good for him. Visit his Web page at www.theclockworkempire.com, and his Twitter feed at www.twitter.com/steven piziks.

Read on for an exciting excerpt from
Steven Harper's next Clockwork Empire novel,

THE HAVOC MACHINE

Coming in May 2013 from Roc

Thaddeus Sharpe loosened his brown leather jacket and shoved his way into the low-beamed tavern. A fire glowed like a captured demon in the long ceramic stove, and the smoky air wrapped itself around him in a stifling blanket. At long tables, men in long shirts and blousy trousers clanked glasses of vodka and thumped mugs of *gira*, the fermented drink made from rye bread and favored by Lithuanian peasants. A heavy smell of sweat mixed with the sharp tint of vodka and the earthy slop of *gira*. The autumn evening was already well under way, and the red-faced men shouted more than they talked. Candles in cracked saucers stood upright on the tables to provide light. Dante cocked his good eye at the room and clacked his brass beak from his perch on Thad's shoulder. Several of the men turned to stare at Thad when he blew in. He tensed and automatically felt for the long knife in his sleeve.

"Shut the damn door!" one of them barked in what Thad assumed was Lithuanian. Thanks to his mother, Thad spoke a number of Eastern European languages, and his father had liked to joke that once you learned three of them, the fourth came free. Thad slammed the door, and most of the men went back to their drinking. Two, however, continued to stare at him.

"Dummy, dummy, dummy," Dante muttered in Thad's ear. "Stare and stare, here and there." He squawked.

"Shut it." Thad's jaw was set in a line. His dark hair curled beneath a workman's cap and his face was free of facial hair, but there his resemblance to the men in the tavern ended. His lean build, long leather jacket, and stout boots made him stand out among the plain Lithuanian homespun. The ratty brass parrot on his shoulder didn't help. Maybe he should duck out and look for a way in through the back.

The two men, both large and callused, got up from their long benches and strode across the sticky tavern floor before Thad could retreat. One of them loomed over Thad, his breath heavy with vodka.

"I have heard of your parrot," he said in thick Lithuanian. *"You are the man who kills clockworkers. Many, many clockworkers."*

The knife was already in Thad's hand. *"What of it?"* he replied, his own accent heavy with British vowels. The blade gleamed silver in the candlelight, though neither man seemed to notice. Thad was already calculating— one slash at the throat to incapacitate the first man, shove him backward into the second man, flee into the street. Dante's forged feathers creaked in his ear as the parrot tensed.

The man clapped Thad on the shoulder. *"I will buy your first drink,"* he boomed. *"And my brother will buy your second. Bartender! Vodka and* gira *for our new friend!"*

Moments later, Thaddeus found himself wedged in at one of the splintery trestle tables with a clay mug by his left hand and a shot glass at his right. A dish of salt and a loaf of dark rye bread sat in front of him. The men at the table raised their own mugs and glasses to Thad, drained them, and wiped their mustaches with their sleeves in one smooth motion.

"So. How many clockworkers have you killed?" asked the first man. His name was Arturas and his brother was Mykolas.

"I keep no count." Thad raised his *gira* mug, tried a gulp, and suppressed a grimace. It was like drinking sour rye bread.

"Liar, liar, liar," Dante croaked in his ear.

"Shut it," Thad said, glad none of the men seemed to speak English.

"Who is this man, Arturas?" asked one of the other drinkers.

"This," Arturas boomed in reply, *"is the man who killed Erek the Terror outside Krakow and Vile Basia in the sewers of Prague. This is the man who killed countless monsters and saved a thousand lives. They say he walks the streets with a brass parrot on his shoulder and a cannon in his trousers."*

The men roared at that, and Thad, laughing but uncomfortable at the attention, raised his mug with an ironic grin.

"This man," Mykolas added in conclusion, *"is a hero!"*

Arturas threw his free arm around Thad and clashed his glass against his brother's. The other men, all half drunk, joined in, slopping *gira* and vodka onto the bread plate. Thad glanced about uneasily and pulled a small card from his coat pocket.

"What brings the mighty clockwork killer into a pisshole like Bûsi Treèias?" Arturas demanded.

"Hey!" the bartender snapped.

Dante cocked his head and Thad glanced down at the card in his hand. In graceful script on one side was engraved:

София Иванова Экк

On the back in black ink was scribbled *7.45 sharp, Bûsi Treèias.* A ragged boy had handed him the card on the streets of Vilnius earlier this afternoon and fled before Thad could even react. Bûsi Treèias was the name of the tavern. It meant "You'll be third," and it was the name that made Thad uneasy, though not so uneasy that he avoided the meeting.

The name on the card was Sofiya Ivanova Ekk, a Russian woman's name, and Russian women did not frequent taverns in the Polish-Lithuanian Union. Neither did Polish-Lithuanian women, for that matter. He thought about asking the men at the table if they knew

Sofiya Ekk, but had the feeling that they might think he was inquiring after a prostitute or, worse, someone's sister.

"I thought I might have business here," he said in his heavy Lithuanian. *"But I seem to have made new friends instead."*

That brought on another smashing together of mugs and more knocking back of vodka. Thad tried the latter this time, and it burned a fiery trail down to his stomach. Tears streamed from his eyes. He hastily snatched up some bread, dipped it in salt, and wolfed it down.

A glass of honest-to-god beer landed in front of him. Startled, Thad looked up. The balding bartender withdrew his hand and jerked his head toward a corner of the bar. A figure wrapped in scarlet sat in a shadow far away from the red-hot stove. Thad clapped Arturas on the shoulder and picked up his beer. *"I seem to have business after all."*

Arturas and the other men didn't seem to mind, though they watched him curiously as he picked his way across the crowded room with his beer.

"Pretty, pretty, pretty boy," Dante said. "Beer and crackers."

When Thad reached the corner, the scarlet figure resolved itself into a woman in a hooded cloak of rich scarlet velvet, unfashionable but not unheard-of. The hood covered the upper half of her face, and an untouched glass of something red sat on the small table in front of her. She had an actual chair instead of a bench, and a matching chair waited across from her. The noise of the tavern seemed to die away as Thad gingerly sat down. He had talked to his share of women in taverns elsewhere, but these circumstances were definitely odd. They were also intriguing.

"Pretty, pretty, pretty," Dante said again.

"Miss Ekk?" Thad put out a hand, half ready to snatch it back.

"I am that woman." She shook hands. Her palm was smooth and soft. Thad wondered if she expected him to kiss the back, but he didn't. Instead, he set his elbow on the table and let Dante walk down his arm. Dante did get heavy after a while. The parrot waddled over to investigate the unlit candle. Gears creaked uneasily through bare spots where brass feathers were missing or broken, and the bottom half of his beak was off-center, as if Dante had flown through a tornado and only barely lived to tell about it.

"I am thrilled you decided to come, Mr. Sharpe," the woman said. Her English carried a Russian accent, and her voice was low and powerful.

"I'm a little surprised to find someone like you in a place like this, Miss Ekk," Thad countered. His eyes flickered up and down her form, trying to assess her, but she wasn't moving and the damned cloak hid everything. He couldn't even tell how old she was.

"Someone like me?"

He gestured at the tavern. More than one person was still staring in their direction. Normally it would have made him more nervous, but right now he found it reassuring to have other eyes on him. "Proper females don't go to bars in the Polish-Lithuanian Union. Or in Russia. They stay behind closed doors and do proper female things."

"Rules are for people who think little, Mr. Sharpe. People like us, we think large. That is why I wished to meet you."

"In a tavern with the name *You'll be third*?" Thad brandished the card.

"I believe the name shows that the place is very popular—there are always two people ahead of you waiting to be served. The name fits, no?"

"It's also the Lithuanian way of saying your luck will turn for the worse," Thad spat. "Did you think I didn't know?"

Sofiya laughed quietly. "You are not superstitious. You use scientific knowledge. You know from experience how the clockwork plague works, for example. These people," she gestured at the room, "think the plague comes from the devil. They think that when someone catches the disease and it turns him into a shambling mound of flesh that wanders through the streets, feeding on garbage until his brain rots away, that God meant it as a punishment. And they think that when the disease makes someone into a clockworker who creates glorious and impossible inventions—"

"—and goes mad and does horrible things to innocent to people," Thad put in.

"Doom, destruction, death, despair," said Dante. "Doom!"

"Shut it," Thad ordered.

"They think this also is a punishment from God," Sofiya finished as if no one had spoken. "Their Church tells them so. But we know it is nothing more than a disease that acts as a disease must."

"The plague is a curse, and the faster we eradicate everything connected with it, the better," Thad spat. He found his left hand was shaking, and he forced it to still.

"I told you we think large," Sofiya said with a nod. "And I am glad to see that you can react as a human being, Mr. Sharpe."

Thad clenched his teeth. "Why are we talking about this? What do you care about the clockwork plague?"

"You have caught my interest, Mr. Sharpe. You are a very interesting person to very many people. *Very* interesting."

That set off several small alarm bells inside his head.

"I don't want to offend," Thad said, now with careful control in every syllable, "but I feel I should point out that the parrot, which has moved to a strategic spot on the table less than eight inches in front of you, can deliver more than two thousand pounds of pressure from the business end of that sharp beak, more than enough pressure to slice open your windpipe. I also have a knife on a spring-load that can open up an artery so quick, you won't even know you're dead before the blade is clean and back up my sleeve. Finally, all those men over there, the ones you were scorning as small-thinking peasants a moment ago, seem to like me quite a lot, and I think they would be very upset if anyone tried something foolish."

"Such a mental condition you have," Sofiya tutted. "I believe the English word is *paranoia.*"

His muscles were growing tight with tension. The situation was unusual. Thad didn't like unusual. It was too much like hunting clockworkers. But tension made fights difficult. He forced himself to relax. "I deal with clockworkers all the time. One can never be too paranoid."

"As you like, Mr. Sharpe. But I do not have a wish to harm you." From the folds of her cloak, she produced a small purse, which she dropped on the table. It clinked. "I wish to hire you."

That got Thad's attention fast, though he made no move to touch the purse. "Dante."

The parrot expertly tore the purse open, revealing the glint of silver and gold coins, a generous offering. "Pretty, pretty, pretty," he said, plucking a coin from the pile with a claw and bending it in half with his beak.

Thad didn't relax his guard. "People don't usually hire me to kill clockworkers. They usually beg me, and I'm usually happy to oblige. Why offer me money?"

"You may do with the clockworker as you wish. It means nothing to me. I want—or rather, my employer wants—something else entirely. That is why we are offering you money."

Now Thad leaned back in the hard chair. "Your employer?"

"I represent a third party. He does not go out in public and needs people to do for him. He heard you were traveling with the Kalakos Circus these days, and when they came to Vilnius, he asked me to arrange for your employment."

"I'm not seeking long-term—"

"This is a single piece of work," Sofiya interrupted. "And it is exactly what you do."

"Money, money," Dante said. "Pretty money." He reached for another coin. Thaddeus absently moved the purse out of his reach and took a pull from his beer.

"You can see my face," he said. "I would like to see yours. So I know who I'm dealing with."

Without hesitation, Sofiya cast back her scarlet hood. Golden hair spilled across her shoulders and clear blue eyes looked out over finely molded features and a sharp chin. The small scar that ran along her left jawline was the only flaw to her beauty. Thad didn't outwardly react, though inwardly he caught his breath. Such sweet loveliness ran a sharp contrast to the dull tavern and its sour drinks—and brought up bitter memories.

"Thank you." His voice stayed carefully neutral. "Who's your employer, if you please?"

"He is a person who hires people like me so he does not need to give his name." Sofiya straightened her thick cloak. It must have been stifling in the heat of the tavern, but she showed no signs of sweating. "You usually kill clockworkers for no money at all, so I would have thought the prospect of having some would be an encouragement, no?"

"I just like to know what's going on," Thad replied.

"Darkness, despair, death," Dante squawked. "Darkness."

Sofiya ignored him. "I will tell you. There is a castle ruin approximately half a day's horseback travel south of Vilnius. A clockworker who calls himself Mr. Havoc has moved into it, fortified it, and made it his own. He is quite brilliant, as all clockworkers are." She paused to sip from her red glass. Was it wine? She had expensive tastes. "He has already managed many dreadful experiments with machines and men. The village nearby is quite terrified of him, but they lack the weaponry to assault his little fortress."

"And you want me to go in there and kill him," Thad finished.

"You are very forthright for such a handsome Englishman," Sofiya said. "But I have already said that my employer does not care if you kill Mr. Havoc or not. He wants you to deliver a particular machine Mr. Havoc has created."

"Is that so?" Thad took another pull from his beer mug. The drink was only of middling quality, but it was beer and not *gira*. "Why doesn't your employer simply wait him out? The clockwork plague will kill this Mr. Havoc of yours in a couple of years, three at the absolute most."

"No. My employer needs the invention now. But I see you are reluctant." She gathered up the purse and made to rise. "I will find someone else, then. Good day, Mr. Sharpe."

He caught her wrist. The skin was smooth. "I didn't say I wouldn't do it, Miss Ekk. I'm just suspicious of strange circumstances and a secretive employer."

"The circumstances are this: you have the chance to rid the world of another clockworker, and make a great deal of money in the bargain by delivering one of his inventions to my employer. Will you do it?"

Dante bit the candle in half. "Done, done, done."

"Done," Thad said.

"Excellent. The invention is a spider the size of a small trunk. It has ten legs instead of the usual eight, and it has copper markings all over it. You will know it the moment you see it. I would approach the castle from the west. Our employer has information that says the west wall of the castle has an old doorway overgrown with ivy. The castle's defenses are also weaker in that direction, which is lucky for you—us. That door will get you through the castle wall and into the ruins. After that, you are quite alone."

"I'm never alone if I have Dante," Thad replied without a trace of irony.

Sofiya got to her feet. "I have a horse waiting in the back, and a basket of food. The moon is full tonight, so you can see. Take the main road south, then turn west when you reach the village of Juodsilai. The ruins are there. The horse is fast and should reach the castle an hour or two before dawn."

"What, you want me to leave now? In the middle of the night?"

"Must you make extensive preparations?"

"No."

"Do you intend to attack Mr. Havoc during daylight, when he can see you coming?"

"No."

She took him by the arm and hauled him toward the back door. "Then we go now, Mr. Sharpe."

"Wait a moment." He came up short. "We?"

"I will come with you, of course." A grim smile crossed Sofiya's face. "I am suspicious as well."

ALSO AVAILABLE FROM

Steven Harper

THE IMPOSSIBLE CUBE
A Novel of the Clockwork Empire

Declared enemies of the Crown, Alice Michaels and
Gavin Ennock have little choice but to flee in search
of a cure for the clockwork plague ravaging Gavin's
mind. Accompanying them is Dr. Clef, a mad genius
driven to find the greatest and most destructive force
the world has ever seen: The Impossible Cube.
If Dr. Clef gets his hands on it, the entire universe
will face extinction.

Available wherever books are sold or at
penguin.com

facebook.com/acerocbooks